WHAT BEATS WITHIN THE TUNNELS

ASHLEY R. O'DONOVAN

What Beats Within the Tunnels

A What Lies Beyond the Realms Novel

By Ashley R. O'Donovan

Map by Kathrin- Instagram: e_kath_art

This is a work of fiction. All of the characters, organizations, and events portrayed in this novel are either products of the author's imagination or are used fictitiously.

ACKNOWLEDGMENTS FROM THE AUTHOR

This book would not be in your hands if it weren't for my incredibly supportive husband, who has constantly encouraged me to pursue my dreams. His patience and understanding, especially during my late-night writing marathons and bathtub brainstorming sessions, have been nothing short of extraordinary. I am equally grateful to my amazing parents for their unwavering encouragement. A special thanks goes to my sister-in-law, Bri, for being an exceptional beta reader and offering invaluable feedback. Lastly, but certainly not least, my heartfelt gratitude extends to you, the readers. Without your interest and support, this journey wouldn't have been possible. I am deeply thankful for every reader and reviewer – your engagement means the world to me.

DEDICATION

To all my readers tempted by their dark side…Consider this your invitation to indulge.

EGU

CLOUDRUM

SHIFTING FOREST

LYCAN REALM

CINDER TERRITORY

SORCERER REALM

TEMPEST MOON

BLACK FOREST

DARK LUNAR REACH

MAD TERRITORY

LAMIA REALM

MORTAL YOUNDER

THE FERAL SEA

WHAT BEATS WITHIN THE TUNNELS

Please Note: What Beats Within the Tunnels is a mature fantasy novel that contains explicit content and darker elements, including mature language, sexually explicit scenes, and violence. If you would like a full content/trigger warning please visit the authors website: www.AuthorARO.com

CHAPTER
ONE

I wake with a gasp, and my nostrils are immediately stung by a harsh, acrid scent.

Instinctively, I recoil, feeling the overwhelming aroma constricting my senses and triggering an involuntary cough. As I blink rapidly and clear my head, a woman comes into focus, a bag of salts in her hands. Even through my disorientation, I can't overlook how stunning she is, her vibrant red hair tumbling over her shoulders in harmony with her crimson eyes.

"Sorry for that," she offers, moving to a counter with a sink close by. "I was growing quite bored waiting for you to wake up."

I rub my eyes, still struggling to find my bearings. This image of my father's blue-green eyes lingers in my mind. I was so close to finally speaking with him in Zomea and then...salts?

"What happened? Where am I?" I ask while trying to sit upright.

I take stock of my surroundings and see I am in some sort of medical facility. I glance around the room, scanning the shelves on my right brimming with bandages and tinctures, yet my gaze is drawn to the shelf holding an assortment of knives. An unwelcome reminder of Samael comes to the forefront of my mind.

I inhale deeply, an effort to bury the memory for now. I return my attention to the woman in front of me.

"Who are you?" I ask. I know she is a Lamia from her red eyes, but the only one I've ever met was Citlali. Gods, I hope Nyx killed her after I left. The thought of her blood on my tongue makes me want to vomit.

"I'm sorry for being rude. My name is Drew," she replies, advancing toward me with a warm smile. Under the flickering candlelight, strands of her hair transition from red to a vibrant shade of violet. My hand involuntarily gravitates to my chest and my thudding heart.

Thoughts of Chepi flood my mind, and I have to swallow the lump in my throat before the tears have a chance to fall down my face. I mentally rebuild the barriers around my heart and remind myself I will get Chepi back.

"Where are we?" I ask again, folding my hands in my lap.

"Do you not recall channeling to my realm? Adira must have hit you over the head harder than I thought," Drew responds, her brows knitting as she looks me over.

"Of course I remember channeling here, but I don't know where exactly we are now. How long was I unconscious?"

"You've been unconscious for a mere few hours. I apologize for the abrupt manner of your capture. Adira has a tendency to hit first and ask questions later. I asked Soren to tend to your wounds while you were out. Despite him being a mortal, he possesses many potent salves and concoctions and is exceptionally adept at stitching wounds," she explains while placing her hand under my chin, guiding me to meet her eyes.

The gesture reminds me of Nyx, and I try to ignore the pang in my chest.

"Ah, yes. There's a touch more color in your cheeks now," she observes, releasing my chin gently.

"Are we underground?" I ask, taking in the peculiar acoustic environment. Our voices seem to resonate uniquely, as if the sound is slightly warped. Rumors claim Drew's castle in the Mad Territory is merely a façade, her true stronghold lurking beneath it. I'd always wondered if the tales of this place were true. The thought of living underground has always been unsettling to me.

Gods, I never thought I would leave Tempest Moon, let alone find myself here. My life since meeting Aidan is like a whirlwind of chaos and heartache. Aidan—his name makes bile rise in the back of my throat. Then I remember his death, and the delicious feeling that memory brings me should probably concern me more than it does.

"You ask a lot of questions. If I am to satisfy your curiosity, perhaps we should relocate somewhere more comfortable so you can see for yourself," she suggests, gesturing toward an open doorway before vanishing around the corner. I scramble to my feet, the room spinning momentarily as I trail after her.

Rounding the corner, I find myself tailing Drew. Gods, she really is tall, slender, and strikingly beautiful. She's gorgeous yet terrifying when I consider what she is. It's hard to imagine she's over a thousand years old but doesn't look a day over forty. Mortal men must fawn over her, ready to offer up their veins in a heartbeat.

We head down a dank, narrow corridor. Moisture seeps from the walls, and a musty scent hangs heavy in the air. I reach the end of the hall and step into an enormous amphitheater. Its scale surpasses anything I've ever encountered. Cascading staircases twine around the walls above and below as far as the eye can see, and countless doorways punctuate the labyrinthine hallways. Wall sconces are regularly placed, illuminating the space. The wavering candlelight projects a sea of shadows, revealing an enormous, subterranean Lamia hive.

The sight and scale of this place take my breath away. I never could have imagined such a place existing. I'm drawn to the edge of the stairs, peering into the abyss below. A fall from here would mean instant death. The bottom, if it exists, is lost in obscurity.

"Keep up." Drew's voice echoes from several tiers below. I hadn't realized I let her get so far ahead of me, my attention lost to the haunting allure of this place. I quicken my pace to catch up with her, all while keeping a close eye on my feet and staying close to the wall. A clumsy step could seal my fate.

We travel down countless tiers, each a carbon copy of the last. At the base of each flight, I glance down the shadowy corridor only to be met with identical damp walls and oscillating candlelight, no other souls in sight. How far down does this underground hive stretch? I used to think the bunker Nyx and I once shared underground was unsettling, but this...this is on a much grander scale and even more terrifying.

Suddenly, Drew veers down a hallway, and I let out a sigh of relief. My legs are heavy with fatigue from the relentless descent, and the further down we go the harder my heart pounds in my chest. The anxious feeling I get from being so far underground is impossible to block out this far down.

In the distance, I see a man leaning against the wall. I match Drew's brisk pace as we approach him.

"Soren, prepare Lyra's chambers," Drew instructs, her tone stern yet infused with a honeyed sweetness that makes me wonder what the dynamic is between these two.

Soren is the mortal man who helped heal my wounds, and the Lamia are known to mate with mortal men. Maybe there's a romantic relationship between them. Soren acknowledges her command with a nod and vanishes down the hallway. I shake the thoughts out of my head. I don't need to waste time trying to decipher their rapport. I need to focus on unlocking the bridge. Drew pushes the towering metal door open, and I trail behind her into the room.

The chamber is magnificent. The polished obsidian floor sprawls before me, reflecting the flickering candlelight that swathes the chamber in an otherworldly glow. In the main room, a collection of robust leather chairs encircle a low table, the surface carved with an array of mythical beings. A grand archway offers a glimpse into the adjoining bedroom. Shrouded in a curtain of darkness, the heavy drapes create an aura of intimacy and secrecy. At the room's heart is a giant four-post bed, the four posts carved into faces of creatures that would cause the average person to have nightmares.

The chamber's atmosphere is heavy and potent, the scent of burning candles intermingling with aromatic incense. The air is stifling, void of windows to usher in sunlight or a breath of the world above, amplifying a palpable undercurrent of danger.

"Sit. No one will disturb us in my private quarters." Drew settles into one of the leather chairs, and reluctantly I find a seat opposite her.

Drew's crimson eyes find mine, and her unwavering eye contact makes my palms clammy. The silence between us draws on, and I refuse to let her unsettle me. Drawing in a deep breath, I grapple with my racing thoughts. I need her help if I'm going to get through the final ceremony and unlock the bridge to Zomea. Time is getting away from me, and I need to get Chepi back, not to mention the threat of the key consuming me if I don't unlock the bridge in time. I'd hoped Drew would break the silence, but her demeanor reveals nothing. I wonder if her silent stare is some kind of strategy to unnerve me. I have to admit it's working. I work at keeping my expression impassive as I evaluate my choices. I decide I'm going to be honest with her and ask for her help. I don't trust this woman, but I'm running out of options and time.

"I came here because I need your help. I am the conduit to unlocking a bridge to Zomea, and there is a final ritual I must perform here in your realm."

I shift uncomfortably in my seat, making a concerted effort to cloak my trepidation.

Her eyebrow arches in curiosity. "What do you require of me?"

"During the blood moon, I must consume the blood of a Lamia who willingly sacrifices her life for the cause. I realize this sounds crazy, but once the bridge is unlocked traversal between the realms and Zomea should be possible. The sacrifice could come right back to life—in theory."

I steady my voice to mask the nerves gnawing away at my insides. I cannot let her know about the powerful relic my family was after. With any luck, she isn't already aware of it. It's best if that secret died with my mother and Samael.

Drew nods slowly, her eyes reflecting the calculations taking place behind them. "What will you do once you have access to Zomea?"

I don't want to unveil everything to her, but some truths can't hurt in trying to gain her trust. "My pet—my best friend really, Chepi—he was murdered, and I need to get him back from Zomea. Also, there's the possibility that if I fail to unlock the bridge by the next blood moon the key will destroy me."

Drew inclines forward, every movement elegant, her eyes a furnace of intensity. "What do you know about the War of the Realms?"

"The War of the Realms, what does that have to do with helping me?" I sit up straighter, taken aback by her question.

"It has to do with why I will help you." A slight curve tugs at her lips, probably because my face is that of utter relief hearing she is willing to help me.

"Okay, I don't know much about the war, only what Nyx told me. A group of Sorcerers set out to unlock Zomea, not a bridge but Zomea itself, and once unlocked it tore Eguina apart. He said volcanoes erupted, and the feral sea split the land, forming Nighthold and Cloudrum. My father was the one who finally closed Zomea, and over time the realms were formed as we see them today."

In the back of my mind, I wonder if Nyx was even telling me the truth about the war. Maybe his version of it.

"I was born long before the war. I am much older than most can recall, and I remember a time many have forgotten. Do you know why the Sorcerers sought to unlock Zomea?"

"No, I don't. As far as I know, all the history books mentioning the war have been destroyed or concealed." I can feel my heart beating faster in my chest.

"Before the war, darkness began to loom over Eguina. Not tangible, but it was something one could feel. Changes were subtle at first. Some plants and trees started dying, creatures that were not regularly seen started to multiply, and Monstrauths and Spider Wraiths wreaked havoc. Some Lamias died before their time, and rumors of Fae magic weakening spread. Lycans were not always able to shift at will, and many died trying to protect their homes from the monsters that infiltrated the lands."

Drew looks away, her brows furrowed, and I wonder what memory she's reliving. I think about the Monstrauths and Spider Wraiths Nyx and I had to face, and goosebumps spread across my skin. We assumed Samael was resurrecting the Monstrauths, but who was doing it back then way before he was born?

Before I can fall into a full-blown spiral of conspiracies, Drew starts to speak again.

"A group of Sorcerers set out to unlock Zomea because they believed Eguina was dying and the fuel for all life and death—all magic—lies within Zomea."

"Was this ever proven? Why then did opening Zomea destroy the lands even more. My father had to close it to save everyone and preserve what was left of Eguina." I brush my hair out of my face, trying to wrap my mind around what she's suggesting.

"I'm not saying your father didn't save us. He did, Lyra. I don't know how he was able to close Zomea, but by closing it the storms settled, the monsters receded, and the realms healed. But those of us who are old enough to remember the war and the things that happened before can feel them now. I feel a darkness again settling over the lands, and it's not Samael. I've seen trees and foliage die for no reason. The monsters that once receded are starting to show up again across the realms, and I don't think it's a mere coincidence."

"What are you saying exactly, another war is coming?" I ask, leaning in closer.

"I'm saying Eguina is dying. Something is wrong, and I think the answer to restoring order is in Zomea. The one person who knows more about Zomea than anyone else is your father, and I'd like a word with him. If Zomea had not been unlocked before, I don't know what would have happened, but I don't have a good feeling about it and am far too old not to trust my gut. I'm going to help you because I'm worried we are on borrowed time, not just you but all of us. I want you to help me figure out why."

"Okay," I muster, absorbing her tale. I've been so focused on stopping Samael and figuring out the ceremony that I didn't notice a larger threat. Could Eguina really be dying?

"I know this is a lot to take in, and the blood moon is in four nights. Tomorrow, we can start preparations. For now, I'll have Soren show you to your room so you can get cleaned up and rest."

DREW PROMISED we'd have a conversation tomorrow, leaving me isolated in the chamber that Soren had arranged for my stay. The silent walk to the room and his wordless departure upon closing the door on me amplified my solitude. Testing the door, I found it unlocked, a small relief in the grand scheme of things. Now I'm perched on the edge of the bed, surveying my new quarters. The ascent of a few flights of stairs to reach this room brought me closer to the surface, making me feel slightly better, but my confinement is still disorienting.

A windowless room beneath the ground makes it hard to even know what time it is.

This room holds a dark and enigmatic beauty. The floors are the same shiny black stone seen in Drew's chambers. Thick velvet blankets of the deepest purple envelop my bed. The same hues are reflected in sheer curtains, extending from ceiling to floor, encapsulating the bed. It reminds me of my childhood days of fort building in my room with my father. The absence of a fireplace highlights the room's cool dampness. I'm sure I'll appreciate the plush blankets tonight.

To my left, a shelf hosts a variety of books and trinkets. To my right, the door opens to the corridor, and straight ahead lies a small archway leading to a bathroom. Exploring the area, I discover a black clawfoot tub, a matching sink, and an ornate gilded mirror suspended above. Over the tub hangs a chandelier loaded with candles, the warm glow animating the room.

I pause before the mirror, taking in my own image for the

first time in what seems like forever. The white-blonde waves of my hair, which should shimmer like moonlight on water, hang dull and dirty, spilling down to my hips in unkempt waves. The sheer slip that Citlali made me wear still clings to my curves, my breasts almost spilling out beneath the thin fabric. Gods, I would normally be horrified to have walked around like this, but I'm thankful that only Soren and Drew have seen me.

Silently, I remind myself to ask about Citlali in the morning. The image of the obedient Lamia, who so reverently regarded Samael as her master, revolts me—yuck. I shed the filthy garment with haste and lean in closer to the mirror. The blue-green swirl of my eyes reflects back at me like a stormy sea, the colors blending into one another. Even in the soft light, my gaze seems to hold an inner fire, betraying the Fae magic that flows through my veins.

I scan the healing marks on my body—Soren's handiwork. The vicious gashes that once marred my skin are now reduced to thin, angry red lines. The stitches that zigzag along my side show a precision that speaks of his care, each one a meticulous testament to his skill. But the realization that Soren had to undress me to tend to my wounds washes over me, leaving a mix of horror and embarrassment. I try to shake off the feeling because I am grateful for what he did. I'll have to remember to thank him the next time I see him.

I fill the bathtub with warm water, adding some sandal-wood-scented soap. I'm careful not to soak my stitches as I clean myself and my hair. Once purged of all the grime and haunting reminders of the day, I towel off and pick through the clothing Soren left. I don a silky white nightgown and robe then quickly slip under the thick blankets to keep warm.

Alone in bed, sleep feels impossible. The silence of the room makes my mind spin with worry. I can't believe Chepi is gone. Images of his broken wing and Samael stepping on him keep flashing in my mind, causing tears to stain my cheeks. The only thing that keeps me from breaking completely is knowing I have a chance to get him back.

My mind can't stop replaying all the things I don't want to think about right now. Nyx...Why did he have to lie about so much? Did he ever really care for me? His last words linger fresh in my mind. "I love you," he said as the wind picked up around me. I heard it right as I channeled. They weren't enough to stop me, because I think I had loved Nyx, but after everything, after all the hurt and all the lies, I don't even know if my heart is capable of love anymore.

My chest squeezes at the thought, and the lump in my throat starts to hurt again. Everyone I have ever loved has hurt me, and everyone I have ever trusted has betrayed me. Going forward, I can only truly trust myself, and I don't know if I'll ever be able to put all the pieces of my heart back together. I can't let that happen again. I can't take the pain.

I roll onto my side and curl up in a ball, deep inside wishing Nyx was wrapped around me and Chepi was sleeping at my feet. I let the tears run freely until eventually sleep claims me.

I'm jolted out of bed by a loud knock on my metal door, the sound echoing across the room. My internal alarms go off as I frantically search for a weapon, realizing the door doesn't even have a lock. If it were an attacker, they wouldn't be knocking.

The heavy knock resounds again. With a held breath, I turn the handle and pull the door open. The sight that greets me is as surprising as it is concerning – Nyx, drenched in blood.

CHAPTER
TWO

Nyx wraps his arms around me, and our lips crash together in a frenzy. I lose myself in his embrace, savoring his taste and scent. Thoughts of getting lost against his soft lips and warm skin erase any notion of what I should be doing.

A tugging sensation at my leg snaps me back to reality. Pulling back from Nyx, I glance down to see Chepi and can barely believe my eyes. I drop down to the ground and scoop him into my arms. I shower him with kisses, and a sob escapes my throat as my cheeks feel a wide grin.

"How is this possible?" I manage to say, clearing my throat.

"Chepi is a glyphie," Nyx explains, bending down and touching the stone pendant on my chest. "His existence is bound to the safety of that stone. I intended to tell you, but you channeled before I could explain anything."

Instinctively, my fingers trace the stone's cool, smooth surface. "How? I don't understand."

"It's a bloodstone harvested from the Dream Forest." Nyx settles down on the ground next to me. "Its magic is intrinsically linked to Chepi's life force. As long as this stone remains intact, he'll be reborn, time and again."

"And if the stone gets destroyed?"

"Chepi wouldn't die, but it would signify his final life," he explains.

My father did give me Chepi and the necklace at the same time. No wonder he told me never to take it off. Chepi licks my cheek again then curls into a ball on the ground.

"Snoring already." I turn to Nyx and giggle. "He must be as relieved as me to be back. Poor guy is exhausted."

Nyx pulls me against him, and I let my leg wrap around his. He brushes stray curls from my face and tangles his hand in the back of my hair, coaxing my mouth closer to his. Our lips connect again, and when he pushes his tongue between my lips I open for him, welcoming the feel of him as he explores my mouth. I let my robe slide off my shoulders and fall to the ground. Nyx slides one hand under my ass. With the other still pressed against the back of my head, he sits me down on the edge of the bed. Then he's pushing me back, and his hands are working their way up my nightgown. All the while, he kisses me utterly senseless.

I give into him fully until he inches away from me long enough to pull my nightgown over my head and toss it to the floor. He looks down at me, his gray eyes glowing bright in the dark room. Dipping his head, he places another kiss on my mouth and then starts his descent down my body. He trails kisses down my neck, pausing to take each of my nipples into his mouth before kissing my stomach and spreading me wide.

His mouth presses to my center, and he feasts on my pussy, sliding his finger in and out of me. I lose all train of thought, my mind unable to focus on anything else except for the heat of his breath on my clit.

I feel as if I might explode from the pleasure. Then he pulls away, giving me a moment to catch my breath as he pulls his pants down and reveals his cock. Coming closer, he thrusts it inside me. He moves slowly, teasing me and drawing out my pleasure one embarrassing moan after another. I wrap my arms around his lower back, pulling him into me, coaxing him to move faster and harder. I find my release, the orgasm washing away the tension in my body. Nyx presses inside of me one last time, finding his own release and then falling off me onto his back.

We both lie there in silence, staring up at the ceiling, breathing heavily. My mind clears from the pleasure stupor I was stuck in, and I realize I don't know what the fuck I'm doing. Nyx is a liar, and I just promised myself I wasn't going to get sucked back into his lies. Then he shows up here caked in blood, and I spread my legs for him. I need to get control of this situation before my heart betrays me again.

Nyx's voice pulls me from my thoughts. "That was—"

"A mistake," I interject, and he turns onto his side to face me. I don't look him in the eye. I'm a coward and focus on the ceiling.

"What? Why? Lyra, I love you," Nyx says, and my heart does a pitter patter in my chest, but I shut it down.

"It's not enough... You betrayed me, Nyx. I gave you my trust, only to discover it was all a lie. I don't know who you truly are. You've had so many opportunities to be honest with me, but every time you lied. Our entire relationship was based on lies."

He sits up, tugging on me until I sit up and face him. "Lyra, I'm so sorry I hurt you. Please give me time, and I will make it up to you. I will earn your trust again." The look in his eyes makes my throat constrict, and I swallow that lump I can feel forming again. *I will not cry. I will not cry.*

"I need space. I need distance. I offered you a chance to

explain, and all I received were more deceptions and half-truths. Gods, you killed my father, Nyx. I know he killed your parents, but that's part of it. Everything is so fucked up. I need time to myself to think."

"Lyra, I can't leave you right now, not with the blood moon coming and the ceremony about to happen."

"I don't need you here. I have Chepi back, and I'm so grateful you brought him to me. I have Drew here too, and she's agreed to help me. I'm going to be okay, Nyx."

"You can't trust Drew. You don't even know her."

"You have no right to say who I can or can't trust. Please, I need you to walk away." My voice breaks, and I can feel the tears welling up in my eyes. A part of me yearns for him to draw me in, but I know better. I need to be strong. I blink back the tears, clearing my vision. "If you've ever cared for me, respect my wishes and leave. I'm not at my strongest and can't be around you right now. Please..."

He reaches out to touch my cheek, his thumb lightly brushing away a traitorous tear.

"Tell me right now you don't love me, and I'll leave."

I'm forced to take a slow inhale before I meet his gaze again.

"I don't love you, Nyx." I make sure I say it clearly before my quivering voice can betray me. Nyx gets to his feet, puts on his clothes, and walks to the door. My heart sinks as I stare at his back walking away from me. He pulls the door open, but before he leaves he turns back to find me in the dark, his eyes glowing bright again.

"Now who's the liar, Lyra?"

The door closes behind him, sealing his departure for good.

I pull a blanket off the bed and slump onto the floor, a harsh sob clawing at my throat. I find Chepi where he fell asleep curled into a ball and pull him against me. He licks away my tears and nudges close to me, resting his head against my neck. My heart wages a battle between elation at Chepi's return and the anguish of Nyx's departure.

I HAVE no idea what time it is, but I'm still in disbelief about last night.

Chepi rolls over, and I rub his belly, relieved to have him back with me. "I was so worried about you, squish," I murmur to him, and he yips in response, his tongue lolling out of his mouth as he soaks up all the attention.

I get to my feet and head to the bathroom, my body sore from the night's uncomfortable rest. As soon as I step in front of the mirror I'm taken aback by my reflection. I have dried blood clinging to my skin in random smears across my body. It was dark last night, and once Nyx started kissing me I forgot all about the blood on him. I quickly brush my teeth and draw a bath, scrubbing my body clean.

I rummage through the clothes left on the sink and find a simple black gown. I braid my hair into a single large plait and toss it over my shoulder, contemplating whether to stay in my room until someone comes knocking or to venture out and explore this mysterious hive. Before I can contemplate it any further, there's a quick knock on the door. Soren peaks in.

"Good morning, Lyra," he says, eyeing my disheveled bed that is also smeared with blood. Great...

"I'm supposed to escort you to Blood Lake. Are you ready to go?"

"Absolutely. Let's go, Chepi," I say, quickly pulling on my boots. Chepi's wings manifest, and I see Soren's eyes widen, but he doesn't say anything.

We follow Soren up countless flights of stairs, my thighs

WHAT BEATS WITHIN THE TUNNELS

protesting against the exertion when we finally reach the uppermost level. The never-ending corridors are still candlelit, but eerie sounds disturb the silence, stirring my curiosity about where all the castle's inhabitants might be.

We ascend a narrow stairway that seemingly leads to a ceiling. However, upon our approach, a large hatch swings open automatically, exposing us to the daylight—a startling contrast to the hours spent in the subterranean gloom. The castle above thrums with life, and I let out a breath of relief at finally seeing other people around. We remain inconspicuous, Soren guiding us through a set of double doors and down a rocky slope toward Blood Lake.

The outside air greets us with its crisp coolness, a stark change from the musty chambers underground. Negotiating the rugged, uneven terrain demands my full attention, ensuring I don't stumble. I've had enough injuries lately to last a lifetime. Chepi appears thrilled, energetically hopping from stone to stone, his wings flapping in pure delight. Upon reaching the base of the hill, I notice the lake is stunning. Its waters are a haunting deep red. No wonder it's called Blood Lake.

"Wait here. Drew should be around shortly," Soren says, turning to leave us.

"Hey, Soren, before you go, I want to thank you for healing me."

He doesn't respond. I get a slight nod, then he starts to make his trek back to the castle. He really isn't very talkative, at least not with me. I mean, I haven't tried to hold a conversation with him either, but he seems very closed off.

I venture closer to the water's edge yet maintain a safe distance, wary of the unknown creatures that might lurk beneath. The intensity of the crimson hue is mesmerizing, unlike any water I've seen.

"Eventful night, was it not?" Drews voice startles me from

behind. I turn to face her, and she glides over to us, her movements always so graceful that it's like she's floating instead of walking.

"Yes, you could say that," I reply, sitting down on one of the large rocks by the shore.

"I see you have your friend back. Chepi, is it? I hope that doesn't change your mind about going to Zomea."

"It doesn't change anything. I need to unlock the bridge, and if you are right I want to get to the bottom of what's happening to Eguina before it's too late," I say, pulling Chepi into my lap.

"Glad to hear it. I don't want to overstep, but I may have overheard you speaking to King Onyx last night. You see, he knocked out three of my guards, and instead of intercepting him I decided to see how things played out. Plus, Lamia hearing."

She points toward her ear, a furtive smile playing on her lips. I wince, the memories coming back to me.

"I'm sorry about your guards."

"Nothing to be sorry about." Drew shrugs. I feel my cheeks heating at the thought of her overhearing us last night. My moans while he was over me with my legs in the air and the conversation afterward.

"He is a liar, you know. You're right not to trust him. He does have a good heart though, I think, and has always tried to be the noble son. I prefer the other brother, personally, but then again I've always had a thing for the bad boys," she says, winking at me.

"Nyx has a brother?" I exclaim, my mouth practically falling open. Gods, he really is the biggest liar. I don't even know who Nyx is.

Drew clicks her tongue. "Tsk, tsk. King Onyx keeping secrets. Although this might be one that's been kept from him."

"What do you mean by that?" I question.

"Forget I mentioned it. I may be confusing him with someone else. How was it so easy for him to lie to you about so much? Do you know nothing of our histories?" she says.

"I am slowly coming to the realization that my childhood education was lacking. No, I guess I don't know a lot about history. No wonder it was so easy for him to lie to me. I ate it up," I say, shaking my head. It's easy to talk to Drew as if she's a friend, but I silently remind myself to watch my tongue. I don't have any friends here.

"Let's not speak of him anymore. There is much to be done before the blood moon." Drew sits on a rock near mine and places a sack I hadn't realized she was holding between us.

"I've brought you a couple of books from our library that I think might be helpful. I thought you would like to read out here by the lake. I know being underground takes some getting used to."

"That's for sure." I laugh, thinking about those endless, dark staircases. "What are the books about?"

"One is a book your father used to own. It's about Fae magic. I gather you are new to magic, and I think it may be useful. The other book is one I think you should find most interesting." She smiles fully, and it's the first time I've seen her sharp canines on display.

"Thank you." I let Chepi go and pick up the sack, ready to take a closer look at the books she brought. Drew gets to her feet. "Oh, Lyra, I have an old friend coming to help you with your magic, should be here by nightfall." She doesn't give me a chance to respond and glides back up the hillside.

Old friend to help me with my magic, who could that be? And she sounded rather cryptic about the second book, something that does catch my interest. I take the sack, settle down on the grass, and take out the first book. It's a thick leather-bound book with a tree carved into the cover, its roots extending to the edge of the binding. Lying on my stomach, I crack open the book and right away realize this is the book about Fae magic, the one she said belonged to my father.

Chepi plops down next to me, rolling on his back in the grass. An uneasy feeling tugs at my gut. When my father spoke through Samael, he told me Chepi was in Zomea waiting for me, but it was a lie. The thought that my father may not be the man I thought he was keeps creeping into my mind, but I force it aside. It doesn't matter. It won't change what I have to do. If all goes well, I'll be able to question him soon enough.

I lose myself in the book for what feels like hours. The pages seem to come alive under my fingertips, as if the words and images are leaping off the pages and into my mind.

As I read, I become more and more fascinated by the origins of Fae magic. Legend has it that the first Fae beings walked among the gods and were born from the light of the Dream Forest. They possessed such powerful magic that they could control the elements, bend time and space, and even create life. Over time, the Fae beings learned to harness and refine their magic, passing down their knowledge and skills to future generations. It's hypothesized that some of the more powerful Fae lines may be that way because they mated with the gods. Living among the gods—what an amazing time to be alive. I wonder what it was like then.

There are many different types of Fae magic, unlike Sorcerer magic, which is either dark or light. Elemental magic allows one to control the forces of nature, such as fire, water, earth, and air. Mind magic involves mental powers, like telepathy, mind-walking, and midnight mind. Illusion magic can alter one's perceptions of reality, while healing magic can soothe and mend injuries. And then there's necromancy, which involves communicating with the dead and interpreting omens and prophecies. The list seems endless, and I know I have a lot of studying ahead of me.

Soren arrives with a tray, my mind still spinning with everything I've learned about Fae magic. I feel the magic inside me pulsing with every beat of my heart, almost as if it's urging me to learn how to wield it. To my surprise, Soren sits down next to me, revealing a small bowl of diced meat for Chepi and some strange food for me.

"Would you like some company while you eat?" Soren asks, and I have to consciously wipe the silly look off my face. He's been so distant until now.

"Some company would be great. What is all of this?" I inquire, eyeing the tray of food suspiciously.

"I bring you nightshade salad, venomous noodles, and shadow fish caught from this very lake," Soren replies. I gulp, examining the contents of the tray.

"Could you please explain in more detail what each one is?" I give Soren a weak smile. I mean, venomous noodles sound anything but appetizing, and nightshade salad is rather ominous. Shadow fish sounds harmless enough, but it came out of Blood Lake and has a massive mouth of sharp teeth. I half-imagine it coming back to life and biting me.

"Sure," Soren says then chuckles, the first time I've seen him smile. He has hard features, slicked-back dark hair, and hazel eyes. With his smile, his face lights up, and I can under-stand how someone could be attracted to him. "The venomous noodles are exactly what the name suggests. They are noodles infused with the venom of a deadly serpent, giving them a slightly spicy kick. It is said to have healing properties but can be dangerous if not prepared properly. Don't worry. I made sure they were prepared with care.

"The nightshade salad is one of Drew's favorite things to eat. It's harmless, with dark leafy greens, fresh berries, and crumbled cheese. Lastly, the shadow fish may look scary, but the murky red water gives it a rich, oily flavor that's quite good. We usually eat it grilled like this."

"Are you going to eat anything?" I ask, wondering if he poisoned my food, but would he have any reason to do that?

"Yes, I figured you could use the company. Here, I'll show you how I like to eat it." Soren grabs two bowls and fills each with some salad then tops them with a handful of noodles and a few chunks of fish. "It tastes best all mixed together, trust me," he says, handing me one of the bowls and a fork.

I watch him start shoveling food into his mouth, and my nerves instantly relax. I start eating the food and am surprised by how good it tastes. There's a bit of spice from the noodles and sweetness from the berries, creamy chunks of cheese, and the fish is rich and oily, making everything go down smoothly.

"Have you known Drew for a long time?" I ask between bites.

"All my thirty years of life," Soren replies.

"Do you work here at the castle? Are you like her assistant or something?"

Soren pauses, looking over at me. "'Or something' would be more accurate," he says, cryptically. Interesting. I knew there was something between them. I sensed a weird sexual tension. We finish eating in silence, and even Chepi devours his bowl of food.

"Do you mind showing me back to my room?"

"Sure, I'd be happy to."

As we walk, Soren tells me more about the castle and the surrounding area. Apparently, the Lamia realm is known for its natural hot springs, which have anti-aging properties. He also tells me about the different kinds of creatures that live in the forests here, some of which are dangerous.

We finally reach my room, and Soren departs. Someone

tidied up my chamber while I was out. The bed has fresh sheets and clean blankets on it, no blood, a welcome surprise after last night. I prop up all my pillows and make a cozy spot to continue reading. Chepi quickly falls asleep at the end of the bed until a knock sounds at the door.

CHAPTER
THREE

"I t's me again." Soren pops his head back in, and I sit up to see he's carrying a small wooden trunk. "Drew is having a dinner party tonight and wants you to attend. I'm supposed to drop this off for you and let you know I'll be back to escort you to dinner later."

"Er, thank you." I take the wooden trunk from him and close the door, placing the trunk on the end of my bed. I unlatch it and lift the lid to find some black fabric with a black bow tied around it folded neatly inside. I pull the fabric bundle out and untie the bow, carefully unfolding the fabric. The most exquisite gown lies inside. It's woven from the most opulent champagne silk, bedecked with intricate patterns of rose-gold gems that shimmer in the candlelight.

With delicate hands, I lift the dress, its luxurious fabric smooth as liquid silk against my skin. Admiring its breathtaking design and craftsmanship, I can't suppress the thrill it incites. What kind of dinner party is this?

I peek back inside the trunk, and in the corner a tiny envelope lies nestled beside a pair of heels, their sparkles matching the dress. I grab the piece of parchment, tearing it open to reveal a cryptic message, "Wear me." I chuckle at the mysterious note, wondering what surprises await me at dinner tonight. Why would Drew send me such a dress? So unusual. This better not be some scheme on Nyx's part trying to earn my forgiveness, because it would take a lot more than sending me a fancy dress. If he didn't leave the Lamia Realm, Drew would have said so this morning. There was a time when I thought Nyx was a good communicator who made me feel so safe and happy. That seems like so long ago now. So much has happened that I don't even feel like the same person anymore. That girl gawking at the mysterious man in Tempest Moon over dinner seems like a stranger to me now.

It's still early, and I have plenty of time until I need to get ready for dinner. I climb on the bed and settle into the pillows. I put the book on Fae magic aside and grab the sac to look at the other book. I meant to look at it before, but everything about the Fae magic was so interesting that I got distracted.

Drew was kind of cryptic earlier when she spoke about the second book. I hesitantly pull it from the sack and give it a look. It's old and dusty, the cover fashioned from aged leather, supple and worn with time. The vibrant black hue has faded to a rich, dusky shade with faint creases and subtle wrinkles. The cover appears to be blank, but on closer inspection the spine reveals faded, gilded lettering in an ancient script, possibly inlaid with remnants of tarnished gold leaf.

I open the book, and I'm not sure why but an unusual feeling spreads across my skin and up the back of my neck, like I'm being watched. This book appears far older than the other, the delicately yellowed pages, their edges rough and uneven from years of use. The aroma that emanates from the book carries the scent of aged parchment and a faint hint of herbs. I'm not sure it's even possible, but I swear an energy seems to pulsate from the book, as if the very essence of magic still lingers within its pages.

I shake my head and sit up straighter, trying to ignore the odd feeling that washes over me as I begin reading.

As SHADOWS DESCENDED upon the land, the last known dark Sorcerer emerged as a formidable force, unmatched in command over the realms of dark magic. The very presence radiated an air of arcane supremacy, a palpable aura that both mesmerized and terrified all who beheld it.

Through the forbidden rituals they undertook, the Sorcerer unlocked depths of power that were dormant within the darkest recesses of the magical realm. They harnessed energies that defied comprehension, weaving spells of unrivaled potency and devastation. Not even the strongest of Fae magic was a match for this. The Sorcerer even possessed an innate ability to manipulate the very essence of shadows, shaping them with a mere flicker of the fingers.

Among the extraordinary repertoire of abilities, the dark Sorcerer possessed the unnerving talent of veiling within the ethereal shroud of darkness itself, moving silently through the night, undetectable and unseen, leaving behind only a lingering chill as evidence.

The Sorcerer's command over elemental forces was equally formidable. Flames danced on fingertips without the need for kindling. The very earth trembled, tearing open with a wave of the hand. Even the winds answered the Sorcerer's call, delivering messages on unseen whispers.

But perhaps the most chilling of these abilities was the art of ensnaring and manipulating the minds of others. The dark Sorcerer possessed a sinister charisma, a power to bend the wills of unsuspecting souls to their desires. Whispering dark secrets into the minds of enemies sowed seeds of doubt and discord that festered like a poison.

The mastery of dark magic was unparalleled, leaving a legacy of destruction and awe. Legends speak of this power as a force that eclipsed the sun, casting the world into an everlasting night, where the wicked thrived and the righteous trembled in fear.

Let the tales of this dark Sorcerer serve as a testament to the immeasurable power that can be attained through the shadows. But beware, for such power comes at a grave cost, entwining the wielder in an inescapable web of darkness.

WELL, that was a disturbing passage if I ever read one. I don't know if there's a chill in the room or if I'm unsettled by the book, but I seek comfort under the covers and continue reading.

I go on to learn about the Luminary Council. All the most powerful beings of the time had to come together to defeat the dark Sorcerer. The Luminary Council was born out of necessity, but its formation was not without challenges. Personal agendas, different perspectives, and ancient grudges threatened to unravel their delicate alliance. However, their unwavering commitment to the greater good prevailed, overcoming their differences and binding them in a common purpose, to eradicate dark magic from Eguina and kill the dark Sorcerer.

The council knew that only by pooling their collective forces, drawing upon their noble virtues, and synchronizing their abilities could they stand a chance against the dark Sorcerer's might. Together, they were a radiant force that pushed back the encroaching darkness, reclaiming the balance that had been disrupted.

At least that's how the book reads. It sounds to me like they killed the dark Sorcerer and then murdered a bunch of innocent Sorcerers who had dark magic but weren't doing anything nefarious. How have I never heard of this council before? It seems like something every Sorceress should be taught. Why did Drew give me this? She must suspect I may inherit dark magic. Why else would she think I should read a book about a dark Sorcerer and a council of murderers? How could she suspect unless Nyx told her something? I don't think he would do that, but he's the only one I've ever spoken to about my fears of inheriting dark magic on my nineteenth birthday.

I think Drew knows far more than she's leading on and might be more clever than I've given her credit for. I want to read more, but I need to get ready for dinner. Drew and I have more to discuss than I thought.

Proceeding to the bathroom, I untangle my wavy hair, throwing it over my shoulder. Taking a deep breath, I don the gown, the silk hugging my curves until it flares out below my hips, cascading to the floor. My reflection in the mirror leaves me speechless, looking every bit a queen adorned in such a stunning ensemble.

Delicately, I perch on the bed's edge, mindful not to crumple the dress, and reach for the book again. As I revisit its pages, my free hand idly massages Chepi, scratching his back in rhythm with my reading.

Usually a Sorcerer needs to cast spells or preform rituals. I've never heard of a Sorcerer who can bend the elements. That is usually something only the more powerful Fae can do, and not to the extent the book speaks of. And for the bending of shadows, I look around the room, unsettled by the idea that a person could hide in the darkness of the shadows, let alone bend them to their will.

The sudden knock at the door catches me off guard, causing me to leap to my feet and Chepi to take to the air. That book really has a way of pulling me in. I tuck it safely under my pillow and glance at myself in the mirror one last time. I'm surprised Soren hasn't barged in like he normally does. The thought makes me slow my steps as I approach the door.

Opening the door, I find myself face-to-face with...Colton. He possesses a frustrating allure. There's an undeniable magnetism to his chiseled frame, sandy blond hair, and those piercing emerald eyes that seem to challenge and beckon all at once—undeniable and annoying.

"You..." I draw out the word with disdain in my voice.

"If it isn't little Miss Stardust. Come now, Lyra. Is that any way to greet the man who came all this way to help you? Not to mention the gift you're wearing." Colton eyes me up and down. He brought me this dress, disgusting.

"I didn't ask you to come here, and I don't want your help or your gifts," I retort sharply, pushing past him and heading into the empty hallway.

"Well, if you don't like it, feel free to take it off."

"Very funny." I start walking down the hall toward the stairs, I slow my pace when it hits me that I have no idea where I'm going for dinner, fuck. I can hear Colton catching up behind me. "Come on, Lyra. What's got you so upset? I didn't give you the stardust to drink. Besides, I already helped you once, don't you recall?"

"I'm not upset. I just don't like you." He may have given me one of Callum's journals, but I don't know what his goal was. "I don't know if I would consider that helping me."

"I don't see Nikki boy around, so I'd say it was a push in the right direction, my dark enchantress."

I crash to a halt, turning around to face him, "Shh, don't call me that. As a matter of fact, don't call me anything, and don't talk about Nyx," I say in a hushed voice, not that anyone is around to hear me. The last thing I need is rumors swirling in the hive about me inheriting dark magic.

"Sounds like I struck a nerve. Which part exactly? Nikki

not being here to protect you or the part about your dark magic?"

"I don't have dark magic, and for your information I told Nyx to leave. Now if you'll excuse me, I must be attending dinner."

"Precisely why I'm here to escort you," he says with a wink. I roll my eyes but take the elbow he offers me. I do need someone to show me the way to dinner, and walking all these flights in heels is risky for me without an arm to hold on to.

I look over at Chepi, and he's just flying next to us, amused as ever by this awkwardness, I'm sure. He always has been able to understand me. I'm not sure how exactly, but we've always been able to communicate. We traverse down at least ten flights of stairs before we finally turn down a corridor. Colton stays silent next to me the entire time, so he must know what's good for him. As we reach the end of the hall, I pause and give Chepi a meaningful look, silently communicating the need for him to stay close to me tonight. He responds with a wag of his tail, and I turn my attention to the large double doors in front of us. With an assertive stride, Colton moves ahead, pushing them open to unveil a spectacle that steals my breath.

The initial wave that strikes me is an intoxicating melody, an otherworldly symphony plucked from a lyre, which suffuses the room and weaves an additional layer of mystique into the ambience. The chamber extends in all its grandeur, a dining room befitting of this giant hive.

At the heart of the room sits an imposing table crafted from ebony wood, its surface decorated with delicate candelabras. Chairs with lofty backs and lavish cushions surround it, populated by Lamias and mortals engaged in vivacious chatter and laughter.

However, my gaze is involuntarily drawn upward toward the ceiling, where a series of ornate cages swing, each inhabited by a man garbed in leather executing acrobatic feats with the grace of a seasoned performer. The synchronized twists and turns of their bodies, flowing seamlessly with the rhythm of the enchanting music, create a mesmerizing sight.

"Do you need me to pick your jaw up off the floor, or are you going to be alright?" Colton chuckles next to me, and I snap my mouth closed. "You're more sheltered than I thought, little enchantress."

"I'm sorry. I didn't realize watching half-naked men dance in cages was a common occurrence, my mistake." I turn my attention away from the dancers and back to surveying the room.

"It's one of my favorite pastimes," Colton whispers, brushing past me, and I can't help the smirk that crosses my face. Lamia women and mostly mortal men dressed in their finest attire congregate around these aerial performances in clusters, some entranced but others immersed in their conversations. Colton approaches one of the smaller clusters and speaks with Drew.

I'm about to join them when a low voice jars me from behind.

"Nice to see you on two feet again," says a broad, fit woman with blonde hair pulled back into a tight bun, her fiery red eyes looking me up and down.

"Excuse me?" I reply, unsure how to react to that comment.

"Lyra, this is Adira. She's the one who hit you over the head when you first arrived. Don't mind her. She has no manners," Soren explains, appearing beside me.

"Oh yes, and I'm glad you've become so well-acquainted with Drew's favorite pet," Adira says then chuckles softly as she walks away. I can see Soren's cheeks flush next to me, and I almost feel sorry for him.

"Soren, do you know the Lamia named Citlali?" I ask, changing the subject.

"Shh, don't speak her name here. That's Drew's daughter. She was exiled, and it's forbidden to speak of her," he warns me. I nod, pressing my lips together in a tight line to let him know that my lips are sealed. I want to know the full story though. Maybe I'll ask Drew myself when we are alone.

Soren guides me to the table where Drew is now seated, looking regal in a dark-green gown that contrasts her fiery red hair. As we approach, she rises gracefully from her chair to greet us. "Lyra, you look absolutely stunning," she says with a warm smile. "I see you've already been introduced to Colton."

"Lyra and I go way back. It's a funny story how we met actually—" I elbow Colton in the ribs before he can say anything else.

"Ahem, no, it's not. It's a very boring story," I say, a nervous smile tugging at my lips.

A fleeting expression of confusion crosses Drew's face, but before I can dwell on it a woman at the table asks her a question, and her attention is diverted.

I find a seat further down the table. Colton sits on one side of me, and Soren sits on the other. I don't recognize anyone else other then Drew and Adira, who is sitting next to her. The table sprawls the length of the room and easily holds the several dozen people here tonight.

"Would you like a drink?" Colton asks, a slight glow to those emerald eyes of his. I simply turn away from him, ignoring his question. He has to be mad if he thinks I'm going to trust him to give me another drink after last time. I look to Soren, who is eyeing the man holding a tray of cocktails behind us.

"What are they exactly?"

I survey the server wearing black leather pants that don't

leave a lot to the imagination, and that's all he's wearing. I never would have thought the Lamias were so—libertine.

"Venomous Vixen is the bright-green cocktail, made with a mixture of exotic fruits and herbs and infused with Lamia venom," Soren explains. I must make a face, because he pauses before adding, "The venom won't harm you. It only intensifies the buzz."

"And the other?" I ask, hoping for a more palatable option, pointing to the darker-colored cocktail.

"We call it Black Sun. It's a red wine with a smoky flavor, aged in barrels made from trees that only grow here in the Lamia realm," Soren answers.

"I'll take a Black Sun, please," I say, extending my hand to take the glass of wine from the server. I'm not sure I'm ready for venomous cocktails, especially after my experience with Stardust at the elders' palace dinner party. I take a sip of the wine and can't help but squint at the potent, smoky flavor that coats my tongue. It's not exactly my favorite, but it's better than nothing. I much prefer the sweet wine in the Faery Realm, but I'm not going to complain.

More men clad in black leather pants emerge, and they begin to place trays of food on the table. Despite the appetizing aromas wafting up from the dishes, I'm completely lost as to what anything is. Chepi perks up next to me, no doubt enticed by the scents of the various dishes as well.

Drew has been engrossed in conversation with Adira, and I can't help but try to eavesdrop on their conversation. Soren notices my distraction and offers to explain some of the dishes to me. However, I find myself zoning out midway through his explanations, the descriptions of snake tongue soup, roasted bat wings, and blood orange shadow fish doing little to stimulate my appetite.

In the end, I opt for a plate of ice berries and nightshade

salad, using my fork to push my food around as I try to turn my attention to the other conversations taking place.

"Why aren't you eating anything?" Colton's hand nudges my thigh under the table, and I suck in a breath at the feeling. A ripple of warmth seems to spread through me and then dissipate.

I had a similar feeling when he touched my leg at the party before, but I assumed it was from the stardust. I quickly glance around the table to see if anyone is acting different from the cocktails, but everything seems to be normal. He doesn't appear as though he felt the unusual sensation but is watching me carefully.

I clear my throat. "I'm still getting used to the food here. Besides, I'm not that hungry." He furrows his brows briefly but doesn't push the topic.

Suddenly, a voice overwhelms the chatter.

"How can you all sit here dining with her when you know what she is?"

The table falls silent as the woman across from me lashes out, pointing at me. I hadn't noticed her before, but look down at Drew's end of the table to see her giving me a death stare. I set my glass down, placing my hands in my lap and trying not to fidget.

"I'm sorry?" I ask, hoping I didn't hear her right. Gods, I definitely heard her right. I hate that all eyes are on me in this moment. I gulp and subtly wipe my clammy palms in my lap.

"You all welcome her here with open arms. We should end—"

"Enough!" Drew gets to her feet, and the entire room goes utterly still. "Adira, please help Bella back to her room." She takes her seat again, Adira nods, and Bella throws her napkin down at the table.

"I'll see you again," the woman growls. It sounds like a

threat, and before Bella can say anything else Adira ushers her out of the room. The chatter around the table starts up again instantly, and I feel incredibly uncomfortable now. I glance over at Colton as he sets his fork down. It shatters into pieces. He quickly places his napkin over it, and I look away, pretending I didn't see.

What in the gods is happening tonight? I need to get out of here and want to get back to my room and finish reading my book. Now I'm wishing there was a lock on my door. I'm going to have nightmares about Bella coming to suck my blood in my sleep tonight. Why did she say that, and what does it mean? Does she have something against Sorcerers? Does she know I am half-Fae, a mixed breed, or can she see something darker might stir within me?

CHAPTER
FOUR

"Hey, are you okay?" Soren drags me from my thoughts.
"Yeah, I'm fine. Tired."

"You don't have to stay here. These dinners go on for hours. I don't think you're adventurous enough to try the dessert either." Soren laughs, and I'm about to tell him he's wrong, because I love anything sweet, but Colton gets to his feet, causing us both to turn toward him. I hold my breath, hoping he's not going to have an outburst too, but he just extends a hand to me.

"Let me walk you to your chambers," he says, and normally I would roll my eyes and blow him off, but I can't wait to get out of this room and away from all the awkward stares after Bella's confrontation. I take his hand and ignore the warm ripple that spreads up my arm, faint but enough to know it's not because his hand is warm. It's a peculiar feeling. I nod to Soren in farewell and glance at Drew as we pass by, but she doesn't look our way.

Once the dining room doors close behind us, I release

Colton's hand and start to walk to the stairs, anxious to get back to my room.

"What, no 'thank you, Colton, for getting me out of there?'" he says, and I huff, pulling my heels off and deciding it will be much safer to take the stairs barefoot. I wonder how many people have fallen to their deaths on these stairs over the years.

I finally reach my room, and Colton must sense I'm in a mood, because he doesn't try to tease me or have small talk. I don't think he's going to say anything, and I'm kind of surprised. I push my door open, and Chepi plops down on the bed. When I step inside, Colton grabs my arm, not hard or anything but firmly enough so I turn to face him.

"My room is over there if you need anything. I'll see you in the morning," he says, pointing to a room down the hall. He seems much more serious now, and I don't know whether I should be worried or thankful. I lift my chin and close the door, tossing my heels on the floor and slipping out of my dress and into a nightgown. I climb into bed and get comfortable under the covers. I feel anxious, and my nerves won't let go of me.

Of all the Fae in Eguina, why would Drew bring Colton here to help me with my magic? I guess Nyx was out of the question after I basically ended things with him and told him to leave. I keep thinking maybe I was too harsh with him, but then I remember all the lies. I don't think I really know him at all. It doesn't change the fact that I miss him deeply and the thought of him makes my heart hurt.

Drew doesn't strike me as the kind of woman to do something without a purpose. Gods, thinking everyone is out to get me is exhausting. I'm tired of all the secrets and deception. I tell myself I don't care and that it doesn't matter. I'd be going to Zomea anyways and have more important things to worry about. I grab the book and set my mind on finishing it tonight.

I read until I can barely keep my eyes open, but then I

come across probably the most interesting passage in the book thus far, and by interesting I mean disturbing.

When the moon's shadow fades on the nineteenth dawn of the tenth cycle of the third Grand Cycle, dark power shall reawaken in the blood of the Fae. After countless generations lying dormant, the ancient magic, unseen since the time of the last dark Sorcerer, shall emerge once more. Two bloodlines, both ancient and pure, will intertwine and birth a harbinger of the old magic. She will be of Fae and Sorceress, the child of light and dark, who brings balance or chaos, based on her heart's choosing.

This child will be the Mirror of Eguina, reflecting the world's truth and darkness. With the passing of each phase of the moon, her powers shall grow. She shall have the strength to rebuild or destroy, to love or hate, to offer salvation or damnation.

On her skin, she will bear the mark of the cosmos, a sigil known only to the Luminary Council, the silent sentinels of the arcane. They who extinguished the flame of dark sorcery will see it reborn, stronger, more potent, and yet vulnerable all the same. It is their duty to guide or misguide, to protect or threaten, depending on the path the Mirror of Eguina decides to tread.

Her destiny is her own to forge. Her choices will reflect in the heart of Eguina. She must understand that the power she holds is not evil, nor is it good. It is a reflection of the self, an echo of her heart, her intentions, and her actions. As she decides, so goes the fate of Eguina.

But be warned. Dark magic is a slippery path, for it is ancient, powerful, and yearns to claim her. Its seductive whispers will echo in her ears, offering power, control, and domination. It will seek to consume her light, to draw her into its shadowy embrace, to sway her from the path of balance.

And in this journey, she will not stand alone. For the prophecy foretells the presence of a beacon, a Light Bearer whose spirit remains untainted by the shadow. This guide will shine brightly in the darkness, a testament to the strength of the light. Only with this light can the Mirror of Eguina withstand the temptation of the darkness, keeping her heart true and her intentions pure.

I DON'T WANT to accept that this is about me. Drew must think it's about me, or at least the possibility of it being me. Why else would she give me this godsforsaken book? I don't want to inherit dark magic or be the mirror of Eguina, whatever that is. And if this is me, then this council must already be on the lookout for me. This was a very long time ago, hundreds of years. Maybe the council has fallen apart and forgotten about all of this. The nineteenth dawn of the tenth cycle would be October 19th, my birthday. A grand cycle is a hundred years. The third grand cycle would make it three hundred years. Has it really been that long since this dark sorcerer lived?

What Drew said about things dying and the War of the Realms, could that have anything to do with this? The power to offer salvation or damnation, but why me, why now? I hope my father will have answers. Every time I find an answer to something, I get at least ten more questions piling up. It is still several months until my nineteenth birthday. Nothing will be definite until then.

The part about needing a Light Bearer so the darkness doesn't destroy her everything, that part lines up with what Callum's journal has, and a sick feeling begins to churn in my stomach. Is Nyx really going to be the one to save me? It says his light can save me, or at least that's how Callum interpreted it. Fuck, I wish I still had the journal. I'm trying to recall exactly what it said, but all I remember is the last part of it, the most important part, I suppose. "Can his light save her? Or will her darkness destroy him—destroy us all..."

I stare into the darkness, thinking about my darkness.

SOMETHING'S COMING! The whispers grow louder, more distinct, more menacing. The air is heavy with a noxious odor that clings to my skin and chokes my breath. I look around frantically, but all I see is darkness. Shapes move in the shadows, coalescing into forms that shift and twist as I try to focus on them. The whispers turn into laughter, cold and mocking, and my skin prickles with goosebumps.

I realize that I'm standing at the edge of a bottomless pit, surrounded by tunnels that lead to nowhere. The whispers become screams, filling my mind with terror. I turn to run, but my feet are leaden and unresponsive. Something grabs me from behind, its grip icy and unyielding. I struggle to free myself, but the thing drags me back toward the pit.

I hear the whispers again, closer now, and I know that I'm running out of time. I manage to break free and run down one of the tunnels. I don't know where it leads, but I keep going, fueled by pure terror. The whispers follow me, echoing down the tunnel, bouncing off the walls and amplifying until they become a deafening roar—then silence. It's so quiet I think I can hear the beat of my heart, no, not my heart, but something. Every beat is slow and deliberate, each pulse dragging the silence out into an eerie elongation, thickening the air with tension. It sounds primal, as if it's a piece of me, ancient, like the ticking of a monstrous biological clock, the heartbeat of the tunnel itself, as though the cold stone walls are alive and breathing.

I wake, my hands instinctively reaching for my throat as I

sit up, gulping down air, soaked in sweat. Zomea...or some other nightmare. I can't be sure, but it felt so real, felt like the burning forest but more pressing. I can still hear that sound beating in the recesses of my mind.

I shiver, trying to rid myself of the eerie thumping. What was that place, what happened to the burning, bleeding trees? I need help controlling this midnight mind. That's what I really need.

My throat feels raspy. I must have been screaming in my sleep. I hope no one heard me. Chepi is still asleep, so that's a good sign.

I can't see the sun, and there is no clock in my room. This is extremely frustrating having no clue what time it is. There's no way I'm going to be able to fall back asleep after that dream. I leave Chepi under the covers and wrap my robe around me. I need to move. I need to distract my mind with anything else right now.

I silently step out into the hallway and close my bedroom door, leaving Chepi to sleep a while longer. The silence that greets me in the hallway gives the impression it's the middle of the night, but I haven't seen another soul roaming this hive since I got here except for at dinner, so unusual for a space that houses so many. Maybe not all the Lamias live here.

I pause in front of Colton's room and push my ear against the door. I don't know what I was expecting, but I feel slightly let down by the silence that greets me. I meander further down the hall away from the stairs, a direction I have yet to explore. I pass several more doors, and they all look the same. I am half tempted to open one, but with my luck it would be Bella's room, and that's the last thing I need right now, another run-in with her.

I finally reach the end of the hallway, and to my surprise there are more stairs. This is different though and doesn't open up into a giant hive like the others. There's a single dark stairwell going down. I know I should go back to my room, but curiosity tugs at me, and before I know it I'm several steps down. The bottom of the stairs is met with a large, imposing door standing slightly ajar, unlike all the others. Tempted, I push the door open, revealing some kind of ancient library. The air here is heavy with the scent of old parchment and dust. Tall, dark mahogany shelves reach up into the shadows, lined with books bound in leather, covered in dust.

I try not to choke as I move further into the dimly lit room. In the center of the room, there's a huge map spread out on the table. It's detailed with intricate ink drawings, perhaps an old layout of this hive. I move past it and around a shelf, curious about what light source is casting the library in a faint red glow. Off to the side of one shelf, as if it's a bookend, rests a peculiar artifact— a large, crimson crystal orb, softly pulsating with an inner light.

What kind of magic is this? The Lamias are not really magical beings. They drink blood and have incredible strength and speed but not magic like the Fae. What an odd thing to find hidden away down here. The sight of it fills me with an indescribable feeling. I can't resist reaching out to touch it.

I let my fingers graze the surface, and an abrupt chill runs up my arm, causing me to gasp. I try to pull my hand back instinctively, but the orb only pulls me in, trapping my hand onto the surface. It illuminates, bathing the entire room in a bloody red glow. The chill up my arm intensifies, and I begin to tremble. My head falls back, and suddenly I'm no longer in the library. The library around me has dissolved into nothingness, replaced by a maelstrom of visions.

I'm plunged into an all-consuming darkness, an abyss so unfathomable it seems to devour every shred of light. Fear courses through me, an icy dread that roots me to the spot. It feels like a portent of doom, a threat lurking beyond compre-hension.

Faces flash before me in a rapid disorienting flurry. Nyx and Colton appear, their expressions etched with a potent blend of fear and resolve. They're locked in a fierce battle with an enemy I can't see, their every movement desperate.

Interspersed with the chaos, the menacing rhythm of a heartbeat reaches my ears. It resonates like a war drum, growing louder and drowning out the other sounds, amplifying the unease within me.

Then I see myself, but not as I know myself to be. My eyes are voids of black obsidian, devoid of all warmth, all humanity. From these dark pools, black veins spread like tendrils of night, coursing across my face, and shadows spew from my hands. I look monstrous, a creature of nightmares, unrecognizable as the girl I am.

A hand clamps down on my wrist, and as abruptly as it started the onslaught of visions ceases. I'm back in the dimly lit library, the red light of the orb comes back into view, and a hand is now wrapped around my wrist.

"You're going to wake the whole godsdamn hive with your screaming. First in your room and now down here, wherever the fuck this is." I turn to see Colton is the one gripping my arm. I try to move, but my steps falter, my mind still trying to make sense of what I saw.

"Here, sit down." He helps me to the floor, and we both sit and lean against one of the bookshelves.

"What are you doing down here anyways?" he asks, and I close my eyes, replaying what happened in my mind. I can't help the shiver that spreads over my skin, and when Colton puts an arm around me I don't push him away.

"You're shaking and cold to the touch. Come, I'll help you back to your room." I can't find the words, so I nod and let him guide me back up the flights of stairs and into my bed chamber. Once I'm back in my bed, Colton pulls a blanket around my shoulders and sits next to me. "Are you going to tell me what that fucking echosphere showed you now?"

"Echosphere, is that what that red orb is called?" I ask, finally finding my voice.

"Yeah, Drew's had it for ages. It's how she knows so much. It reveals traces of possible futures."

"It showed me...me. Only it wasn't me, not as I am today." I look over at Colton and snap back to reality, "It doesn't matter. Get out of my room." I shove at him until he gets off my bed.

"Okay, okay, enchantress, I'll leave you be, but I'll be back first thing in the morning, and we are training with magic whether you like it or not." I wish I had something harder within reach. I settle for a pillow, throwing it at him only for it to collide with the door as he closes it and fall to the ground. Everything about him gets under my skin. I don't care if he's trying to be nice. I don't like him and don't trust him.

I fall back onto the bed, pulling the covers over my head and seeking to warm my feet where Chepi still sleeps. I may have seen myself through that orb, but I also saw Nyx and Colton. I wish I knew what it meant, what were they battling. And that heartbeat, the sound was like the loud pulse I heard in my dream, in the dark tunnels—what beats within the tunnels? I can still hear the faint sound in the back of my mind like it's a piece of me.

CHAPTER
FIVE

Perched on a stump amidst the forest that encircles the castle, I wrestle with my mounting frustration. Evidence of my failed attempts at igniting a fire with my magic pepper my surroundings. Little wisps of smoke curl up from scattered piles of leaves, each sporting a few blacked edges where I was almost successful.

Sleep had eluded me again, leading to my decision to venture into the woods with Chepi before dawn's first light. Thankfully, escaping the hive was simple. All we had to do was travel up.

Beyond Blood Lake, the woods reveal themselves in all their breathtaking splendor. In any other circumstance, I'd be drinking in the beauty of this place – the trees displaying a symphony of auburn and pale green, crisscrossed by deep red veins etching patterns on the bark.

Drawing my knees up to my chest, I let my face sink into my hands, feeling defeated. Days ago, I had been a force to be reckoned with in the shifting forest. I'd even defeated Samael. Now, my magic is a pitiful shadow of its former glory, unable even to kindle a simple flame. I don't get it. The power I had now feels like a distant memory, replaced with this frustratingly weak trickle of Fae magic that pulses from time to time.

I need to focus, and my mind is too busy being anywhere but here. Thoughts of Nyx, the blood moon, Zomea, the nightmare I had, and the fucking echosphere visions keep flooding me with anxiety. I focus on my breathing and tell myself I need to bury this. I need to focus on one thing at a time. Nyx is gone. I can't prevent my midnight mind from taking over my dreams, so it's pointless to waste my energy stressing over it. The blood moon is eminent, and unlocking the bridge to Zomea needs to be my number one focus right now. I should forget anything that echosphere showed me. I shouldn't have been meddling with things I don't understand.

I'm trying to wrap up this mental pep talk when I hear footsteps approaching. I know it's not an attacker, because Chepi's tail starts to wag, whacking me in the side. I look up to find Colton sauntering over, a smug grin plastered on his face.

"Having trouble, Lyra?" he teases, his voice echoing through the tranquil forest.

"I'm just getting started, thank you," I retort, rolling my eyes at him. He chuckles, his emerald eyes glinting with mischief. "Allow me to offer some assistance then, Princess." He sits down on the ground beside me, his close proximity sending a jolt of awareness through me.

"I don't need your help, Colton," I say, getting to my feet.

"Your pride says one thing, but your aura says another," he muses, his gaze fixed on me. Nyx could read auras too. I wonder if that's an ability I may have one day.

"And you're suddenly an expert on reading auras?" I turn away from him, my cheeks heating.

"Oh, I'm an expert on many things, my little enchantress."

"Apparently not an expert at winning over the ladies." I can't help the smile that curves my lips.

"Funny, you are a real charmer," he says, getting to his feet and moving directly in front of me. I don't shy away from him. Instead, I hold his eye contact, no matter how uncomfortable this close proximity makes me. "Give me your hand."

"No. Why?"

"Give me your hand. I'm not going to bite, not unless you ask me to." He winks, and I give him a vulgar gesture before he takes my hand in his, laughing.

"You are a little spitfire, aren't you? I bet Nikki boy didn't know what to do with you," he says, shaking his head. I pull my hand away and for the first time take a step back.

"Let's get a few things cleared up. I don't understand what you're playing at with wanting to help me, but I don't trust you. Not only do I not trust you, I don't like you. However, if I am going to allow you to assist me with my magic, then you are going to stop bringing up Nyx, you got it?"

"It's a deal, Princess." He takes my hand, his grip firm, a jolt of electric shock shoots up my arm, and a light bursts from my palm as my fire rushes to the surface.

"What the fuck was that?" I exclaim, darting my eyes from my hand to Colton's face.

"I'm sorry. Did you think you could learn defensive magic without a little pain involved?" He reaches over, petting Chepi and laughing at me, and I can't help but gape at him.

"A little pain? That really hurt." I rub my hands together.

"But did you notice how quickly your magic reacted, ready to defend you? It's easy to let it come to the surface when you trust it and get out of your own damn head." He presses his finger to my temple, and I pull away, giving him a dirty look.

"I really don't like you."

"Lucky for you, you don't have to like me for this to work.

And by the looks of it, that's the most fire you've been able to conjure all morning." Colton glances at the wisps of smoke still scattered around us. I won't admit it to him, but he is right.

"I'm listening." I cross my arms, my eyebrows raised.

"You don't have time to learn to control your magic right now. It might be dangerous in Zomea, and if something comes after you I want you to act first and think about it later. You need to have terrible, sad, and infuriating memories at the ready, and when you need your magic you go to the deepest darkest place you can find within yourself and let it out. Fae magic will always run off emotions. Emotions are your friends right now. Don't be afraid to get upset."

His eyes never leave mine, and I don't like what he's saying. I let out the breath I hadn't realized I was holding, realizing I'm going to have to think about things I'd rather stay buried forever if I am to survive this.

"Yeah." I look down at my feet.

"Hey, after you unlock the bridge and make it back from Zomea, I'll teach you anything you want to know about Fae magic. That is if you haven't killed me yet," Colton says, his voice a bit softer for a moment. I let my lips turn up on one side of my mouth. It's a nice thought—if I make it back from Zomea.

"Let's get started." I clear my throat, looking up at him. I can't help but take a closer look at Colton's appearance. His sandy blond hair, cut short but with longer, wavy strands brushing his shoulders, adds to his striking appearance, augmenting his rugged handsomeness. Meanwhile, the stubble adorning his jawline enhances the overall air of hardiness and virility that is characteristic of a seasoned warrior. He is built like no man I have ever seen and would be a force to reckon with even if he didn't have any magic. I know close to nothing about this man and can't help but be curious about his past.

I shake my head, pushing these useless thoughts out of my

mind and square my feet in front of him, ready for whatever he's going to throw at me next.

Colton begins to circle me like a predator stalking its prey. "Ready, Princess?"

"Stop calling me that," I retort, annoyed with all the nicknames.

"Then show me you're not one. Show me the dark enchantress I know you are," he teases. "Show me you can handle a little attack."

In an instant, he thrusts his hand forward, fingers splayed wide, and a gust of wind rushes toward me with startling force. It takes me by surprise, and I stagger back a few steps, bracing myself against the invisible onslaught.

"You need to anticipate the attacks, Lyra," he instructs, still circling me.

"Easy for you to say," I snap, brushing a wild strand of hair from my face. As if on cue, he raises his other hand, and the earth beneath me starts to tremble. Roots erupt from the ground, snaking toward me.

"Oh, come on!" I exclaim, evading the roots with a swift jump.

"React, Lyra!" he urges, his tone firm yet encouraging. "Let your emotions guide your magic. Don't hold back! Those roots should be ashes right now." His hand slices through the air, drawing moisture from the environment. Droplets coalesce, forming a swirling sphere of water. He thrusts it toward me, fast as an arrow.

"Block it!" he shouts, but that water arrow was already too close, spraying me with its icy touch. I narrowly evade the full force of it. Gods, I wish I could manipulate the elements with such ease. Frustration bubbles up, followed by a growing spark of determination. As he sends another gust of wind my way, I close my eyes and call on the fire within me. I let it rise, stoked by my emotions, and send a wall of flames toward his wind.

To my satisfaction, the flames meet his gust head-on, causing a burst of heated air and steam. I open my eyes to find him grinning at me.

"Good. Again," he says, his eyes alight with excitement.

"Well, look at that," I say, raising an eyebrow. "Mr. Know-It-All is capable of praise."

"I'll praise more than your magic. Give me some time," he says, smirking, and then the earth beneath me starts to tremble once more. This is going to be a very long day.

BY THE TIME we stop for a break, I'm exhausted. I plop down on the ground next to Chepi and lean against a fallen-over tree. I never realized using magic takes so much energy, physically and mentally. Colton continues pacing around in front of me, laughing at my state of exhaustion. I think he finally realizes I'm going to need more than a minute and sits down next to me.

"You're doing good, better than I anticipated," he says, and I don't know if it's to make me feel better or if it's what he actually believes.

"The blood moon is tomorrow night. I don't know what Zomea is going to be like, but, gods, I hope I'll be ready." I let my head fall back against the tree, looking up at the sky above. It has to be getting close to dinner time. The sun has started its descent.

"Why are you only using elemental magic with me?" I ask, looking over at Colton, who appears to be deep in thought.

"Because elemental magic is what you are most powerful with, at least for now. Your fire is strong, and we don't have time to explore other things." He places his hand on my leg, not in a handsy way, a reassuring touch. "You're going to be ready, I promise."

"Don't make promises you can't keep," I tease.

"I'm not. You're ready now. You are much more powerful than you give yourself credit for." He takes his hand off my leg and stretches, kicking his feet out to get more comfortable. "If we are going to take this long of a break from practice, I should at least be teaching you something."

"By all means then, fire away, professor." I laugh.

"I'm serious. You grew up with a Sorcerer as a teacher. They would have taught you very little about Fae magic, and most of it was probably incorrect."

"I was never taught anything about Fae magic. I didn't even know I was half Fae until recently." I kick my feet out to mirror his.

"Elemental magic is extremely powerful on its own but can be more powerful when used near its corresponding element. For example, fire magic is strongest when used near a source of fire or heat, while water magic is most potent near a river or lake. All Fae magic runs off emotions, not just elemental magic. But one important thing to always remember is that Fae magic can have a mind of its own. It's important to learn to navigate and control your magic, but you also need to trust it."

"What do you mean by 'trust it?'" I ask.

"Your magic is a part of you. It lives within you and will always seek to protect you. You have to let it." The silence stretches on between us, and I enjoy the peace while I can.

"Tell me what you saw in the echosphere that had you so shook up last night," he says.

"I'll tell you what I saw if you tell me what you're doing here. Why are you trying to help me? Why did you come?" I sit up straighter, looking over at him. His eyes catch mine, sparkling with a force that can both rattle and charm at the same time. There's a fleeting moment where his features soften, seeming thoughtful. But if I wasn't paying close attention, I would have missed it. As quickly as it came, it's gone, replaced by a confident grin.

"I owed Drew a favor," he says. "Helping you squares us up." I figured it had to be something like that. Why else would he help me when he clearly dislikes me, especially considering my past with Nyx, a past that's over now. But then why bring me the dress, why give me Nyx's father's journal? Part of his task for Drew? Maybe the journal was just to piss Nyx off and cause a rift between us, because they clearly don't care for one another. But the dress...

"Your turn, Princess," he prods, pulling my focus back to him.

"Why'd you call me a dark enchantress?" I inquire.

"I read the prophecy in Callum's journal. I know you're Euric's only child," he explains. "I've heard the murmurs over the years. You're the one they've been whispering about, the shadowmancer, the dark Sorceress, Eguina's mirror, the dark enchantress. Pick any name, they all point to the same meaning."

My stomach twists with unease.

"But how can you be so sure of this when I'm still questioning it? And please don't spread this around," I retort, slightly annoyed.

"Whether you believe it or not doesn't change the truth," he says, causing me to draw my lower lip into my mouth, clamping down on it in sheer frustration.

"And Nyx...he was aware of this too?" I question, my voice barely above a whisper.

"I thought we weren't talking about him anymore," he shoots back.

"We're not. This will be the last time, so answer me." I start chewing anxiously on my bottom lip. I dread hearing the confirmation and don't want Nyx to have known about this. But I already know the truth. Nyx told me he was supposed to kill me before I inherited my dark magic. I had almost forgotten everything he said after Samael's death, being too overwhelmed with emotions. But because Nyx and his crazy father believe I am going to be dark doesn't mean it's true. I pull my knees to my chest, burying my face in my lap. I don't want to, but I need to start accepting all of this. I may be a dark Sorceress, but I don't know what that truly means yet. I need to find my mother's grimoire. Fuck, I am so overwhelmed. Everything keeps mounting up.

Lyra, get a grip. You're unlocking the bridge to Zomea, one thing at a time, I remind myself again.

"Yes, Onyx knew about it," he admits reluctantly. "Callum was obsessed with that prophecy, harped on about it for years before his demise. It's why he exiled Euric from Nighthold and Nyx... Nyx was his perfect son, feeding into everything daddy told him. I'm sure he's had plans for you long before you were born. Whether those plans changed after he met you, well, that I don't know, to be honest. But as much as I can't stand the asshole, I will say he does always try to do the right thing, what he thinks is the right thing at least." He pauses, sighing. "I gave you that journal not because I wanted to break you two up. I gave it to you to wake you up, but here you are still in denial." He ruffles his hair absentmindedly, and I watch as the unruly locks fall back onto his face.

"He told me he was supposed to kill me before I inherited my dark magic, but he said he couldn't do it. He said he loved me," I admit.

"That piece of shit—"

I'm not sure if Colton's mad about the idea of Nyx killing me or loving me.

"Stop." I cut him off before he can say anything else bad about Nyx. I can't bare it, no matter how much he hurt me.

"You stop. Stop defending him," Colton spits back.

"Let's go back to not talking about him," I say, quickly trying to ease the tension.

"Thank the gods. Going the rest of my life without hearing about that prick wouldn't be long enough." Colton relaxes against the tree again. I want to ask him why they seem to hate each other so much, but I think it's best for both of us if we don't talk about him anymore.

I pull Chepi into my lap and start scratching behind his ears when Colton says, "Have you ever heard of the Luminary Council?"

"Not until recently. Drew gave me some books to read, and one of them details the history of the Luminary Council and how they killed the last dark Sorcerer and eradicated dark magic from Eguina," I admit, my voice heavy.

"She would slip that in without an explanation. Drew is on that council, or at least she was. Who knows when they last convened. It's probably been over a century. Callum was also on the council, when he was alive."

"Do you think Drew believes I am going to be this dark Sorceress after my nineteenth birthday? Is that what Bella was talking about at dinner last night when she said they all knew what I was?" I want to ask if Nyx took his father's place on the council, but I decide it's better I don't ask. It doesn't matter anyways.

"Bella is a lunatic, and no one will listen to a godsdamn thing that comes out of her mouth. She shouldn't have made you uncomfortable like that. As far as what Drew believes, I can't be sure, but I do trust her. She is only trying to help you."

"Why do you ask if I know about the council then?"

"I thought it was something you should be aware of, given

you are going to be the great shadowmancer." He holds his hands up, making his best effort at a scary face, but he only looks foolish.

"You're not funny." I look away, not feeling much in a joking mood, especially not about this. I close my eyes, and a flash of myself with those swirling black eyes makes me shiver.

"Do you think this council is good? Even though they killed the last dark Sorcerer? I mean, from what I've read, he did do some pretty bad stuff, but did they even give him a chance? I can't believe that dark magic inherently makes everyone evil—I won't." My voice trails off. I worry that dark magic does exactly that, but I have to maintain hope that it can't truly change me if I am to inherit it.

"No, I don't think the council is good," Colton says with a laugh that doesn't suggest amusement. "I think the Luminary Council is just like any other council or collection of leaders. They're all power-hungry and out to achieve their own agendas by any means possible. Drew is the only exception, and that's why I trust her," he continues.

"Then why is Drew on this council, if it even still exists? If she's not corrupt and power-hungry like the rest, then why associate with them?" I ask.

"I imagine it's because she thinks she can change them, perhaps make up for the past," he replies.

"What do you mean by 'make up for the past?'" I press.

"Drew gave you those books. You've read it yourself—they killed the last dark Sorcerer and then proceeded to eradicate all dark magic. I'm sure innocents were killed, and I think Drew still carries guilt from those days. They were dark times," he says, staring off as if recalling a memory, and I wish I could see into his mind. "Drew is a good person to have on your side, and if the council is convening again, and you are to be the great dark enchantress, then she will try to sway the others. She will try to prevent history from repeating itself. You can trust her," he says, and I look down into my lap, absorbing the information.

"Cheer up, Princess. Come on, it's late. I'll walk you back, and we can train some more tomorrow." He gets to his feet, and I take the hand he offers to help me up. That strange feeling happens again when our skin meets, but he doesn't seem to notice, so I ignore it.

CHAPTER
SIX

The entirety of the following day, Colton and I immerse in relentless training. Over and over, he barrages me with a series of attacks until I manage to summon my fire on command, each successful draw pulsing confidence through my veins. We dabble a bit with the other elements, but Colton insists that my focus remains undivided — all on fire, for now.

The ceremony is set to occur tonight. Or more precisely at three in the morning, the hour often branded as the peak of magic, the apex of supernatural activity, when magical powers surge with unparalleled strength and rituals yield their most potent outcomes. Drew, insists it's the perfect time for our ceremony. I, for one, am not inclined to disagree with her. I'll need every possible advantage aligning in my favor to ensure this works.

The sun has already long set by the time we get back to my chambers and scarf down some soup that Soren delivered. Now we sit on the ground with our backs against the foot of the bed. Chepi lies on his back between us, screaming for attention, and we both take turns scratching his belly.

"Maybe you should try to get some sleep," Colton suggests.

As he moves to stand I blurt out, "I can't sleep." I pause as he looks over at me. "My mind won't calm down. I'm too anxious about what's going to happen at the ceremony and after." I look down and feel my face flush. Colton readjusts himself.

"Well, then we won't sleep together." He crosses his arms, leaning his head back on the end of the bed. "Once you unlock the bridge, what do you plan to do?" he asks.

"I need answers, I need to find my father, I need to know why he did this to me, and I need to know why he did a lot of things and if he knows anything about the state of Eguina. Drew told me about how things are dying and magic is weakening. She said it reminds her of a time before the War of the Realms took place."

"Yeah, she's shared her concerns with me as well."

"Do you know what will happen at the ceremony? Do you know what unlocking the bridge will be like?" I ask. I've avoided asking anyone until now, afraid of what the answer might be. I'm not sure if it's better to know or not. I imagine it will not be good either way.

"I wish I could tell you," Colton responds, his voice heavy with uncertainty, "but honestly I don't know. It's never been done before, so all of this is unknown territory." He pauses for a moment, his gaze fixed on the wall. "But I can tell you what I do know of Zomea."

I turn to face him, resting the side of my head on the bed.

"Please," I urge him, desperate for any information.

"I'm hesitant to tell you anything, because I don't want you to think I lied if it turns out not to be true. Everything I know is all hearsay. I've never been myself, so I can't tell you facts from personal experience."

"It's okay. I won't hold it against you if whatever you tell me turns out to be false when I get there," I tell him, hoping he'll keep talking.

"My father used to tell me that the Gholioths are the guardians of Zomea," he says.

"Athalda told us that the Gholioths are the oldest creatures to ever exist in Zomea, that they have never entered these realms, and that somehow my father put Gholioth blood in me. It's making Zomea unstable. It's also part of the reason why I am the key."

"Interesting. Well, my father said that Gholioths were once people, once beings that lived among us, but after death they were greedy and power hungry, trying to steal magic and cause havoc in Zomea, so the gods punished them, turning them into monsters and sentencing them to an eternity of work as guardians, never allowed to find peace."

"That sounds horrible," I admit. Colton's father is an elder, so I would be inclined to believe him, but where did he get that information?

"What are you going to do with Chepi when you unlock the bridge and all?" he asks.

"I imagine I'll take him with me. Actually I'll let him decide." I look down at Chepi, whose ears are perked. "Hey, boy, do you want to go with me to Zomea, even though it will be dangerous, or would you like to stay here? Colton can watch you." I smile, looking up at Colton. I'm joking, at least I think I'm joking. I don't know if I could trust Colton or anyone here with Chepi, nor do I know how long I'll be gone. Or, gods, what if I can't get back? Chepi jumps into my lap, pawing at my chest and licking my face.

"See, he wants to go with me." I laugh, looking over at Colton petting Chepi.

"Good, he can protect you. Use his invisibility to hide. Only fight if given no other choice."

"I'm hoping I don't have to fight anything, but maybe that's naïve." I run my hands down my face, letting out a heavy sigh. I can't help but feel my thoughts spiraling into an abyss of what-ifs and uncertainties that make my stomach churn with anxiety. The thought of my father, the man I once looked up to, now a mere ghost from the past, stirs a knot of emotions deep within me. Excitement, fear, longing, and resentment all jumble together in an incoherent mess. How did I get here? How did everything come to this?

Every passing second brings me closer to the reunion I've both yearned for and feared in equal measure, the latter not until recently. The father I once knew, loved, and admired had become an enigma, his actions painting a different picture than the memories I held on to. Will I be greeted by the man who used to carry me on his shoulders and tell me bedtime stories? Or will I be met by a stranger, a man led astray by his quest for knowledge and power?

My heart pounds in my chest, each beat echoing the count-down to the moment I've both dreaded and anticipated. The moment when I unlock the bridge and cross the threshold into Zomea, into the unknown. The tales and warnings about Zomea play out in my mind like some grotesque theatre, filling me with a sense of impending dread. What kind of world awaits me there? What lies beyond the realms? It's something I never thought I'd find out in this life at least, and here I sit on the precipice of it. Will I disappear and be dropped into the burning forest that haunts me in my sleep? Will I see Luke, my mother, or—gods forbid—will Aidan be there?

My breathing quickens, and I can feel my heart fluttering in my chest at the mere thought of all this. And the ceremony, only a few hours away. The key, the magic, all the death—it all lead me to this point. But what if it doesn't work? What if all the ceremonies, the preparations, the sacrifices were for naught? The idea tightens a vice around my chest, stealing my breath.

"It's not naïve to think that. Sometimes it seems easier to believe the bad stuff. I like that you try to believe the good." Colton elbows me, pulling me from my silent spiral of panic.

"Why are you being nice to me? I don't think that was part of the deal you made with Drew." I smirk.

"Why do you make it so hard to be nice to you?" Colton nudges me again as a low chuckle leaves his lips, and we relax into a comfortable silence. Despite the fear and anxiety, there's this part of me that can't help but feel a spark of excitement. A flicker of curiosity. This journey, as terrifying as it may be, offers answers to questions that have been gnawing at me for far too long. It's a chance to know my father, to understand his actions, and maybe, just maybe, to mend things.

I hold on to this thought, this flicker of hope, as I brace myself for what is ahead. For as terrifying as the unknown may be, it's the only path that leads me to the truth. And for that, I'm ready to face whatever awaits me in Zomea.

"It's time." Soren's voice jolts me awake as my door swings open, and he eyes me and Colton. "I'll meet you by the lake. Get ready." My door slams shut behind him, and I sit up quickly, realizing I dozed off and fell asleep with my head in Colton's lap. By the looks of it, I think he fell asleep too. I rub my eyes, trying to clear the fog in my head. Colton gets to his feet and extends his hand to me. I take it, and he pulls me to my feet.

"Ready to kick some Zomea ass, little shadowmancer?" Colton asks, making me laugh. At least I can count on him to lighten the mood, always with the nicknames.

"Ready as I'll ever be." I shake my head, but a smile tugs at my lips.

I'M NOT sure what I was expecting, but as we reach the first floor of the castle, only Drew is waiting for us. She's draped in a long crimson cloak and kindly hands one to me as well. I quickly slip it on over my red gown, grateful for the warmth, as we prepare for the ceremony. Colton, on the other hand, seems unfazed by the chill, clad in black pants and an off-white tunic.

As we step outside, my eyes are immediately drawn to the blood moon, hanging in the sky like a captivating omen. It's stunningly beautiful, with an enchanting allure that I can't help but find fascinating. The moon appears to be closer to the realms tonight, larger than its normal size. I'm mesmerized by its crimson glow until Colton tugs on my cloak, urging me to keep moving.

We hike on in somber silence for the next hour, the crunching of leaves and twigs under our boots punctuating the occasional hoot of an owl. The canopy of the forest is thick and foreboding, casting us in darkness. My senses are on high alert, my ears straining to pick up any sounds out of the ordinary. I tuck Chepi under my coat and carry him with me. I know he can fly, but the poor guy has to be exhausted. He's had as much sleep as me, and that's not much.

We finally stop at the edge of the forest, the top of a rocky cliffside overlooking the sea. I can hear the feral waves crashing against the shore in the distance, their unrelenting power adding to the already tense atmosphere. Normally, the sound of water would be soothing to me, but right now it only serves to amplify the dark pit in my stomach, ready to devour my racing heart. The feeling of utter anxiety and fear threatens to take over my mind and body, but I fight to bury it deep down, determined to keep it locked away. I have no other choice but to complete the ceremony and unlock the bridge. Being afraid will do me no favors.

"Soren, dear, can you come out now?" Drew calls from the forest. Soren emerges, a small figure trailing behind him. As they draw closer, I realize with a sinking feeling that it's a child. A little girl, no older than ten, with curly brown hair and big red eyes. My heart sinks at what this might mean.

"I don't understand. What's this about?" I ask Drew, my voice shaking.

"Lyra, did you really think I was going to sacrifice my life willingly for the cause? There are too many unknowns attached to it. I cannot leave my people without a leader," Drew says, her eyes fixed on me.

The young girl looks up at me, her eyes wide and innocent. I feel sick to my stomach, knowing what is about to happen. "But she's a child. You can't sacrifice an innocent child," I protest weakly, backing up, my feet perilously close to the edge of the cliff. The wind whips through my hair, and I can feel the chill of the sea spray on my face.

"She has offered herself willingly," Soren says softly, his eyes fixed on the ground. My mind struggles as I try to think of a way out of this, but I know there is none. I must complete the ceremony and unlock the bridge. And to do that, I must drink the blood of this innocent child.

The answer comes instantly and clearly. No.

I look around frantically, feeling like I might be sick or pass out. A part of me considers running away or even ending it all and jumping off this cliff right now, but I know I can't. Zomea's fate hangs in the balance, quite possibly Eguina's too, and if I don't unlock the bridge souls will be lost forever in a limbo of nothingness. The weight of responsibility is crushing, and I feel like I'm about to crumble under it. I can't even be sure if the prophecies are true, but I have to try. Yet, can I really take a child's life for the sake of others? How will I ever live with myself? I can feel the darkness closing in on me, threatening to consume me whole.

My heart thumps rapidly against my chest as I try to wrap my head around what's happening. I glance over at Colton, hoping for some kind of reassurance, but he looks as troubled as I feel.

The little girl releases Drew's hand and steps forward. I find myself crouching down to meet her gaze. I feel a tear fall down my cheek, but I quickly clear my throat and ask, "What's your name?"

"Anya," she says in a small voice. She reaches up and wipes away my tear with her thumb. "Don't cry for me, Lyra. This is what I want."

Another sob escapes my throat, and more tears fall down my face. "But why, Anya? Why would you want this? Why would you want to die?" I ask, my voice shaking with emotion.

The girl looks up at me with a wisdom beyond her years. "I want to be the one to help you unlock the bridge. I want to be a part of something bigger than myself, something that will help everyone. I want to be remembered for doing something important."

It hits me like a punch to the gut. This child is willing to sacrifice herself for the greater good, something I couldn't even fathom doing at her age. The weight of the situation crushes me, and I struggle to catch my breath. Can I really take the life of a child for the sake of unlocking a bridge? Is the fate of Zomea worth this cost? The tears keep streaming down my face, and I realize I'm not just crying for Anya. I'm crying for myself, for the loss of innocence, for the weight of responsibility, for the sacrifice that must be made.

"If it makes you feel any better, my family is in Zomea. I lost my mother and father and am looking forward to being reunited with them," she says, and I try to regain control of my emotions.

If I am successful at unlocking the bridge, then Anya and her family may even be able to travel freely back to the realms if they want. I reach for any positives I can, wiping the tears from my face. I can't give up now, not when the fate of so many souls is at stake. I look out at the horizon, where the blood moon casts a crimson glow over the land. It's a stark reminder of the urgency of the situation. Without Zomea, these souls will be lost forever.

"Why can't someone older do it? Lamias live for centuries. She hasn't even started to live her life. There has to be someone old up for the task," I press, squeezing Chepi tighter and looking to Drew.

"Lyra, she is far older and wiser then she looks. The Lamia do not age as you do. Let her do this. Let her honor her people and make this choice for herself," Drew says, but I don't want to accept it. I swallow, dropping my chin in reluctant defeat.

"It's decided then. Lyra, you must reunite this child with her family." Drew's urgent command hangs heavy in the air. I know time is running out. Soren steps forward and places a small dagger in my trembling hand. I release Chepi, and he stays close, flying right next to me. The weight of the blade brings a harsh reality crashing down on me. I drop to my knees, struggling to keep myself together. Anya steps forward and wraps her arms tightly around my neck, almost knocking us both backward off the cliff.

Her small body feels fragile in my embrace, and a sense of dread washes over me. Suddenly, I realize the dagger is no longer in my grasp. As I look down, I feel wetness soak into my gown. Horror seizes me as I see blood pooling around my knees. I pull Anya back, supporting her neck, and notice her wrists are already slit. Panic rises within me, and I hold her close as she coughs weakly. Her eyes meet mine, and I see fear and panic etched in her red irises.

"What have you done?" I cry out in despair, cradling her limp body. With one final effort, she reaches up to touch my face before her eyes close forever.

"Quickly now, there's no time. You must drink her blood." Drew's voice snaps me back to reality. I rebuild the barrier around my heart as I grab her wrist and drink.

The first drop of Anya's blood hits my tongue, warm and metallic, and an intense heat spreads through my body. I squeeze my eyes shut as I force myself to swallow, trying to ignore the sickening feeling in my stomach. As I drink more, the ground beneath me begins to tremble, and I release Anya, setting her gently on the ground. The tremors become more violent, and I look up, catching Colton's movement out of the corner of my eye. I grab Chepi and hold him close tucked under one arm. I hold my other arm out in front of me, trying to brace myself for whatever is about to happen.

That's when everything changes.

The air above starts to ripple and warp like a heat mirage. An icy wind gusts down from the distortion, whipping my hair around my face and causing the others to shield their eyes. I can feel a raw, primordial power humming in the air around me. It's terrifying, and I have to swallow back the fear rising in my throat.

Then I notice the cracks forming in the ground, a perfect circle becoming visible beneath me. Suddenly, a vortex of shadow appears in front of me, spinning faster and faster, all around me before crashing into the ground and seeping into the cracks. I gasp as I realize what's happening. Colton lunges forward, grabbing my hand as the ground disappears below me. A bottomless pit seems to open up in the earth, and I dangle over the edge, too afraid to look down.

Colton leans in close, his lips brushing my ear. "Did you think I was going to let you have all the fun, my little enchantress," he whispers, and I squeeze his hand tighter, my heart pounding. Gods, he really is crazy.

"Are you ready?" Colton asks, and I look up at him, his green eyes glowing with a fierce intensity I've never seen before. The ground continues to shake, and I swallow hard, determined not to let my own fear consume me.

"Yes," I force myself to say, my voice scratching my throat.

Colton leaps off the edge, wrapping himself around Chepi and me. I bury my face in his chest as the shadows swallow us whole.

CHAPTER
SEVEN

A fierce gust of wind roars upward, delivering a putrid stench that invades my senses and rattles my stomach. The gust seems to cradle us momentarily in its grasp, slowing our fall then vanishing as swiftly as it came, dumping us onto a hard surface. Pain ricochets through my body as we collide with the ground below.

"You're welcome for breaking your fall," Colton says, coughing beneath me.

"Shh," I whisper, feeling Chepi to make sure he's okay. I blink against the pervasive darkness that engulfs everything, swallowing all the light and leaving nothing but an impenetrable void.

"Stay close, boy," I say to Chepi in a hushed voice as I struggle to get to my feet. I wipe my damp hands on my clothes, the slick rock beneath us adding to the discomfort. An eerie squelching sound accompanies every step we take on this wet surface. Water murmurs in the distance, bouncing off the cave walls, disorienting me further.

"Let me go first. Take my hand." Colton steps in front of

me, and I reluctantly take his hand. I guess it's not the time to be difficult right now. We take slow measured steps until small patches of light appear and help my eyes to adjust. The walls and floors are slick with moss, which glows with a faint bioluminescence, casting eerie green splatters of light across the dank space.

As we move further into the tunnel, the space seems to open up ever so slightly ahead. I quicken my pace, eager to escape this claustrophobic place, but Colton squeezes my hand, steadying me next to him. We emerge from the darkness, and I freeze in terror. The cave branches off into three openings, and there's a bottomless pit in the center of the path in front of us. The realizations hits me like a punch in the gut. These aren't just any tunnels—they're the tunnels from my nightmare. Why did my midnight mind show me this place for the first time only right before unlocking the bridge? This can't be a coincidence. What was my dream trying to show me? I try to remember it more clearly, but the memory is fuzzy now. Something was after me, and the whispers... A chill spreads across my skin. I try to shake off the uneasy feeling.

"I've been here before," I say quietly. Seems like something I should share with Colton, since we are now in this together because he's absolutely insane and decided to jump into the earth after me.

"What do you mean? How?" he asks, coming to a stop before the dark hole in front of us, peering into it carefully.

"I don't think I told you, but I have midnight mind and have been seeing Zomea for some time now. Only once and only recently was I brought here in my nightmare." I shiver, stepping closer to him. "Colton, something was after me," I whisper.

"What was after you?" He finally looks at me, his attention fully mine. In the shadowy ambiance of the tunnels, his emerald eyes gleam with a sharp intensity. His dirty-blond hair falls in a disheveled mane around his face and shoulders, complementing the ruggedness of his features. With broad shoulders set back, and a stance that speaks of natural, athletic strength, he carries an undeniable presence—graceful yet formidable. I won't admit it aloud, but by the gods, am I relieved to have him by my side right now.

"I don't know," I admit. We stand silently before the three tunnels, their dark maws beckoning me with the same ominous emptiness.

"I think we should take the left tunnel." I take a step forward, tugging Colton's hand as I inch around the dark pit in the floor. Chepi stays close, hovering right over my shoulder.

"Why exactly do you think we should take the left tunnel, Princess?"

"Intuition." I shrug, stepping into the tunnel. I'm not exactly sure why I chose the left one, but my choice was driven by an inexplicable urge. The sound of trickling water echoes all around us. I don't like it. The idea that this tunnel system could be beneath some sort of body of water makes me really uncomfortable. The thought alone gets my feet moving faster, drawing me forward.

I stop dead in my tracks when I hear it. A distant throb undulates through the dank air of the tunnels, a rhythm so primal and elemental that it resonates within my own chest. It's a heartbeat—a relentless thud...thud...thud...echoing through the darkness, disorienting me.

"Colton," I exhale, my voice a thin wisp of sound, trembling in the darkness.

"What's wrong?" His voice, instantly edged with alarm, cuts through the silence.

"Do you hear it?" I say quietly, clutching his hand tighter than I'm proud of.

"I don't hear anything. Lyra, what do you hear?" he whispers.

The thud is maddening, each beat reverberating in my skull. I can't block it out. It's a heartbeat, a rhythm, a reminder that something unseen and unknown lurks in the foreboding depths of these tunnels.

"Let's keep moving."

I hurry our pace, not knowing where we are going, but I have a strange sensation of something pulling me toward it. The feeling grows more intense with each step, urging me to go deeper into this maze of tunnels.

Suddenly the whispers start, so faint at first that I almost think I imagined them.

"Now *that* I can hear," Colton says, moving past me to take the lead but not releasing my hand. We keep up our pace, and the whispers grow louder, carried on a gust of wind that seems to guide our path. We pass through several more openings, each leading to a new tunnel, and every time we step into a new one, the whispers become louder, as if they're closing in on us from all directions. I can no longer hear the heavy beating as the whispers turn to screams, dozens of them, all echoing around us. Adrenaline takes over, and I start to run as fast as I can, my heart pounding out of my chest. Colton keeps pace next to me, and I cradle Chepi under my arm, not comfortable with him flying on his own.

We reach a dead end, and the screams grow even louder. I want to cover my ears, but instead I release Colton's hand and slam my palm into the rock wall, silently begging for a sign, anything to help us before the voices reach us. I slam my palm into the wall again, harder, and squeeze my eyes shut, unable to think straight with the sound closing in on us.

"What the actual fuck?" Colton causes my eyes to fly open, and that's when I see it. The wall starts to bleed, and at first it's just a few drips. But soon it's pouring out of the cracks in the rock. We both step back in horror as the wall melts away in front of us and blood pours from the stone, until we are left staring into a shimmering, wobbling wall of liquid crimson.

The voices are still fast approaching, but time seems to slow down as I stare at the shimmering veil. I can't resist the urge to press my hand against it, and I sink my fingers into the warm, viscous fluid.

"Shit, why did you have to touch it?" Colton says, but I barely hear him, totally entranced by the wall before me. Suddenly my fingers feel a warm breeze, and the wall seems to part before me. It's a portal or maybe the bridge we've been searching for. I lift my foot and press it into the blood, which seems to open up for me, allowing me to pass through it without a single drop sticking to me.

Colton grabs hold of my leg, and we lock eyes. He looks alarmed, but I can't describe the feeling I'm having right now. The crimson wall begins to melt away, and then I hear his voice from behind. Before I can pass through the wall, his hand clasps down on my shoulder, and an icy wind with a hint of sulfurous decay envelopes us.

"My Pixie." A voice echoes through my mind as we channel.

My feet hit the ground, and I whirl around to face him— my father. I stare at him, unable to speak, my mind racing and not quite believing what I'm seeing. Why did he smell of decay? Or was it the portal that smelled? And how did he channel? How did he know we were here? I know he admitted to killing Nyx's parents, and a part of me is weary of his intentions, but the other part of me just wants to hug him and trust him.

I decide to be cautious, molding my face into a façade of calm as I look him over. He looks exactly as I remember him, like he did the last time I saw him, only this time I know there's more to him than meets the eye.

He's a regal-looking Faery. My father is a vision of charm and grace, his golden countenance masking the darkness that lurks within, the darkness that allowed him to kill Nyx's parents, his friends. His well-proportioned body conveys an air of noble elegance with toned muscles and a graceful stature that commands attention. His skin is warm, a radiant shade of gold, and devoid of any imperfections.

His face is striking, with sculpted cheekbones and a strong chiseled jawline. Looking at him now, I can't imagine how anyone would look at him and believe he was a mere Sorcerer. His eyes, my eyes, the emerald and cobalt melding together, sparkling with a deceptive warmth, making it nearly impossible to see the cunning that must hide beneath the surface.

His lustrous golden-blond hair cascades down his broad shoulders, framing him like a halo of sunlight. He is dressed in luxurious, finely tailored garments that accentuate his regal bearing, or what was once his regal bearing. The rich fabrics, in shades of gold, sapphire blue, and deep crimson are embroidered with intricate patterns and embellished with sparkling gemstones. Each piece of clothing is crafted to further enhance his magnetic presence, distracting from the sinister intentions hidden beneath the surface. To everyone else, he is a picture of benevolent royalty, but beneath the golden façade I know this male Faery, my father, harbors sinister secrets that only a select few would ever come to know.

"You've grown up. You're a lady now," he says, a wide smile plastered on his face. "Come on, Pixie. I've been waiting for this very moment for so long. Can I get a hug?"

I hesitate for a moment, and so does Colton. It's the first time he's moved since we channeled. I feel him take a step closer to me, but my father doesn't take his eyes off mine. I can't help but want to believe he's good. I wrap my arms around his neck and let him pull me into a hug. He squeezes me tight, lifting me into the air as he used to. I breathe him in, smelling his hair as I hug him. He has the same smell, a warm aroma of leather and sandalwood. A hint of decay still lingers in my nose too, reminding me to be cautious. I release his neck, and once he lets my feet hit the ground I step back next to Colton again.

"It's been a long time, my boy," my father says, extending his hand to Colton.

"Indeed, it has," Colton says, shaking his hand.

"I see you've been protecting our girl as well." My father pats Chepi on the head.

"Where are we?" I inquire, my eyes finally adjusting to the surroundings. The scene is reminiscent of the burning forest I encountered before, but without any traces of fire or blood. A thick swirling fog cloaks the forest floor, creating the illusion of a living, breathing ground. Ancient, gnarled trees encircle us, their twisted limbs weaving together overhead and casting ghostly shadows through the mist. The bark is an eerie dark gray, nearly black, while the leaves boast a crimson hue, bathing the forest in perpetual twilight.

The trees here don't bleed, and the foliage is lush. Perhaps this is what the burning forest once resembled.

"We're in Zomea. You've succeeded, Lyra. You unlocked the bridge. I sensed your presence the moment you crossed over. We have much to discuss, all of us. Allow me to take you to my dwelling," he says, draping an arm around my shoulders, urging me to walk with him. I glance back at Colton, who gives me a weary look and keeps pace behind us next to Chepi.

The forest is unnervingly quiet, and the sky above is an angry blend of gray and black, making it impossible to discern the time. Navigating beneath the tree canopy is disorienting due to the dim light and oppressive fog.

After a brief hike, we encounter a magical barrier that blocks our path. The mystical force, appearing as a swirling, dark mist, parts enough to let us pass as we approach.

"Don't be alarmed by the dark mist," he reassures us. "It serves as both a protective measure and a means to conceal the palace from those I wish to keep at bay."

I step through the dark barrier of magical mist and find myself awestruck by the sight before me—a palace carved into the heart of a volcano.

Its majestic architecture fuses seamlessly with the rugged, volcanic terrain, looming ominously over the surrounding landscape. Molten lava flows down the sides of the mountain, forming glowing rivers that illuminate the palace's dark, imposing facade. A fiery moat encircles the structure, acting as a second barrier to protect it from unwanted intruders.

The exterior walls of the palace are hewn from the very rock of the volcano, their rough texture contrasting with the intricate, fiery patterns etched into the stone. As I move closer, I notice the entrance is flanked by two colossal statues, each depicting a fearsome creature, maybe even Gholioths. Their stony eyes seem to follow my every move, and it gives me the creeps.

We all cross the bridge of volcanic stone that spans the fiery moat, and I can feel the intense heat beneath my feet. My father pushes the colossal doors in front of us open, and we make our way inside.

The moment I enter, I'm struck by the contrast between the dark, volcanic exterior and the opulent, glowing interior. The walls are adorned with precious gemstones that shimmer in the volcanic light, casting a warm, flickering glow throughout the vast halls. The floors are covered with elaborate mosaics, and streams of lava flow through channels carved into the palace walls, providing both light and heat.

We silently venture deeper into the palace, following my father as he leads us into a sitting room. I step onto a plush, dark carpet, feeling as if I'm walking on a cloud. In the center of the room, I see a short table with a polished surface reflecting the warm glow of the volcanic light. I can't help but admire the deep-red, velvet-upholstered armchairs that surround the table, each chair decorated with peculiar swirling patterns, mimicking the movement of the fiery rivers flowing through the palace.

Following my gaze, he gestures toward one end of the room, where a grand fireplace roars to life. Its flames lick at the edges of a magnificent mantle, carved from a single slab of volcanic rock. The fire's warmth fills the room, creating a cozy atmosphere that contrasts with the raw power of the volcano just beyond the palace walls.

I take a seat in one of the chairs, Colton sits next to me, and Chepi curls up on my lap.

"Are you well?" my father asks while lowering himself into a chair across from us.

"No, I'm not well. I am far from well, Father."

"I know. I imagine this is a lot to take in, and a lot has happened. You've grown up after all."

"A lot to take in." A high-pitched laugh makes its way up my throat as I think about how casual he's being and everything I've gone through.

Colton reaches over and places his hand on my knee, squeezing it slightly. "Do you want something to drink, Lyra?" he asks, giving me a look telling me I need to relax.

"Yes, I should have asked all of you that first. Let me grab us some drinks." My father moves across the room to a cart filled with different decanters and glasses.

"Breathe," Colton whispers in my ear. My father returns

with three glasses, handing one to each of us and reserving one for himself.

"Please tell me about yourself. Tell me about your life," he says, and I take a sip of the amber liquid he gave me, clearing my throat and letting the warm liquor settle my nerves.

"I'm not going to tell you about myself, not right now. I need answers, Father."

"Then please ask me anything." He moves his leg to rest his ankle over his knee.

"Well, for starters, what was that place, those tunnels we were in?" I ask.

"Those are the Tunnels of Mystweave, and they run beneath Zomea," he says but doesn't elaborate.

"And the wall of blood, the portal Lyra was about to step through before you encountered us?" Colton says, taking a drink from his glass but keeping his eyes on my father, Euric.

"That was simply a portal from the tunnels to Zomea. There are many of them found all throughout the tunnel system that bring you to the surface," he explains.

"What about the beating, the consistent thud that echoed all around us?" Colton turns his head to me, and I remember now that he couldn't hear it. My father's eyes narrow for a brief moment. "I don't know of any beating. Maybe you hit your head when you unlocked the bridge."

I have to resist rolling my eyes, because now they are both looking at me like I'm crazy.

"What about the whispers and screams? It sounded like they were chasing us. You heard them too," I say, turning to look at Colton, who nods in confirmation.

"The tunnel walls are lined with a unique mineral that enhances the voices of the deceased, producing a haunting symphony from time to time. The whispers you hear are the dead voicing their secrets, regrets, and hidden desires."

"That's creepy." I pause, shaking my head. "I don't understand. I thought Zomea is where everyone goes in the afterlife. Why would anyone down here be dead, and for that matter isn't everyone down here technically dead?" I ask, rubbing at my forehead.

"Zomea is not the afterlife, not in the way you are made to believe it is back in the realms. When you die, your body drops into the most dangerous section of the tunnels. We call it the Abyssal Chasm. You have to fight your way into Zomea or choose to die the final death."

I reposition in my chair, unsettled. "What happens if you die the final death, and why would anyone choose that?"

"One may choose to die because they want peace, or one may simply not pass the tests to get out of the Abyssal Chasm, losing the fight," he says, his eyes drifting to the fireplace.

"What happens to those who die the final death, and what do you have to fight to make it to Zomea? Why didn't we have to fight anything?" Colton asks.

My father seems to watch the flames lick the edges of the mantle, looking deep in thought. "Those who die the final death, only the gods decide what happens to their souls. All I know is they don't make it to Zomea. As for your other question, what one may face in the chasm is unique to them. Everyone experiences something different, and everyone is tested in a way that uniquely caters to them. It's decided by a higher power, one I do not fully understand myself, and before you think about asking what I faced, don't. It is for me to know." He takes a long drink from his glass before turning back to face us. "What do you think of the spirit?"

He holds up his glass, eyeing the liquid.

"It's different. What is it exactly?" I ask, lifting my glass and taking another sip. It warms me from the inside out, and I hadn't realized how badly I've needed to ease my nerves.

"It's called Magma's Kiss. Some fool named it. It's aged in casks made from porous lava rock. The flavor grows on you." He downs the rest of his spirit and places his glass on the table between us. "You didn't have to face anything in the tunnels because neither of you died. You didn't pass through the Abyssal Chasm. Instead you unlocked a bridge straight from the Lamia Realm into the Tunnels of Mystweave. You did the very thing I have been working most of my life to achieve, and you cannot possibly understand how extraordinary this is, Lyra."

His lips curve up, and a softness settles into his features that would make anyone want to trust him, but I quickly remind myself my father is the most powerful king to have ever ruled over Cloudrum, one of the most powerful Fae and now quite possibly the ruler of Zomea. He clearly has an undeniable skill for getting people to trust him, believe in him, and follow him. I will not let myself fall for his cunning.

"Why did you kill Nyx's parents, Callum and Scarlett, when they were your friends?" I ask, straightening my back in my chair.

"That is a very long story, Pixie, and there is a lot of history there that you don't understand."

"Then make me understand. We have plenty of time." I stroke Chepi's back, and he rests his head on my knee but keeps his eyes locked on my father, as if he's judging him too.

"Callum was once a friend, indeed, but over time he grew envious of my midnight mind and my foresight abilities. There was even a time when he was obsessed with your mother, Elspeth, and her mind abilities." He pauses, nodding at Colton, but Colton doesn't say anything, just studies Euric while he continues talking. "Our friendship soured, and he developed a personal vendetta against me. Callum became obsessed with prophecies, far more than my healthy curiosity would allow.

He stumbled upon a prophecy that he believed was about you. According to his interpretation, you would inherit dark magic, and the darkness within you would threaten his son and the realms. You hadn't even been born yet, and I thought he was losing his grip on reality.

"Knowing he couldn't defeat me, Callum and Granger decided to banish me instead, and I allowed it to happen. I started anew in Cloudrum with your mother under the false pretenses that I was a Sorcerer."

"But how? How did you suddenly claim the right to rule in Tempest Moon?" I ask.

"I used my magic to trick most of the Sorcerer Realm into believing I was always in Cloudrum. Once you were born, I had no choice but to eliminate the threat. I was well aware that it would lead to my death, which is why I made you the key. I devised a way for us to be reunited, but my priority was to protect you. In taking the lives of Nyx's parents, I set the stage for my own demise, ultimately falling at the hands of Nyx."

He lets out a long sigh and runs a hand through his hair before going on.

"You have always been everything to me, Lyra. I may have done horrible things, but I did them from a place of love. I only did what I believed was right, what I had to do to protect my family— to protect you."

I'm not sure what to say. Thankfully Colton speaks before I do. "Don't try to make Lyra feel guilty for something you did. She's gone through enough because of you." I'm shocked for a moment. Why is Colton sticking up for me like this? I don't know, but I like it.

Euric clears his throat. "I'm sorry, Pixie. I know you have been through a lot, and I hope one day you will feel comfortable talking to me about it. You should not feel any guilt for my actions. Colton is right." I'm even more shocked he didn't snap back at Colton, instead agreeing with him.

"Where are Nyx's parents now? Are they here in Zomea?" I ask, thinking maybe I can fix all of this and reunite Nyx with his family.

"If they are, I have never seen them. Zomea is much larger than Eguina. You must remember that this is not the afterlife. This place is simply another continent, almost like a second chance at life if one is able to get here."

I still can't quite wrap my head around this place and the tunnels. I need to digest things. It feels like everything we were taught to believe of the afterlife is false. I don't even know what to believe of the gods now.

My father looks me over and must sense my exhaustion. "Why don't I show you to a room where you can rest and get cleaned up? We have plenty of time to have more discussions. So much has been said already. Maybe it's best you take some time to process it all. I promise I will answer every question you have, in time." He gets to his feet, ready to lead us to our rooms.

"Wait, I have one more question I need you to answer." I rise, and he watches me patiently. "Actually, two more. How did you speak to me through Samael, and why did you lie and tell me Chepi was here when you had to have known he would come back to life?"

I don't look away from him for a second.

"I will always tell you the truth, even if the answers are not always easy to hear. I was able to contact Samael through powerful magic that I cannot explain to you right now. I know Samel is deranged, but we had a common interest, and I needed him to kill Onyx. You have to understand that I do not want you to be anywhere near him. He needs to die. I offered Samael the spell that would subdue Onyx's magic with the proper restraints in exchange for a piece of his soul. That is how I was able to speak through him. As for Chepi, I had to say anything to get you to unlock the bridge before the key could harm you."

He moves to touch my arm, and I take a step out of reach.

"You cannot kill Nyx. I don't care if he is the reason you're in Zomea. You killed his family. What did you expect him to do?" I feel heat rise to my cheeks as my anger starts to come to the surface.

"Pixie, please don't be upset. There is history there you will never understand, and I cannot allow you to be with him." He steps toward me again, and I back away.

"Please, don't. I may not be with him, and he may have hurt me, but I still care for him deeply. Causing him pain will only bring me more suffering. My heart aches enough as it is." I feel my eyes fill up with tears at the thought of a life where Nyx doesn't exist, and I swallow hard, trying to bury my emotions.

"Okay, Lyra, I will not kill Onyx. I do not wish to cause you more pain. Now don't get upset. Come rest." He reaches for me again, and this time I let him wrap his arm around my shoulders and guide me out of the room, Chepi tucked tightly under my other arm, nudging me softly with his wet nose. That was far too easy, and I don't even know if I believe him, but for now at least I know Nyx is safe, away from this place.

He leads us down a series of corridors until we finally pause. He opens the door for me, and I step into the bedroom. The walls catch my eye. They are sleek, polished volcanic stone, their dark hues offset by the flickering light from the wall-mounted torches. A canopy bed stands in the center of the room, draped with luxurious fabrics that complement the fiery surroundings.

The floor is covered in a plush, obsidian-hued carpet that feels surprisingly soft underfoot. A large window offers a mesmerizing view of the volcanic landscape outside, with plumes of smoke and the distant glow of molten lava painting a dramatic scene.

In the corner of the room, a small seating area is arranged around a table carved from volcanic rock, and I can see a small doorway past the seating area that must lead to a bathroom.

"I'll leave you all to rest and get cleaned up." He turns toward the door.

"Wait, we are not sharing a room," I say, quickly looking at Colton, who's already made himself at home by the foot of the bed— the only bed.

"My mistake. I just assumed you were together. The other side of the palace is unstable, and this is the only other bedroom available right now. Colton is welcome to sleep on the rugs downstairs." I cringe. I can't have Colton sleeping on the floor downstairs. He did risk coming here with me after all.

"No, we will make do," I say, hesitantly.

"Very well, whenever you're ready for dinner, come find me downstairs. Take your time and make yourself at home, Lyra. I want you to feel comfortable and safe here. We're together again, and my heart is overjoyed." He gently touches my cheek with his hand and offers me a soft smile. However, I catch a fleeting glimpse of something in his eyes—a possessiveness that makes my skin crawl.

"Thank you, Father. I'm happy to see you too. I look forward to continuing our conversation at dinner," I assure him, trying to muster a convincing smile. But as he leaves the room, the unsettling feeling within me lingers.

CHAPTER
EIGHT

I stare at the shut door for a moment, waiting for the uneasy
feeling to subside. Turning back to the room, I see Colton is
still sitting on the end of the bed petting Chepi. I walk around
to the other side, kick off my boots, and fall back on the bed,
exhausted.

"I know I promised to quit bringing up Onyx," I vent, the
weight of my words hanging heavy in the air, "but do you
believe he'll make another attempt on his life? Can I trust
him?" A deep exhale follows my question. I harbor doubts
about Colton as well, yet as much as I hate to admit it, I would
feel utterly alone without him right now.

"Why should it matter?" he snorts. "Why are you bothered
by his absence? He left, didn't he?"

"He left only because I asked him to," I correct him swiftly.

"If you were mine, Lyra..." He lies back on the bed next to
me, and his eyes find mine, shining a brighter shade of green.
"...it would take far more than a mere request to make me leave
your side. Onyx is a self-righteous nuisance. You're far better
off without him, and the sooner you come to terms with this

and untangle any lingering feelings, the better. From what I gather, you haven't even seen the real Onyx. Consider yourself lucky."

"What is it with you two? I've been biting my tongue, but I need to know. Why do you both hate each other so much?" A heartbeat passed.

"We were friends once, you know. But he did something unforgivable. Over the years, we learned to tolerate each other, but after his parents died and he became the king of Nighthold and inherited even more power, he changed."

Searching his gaze, I waited for him to elaborate, and when he didn't I couldn't help but open my mouth again. "I think the death of a parent changes everyone. I would know."

"I'm sorry. I know you would. He didn't change in the way you are thinking." He coughed, turning his head away from me to study the ceiling. "Besides, we have much more important things to discuss right now, like what your father is up to and what the fuck this place is—this Zomea."

"Right...not the afterlife exactly, almost another realm connected to Eguina but not at the same time," I muse. "You knew my father before when he lived in Nighthold?"

"I did."

"What was he like? I only remember the good things a young girl would remember about a father. But with everything that's happened, I am starting to think he's not the man I thought he was. I don't know if I allowed Nyx's influence to cloud my judgment, and I need to give my father the benefit of the doubt. We used to be so close when I was little, but now all the secrets and superstitions I've heard from others have soured things. Not to mention killing Nyx's family. I mean, he has done unforgivable things...and I can't deny the uneasy feeling that tugs at my gut when I'm in his presence." I inhale deeply, wishing things weren't so fucked up.

"I know it's easy to fall prey to the influence of others. Don't think about that. Forget everything you've heard from other people and follow your gut. If you have an uneasy feeling, don't ignore it. It's there for a reason."

"I know." I sigh.

"As far as what he was like before, he was intelligent and fierce. Powerful and cunning, there's a reason most of the Fae feared him. He was always nice to me, but I know he has a hunger for power, always wanting to be the one who runs the show. Some would say he has questionable judgment when it comes to getting what he wants and risking the lives of others, but you already know that." He rises from the bed, kicking off his boots and pulling his off-white tunic off over his head. "Can you trust him? Only you can answer that for yourself."

"What are you doing?" I ask, not liking the lack of restraint I have when taking in his bare upper body. He is built like no man I've ever seen, the body of a real warrior. But what battles had he ever fought? I always assumed Colton was a pompous, privileged child of the elders, attending Faery parties and drinking too much, but his body speaks to a darker past. I let my eyes linger over a scar that extends across the right side of his chest. It spreads from his collarbone to his belly button, jagged across those glorious abs.

"I'm going to get cleaned up." He smirks, moving into the bathroom and closing the door before undressing the rest of the way. Gods, what is wrong with me?

I clasp my hands over my face, closing my eyes. I was just with Nyx, and now I'm letting my mind linger on Colton's extremely built figure. I let out a strangled laugh. Everything is so screwed up right now that it seems only fair to laugh about it. A part of me wishes Nyx was here instead of Colton, but then a part of me is also undeniably enjoying Colton's company. I never thought I would be enjoying anything about Colton, but he's not so bad.

I OPEN MY EYES, searching the darkness of the room, disoriented for a moment. It's late, pitch black outside the window now. I can feel Chepi curled up next to my feet, and I relax a bit. Wait, someone tucked me in the bed. I wasn't under the covers before, but I am now. I must have fallen asleep while Colton was in the bathroom. I must have missed dinner. Gods, I wanted to keep questioning my father, but I was so tired. I throw my arm out in frustration, and I'm momentarily shocked when it hits a solid chest.

I forgot I was sharing a room. I blink a few times, my eyes trying to adjust to the darkness. Colton is lying on his back above the covers with all his clothes on. Hmm, maybe he is more of a gentleman than I thought. He tucked me into bed then slept fully clothed with layers of blankets separating us and as much distance as possible without him falling off the bed.

"Ouch," Colton drawls in a low voice.

"Oh stop, there's no way that hurt you," I snap.

"I think you're stronger than you realize." He chuckles lightly, turning over to face me.

"Did you go to dinner? Why didn't you wake me?"

"You looked so peaceful, and you needed rest. I couldn't bring myself to disturb you. I didn't go to dinner, but I did venture downstairs and spoke to Euric briefly."

"What did you talk about?" I move, turning to lie on my side to face him. I quickly move onto my back again when I realize my stitches are still too uncomfortable to rest on my side like that.

"Not much, he said he's going to take us on a tour of Zomea tomorrow. There's something he needs us to see before he can talk about it. Whatever the fuck that means." His brow pinches. "Why did you make that face?"

"What face?" I ask.

"You made a face when you faced me, then you rolled back and looked away." He is way too observant for my liking.

"Oh, that. I didn't think I was making a face. I turned on my side, forgetting my stitches are still healing, and it's not quite comfortable to lie like that yet." I paused, running my teeth over my bottom lip. "I wonder what he wants to show us tomorrow, if it has to do with my midnight mind and the burning forest I told you about. Or if my mother is here. It could be any number of things." I also think of Luke but don't mention that part to Colton.

Luke warned me to stay away from this place.

"Why didn't you tell me? I can heal you." He moves to sit up on his elbow.

"Oh, no, that's okay. Soren did what he could, and I'm feeling much better."

"The mortal," he says, eyebrows raised. "Show me your side."

I'm thankful for how dark this room is right now, because I can feel heat rising to my cheeks. I contemplate how to show him my side without getting naked, and it would be nice if he could heal me the rest of the way. The only reason it's taken this long is because it was such a nasty wound. Colton makes some hand gestures for me to hurry up, and I slip out of bed, letting my feet hit the ground. I pull my gown over my head but keep my under slip on.

"What happened to your back?" He moves before I can answer, and I feel the tips of his warm fingers trail across the visible skin on my upper back.

"Who did this to you?"

"Don't you already know?" I turn to face him, self-conscious with him so close.

"Did Nyx do this?" He clasps my shoulder so I can't turn away.

"Nyx would never do something like that. Didn't you know we got captured by Samael and were tortured..." I don't want to be talking about this right now.

"Drew was not specific, only saying you and Nyx got into some trouble, you ended things with him, and you needed someone to help you with Fae magic. There was no mention of torture. Did Nyx kill the bastard at least?"

"No, but I did. Anyways, my back is almost healed completely, last I checked, only some red lines," I say, sounding defensive, although I don't know what I'm being defensive about.

"Your magic should be able to heal any petty wounds you get so for these marks to still be here, your wounds had to have been substantial. And Nyx left you like this, still hurt."

"Nyx has always said he's not a good healer, and he didn't leave me hurt. I asked him to leave because I needed space, and he did. He was respecting my boundaries," I retort, although I don't know why I'm defending Nyx now.

"Show me your stitches. Wait, turn back around first." I stare at him for a moment, and he releases my shoulder. I debate not turning around again because I don't want him seeing the marks on my back again. I feel awkward, but I'm not sure why. I sigh, turning away from him so he can examine me.

"I'm fine, really," I insist. A soft glow lights up the room from behind me, and I can feel Colton's fingertips trail across my skin again. A warm tingling sensation follows his every touch as he traces the marks on my back. He tugs at my slip, and I slide my arms out and let it fall to my hips. He's behind me, so he can't see anything, and surprisingly I don't think he's trying to. Once he's finished with my back, he presses a palm to my side, and I suck in a breath, not because it hurts but because this close contact and the heat from his body touching mine are doing something to me. I push those thoughts out of my head, quickly reminding myself I don't know what is going on with Nyx and I.

I did end things with him, but I don't know if that's really what I want.

I can feel it the moment Colton's done, and I look down at his hand as the soft white glow dissipates, and I'm left with unscarred flesh. He takes each of my straps and works them back up my arms, taking his time until my slip is perfectly back in place. Then he lies back on the bed.

"Thank you," I whisper as I crawl back into bed.

"Get some sleep." He inhales deeply, and I sneak a peek at him. His jaw is set hard, and I don't know what else to say.

CHAPTER
NINE

Morning finally comes, and I awake to Colton sitting on the end of the bed, leaning against the bed post, watching me.

"It's too early for you to be creepy," I murmur, stretching.

"I'm enjoying coffee...and the view." He smirks, and I look down remembering I'm only wearing my slip. I pull the blankets up my body.

"Very funny, and how did you get coffee?" I rarely drink coffee, which always tastes bitter to me, but I guess I should start drinking more of it if I'm going to keep losing sleep. Colton seems to read my thoughts and brings me a cup.

"You are quite the heavy sleeper once you actually sleep. A lady was here. A Lycan lady to be precise, she left some clothes for each of us and a tray of coffee and fruit." He ran a hand through his hair, tucking it out of his face, looking down at the tray resting on the bedside table. "Oddest-looking fruit I've ever seen, but you're welcome to test it out for us."

The coffee is dark as night, and I have to choke it down. It's still hot, so that helps. As for the fruit, it does look unusual, but

I imagine Zomea is like all the other realms, each having food vastly different from one another. In fact, the only constant amongst the realms seems to be whiskey and wine. I grab something that resembles a banana, only it's red and fuzzy. Peeling back the outside reveals a creamy sweet inside that tastes very similar to a banana but softer and sweeter. I take a few bites and head into the bathing chamber to get cleaned up.

I'm quick about it, eager to get the day started. I braid my hair into one large braid and wash up quickly, popping my head out to see Colton still poking at the fruit like it's going to bite him.

"Hey, you said something about clothes?" I ask, getting his attention. He hands me a folded stack, and I duck back into the bathroom.

Glad to be clean and out of the heavy red gown I was wearing, I look through the small stack of interesting clothes this Lycan lady left. I wonder where they came from while sliding into a pair of black hosen, the supple leather hugging my legs and promising easy movement. I don a bright-blue tunic next, its vibrant fabric embracing my form. Over this, I secure a black leather bodice, cinching my waist and enhancing my appearance to seem more composed and formidable than I feel.

I step back into the bed chamber, ready to go find my father. A wicked smile spreads across Colton's face as he looks me over. "Who's looking all dark enchantress-like now?"

"Not another word," I scold him. He laughs, and I pull the covers back off the bed. Chepi stretches, rolling onto his back. Colton and I both lean in to give him belly rubs at the same time, and all we accomplish is smacking our foreheads together.

"Gods, are you ready to go?" I huff, rubbing my forehead and giving him my best impression of an evil eye.

"After you, my little shadowmancer." I'm pretty sure I'm never going to get away from the nicknames, so I just ignore him, giving Chepi some love and heading to the door. Chepi hops down and trails after me. Once into the hall, I glance around to get my bearing and realize I have no idea how we got to this room.

"Alright, squish, go find father," I tell Chepi, and he takes off down the hall. Colton and I have to keep a brisk pace to keep up with him. He doesn't take us back to the main sitting room we were in yesterday, and instead we end up on the other side of the palace, I think. It's slightly more rundown looking, and I find myself slowing my steps as the corridors go from warm and grand to dark and decrepit.

Chepi stops in front of a closed wooden door, rot setting into a few of the boards, and the handle appears rusty. Colton gives me a look, and I lift my hand to knock on the door, but a voice stops me.

"You have to tell her everything or she's never going to go along with it," Athalda says. Her voice is low and muffled through the door, but I know it's her.

"I'll tell her everything she needs to know. There's still plenty of time," my father says.

"Lyra, you're awake. I hope the coffee and fruit were to your liking," a woman's voice calls from a few feet away, much louder than necessary for us to hear. This must be the Lycan lady Colton was referring to earlier.

"Yes, thank you. And you are?" She has soft features and those piercing blue Lycan eyes. She fiddles with her long brown hair, twirling it in her fingers as she walks toward us. She looks far too young to be in Zomea, and I wonder how she died, how she fought her way here, and how the hell she ended up here working for my father.

"Forgive me, my name is Anika. I help your father out around this place when I can. I'm pleased to see the clothing fits."

I glance down at myself. "Er, yes, it does. Thanks."

The door opens, and my father is standing there, dressed as impeccably as yesterday. I turn back to look at Anika, but she's gone. Instead I see Colton furrow his brows at me. My father steps out of the room, closing the door and forcing us to back up into the hallway. I try to peer around him to see if the voice I heard was Athalda's, but I can't see anything.

"Athalda will meet us later." I snap my eyes back to him. So she is here. He nods, seeming to know what I'm thinking.

"Come, I want to show you around." He proceeds to walk back the way we came, and we follow him, but not before Colton and I exchange another look. I can't read his face, but he must be feeling uneasy about what happened...because I am. Anika clearly was alerting them that we were eavesdropping, but why, and why didn't Athalda come out?

We stop outside the sitting room in the grand hall. "Are you ready to see what Zomea has to offer?" My father holds out both hands for us to take. Colton reaches over, clasping my hand, and instead of taking my father's I bend down and pick up Chepi. I let Colton pull me in close and wrap an arm around my waist. He nods to Euric, who then clasps him on the shoulder. An icy fog kicks up around us as we channel.

The instant my feet touch the ground, the surrounding fog and chill dissipate. I'm standing at the edge of what once was the burning forest, now transformed into a desolate, smoky wasteland. Trees that once towered high stand charred and skeletal against the gray sky, their blackened branches reaching out in a silent accusation. Every verdant trace that once hinted at life has now turned to ash, settling over the land like a grim blanket of gray snow. The world before me is drained of color, dominated by shades of black, white, and the deepest gray.

A heavy silence hangs over this devastated landscape, devoid of any sign of life or the usual chatter of forest inhabitants. The lack of sound is unnatural, eerie, broken only by the occasional mournful sigh of the wind. As I inhale, the air tastes of char and smoke, yet beneath that there's the ghost of a scent, a faint echo of the vibrant forest that once was — wildflowers and fresh sap. It's faint and fleeting, yet it clings stubbornly to the barren air.

I feel the absence of magic deep in my bones, an uncomfortable void where once there was a vibrant thrum of life. "The burning forest," I murmur under my breath to myself. The words taste bitter.

"You've seen it," my father says, his voice solemn.

"I have. But I have a feeling you already knew that." I pause, turning to look at him. "The trees aren't bleeding anymore."

"No," he confirms, inhaling slowly. "I'm afraid this section of the forest is past that stage."

"What happened here?" Colton asks, his voice barely more than a whisper. I realize he still has his arm wrapped securely around my lower back. We're both struck speechless in the worst way, staring out at the ruins.

This place feels haunted, like a graveyard of nature where every scorched trunk and desolate patch of ground echoes the torment of what used to be. I'm standing in the remnants of beauty, now twisted and corrupted into a stark picture of devastation.

"Zomea is sick because I have the stolen blood of a Gholioth in me," I say, recounting my conversation with Nyx and Athalda.

"Well, that isn't exactly true," my father replies, exhaling a long, weary breath.

My eyes lock onto him, aghast. "What do you mean it's not exactly true?" I ask in confusion. He shifts his gaze to meet mine.

"Athalda...didn't exactly lie to you, Lyra, but there's more to the story."

Colton pivots to face Euric, a hardened edge to his voice. "What's the rest of the story then? And why has it led us here?"

With Chepi held tighter to me than before, I draw in a shaky breath, bracing for the revelation my father is about to deliver.

"It's not stolen blood," he begins, sounding heavy with regret. "Moirati is the oldest Gholioth to inhabit Zomea, and he didn't lose his blood unwillingly. We made an agreement, a deal. He willingly offered some of his blood as payment. At the time, neither of us could foresee the disastrous chain of events that would follow when I fed you his blood."

His confession sends a shiver of revulsion down my spine. "I still can't believe you fed me blood as a child."

"I know," he sighs, his gaze darkening. "I made choices, some of which I am far from proud of. Yet they were necessary. Look at us now, here together with the bridge unlocked."

"But Zomea is dying," I retort, my voice rising in frustration.

Colton interjects before I can continue, "How can we save it?"

"Athalda suggested there could be a way to separate the blood, to return it to Moirati. That could stabilize Zomea. Is it possible?" I shift my gaze from Colton back to my father, searching for answers in his eyes.

"Indeed." He nods slowly. "That is part of what we must discuss, Lyra. I'm aware that you've let Elspeth access your mind and unleash your Fae magic."

His assertion feels like an accusation, leaving a sour taste in my mouth. "You mean the magic that you kept hidden from me. My own magic," I respond through gritted teeth.

"Yes, I hid it for your own protection," he says, making it

sound like a confession. "The reasons why can be addressed later. What's important now is to understand that, despite being new to your Fae magic, you aren't powerful enough yet. You're my daughter, and I know you have the potential to wield incredible power. But as things stand, if I attempted to extract the blood, it might stabilize Zomea but at the cost of your life."

Colton's response is swift and firm, his grip on me tightening as he retorts, "There's no way you're trying that then."

I'm not sure why I let him touch me so intimately in this moment, but there's something comforting about knowing he's here, that he's on my side.

"I would never intentionally put your life in danger," my father assures, his gaze intense. But before I can respond, Colton says, "You mean you wouldn't intentionally put her life at risk again."

I swallow hard, expecting my father to retaliate, to argue with Colton. But his demeanor remains calm, collected. "What's essential for you to grasp — something I suspect you already know but I'm here to affirm — is that you'll inherit dark magic on your birthday this year. You'll be the first of your kind to gain such power in centuries. My dear, you are destined to be unstoppable. The power you'll wield is immeasurable, and once you awaken your dark magic, you can return to Zomea. Only then will you be powerful enough for me to remove the blood, thus allowing Zomea to start healing." He ignores Colton completely, his focus solely on me.

I feel a jolt of realization as my father's confirmation of my destiny sinks in. I've been secretly hoping none of it is true, but hearing him say it... The inheritance of dark magic is no longer an abstract concept; it's real, imminent, and I find myself taking a ragged breath to steady the racing of my heart. I force myself to push aside the fear, refusing to be intimidated by the vision from the echosphere. The black eyes, the shadow tendrils, they're a part of me, and I will not shy away from them.

Chepi's gentle nudge pulls me back, and I ask, "Once you remove the blood, do you truly believe Zomea will be restored? And what about Eguina? Drew told me that things there have started to die, that magic has become unstable in certain parts of the realms."

"Zomea will be restored," my father assures me, firm with conviction. "It will take time, of course, but the dying will cease, and healing will commence both here and in Eguina. The stability of Zomea is vital for the health of all the realms."

"Lyra needs more training, more guidance," Colton interjects, sounding concerned. "She needs to be prepared for what dark magic will entail. I don't have enough knowledge about dark magic to help her."

My father's eyes meet Colton's before shifting back to me. "I'd like you both to stay here for a while, if you will. Colton and I can train you physically, help you harness your Fae magic. As for dark magic, Athalda may not possess it herself, but her wisdom will be invaluable in preparing you."

I nod, understanding the gravity of the task ahead. "How long do you want us to stay?" I ask, my voice barely audible.

"As long as it takes," he replies, his gaze unwavering.

"How much of Zomea has been impacted?" Colton poses the question with a calmness that seems to contrast the gravity of our situation.

"Roughly twenty percent of Zomea mirrors this landscape of death. An additional ten percent is aflame, the fire spreading gradually with each passing day," Euric says.

A chill creeps over me at the thought of Zomea decaying further. It's only January. "How much more will be lost by the time we return?" I question, a faint tremble in my voice.

"Don't concern yourself with that, Pixie. The deterioration

has been slow, and what's lost can be replenished in time. Your early arrival here is a win. It gives us time to properly train and prepare you."

"So when do we start?" Colton says, cutting to the chase.

But before my father can reply, I voice my own pressing queries, "Are we going to see more of Zomea? Is my mother here? I've had dreams about her...in the burning forest."

Euric answers Colton first. "We begin today." Turning to me, he continues, "Zomea is vast and dangerous. In time, you'll see more of it. Until then, unless you're accompanied by me or Athalda, all training should take place within the protective veil near the palace. Regarding Macy... I haven't laid eyes on your mother in many years. The midnight mind is complex, especially for one as new to this as you. Sometimes we see things as they transpire; other times, we see things as we wish they were. Visions can't always be trusted."

Before I can process this, Colton chimes in. "What about the Lycan blood ceremony? My father mentioned Lyra might start exhibiting the Lycans' abilities."

That takes me by surprise. Of course, Colton, being Granger's son, would be privy to more about my situation than I'd anticipated. I know Nyx trusted Granger, and, gods, he shared more with him then I would have liked.

"Yes, I believe Granger is correct," my father admits. "However, the open consumption of Lycan blood is a rarity these days. Perhaps Anika might have more insight. I'll speak with her later." He appears thoughtful, his brow furrowing as if contemplating a deeper enigma.

Attempting to steer the conversation back to the present, I ask, "So what's your plan for initiating my training?"

His features shift, a determined glint igniting in his eyes. "We begin here and now. I need to assess your current abilities."

"And how do you plan to do that?" I ask.

He maintains a steady gaze as he answers, "I intend to put you through a simulation. It won't be reality, but it will certainly feel that way. You must be prepared for that."

I swallow hard, my body thrumming with nervous energy. Chepi chitters anxiously in my arms, prompting me to glance down at him. "It's okay, boy."

"Euric," Colton interrupts, stepping forward, "if it's not real, how will we monitor her progress?"

Euric's response is calm and assured. "I can project an illusion for her to experience, but through the same conduit of power we will be able to observe her progress. Essentially, we will be peering through a window into her trial."

He then pivots his attention back to me, his gaze softened, offering an encouraging smile.

"Lyra, I've been preparing for this far longer than you. I understand this might seem overwhelming, but this trial is specifically designed to test your magical instincts, your resourcefulness, and your mental strength. Although it will feel like you're alone, you won't be. Colton and I will be observing from here, and Chepi should remain with us as well. This is only the first of many trials I have ready for you."

Gods, Fae magic never ceases to amaze me. The fact that he's crafted a simulation for me feels impossible, yet here we are. I'm determined to prove to them I can handle this. I press a kiss onto Chepi's head before releasing him. He immediately flies over to Colton, ready to watch whatever this is from the sidelines. "So how do we begin? What should I do?"

I watch as my father extends his hand, eyes glowing intense as a ripple of energy arcs from him and a white veil appears. "Once you step through this portal, the simulation will begin. We will be able to watch you through this veil, which will act as a one-way window. We will be able to see and hear what is happening, but we cannot intervene until I end the simulation. Do you understand?"

"I understand." I nod, trying to swallow down the anxious feeling starting to fester in my chest. "But what happens if I fail?" I ask, the uncertainty clear in my voice.

"Then everything I've devoted my life to—and yours—will have been for nothing," my father replies, his words amplifying the tightness in my chest.

"I did some training with Colton the other day," I tell him, attempting to redirect the conversation to less daunting prospects.

"I heard about that," he says with a dismissive tone. "If that's the extent of your abilities, we might as well give up now." His blunt assessment provokes me, and my eyes narrow in response.

"It's not," I say firmly, my gaze still locked onto his.

"Well then," he challenges, "show me what you can do."

I look over at Chepi and Colton one last time. Before I can second guess myself, I jump into the veil.

CHAPTER
TEN

A cool tingle brushes across my skin, and for a fleeting second darkness engulfs me before a sudden burst of light blinds me. I feel weightless as my vision clears and look down to find I'm descending into a maze of sorts. As far as I can see, a giant labyrinth of illuminated hallways spans out all around me. My body slowly lowers, dropping down into the center of the maze until my feet hit the ground.

The walls of the maze are not made of stone or foliage. They shimmer and light up with moving images—images of me, my life. Vibrant moving pictures of my past, my present, and potential futures... It's as if time itself has been melted down and shaped into tangible, glowing walls.

One moment, I see my own face reflecting back at me, a face full of childhood innocence, then the scene shifts, and now it's the determined gaze of the woman I've become. Occasionally, the images morph and don't make sense, but when the image of myself with stirring black eyes and shadow tendrils veining across my skin appears I know it must be showing me possible futures. Or maybe it's pulling from my mind, and since

WHAT BEATS WITHIN THE TUNNELS

I've seen this image through the echosphere it's projecting it here. I can't be sure, but either way it's no less disturbing. They're so vivid, so real, that it feels like I could step right into them.

The maze breathes with life, teeming with dream-born flora and fauna. I tread on a carpet of luminescent grass that pulses beneath my feet. Flowers bloom around me with each step I take, and trees tower above. But I follow their tall branches up and see only darkness. There is no sky, no stars, only utter darkness beyond this maze of dreams.

I keep walking, assuming my goal is to reach the exit somewhere. It looked like I was dropped right in the center of the maze, so I need to work my way to the outside. I try to ignore the images flashing around me, but it's impossible when I see myself as a child.

I have to pause to see what I'm doing, because it's something I don't remember. I watch as Lili brushes my hair on one wall. I must be no older than five. I turn to my right and on the other wall see Nyx. Oh, gods, he's on top of me, inside me. I feel my face flush and quicken my steps. *Please let Colton and my father not be able to see what I see in the walls.*

I keep a fast pace, trying to escape the images that are starting to surround me. Images of Nyx, not just images but sounds. I see him chained to the table in Samael's throne room, blood splattered across his chest. I look down, and the pulsing grass has changed into pulsing images that seem to appear and disappear as fast as the air I breathe into my lungs. I see Nyx carrying me out of Tempest moon after Samael locked me in my room, then I see him devouring me in Drew's hive while his voice echoes all around me. "Who's the liar now, Lyra?"

How does this have anything to do with my magic? I start to jog, trying not to get distracted by the visions rapidly playing all around me. I can feel my heart rate increasing. If I keep moving, I will find the way out eventually. I turn a corner and smack into a dead end.

The wall feels like hard jelly, and the image of Luke's throat being torn open distorts when I make contact. No, no, no, I shake my head as I swallow down the lump in my throat. I blocked these things out, buried them. I turn back the way I came then go down a different hall, running now as the images around me blur together as a rainbow of bright lights.

I hit another dead end, and suddenly all the halls surround me with the same image playing. The trees are bleeding, and the grass underfoot has turned to blood. It crinkles with every step as I run. "Something's coming, Lyra."

A whisper travels on the wind in a voice I don't recognize, but it sends a chill down my spine that gets my feet moving faster. The path is so long, the end of the hall barely visible, and the images of bleeding trees all around are disorienting. I feel like I'm going to smack face-first into another wall if I don't slow down. Piercing blue eyes catch my attention, and I turn my head to the right. My toe hits the ground, and I stumble then try to regain my balance, but it's too late. I put my hands out, reaching for anything, then I slam into the ground hard.

I roll onto my back, squeezing my eyes shut as I try to gulp down air. I open my eyes, blinking rapidly at the trees. I no longer see bark, but the trees are covered in moving pictures now too, just like the walls. The bleeding forest is gone, and Aidan surrounds me, a different image of him plays in every direction I look. I jump to my feet, and his voice makes me cringe.

"You like when I fuck you like this, don't you?"

Tears start running freely down my face. "No!" I scream, turning down another path, and clasping my hands over my ears. "Cheeks, where are you, Cheeks?"

"Stop. Stop now!" I scream as the sound of his voice grows

louder. I fall to my knees, closing my eyes and clamping down on my ears harder. I can't bear to see anymore. I can't take it. Breathe. I focus on that one word and repeat it again and again in my head slower and slower until I match my breathing with the pace of the word.

I am not alone here. This is not real. You are rational, Lyra, so get it together and think about this logically. What is happening? The labyrinth is shaped by my thoughts, my emotions. This is no ordinary trial. It's a journey into the core of my being, and it is trying to break me.

This maze is more than a test of navigation; it's a test of controlling my inner world. My thoughts, my memories, and my emotions are the forces that shape this reality. The challenge here is not about finding the right path out but rather finding the right state of mind. I must breathe. I inhale a long slow breath through my nose, hold it in for several seconds, then exhale a long slow breath out my mouth.

I can feel my pulse slow, and I take my hands away from my ears, wiping the lingering tears away. I am strong, I am powerful, and nothing will break me. I slowly build the wall back up around my heart and bury everything that threatens to undo me. Then I open my eyes. The images around me have slowed, and I see Chepi belly crawling across my old bed in Tempest Moon and Lili helping me give Chepi a bath. I smile as I get to my feet. The walls melt away until darkness envelopes me once again, leaving me weightless.

The brightness causes me to slam my eyes shut as I fall back out of the veil, and Colton catches me before I hit the ground. I look up at him and think I see something akin to regret on his face as he helps me to my feet.

"That's enough for today. This was only an emotional test, Lyra, and it took you far too long to get control of yourself," my father says, looking me over.

"Don't be an asshole," Colton retorts quickly.

"It will only get harder from here, so I suggest you get a grip and start coming to terms with some things you may be afraid to face. I'll take you back to the palace for now." He clasps a hand on my wrist and one on Colton's shoulder. Chepi jumps in my arms, and the icy wind picks up with the fog.

"READY TO TALK ABOUT IT?" Colton poses the question from his seat at the table in our shared bedroom shortly after channeling back to the palace.

"There's nothing to discuss," I retort, my footfalls echoing in the room as I pace restlessly.

"Clearly," he counters, a touch of sarcasm in his tone. "Looks like you're totally fine, nothing on your mind."

I huff, frustration leaking from my every pore. "I'm livid with myself," I admit, collapsing into the opposing chair with a groan.

Colton arches an eyebrow, a hint of amusement playing on his face as he watches me squirm. "Please, do continue to take it out on the furniture."

"Ha ha. Very funny." I roll my eyes and slump further into my chair, expelling a heavy sigh.

Colton retrieves two glasses from the drink cart and returns, handing me both. Water in one hand and whiskey in the other. I set the water aside, downing the shot of whiskey with a determined gulp.

"So, it's going to be that sort of night then?" He flashes a wry grin, grabbing the decanter of whiskey and setting it between us, refilling both glasses.

"I embarrassed myself today, Colton. I'm stronger than what I showed. I let upsetting memories unravel me. What if it had been a real test? How am I to control my dark magic, to stop it from controlling me, when I can't even handle my own emotions?" I run a hand through my hair, detangling the knots in my waves with frustration. "I am better than this. I cannot, will not, fail."

"Lyra," he interrupts, catching my hand mid-tug, stopping my hair-pulling antics. His gaze is intense, serious. "I happen to enjoy looking at your hair. Please stop tormenting it."

I huff, dropping my hand back into my lap. "I'm not tormenting it. It's just tangled—"

He cuts me off. "Leave it. Let's talk about what's really bothering you."

My heart sinks. "How much of today's events in the maze were you able to see?"

His answer is soft, understanding. "Everything."

"Great," I mutter, embarrassment flushing my cheeks.

"Lyra, you have overcome enormous obstacles in your life, endured things no one your age should have. Fae magic thrives on emotions, and by gods you have enough to fuel yours," he encourages, holding my gaze.

"But those emotions aren't serving me right now. Sure, if I want an outburst to set something on fire, but not when I'm trying to gain control. Not when faced with a situation like today," I say, swallowing another mouthful of whiskey, hoping the warmth will help dull the memories of the day.

"Damn it, Lyra, you're missing the point. You can't keep bottling up your emotions until they explode. If you want control, you need to embrace your emotions. Face the things you've been running from," Colton insists, his tone firm.

"I am not running away from anything, Colton," I snap back, trying to keep a lid on my temper.

"Really? When you told Nyx to leave, did you give him a chance to explain? From what Drew said, it didn't sound like there was much communication that night," he counters, riling me up.

"Why would you even bring that up right now? That's none of your business," I say, unable to hold back any longer.

"That's your issue, Lyra. You keep everything inside. Bad things have happened to you, and you keep it all locked away. You don't trust anyone apparently. You didn't even trust Nyx before you found out he's a liar." He pauses, his eyes glowing brighter by the second. "You don't have to trust me or even like me, but for fuck's sake you need to start dealing with your issues or you won't stand a chance when your birthday comes around."

His rising voice makes me wonder why he's getting worked up about it.

"Why are you so upset? Why do you even care?" Now my temper's flaring.

"Is it so crazy to believe that I might care about you? That I might be a decent person who's genuinely concerned about what happens to you?" he shoots back, his words punctuated by a heavy sigh.

"You don't care about me. You came to help me because you owed Drew a favor. And I have no idea why you followed me here. Probably to find something to steal in Zomea," I say, brushing my hair back from my face.

"I didn't owe Drew a fucking favor, Lyra. I lied. I came because I wanted to help you with your Fae magic. I wanted to help you back when I gave you Callum's journal. Believe it or not, I'm not the asshole you think I am, and I do care about what happens to you."

"Exactly what do you want from me, Colton?" My voice escalates, threading through the tension in the room.

"I want you to confront what you've been running from. Unearth those fears, the ones you've locked deep within yourself before they consume you completely. Afterward, if you still wish, we can drain the entire decanter together." His gaze meets mine, and I find my resolve crumbling.

"I did trust Nyx, you know. I let him in, up to a point. I shared things with him. So don't you dare insinuate I'm incapable of expressing my feelings. It's... I was weak for too long. Again and again, I was manipulated and exploited. The things I've locked away, I've done so out of necessity. I refuse to be weak anymore. I'm tired of crying." My voice quivers, the dam of my patience cracking.

"Lyra," he says gently, "emotions are not a weakness. They're a testament to your strength."

"Well, I certainly didn't feel strong today when I collapsed in that maze," I say, my voice steadying as I regain my composure.

"That's because you keep everything bottled up until you break. You need to let it out, face it head-on. Familiarize yourself with the discomfort, confront the things that cause you pain, embrace the pain, and allow yourself to feel. And today in that maze, I don't care what Euric said, I was damn proud of you when you got control of yourself. I mean, an image of me instead of Chepi at the end would have made it better." He pauses, letting out a quick laugh followed by a sigh. "In the spirit of fairness, ask me anything, and I'll answer truthfully."

"But why?" I ask, unsure what his motives are.

"I want you to feel comfortable sharing your burdens with me. To do so, I'm prepared to do the same." He counters, firm but gentle.

Silence hangs heavy in the room, my lips pressed firmly together as I grapple with what to say. What do I want to ask him? I need more time to sift through the chaos in my mind. However, before I can voice my thoughts, he speaks up.

"I know Nyx hurt you. I may not know the full story

between you two, but I do know he's not to be trusted. He'd stoop to any level to secure his own desires. And it's clear that you've endured more than your fair share of pain. From what I glimpsed in the maze, it's even worse than I feared." He pauses, running a hand through his hair. "You've likely heard this before, but I want you to understand…you can trust me. You might not believe me now, but in time you will."

I fidget with the laces on my bodice, letting them twine and untwine through my fingers. "I hardly know you, Colton. Lately, I hardly know myself," I admit, almost mumbling. Can I trust Colton? Perhaps. It's undeniable that a sense of closeness has grown between us, likely born from his unwavering and unwanted support in one of my life's lowest points. Now, he's claiming he didn't come out of obligation to Drew but because he genuinely wanted to help.

"I see your struggle. I see how you've been projecting an image of strength to the world despite feeling shattered inside. Let me reassure you that you don't have to put on that act with me. I don't know whether it was Nyx's actions that broke you or if they merely served as the final straw, but one thing I'm certain of is this. The person who shattered you can't be the one to mend you. That healing journey, you have to embark on by yourself. However, I would like to be there by your side, helping you navigate it, if you'll let me."

As he speaks, something inside me swells, threatening to burst.

"Let me be your friend," he urges, and the word reverberates in my mind — friend. That's what he's asking for, friendship.

"Okay," I whisper, forcing my gaze to meet his. As I look at him, I realize it might be the first time I'm truly seeing him. He may have the physique of a warrior and undeniable good looks, but there's potentially more to Colton than meets the eye. I find myself curious, eager to peel back his layers and learn who he truly is. Perhaps hate is too strong a word for my feelings toward him; tolerance may not cover it either.

"Why the smirk? Did I finally manage to crack your tough exterior?" He teases, lightening the mood in the room.

"I'm not sure about that." I laugh. "But I am bored, so getting to know you doesn't sound terrible. At least it will help pass the time."

A smile spreads across his face, clearly amused.

I reach over to refill both of our glasses. He immediately grabs his, raising it to me.

"To helping each other pick up the pieces," he proposes a toast, a glint in those emerald eyes.

"And to finding strength in the broken places," I reply, clinking my glass against his.

"Let's start with that scar I've noticed, the one that extends all the way across your chest," I say.

"You've been eyeing my chest?" he teases, the corner of his mouth quirking up. But then his face becomes more solemn. "That scar... I got it saving three elemental Pixies in the Dream Forest."

My attention is immediately drawn to this. Pixies are mischievous little Faeries, tiny enough to fit in your hand. Nyx once claimed that my father must have nicknamed me after them. "And what were you saving them from? What happened?" I'm brimming with curiosity.

"As the son of two powerful elders, no lie, I lived a life of privilege. My parents are respected figures in our community, which isn't without its perks. They're good people, but I can't say the same about everyone they associate with. Like any other society, not all the Fae are benevolent. There are those dripping in gold who frivolously buy whatever their hearts desire. And then there are those who have nothing and are willing to do anything for a single gold piece," he explains. I find myself leaning in, drawn into his story, sipping my wine.

"In my youth, I was a bit of a rebel and had quite a fiery temperament. My parents planned every moment of my life — intensive training, council meetings, and everything in between. But it felt stifling, a trap. I charted my own path, standing up against the injustices in our community."

"And what injustices were these?" I ask, watching him pause to take a drink.

"It was infuriating to see magical creatures treated as toys by the privileged. I acted against the rules, defied the norm, and ended up with a few battle scars. But I'd do it all over again if it meant setting things right."

"So you've saved more than a few elemental Pixies, haven't you?"

He nods. "Those Pixies had been trapped outside their homes and tossed into a cage with magical bars, set to be sold to some loathsome character wanting to hang them in his house like stuffed birds."

"Why would anyone do such a thing?" I can't help but ask, though I know all too well how cruel some people can be. My heart aches at the thought of the innocent creatures that Samael might have harmed over the years. A fury stirs deep within me. "Anyone who harms defenseless creatures doesn't deserve to live."

Colton looks at me, his gaze turned serious. "Well, Princess, it seems we've finally found common ground."

"No wonder Chepi likes you. He must sense you look out for all magical creatures," I say, smiling as I glance back at Chepi, who's lying on the bed, watching us.

"Tell me the top three things causing you pain right now," Colton says, abruptly shifting the conversation. It catches me off guard. "And I'm not talking about physical pain."

I hold my glass, gently swirling it and watching as the wine sloshes around. Its deep red hue reminds me of drinking blood, and my thoughts drift to Luke again. I don't really want to delve into my issues right now. I barely grazed the surface of these things with Nyx, and that was tough enough. I'd prefer to bury everything, hoping one day to forget. Although that seems unlikely, it's a comforting notion. I realize this is what Colton's been aiming for all afternoon— coaxing me to vocalize my feelings, confront the things troubling me for better control. Yet, I know it's bound to be an emotionally exhausting process.

The influence of whiskey and wine, or perhaps the urgency to take a leap of faith, prompts me to confess, "The murders of Luke and the other young Lycans, Aidan's violation, and the heartbreak Nyx inflicted with his deceit." Saying these things aloud feels almost cathartic. I know none of this is news to Colton, who got a glimpse of it in the maze today, and he must have heard rumors as well. He listens with an intense gaze, a wave of seriousness washing over his face.

"Tell me about them. Let's start with Luke," he says. "Tell me what hurts the most, what wakes you up in the night, and how it makes you feel."

I take a long, slow breath. No amount of alcohol in Zomea could prepare me for this conversation, yet I decide to lay it all bare. No worse can happen, and if this is the path to managing my emotions and mastering dark magic to save Zomea, then I must tread it.

"Luke was the first friend I ever made. He felt like a younger brother in the short time we were together. I was naive and should've seen it coming, but I didn't, and then came the ceremony. Dawn, Yuri, Luke... They all died that night because of me. Witnessing their deaths is something I can never unsee, but locking eyes with Luke as his throat was ripped open, watching him drown in his own blood and maintaining eye contact till his last breath, that image haunts me. I've seen him here in Zomea, you know, through my midnight mind. Despite my father's skepticism, I believe he's here. I believe Luke made it to Zomea."

"Their deaths were not your fault, but I understand why you might feel that they were. Now, tell me about Aidan," he urges, leaning back in his chair and watching me intently.

"Aidan took my virginity, took something from me I'll never get back. He drugged me with moon bread, made me think I wanted it, turned me into a willing participant the first time. It was a horrific experience, but it was nothing compared to the time he raped me. When I think about what he did..." I twirl my glass in my lap, focusing on the red liquid, unable to look at him while I speak.

"I feel dirty, shameful, tainted. I feel an overwhelming fury, not just toward him and what happened but toward myself as well. I blame myself for putting myself in that situation. I think I should have found a way to resist him, to escape. The thought of him inside me churns my stomach and makes my skin crawl. Sometimes, nightmares about that night jolt me awake, my throat sore from screaming in my sleep. And the worst part is, even now, as I share this with you, I feel like a burden. I feel weak and embarrassed. I should be able to handle all of this without feeling broken, yet when I allow myself to feel, 'damaged' is the only word that comes to mind."

"You are not a burden, Lyra, and everything you're feeling is entirely justified. Your feelings matter. I never want you to hold back from telling me something because you think you're burdening me. What he did is..." He exhales, shaking his head. "I wish he weren't already dead so I could exact justice myself. He had better hope he's not in Zomea," Colton says, his knuckles whitening where he's gripping the wine bottle. I look away, taking a deep breath.

I think about my mother, and my heart aches. I wish we could have been closer, and while her death does affect me, and there are times I miss her, she also caused me pain. Not in the same way Aidan did, but a different kind of hurt. I think about Samael too and all the harm he inflicted on me over the years until the very end, but somehow neither of those experiences hurt as much as losing Nyx.

Before Colton can say anything else, I voice my thoughts, "And then there's Nyx. He appeared out of nowhere like some white knight—too good to be true, like something from a book my father used to read to me as a child. He rescued me when I needed it most and made me trust him. He was kind to me, showed me that I could feel good and be happy. He made me feel safe. He made me fall for him. But he lied. He lied about everything, time and time again. Every time I gave him a chance to explain himself, he'd tell me more lies. I was so naive that I believed him, even after catching him in his lies. I didn't want to face the truth." I swallow the lump building in my throat.

"When Samael captured us, and I thought I might lose Nyx, I was out of my mind with worry. But then Samael's last words revealed Nyx's true intentions. He'd been watching me since childhood, had always planned on killing me. Despite all that, I could have forgiven him because he said he loved me. But I don't want that kind of love. You don't lie to the ones you love." I pause taking a few steady breaths.

"So, in the end, the damage was done, and I told him to leave. He brought Chepi back to me, thinking we would pick up where we left off. But too much had happened, and I didn't even feel like the same person. I'm a broken person, Colton. I haven't wanted to admit it to myself or say it aloud, but I think Nyx seized the opportunity to take advantage of my vulnerability, to shape me into whatever he wanted. Maybe he did love me, but in the end it wasn't enough." As I speak, tears stream down my face, and I swipe them away with the back of my hand.

"And it's not entirely his fault. My own desperation for his love, for any semblance of affection, played its part too."

Colton rubs his chin.

"I know losing Nyx might feel like the end of the world right now, but everything you're going through will only make you stronger. And from where I'm sitting, you're already incredibly strong. You will find someone who treats you the way you deserve, someone who won't lie to you, someone who will love you unconditionally and spoil you, because you deserve everything you desire and more." He offers me a soft smile, his eyes glowing for a moment as they meet mine.

I find myself smiling back at him, feeling a bit lighter. I'm not saying I'm back to normal—I'll never be the girl I was before all of this. The girl from Tempest Moon is gone. But for the first time, I feel like I can breathe a little easier, and I can talk about these things without completely falling apart.

"Thank you for this, for—for being a friend, even though I didn't want one." I giggle slightly, releasing some of the tension that's been building up.

"You're welcome, Lyra. This is one small step in the right direction. It's not going to be easy, but I promise I won't let you give up. I'll be here, picking up the pieces with you, until you're whole again," he replies, his commitment bringing a sense of comfort to my heart I wasn't expecting.

CHAPTER
ELEVEN

Sometime later, the door creaks open, and Colton steps inside our room. Earlier, I had confided in him, admitting that my current state of inebriation made the idea of joining my father for dinner rather unappealing. Given the situation, Colton had slipped out with a mission to find us sustenance and to inform Euric we wouldn't be attending dinner tonight.

He strides in with a victorious grin. "Mission accomplished," he declares, placing a tray on the table between us, a hint of mischief evident in his tone. Perhaps he might've indulged a little too much himself.

"The goods, huh?" I chuckle, playfully raising an eyebrow.

He nods enthusiastically. "Given the, shall we say, less than stellar offerings from the kitchen, I decided to opt for something that smelled delicious instead of whatever they were making for dinner. And, of course, more wine." Lifting the lid off the plate, he unveils chocolate cookies, their fragrance wafting through the room.

My love for sweets is undeniable, and while it might be

cliché to say dessert is the way to a girl's heart, it genuinely is the path to mine, especially when chocolate's involved.

"Anika was downstairs," he begins, grabbing a cookie for himself. "She mentioned they're called Shades. The name might be peculiar, but then who can resist chocolate cookies?"

"You've made an excellent choice," I say, reaching out to take one. "And they're still warm." I take a bite, and it's nothing short of divine. The rich, chewy consistency complemented by melt-in-the-mouth chocolate chunks is pure indulgence. Pairing it with wine might not be a conventional choice, and it might haunt me in the morning, but in this moment it feels perfect.

Colton uncorks the wine bottle and refills our glasses. "Now, where were we?" he asks. I quickly lick away chocolate from my lip, and I can't help but notice him watching the gesture intently.

"What's life like in that grand palace of yours?" I probe.

He chuckles, "It's the elder's palace, not mine. Haven't called it home in ages. It's my parents' place, and they're hardly there themselves. I usually drop by when I'm in the vicinity or for one of their interminable dinner parties."

"Where's home for you then?" I ask, my curiosity growing, hoping to peel back some more layers.

His grin widens. "Ever heard of the Dream Forest?" he teases, of course knowing I have.

"Wait, I thought no one lived in there except for magical creatures like Pixies."

"For the most part, you're right, but my compound is there too," he explains.

I lean forward, eyes wide with anticipation. "You have to tell me everything."

His laughter is rich and warm. "When I was a boy, the Dream Forest was taboo, 'far too treacherous,' according to my father. Naturally, that made it the first place I wanted to explore. It's unmatched in its beauty, completely distinct from any other place. But its allure also brings danger—not all of its inhabitants are friendly. That's how I first encountered ravishers."

I frown, puzzled. "Ravishers?"

He exhales slowly. "They're malevolent Faeries driven by greed. They sneak into the Dream Forest, capturing creatures to sell in dark markets of other domains. The first time I confronted them, I almost didn't survive. Your father rescued me, always pulling me out of trouble when I was a kid. That near-death experience changed everything for me. I realized I needed to become stronger, not just with my magic but physically too. I started to take my training seriously to help myself and those who can't defend themselves." He pauses, taking a sip of his wine. I'm completely engrossed, hanging onto every word.

"Looks like you achieved that," I say, feeling my cheeks grow warm.

He smirked, catching the hint of admiration in my tone. "Well, thank you, enchantress. But it's more than about being physically strong. It's about knowing the territory, understanding the creatures, and foreseeing their needs. It's about creating a place of safety in the midst of danger, a sanctuary amidst the wilderness."

"The Dream Forest," I whisper, realizing that he wasn't only speaking of his own journey of growth but also the creation of a haven.

"Exactly. I spent years building it, establishing treaties with the creatures, making sure it was protected. Over time, the creatures started seeing me less as an outsider and more as a protector, and the ravishers learned to fear my territory," Colton explained with a hint of pride.

119

"But how do you maintain such a vast territory? Isn't it exhausting?" I ask, wondering about the logistics of it all.

Colton leans back, gazing into the distance as if recalling memories. "It is, but it's also rewarding. The Dream Forest is alive, ever-changing, and I've learned to adapt with it. Plus, I have allies and friends who help me. The Pixies you mentioned? They're more than just magical creatures. They're watchers, guardians of the forest. They often alert me if there's an intruder or if something is amiss."

"I wish I could see it one day," I murmur.

Colton leans in, his voice a mere whisper, "And perhaps, one day, you will." I smile at that, a nice idea.

I shake off the thought. "Do you think my father would want to reclaim his rule over Cloudrum now that the bridge is accessible?"

His eyes study mine for a moment. "He hasn't given any indication of such intentions. But with Samael gone, you know the crown technically falls to you."

I shake my head. "Not yet. I can't ascend to the throne until after my nineteenth birthday. Our traditions dictate that we can't rule until we fully inherit our powers. By now, I assume the council has stepped in."

He frowns, leaning forward. "That's absurd."

Brushing a stray hair behind my ear, I reply, "Whether it's absurd or not, I don't desire the throne at the moment. Even if it's my birthright, I'm not sure I ever want it."

He places a reassuring hand on my arm. "You don't have to decide anything now. When the time comes, I believe you'll be an exceptional queen. For now, I'll stick with calling you 'Princess.' It has a more charming ring to it." His smirk grows broader, eliciting an eye roll from me.

With a playful pout, I say, "Honestly, I'd rather live in the

Dream Forest, surrounded by its enchanting inhabitants." A yawn escapes me, betraying my exhaustion.

He chuckles, standing up. "Alright, Your Highness, it's evident you've had your fill of wine and conversation. Let's get you to bed." As I try to stand, the room tilts, and I waver, but Colton's arm is there in an instant, grounding me. With a simple gesture, he extinguishes the candles, casting the room into dimness. Making my way to the bed, I shed my restricting attire and quickly slip into something more comfortable.

Soon, we're settled under the covers, the comfort of the bed cradling us both. Colton as always is careful to keep his distance in the bed, and something inside me wishes to be closer to him. Maybe it's the alcohol, but I scoot closer to him, and he raises his arm, making room for me. I rest my cheek against his chest, and he brings his arm around me, holding me close. The contact causes a warm feeling to spread over my body, and a rightness to settle in my chest, but as I drift off to sleep something nags in the back of my mind — a feeling of betrayal.

"COME ON, get yourself right. You're never going to be ready if you sleep all day."

Athalda's voice pierces through my sleep, yanking me back to consciousness. My eyes flutter open, adjusting to the dim light, and I'm met with her piercing black eyes and face marred by scars. The bed beside me is empty—the warmth of Colton's body, which I now question whether it was real or a figment of a dream, is absent. My head throbs, and as I frantically scan the room for Chepi, I find his spot vacant too.

Before anxiety can entirely consume me, Athalda's sharp voice cuts through, "Your new friend took Chepi with him.

They're both alright. Now, up and at 'em. You're my responsibility for the day."

Hastily, I dress, choosing a white tunic similar to yesterday's attire. A flurry of questions storms my mind. Why did Colton take Chepi? Where could they possibly be? I try shaking off the disappointment I feel about waking alone. And as thoughts of the night prior wash over me — the warmth, the closeness, the comfort – guilt gnaws at me. Nyx is probably missing me, worried about me, and I've fallen asleep wrapped in the arms of his adversary. What am I doing? It doesn't matter, because I told him we're done.

"Enough daydreaming! Your boots, now!" Athalda's voice is as impatient as ever. I slide my boots on and trudge behind her, my steps heavy with apprehension.

"Where are we headed? What's Colton up to with Chepi?"

Her voice carries an air of mystery, "Don't concern yourself with them. Today's all about you." She briefly turns, her gaze falling on the empty wine bottles strewn across the table, and smirks. "It's going to be a very, very long day for you."

I pull myself together, trying to brush my tangled hair into submission. How I wish Colton had woken me earlier, allowing me a moment of privacy and a chance to bathe before Athalda's abrupt intrusion. Despite the whirlwind of emotions, one thing is clear – I trust Colton. The realization settles effortlessly, surprising even myself.

As we continue on, the wear and decay become more apparent as we reach the other side of the palace. Before long, Athalda ushers me into a room, the very room we overheard her and my father in yesterday. Contrary to my assumption of it being her personal chamber, the room reveals itself to be some kind of ritualistic haven or sacred den.

The scent of sage and burning wax fills the air as I step into the room. My gaze is immediately drawn to an altar adorned with crystals and scrolls, encircled by flickering candles and plush pillows. By the window stands a long table, laden with drying herbs and a mortar containing an unknown mixture. On the opposite side, floor-to-ceiling shelves overflow with ancient books, mystical artifacts, pouches, and charms.

"What is this place?" I wonder aloud.

"This," she says, her tone ominous, "is where we practice dark magic." I feel a surge of alarm. "You can wipe that look off your face. You think you'll be ready to inherit such magic without any practice?" She scowls, motioning around the room.

"Is this what's causing the decay in this side of the palace?" I ask.

She tilts her head, her eyes glinting mysteriously. "Among other things," she replies. "Now take a seat. It's time to get started." I hesitantly sit across from her on one of the pillows surrounding the low table. There's at least a dozen different crystals spread across the table placed on top of velvety cloth and pieces of parchment. "Do you find yourself drawn to any of these?"

She slowly passes her hand over the table of crystals. I want to ask her why, but I know better, so instead I look over the table and find I'm drawn to one in particular. I can't explain it, but I have an urge to pick it up and feel it in my hand, against my skin, but I resist. I point at the crystal, rich burgundy blending seamlessly with sparkly black pieces.

Athalda meets my gaze with her piercing black eyes. "To understand the power you are to inherit, you must see through the eyes of those who wielded it before. This crystal holds the essence of past dark Sorcerers. In theory, you should be able to experience a fragment of their power, their struggles, and their triumphs."

"In theory?" I question.

"I've been reading about it in ancient grimoires, but none of these crystals have shown me anything. I believe the dark essence will recognize you and reveal itself only to you," she says, and I find myself intrigued and terrified at the same time. "My suspicions are already proving true, because you are drawn to the very crystal the last dark Sorcerer owned. I feel no inclination toward it or any of them."

"Should I touch it?" I ask, unsure of what to do.

"Only if you believe you can handle what it may show you."

I want to roll my eyes. I study the crystal, which looks harmless enough. The moment I clasp the cold crystal, it feels as if the world collapses in on itself. Everything around me disappears, and I'm plunged into a swirling darkness. A whirl-wind of emotions tugs at my very being: fear, exhilaration, curiosity. The darkness subsides, an ethereal landscape taking shape around me.

I'm standing at the edge of a green meadow bathed in silver moonlight. Tall grasses sway in the night breeze. From the distance, the low hum of a chant drifts closer. Drawn to it, I step forward and notice figures emerging from the tree line.

A procession of cloaked individuals, their faces obscured, move solemnly through the meadow. Maybe these are the sorcerers who followed the last dark Sorcerer. They gather in a circle, and at its center a tall, imposing figure appears, veiled in shadows. This is him. I can feel it in my very being. This is the last dark Sorcerer. His silhouette, ever elusive, prevents me from seeing his true form, but there's an undeniable magnetism to his presence.

He raises a hand, and from the ground water begins to pool, forming a pristine silver pond. With another gesture, the water rises, and images start to take shape with its liquid form. A village ravaged by drought, children on the brink of starva-tion. With a mere flick of his wrist, rain begins to fall upon the village, bringing relief and hope. I can't explain it, but I can feel the relief and gratitude emanating from the reflections.

But the vision shifts. Now, the scene is one of chaos. Flames engulf a once vibrant town, people running and screaming in terror. The same tall figure covered in shadows stands atop a hill overlooking the destruction, arms outstretched, drawing power from the very fires he's set. Cries of despair echo, and the shadowy figure's laughter reaches me at the same time the heat from the flames does.

Suddenly, a bright light pierces the scene, and the ground starts to shake as a group of people appear dressed in radiant robes. They start to circle the dark Sorcerer. I think I see Drew and someone next to her who resembles Nyx and could be Callum. A sizzling sound spreads across the sky, and an epic battle ensues. This must be when the Luminary Council kills the dark Sorcerer. Magic collides, and bright white flashes nearly blind me, only to be drowned out by the shadows. The council, united, chants an incantation, trying to strip him of his power, but he resists, his strength evident in the way the shadows continuously morph, trying to outmaneuver the luminescent chains attempting to bind him.

I can feel the desperation in the air. Every strike, every spell cast feels like a weight on my chest. The sorrow of the lost village, the hope of the saved one, and the unyielding hate and determination of the Luminary Council... It's overwhelming.

When it seems the dark Sorcerer might be subdued, he lets out a deafening roar, releasing a force that pushes the council members back. The very ground splits apart, creating chasms that swallow the light, turning the landscape more treacherous.

But then, from the chasms, a hand reaches out, followed by another and another. Souls bound to the Sorcerer's bidding, climbing, crawling, desperate to shield their master. The council huddles together, and as the two forces converge the vision begins to blur, becoming unstable.

Before it all fades, I catch a glimpse of the dark Sorcerer's eyes. Even in the shadow, they're piercing, black and silver, filled with a mix of fury, pain, and determination.

With a jolt, I'm back in the room, the crystal drops to the table, and I pant, trying to catch my breath. It's clear the dark Sorcerer battled with good and evil. I recount everything I saw to Athalda, and she takes notes while I talk.

"I don't understand how this was helpful at all," I say, crossing my arm, my headache worse after that.

"You silly girl, can't you glean anything from that vision?" Athalda scolds.

I take a deep breath before replying, "I saw that the dark Sorcerer performed both good and bad actions, which further proves that dark magic itself isn't inherently evil. It's about the wielder's choices, control, and balance. But I already knew that."

Athalda nods, seemingly deep in thought. "The Luminary Council's attack on the dark Sorcerer is a prime example. It should show you how fear and misunderstanding can lead even those with noble intentions astray. Others might perceive and react to you differently once you inherit your dark magic. It's crucial for you to communicate and show your true intentions." She meets my gaze, her statement heavy with implication.

I ponder that. "You will have many moral dilemmas ahead, girl. When you possess such power, you'll be faced with critical decisions you'll have to grapple with," Athalda continues, watching me intently.

"What do you mean by that?" I ask.

She leans in closer, her voice low and intense. "I mean, when you're the most powerful one in the room, you must decide whether to use your power to intervene, dominate, or remain passive."

I study her, especially the unique hue of her eyes. "You said earlier that your eyes turned black from being in Zomea, but I haven't seen anyone else with black eyes. Did they turn black from using dark magic? Will my eyes change too? Will the color be permanent?" My questions tumble out one after another.

Athalda sighs, her expression unreadable. "Practicing dark magic in Zomea for many years changed my eyes. I can't predict exactly what will happen to you, but I suspect it will largely depend on the choices you make."

"If you've practiced dark spells all this time, why not show me how it's done? Wouldn't teaching me about dark magic be more beneficial than giving me twisted visions from a crystal?" I ask, glancing around the room at all the magical artifacts.

"We've discussed this. It's not the same—"

"I get it. If you have light magic but attempt dark spells, they can never be as potent as when someone with dark magic performs them," I say.

"Interrupt me again, girl, and I'll let your father drop you back into that maze simulation," she warns. I bite back a retort, reminding myself to keep my temper in check and listen to what the old lady has to say.

She explains, "When you possess dark magic, you don't need spells. The dark spells detailed in grimoires are meant for sorcerers with light magic. Dark magic is an entirely different entity. Zomea holds all the magic, and when you come of age, it's released to you. That's how it's always been for Sorcerers, a design set by the gods. It's not immediately passed down through generations like Fae magic."

I nod for her to continue.

"Dark magic resides within you. It's dormant in you even now, but once you come of age and your magic awakens, it will become a part of your very soul, Lyra. You won't need to learn spells; that's not how it operates. You'll be able to bend things to your will. Have you ever wondered why your mother never enrolled you in any ritual classes, why none of your tutors taught you spells, or why she was so distant?"

I always assumed my mother's behavior was a punishment, a result of her misery after my father's death. Later, I blamed it on Silas.

"Did she fear me? Was she worried about what I might become?" I ask tentatively.

"I don't believe Macy feared you. I think she resented you. She likely envied the power she knew you'd one day wield and felt helpless against it," Athalda confesses, leaning in closer.

"There's something else I don't understand, and it was never fully explained to me. I read the first Fae were born from the light of the Dream Forest. Does that have something to do with why they are born with magic and we have to wait to come of age before we get our magic?" I ask.

Athalda exhales deeply, pausing for a moment before answering. "The Fae are deeply bound to nature, they receive their magic from birth as nature instantly reacts to the call of the earth, and they sense their power from their very first breath. It's their lesson in immediate responsibility and balance."

I nod slowly, taking that in. "Alright, but why the delay for all the Sorcerers?"

She rubs at the scars on her face like I would rub my temple if I had a headache. "I imagine the gods intended it as a test of character. Zomea has always held all of our magic until we come of age and it is given to us. I think it keeps a balance, and it's how Zomea stays alive."

"And you say my magic isn't going to be given to me. It's already inside me just waiting..." I muse aloud.

Athalda glances at a nearby shelf, laden with scrolls. "The magic you are to inherit, Lyra, it is the deep and formidable power of ancient darkness. Such power demands not only strength but a profound sense of duty and caution."

I furrow my brows, not understanding her point. "But why is it already inside me, waiting? Why is it not being held here in Zomea with all the other magic?"

"Because dark magic is primal, raw, and unpredictable. The gods decided that, instead of having it held in Zomea like other magic, it should be born within the destined Sorcerer, or in your case Sorceress, waiting for the right moment. This ensures it doesn't fall into the wrong hands or is misused. Some speculate it was the goddess Ryella's way of deceiving the other gods."

"Ryella, the goddess of shadows," I confirm.

"Yes."

I take a moment, letting the enormity of what she's saying settle. "But why nineteen? And how does it awaken?"

Athalda gestures toward the window. "The way the Fae have their connection with the Dream Forest, well, Sorcerers have their bond with the cosmos. Nineteen is the celestial number, aligned with the stars formations that gave birth to magic. For you specifically, when a dark magic Sorcerer turns nineteen, the stars align in a certain pattern, triggering the awakening."

A chill runs down my spine. "So, it's like an internal cosmic clock?"

She nods. "Exactly. And because it's dark magic, its awakening is far more...intense. It's different from all other magic because of its potency and ancient origin. While most Sorcerers discover their magic, you'll feel yours erupt from within."

"At least I have something to look forward to."

"This isn't a joke," she scolds me, and I glare at her.

"Does it look like I'm joking? This is my life. So what's next?" I shrug. I need something to make the pounding in my head go away. She's making me feel grouchy and restless, and I don't like it.

"Growing snippy with me, are you?" Athalda's voice snaps, a venomous edge to it.

I grimace. "It's not my fault you don't know when I'm being serious. Maybe instead of the ceaseless talk and trials of dark magic I should actually see it in action."

Athalda's lips curl in a slight sneer as she pushes herself up, muttering something dark under her breath. I track her movements as she purposefully strides to the room's center. She begins a haunting chant under her breath, her hands weaving patterns through the air.

The room's atmosphere thickens, a coldness creeping in that feels almost malevolent. A mysterious wind emerges, spiraling fiercely before her, coalescing into a visible force.

From this vortex, a spectral serpent rises. It weaves protectively around Athalda before making a deliberate path toward me, its very motion causing ripples in the air and unsettling loose items in its wake.

Athalda's smirk is all malice. "Dark magic is so much more than mere shadows, dear child. It's the skill of twisting the world's hidden powers to your every whim. You'll inherit this might, and unlike me, having to delve into age-old grimoires, you'll merely need to picture your desire. No words, no rituals."

Curiosity overrides my trepidation. I reach out to the approaching entity. It coils up my arm, settling on my shoulders, its ethereal form scrutinizing me. Though devoid of eyes, it seems to study me with an intensity that's unnerving. It looks like a storm contained, chaotic and beautiful. But before I can fully absorb its presence, Athalda's clap disperses the being. I whirl at her, aghast. "Why did you do that?"

Her gaze is piercing. "Becoming fond of dark creations is a dangerous game. Now that you've glimpsed dark magic in action, satisfied? Shall we proceed without your needless complaints?"

She settles on a cushion, her every move dripping with disdain. I bristle, "I wasn't needlessly complaining! And that... that was a storm in the shape of a snake, not the evil I was expecting. It's not like the Monstrauths."

She leans forward, her voice cold and unyielding, "Summoning entities is one of the purest forms of dark magic. And trust me, girl, with a mere thought that serpent could have been your undoing." She pauses, the threat in her gaze unmistakable. "Do not mistake beauty for benevolence."

I'm about to argue but immediately catch myself and stop when she slaps her hand down on the table. "Now let's continue your training."

CHAPTER
TWELVE

Hours later, Athalda finally releases me from her suffocating ritual chamber. As I head in the direction of my bedchamber, the eerie silence of the palace pulls my curiosity, urging me outside. I've been cooped up all day and need the cool embrace of fresh air. The weight of today presses on me—Athalda's relentless probing, her attempts to push me to my mental limits.

She did introduce me to some meditation techniques she claimed would help me have more control of my midnight mind. But her teachings weren't limited to that. Another trial, different from the maddening maze of visions orchestrated by my father, awaited me. This was a haunting forest filled with malicious creatures. Devoid of my magic, I had to navigate through relying solely on my cunning and physical combat skills.

Needless to say, I faltered again and again before she dismissed me with a smug promise of more trials in the coming days. I feel so mentally and physically exhausted but am not going to give up. I need to just keep doing the tests they put me through, and I know I will get stronger. It's going to take time, and I want instant gratification.

I continue walking, crossing the bridge and passing through the protective veil of fog. All I want is a moment of solitude, a deep breath of real, untainted air. I settle down at the base of a tree, letting my back rest against its sturdy trunk. The foggy veil in front of me dances and shifts with the breeze, creating an eerie, mesmerizing view.

It's kind of creepy out here, but I'm drawn to it. There's always been a part of me that relishes that jolt of fear—not the paralyzing fear of real danger but the thrill that quickens the heart and sharpens the senses. Growing up confined in a castle, such moments of excitement were rare. They made me feel alive in an otherwise stagnant existence.

Taking in another deep breath, the cool air invigorates me, chasing away some of the day's fatigue. I can't help but wonder what lies beyond these woods. There's so much of Zomea I've yet to see, beyond the palace walls and this haunting forest. Is my mother out there somewhere? And where is Luke?

The idea of venturing out alone crosses my mind, but exhaustion wins over curiosity for now. I stay put, content for the moment to watch the drifting fog.

I'm jolted awake by the sensation of being lifted. The surrounding darkness tells me night has settled in. I must've dozed off in the woods. The familiar citrus scent of Colton envelops me, and without thinking I snuggle closer to his chest. Though half-asleep, I revel in his warmth, not wanting this moment to end. The fresh, forest air gradually fades, replaced by the more enclosed aroma of the palace as we enter. Silently, he carries me through the winding corridors to our bedchamber.

Gently placing me onto the bed, I lift my heavy eyes to meet his. He brushes a few stray hairs from my face, and his

fingers move to the laces of my bodice. A sudden rush of anticipation fills me, but it's short-lived. He simply undoes my bodice
and deftly removes my boots, leaving me in my tunic and pants.
Pulling the blankets over me, he ensures I'm snug and comfortable. I sense Chepi's familiar weight settling at the foot of the
bed. I want to ask them about their day, about how he found
me, but the weight of sleep pulls me under once more.

I rouse myself sometime later, realizing I'm alone in bed.
Pushing myself up, my gaze drifts across the dimly lit room,
finally settling on Colton. He sits near the fire, nursing a drink
in his hand. "Are you alright?" I ask, shedding the blankets and
moving to stand.

"I couldn't sleep. You should rest. You've had a long day,"
he replies, but I feel drawn to him, needing to close the space
between us.

"What's on your mind?" I ask, noting the distant look in his
eyes as they focus on the dancing flames.

His voice carries an edge I haven't heard before, "You were
so drained after being in Athalda's fucking ritual chamber that
you fell asleep alone in the woods, where no one could find
you. Do you realize how dangerous that was?"

His words sting. "Are you angry with me?" I venture, taking
cautious steps closer him.

He runs a hand through his hair, frustration evident in his
movements. "I'm not angry with you, but I don't know if I can
bear to watch you endure this daily." The silence stretches
between us. "When I found you in the woods, covered in
marks... It took everything in me not to confront Athalda. I
wanted to find out firsthand what happens when you kill
someone in Zomea."

I look down, surprised. I hadn't noticed any marks. A quick
look in the nearby mirror reveals cuts and bruises marring my
skin. "I went through another simulation a few times, fought a

bit, but I'm fine. I can handle this. I'm not as delicate as you think."

"I don't see you as fragile, Lyra," he starts but stops to take another drink. "Somewhere along the way, my feelings shifted. I can't stand seeing you like this. Your father gave me a tour today, showing off the tests he plans for you. He speaks about you as if you're a tool, not his daughter. I can't stomach it."

My thoughts whirl. Feelings? What kind of feelings? Before I can speak, he gets up, removes his shirt, tossing it aside, and reclines on the bed.

Breaking the tension, I approach him. "Can you heal me?" I ask, wanting to snap him out of this mood he's in. I pull my leather pants off and lift my tunic slightly, turning away from him.

He sits up, a soft white light emanating from him as his fingers trace my injuries. The gentle warmth of his touch is comforting. He doesn't speak, just runs his hands over each mark. Once he's done, I let my tunic fall back to my thighs and turn around to face him. His eyes blaze with the fierce intensity of a raging forest fire, yet all green and untamed. My breath catches in my throat as he cups my cheek and runs his thumb across my lower lip. His thumb lingers there, pressing gently until his light disappears and he lies back on the bed again.

Without thinking, I pull my tunic off over my head and climb on top of him. My breasts pressed against his warm chest is a shock to my senses. His large hands explore my body immediately, as if reacting on instinct. One cups my ass, warm and rough. The other grazes my cheek then runs through my hair, griping it slightly as he stares up at me, his eyes locked on mine.

"Fuck, Lyra, you can't do this," he says, suddenly using his hands to lift me off him and place me back on the bed next to him. As soon as he says that, I feel heat rush to my face. He doesn't want me, and I suddenly feel a mix of emotions I wasn't expecting—sad, embarrassed, foolish.

I don't know what I was thinking. I reach down and pull a sheet up over my body, and he lets out a frustrated breath.

"When I'm inside you for the first time, it's not going to be under your father's roof where you have to conceal your screams of pleasure, and it damn sure won't be while you're still thinking about him," he says, and I stare up at the ceiling. Him...Nyx.

Lying beside him, a realization hits. For the first time, another wasn't clouding my thoughts. Today, especially in this heated moment, he was the only one on my mind...Colton.

IT'S BEEN twelve weeks since I started my training in Zomea. Twelve relentless weeks filled with unending simulations and tests. I've never felt stronger; my body is more defined, toned with newfound muscles. Mentally, I've learned to harness my emotions better and to navigate through past traumas with a firmer grip. But despite these weeks, Colton and I haven't addressed that night. The night he confessed his feelings and I, in a moment of vulnerability, bared myself to him, only to be denied.

When I train with my father, both Colton and Chepi accompany me. However, when it's Athalda's turn to train me, they venture off, leaving me alone in her ominous grip. Thanks to Anika's guidance, I've begun to master the secondary Lycan abilities I possess. My skills as a tracker, once nonexistent, have now considerably sharpened.

Colton, ever eager, challenges my Fae magic and spars with me frequently. Sometimes, I think he takes a bit too much pleasure in our physical duels, but then again perhaps I do as well.

Over these months, we've become friends. I've learned so much about Fae magic from him, and it constantly amazes me all the different things Fae can do depending on their gifts. Colton is not only built like a freaking warrior who can bend the elements to his will, but he can create illusions and manipulate light as well.

All the rigorous training has been exhausting me daily. Nights have only been for rest, not intimacy. Yet, every dawn, I find myself cocooned in Colton's embrace. It's a silent agreement between us — seeking each other in the night, yet never acknowledging it by day.

The past weeks have been focused, driven. I feel empowered, ready, and equipped for whatever comes next. For whatever awakening my dark magic brings.

I reach down, picking up a stick. It's already been a long day, and the setting sun is mesmerizing. Positioned perfectly at the edge of the clearing, it starts its descent, casting a golden hue over everything. The red leaves appear as if they've been set ablaze, their colors intensified by the sun's glow. Long shadows stretch across the vast expanse. Our own secluded clearing in the dense forest, away from prying eyes where Colton and I like to train together.

Colton stands a few paces away, his green eyes locking onto mine, that familiar, playful challenge evident. "Think you can surprise me today?"

I smirk, twirling the stick I've picked up for our spar. "I always do."

In a flash, he lunges. But I've grown. I've learned. Anticipating him, I duck and spin, my movements more fluid than before. "Too slow," I tease, poking him with the tip of my stick.

His eyebrow arches. "Impatient, are we?" He pauses. "Ready for a different kind of challenge?" There's a hint of mischief unmistakable in his voice.

I raise an eyebrow. "Always. What have you got in mind?"

Without responding, he waves a hand, and suddenly there are three Coltons standing before me, each wearing a cocky grin. I stifle a laugh. "Really? The old multiple illusion trick again?"

The middle Colton chuckles. "Thought I'd give it another whirl. See if you can determine which one is real."

The Colton on the left winks. "Pick wisely, my little enchantress."

The one on the right stretches and cracks his knuckles. "Unless you want to owe me another favor."

I roll my eyes playfully, circling the three of them. "Okay, let me think. Which one of you is the real, overconfident Faery boy."

Each of them begins to move, adopting different stances. Left Colton starts to dance playfully, making me laugh. Middle Colton is trying to look serious, attempting to throw me off, while right Colton is merely flexing his muscles exaggeratedly. Taking a deep breath and concentrating, I reach out with my senses, feeling the undercurrents of magic. But I decide to play along. With a dramatic sigh, I say, "This is too hard. Maybe I should just..." In a swift motion, I launch a small burst of flames toward the right Colton, who dissipates into thin air.

The left one claps. "Nice try! But you still haven't found the real me." Using the element of surprise to my advantage, I spin around and launch my stick at the middle Colton, and it passes right through him. He laughs his illusion fading, leaving the dancing Colton. "Got me. That was impressive."

"You know," I tease, walking up to him, "for someone who can make copies of himself, you're not very good at hiding your true self."

He pulls me close, his breath tickling my ear. "Maybe I didn't want to hide from you."

I seize the moment to catch him off guard, sweeping his feet from beneath him. He's too slow to react, but in a twist he grips me, dragging me down alongside him. His back crashes against the dirt, and I land squarely atop him. Our laughter intertwines with our heavy breaths, echoing through the forest. Slowly, I shift, lying beside him, our gazes fixed on the twilight sky. I let my hand brush against his, finding solace in the touch.

Our bond is evolving. While Colton has kept a respectful distance, most of the time since the night I basically threw myself at him, his protective instincts and playful flirtations are evident. We might label what this is as friendship, but a gut feeling tells me there's an underlying current suggesting something deeper is budding between us.

"How much longer do you think we should stay here?" I ask.

"We can sleep here if you want, but I imagine it's going to get colder as it gets later," Colton says, chuckling softly. I elbow his shoulder and turn onto my side to face him. "I'm being serious."

"We can leave Zomea whenever you want. This has always been your decision. I'm just along for the ride." He turns his head to look at me. I mean, I have been enjoying my time in Zomea, but it's been exhausting, and I want to go back to Eguina. I don't really want to go to Tempest Moon and face the council yet. I don't even know if I'm ready to be a queen. I want to have fun and enjoy life a little bit before my birthday comes. Once I get my dark magic, I don't know what changes will come with it. I'm not afraid of it like I used to be. I've accepted it, embraced it even. I want some time to simply be, before things change.

"What are you thinking?" Colton grazes his fingers against the back of my hand, and I look down at the movement.

"I'm thinking I've had enough training here. I've done the

simulations with my father a million times, and Athalda has put me through enough wacky stuff to last a lifetime. You and I can keep training after we leave. I can keep getting stronger, working on my Fae magic, and kicking your ass from time to time." I smirk, raising my eyes to his.

"Where do you want to go, Princess? I'll take you anywhere you want."

"I want you to take me to your home. I want to see the Dream Forest." I glance around, anxious for his response. He leans in close, his lips lightly brushing my forehead. "Then let's go tell Euric this is our last night in Zomea."

THIRTEEN

"Where do you plan to go once you cross the bridge?" my father asks from across the dinner table. Once we told him this was our last night in Zomea, until we return at least, he insisted we all have dinner together.

"I'm taking her back to Nighthold with me, at least until after her birthday. I'll be able to make sure she's safe if anything should go wrong when her dark magic awakens." Colton squeezes my leg under the table, and my heart does a little flutter at the comforting touch.

"I'm sure your boyfriend will be happy to see you again. I wonder what King Onyx has been up to all this time, probably beside himself without you." Athalda winks at me from across the table, always stirring the pot. She knows we're not together, but she likes getting a reaction out of Colton every chance she can.

"Were you ever able to find anything out from the Lycan Realm? Do you know who's taken Aidan's place amongst the packs?" I turn to Anika, ignoring Athalda completely. I've been pestering Anika to find out if Rhett's okay and what is happening in the Lycan Realm after Nyx killed Aidan and we left with things so uncertain. She said she's been frequenting the tunnels, looking for anyone new to show up to Zomea so she can ask, but so far nothing. I know my father has ways of knowing things about Eguina, but he's been tight-lipped about the Lycans.

"Larc has become the new leader of the Lycans," she says, and my head snaps in her direction. Larc was Rhett's pack master, and he seemed like a good man. Rhett liked him. I swallow, feeling relieved to hear this.

"How did you find out? Who told you?" I'm quick to ask, hoping Rhett is okay and still alive back home.

"A Lycan named Zog came through the tunnels this morning. Did you know him?" she asks.

"Yes, I believe he was leader of the pack that covered the shifting forest."

"That makes sense. He had a lot to say about Spider Wraiths and Monstrauths, among several other dark creatures. He said things are becoming more unstable in Cloudrum, and monsters are multiplying at rates he's never seen before," Anika says, and she looks like she's going to continue, but my father speaks up.

"Let's not worry Lyra with that right now. It's a good thing Colton is taking you to Nighthold. Things should be more stable there."

"It sounds like what Drew said is true. Bad things are happening in Eguina. Things are dying, and evil creatures are becoming more prolific. The darkness looming over Cloudrum wasn't just Samael's doing, and it's getting worse. What if it's getting worse at a quicker rate than Zomea?" I feel my pulse start to increase as worry festers in my gut.

"Even if things are happening faster in Eguina than Zomea, it doesn't matter. You are already doing everything you can.

You can't move up your birthday, and there is no way I am letting him attempt to take that Gholioth blood out of you before you're strong enough to survive it," Colton declares next to me.

"Colton is right. Zomea is much larger than Eguina, so it may seem like things are getting worse there at a faster rate than here, but I don't think that's the case. Like I already told you, Pixie, all will be well. Focus on staying strong, and keep training with Colton until your dark magic awakens, then make your way back here as soon as you can. We will set things right. I will fix what I started. I promise."

"The bridge is unlocked now. Why don't you come back with us and go to Tempest Moon and try to stabilize things?" I press, glancing from my father to Athalda.

"I don't think we should make it known to many the bridge is unlocked yet. I want to stabilize things here first or we risk doing more harm than good. I need to stay here until you return," he says, and I quickly interject.

"But—"

"No buts, Pixie. Go to Nighthold, stay with Colton, and return to me when you're ready. Now let's not waste our last night together speaking about things we have no control over at the moment."

I clench my fists under the table, heat rising to my cheeks.

"I don't think there are mass casualties or anything. The Lycan are very capable of protecting themselves and their territory, so are the Sorcerers, and so are the Lamas. Don't let this stress you out," Colton says, squeezing my thigh again under the table, and I take a deep breath. Chepi climbs into my lap, looking up at me with his sweet violet eyes. Sensing my rising frustration, he licks under my chin. I kiss him on the head and give him a plate of food.

"Colton, I need to speak with you after dinner. Alone,"

Athalda says, and I look from her to Colton. What an odd request.

"Of course." Colton nods, and I don't know what is happening right now, but Colton better tell me what she says later.

"And, Pixie, I need to talk to you alone after dinner," my father says, and I nod. They must be giving each of us a pep talk about training and staying safe. I push around my food, not really into all the unusual meat they serve in Zomea. I eat a couple of cheesy biscuits and feed Chepi the rest of my meat. The rest of the dinner is light hearted. Anika doesn't say anything more about the Lycans, probably too afraid to upset my father, and I'm still irritated and don't have much to say. Once we're all finished, I help Anika clear the plates, while Colton and Athalda disappear down the hall for whatever private conversation they are having.

I return from the kitchen and find my father in the sitting room nursing a glass of whiskey. Chepi's sprawled out in front of the fire napping now that his belly's full.

As I take a seat in one of the plush chairs facing the mantle, I lean forward, my curiosity evident. "So, what is it you wanted to discuss?"

His eyes shimmer with a hint of mystery as he says, "It's something best shown rather than told." As he rises from his seat, I instinctively lean to awaken Chepi, but he swiftly catches my wrist, his grip firm but gentle. "It's best if Chepi rests. We should go alone." I retract my hand, giving a hesitant nod. The secrecy of it all makes me even more eager to find out his intentions.

I trail behind him, navigating a labyrinth of hallways in the decrepit side of the palace. He halts abruptly and with a careful maneuver pushes aside a well-worn rug runner, unveiling a concealed hatch amidst the floorboards. As he lifts it, a shadowy, tight staircase stretches out below us.

"Wait for me at the base. I'll need to secure the hatch," he instructs, stepping aside to let me descend. I pause, my imagination conjuring unsettling scenarios. Could he be luring me into a trap? Then I tell myself the fact that my mind is even going there is ridiculous. I may have had doubts about my father, and some of his actions are unforgivable, but I cannot deny that he loves me and wants the best for me.

Gathering my courage, I tread down the creaky, spiral staircase, each step echoing faintly. Three revolutions later, I find myself in a subterranean chamber. I loathe being confined underground, yet fate keeps pushing me into such spaces. I let out a measured breath, resting against the cold stone wall and waiting for his presence. When he finally emerges, he awakens torches with a mere flick of his wrist, unveiling a lengthy corridor. I follow silently until the passage concludes at a solid stone barrier.

Perplexed, I ask, "What is this place? What's behind this wall?"

Without a word, he places his palms on the stony surface. The wall gradually liquefies, reminding me of the tunnel's bleeding walls, but this time it's like a living, moving mirror. He clasps my hand, leading me through the liquid facade, and we emerge into an expansive vault.

"This, Pixie," he says with a hint of pride, "is where I safeguard all that is precious to me."

I run my eyes over the mountainous stacks of items. Towering piles of old books, seemingly defying gravity. Scattered collections of shimmering crystals, glinting gold, and ornate trunks. It's as if I've stumbled upon a trove of treasures from fabled tales.

"These are invaluable texts and powerful artifacts I've

amassed over time," he explains, his gaze scanning the room, evidently searching for something particular. As I trail my gaze, a familiar mask nestles within one pile. The very one from my childhood memory, the mask I saw during my hallucinatory encounter with Athalda. I shake my head, trying to rid myself of the memory of Nyx.

"Remind me again how exactly you got all of this here?" I ask, my fingers grazing a pile of gems.

"I always knew one day I would end up here. With my midnight mind, I could always traverse from Eguina to Zomea. I could hide things here and keep them safe. One day, when your powers grow and you hone your midnight mind, you too could come here in a more controlled manor without using the bridge."

"Why is the bridge even necessary if you could come here without it?" I feel like we already had this discussion, but so much information has been dumped at me lately that I can't remember.

"Because after my death, I could no longer use the midnight mind to travel back to Eguina. It's why you haven't had any nightmares since you've been here," he says, tapping my temple.

I step back. He's right. This is the longest I've gone without having a nightmare.

"Midnight mind only works when you're not in Zomea, but once you die and come here you can no longer travel back and forth. So you collected all of this before your death," I say.

"Exactly. Once you leave Zomea, your midnight mind will start acting up again. It will bring you here and show you glimpses of things that are current, things that happened in the past, and possible futures to come. You need to practice exploring and being in control to hone your ability," he tells me while rummaging through a trunk. Easier said than done.

"Where did you get all of these artifacts and why? What do they all do?" I walk further into the room, stepping around piles of random objects that shimmer and sparkle.

"The artifacts I collect are ones previously owned by the gods. They are extremely powerful and can do all sorts of things. I either plan to use them someday or will simply keep them out of the hands of others, because they can do great harm. Artifacts are fascinating things, especially when I have someone like Athalda who can do spells to activate the ones that need it," he explains, not looking up from the trunk he's rifling through.

It doesn't seem right that one person should have this much power. Nor does it seem right to have this many powerful objects hidden away in the same place. I guess if he's coming from a place of protecting others, but what if some of these things could make life better back home. I've heard of artifacts being able to do unthinkable things. Things you only dream about.

"Why show me all of this now?" I kneel down beside him, glancing into the trunk he's going through.

"I show you all of this now because you are my daughter and I want to share things with you. But I also want you to use this." He pulls out a large piece of dusty parchment and slowly unfolds it, revealing a small tapestry, not much larger than my hand.

"What is it?" I ask. The tapestry is an off-white color with two intertwined trees stitched into it, their branches and roots tangled together.

"This is called the Lovers' Loom. It is a very unique artifact created by Elara herself."

"Elara, the Goddess of Amorists?" I've only studied the gods briefly. Mr. Drogo never seemed thrilled about the subject. He used to say it wasn't important to learn about them since they didn't live in Eguina and would probably never walk the lands again.

"Yes. She made this for her lover, Varik, the God of Discord, a very long time ago. You see, Elara was a controlling lover, and Varik was...duplicitous." He wraps the tapestry back in the parchment and hands it to me while he places all the stuff back in the trunk.

"What does it do? Why give it to me?"

"This tapestry, once activated, will tether two people together. You will always be able to know where the other is located. You will feel each other on a completely different level, and you will know each other's emotions at all times if you both allow it, knowing if the other is in danger or hurt."

I take a step away back. "I don't want to be tethered to you," I say without thinking. It seems like an invasion of privacy, something an overbearing, ultra-controlling parent would do. Gods, I'm glad this isn't something readily available in Eguina.

My father lets out a deep chuckle, shaking his head. "No, dear, I don't expect you to tether with me. I would like you to consider tethering to Colton before you leave Zomea."

I cross my arms over my stomach. I don't know if that's a good idea either. Oh gods, the thought of Colton knowing my emotions at all times is horrifying.

"Why?" I whisper under my breath almost to myself.

He gets to his feet and places a finger under my chin, forcing me to look up at him. "I know you are strong. I know you are more than capable of taking care of yourself, especially after all the training you've been going through. But, Pixie, your life is so important, not just because I love you but because the very existence of Zomea and Eguina depends on it. You need to survive long enough to awaken your dark magic and make it back here so I can extract Moirati's blood, and then together we can restore things before too much is lost."

I search his gaze for anything deceptive, but all I see is worry in his eyes. He goes on, "I trust Colton. I've known him since he was a boy, and he is a good man. I trust him to look after you. I don't care if you have a romantic relationship with him or not. I know he will protect you. Tether to him for me, tether to him for the sake of Eguina."

"How do we get untethered if I don't like it? What if I want it to stop?"

"I would simply burn the tapestry, and the tether would be broken."

I swallow thickly.

"But the tapestry would then be lost forever?" I ask.

"Yes, the only way to break the bond is to destroy it. No more tethers would be made," he confirms. Colton and I are friends. I know I feel something more from him at times, and he hints that he does too, but this will further complicate whatever our relationship is. Or maybe it won't. Maybe it will clear a lot of things up if we both know how the other is feeling. Fuck.

"I'll do it. But how do you know he will agree to it?"

"He would be a fool not to," he says, taking the tapestry from me and leading us back out of the vault.

"How do you activate the tether?" I quicken my steps to keep up with him as we ascend the stairs.

"Athalda has the spell to activate the tapestry and complete the tether in her ritual room."

"Is this why she wanted to talk to Colton? Is she already asking him about it?" I feel my face instantly heat. I don't know why I feel embarrassed at the thought of him considering being tethered to me.

"Yes, we will know his answer soon enough." He pushes open the hatch, and we go to the ritual room.

Once there, we find Athalda skimming through her messy shelves, pulling things out, and placing them on the table.

Colton is leaning against the window, watching her. He looks over at me immediately when we enter the room, a look of concern washes on his features, and I wonder if he told Athalda that he doesn't want to tether with me. Why would she be going through all of her stuff frantically like she's preparing for a spell?

"What's your decision, girl?" she snaps, black eyes looking me up and down.

"Yes, I will do it."

Colton steps away from the wall, moving toward me. A nervous feeling tugs at my gut, but I try to bury it.

"I want the room," Colton declares.

"It's late. There's no time for that, boy," Athalda huffs.

"I don't give a damn. You'll make time. Now give us the room," he demands, and my father gestures for Athalda to follow him out. Once the door closes, he pulls me in close to him, wrapping his arms around me. I bury my face in his chest and let my arms tangle around his waist, breathing in his citrus scent. He rubs his hand up and down my back. "You looked like you could use a minute."

"I'm okay," I say, muffled into his chest. He leans back, and I raise my lashes, meeting his eyes. He raises his hands and brushes my hair out of my face, tucking it behind my ears.

"Don't lie to me now, enchantress." He gets a smile out of me. "You don't have to do this. We don't have to do anything. Your father and Athalda always want to control everything, not to mention they are paranoid that something bad will happen to you. I can't say I blame them after everything you've been through, but tether or not I will be here for you."

"You're making this all about me. What about you? How do you feel?" I ask, not wanting to release him.

"Soon enough, you won't have to ask me that anymore," he teases. I want to say a smart retort back, but he's right. Gods, what if it actually works? I have no idea what that will even feel like to know what he's feeling or how it will work. "Hey, I want to do this too. Don't worry about me." He narrows his eyes like he's trying to read my mind.

I take a deep breath straightening. "Well, let's get started then." He nods and opens the door. My father comes in first and places a hand on my shoulder, while Athalda brushes past us, muttering under her breath like we are some huge inconvenience.

"Come, sit across from each other so you are almost touching." She waves us to sit in a circle of salts she has at the center of the room. We both get settled, crisscrossing our legs on the floor so our knees are almost touching.

"Now intertwine your fingers with each other, then place your hands on top of one another," she instructs, and my father circles us, watching closely. Athalda drapes the tapestry over our joined hands and lets it rest there. I look up at Colton as my heart starts to beat faster against my chest. He winks at me, and I have to hold back a giggle so Athalda doesn't scold us.

She grabs a bundle of herbs, swatting my father away while she ignites it. The smoke is potent, and she walks around us, slowly whispering things under her breath as the smoke seems to coalesce solely within the circle of salts. I want to cough but swallow hard fighting the urge. I'm forced to close my eyes when the smoke becomes so thick they start to water. I can no longer see Colton right in front of me.

Suddenly, the tapestry starts to move. At first I think Athalda picked it up, but I squint through the smoke and see it's levitating above our hands. It starts to circle us, fast. The cloth circles our hands and then circles our bodies several times before falling back onto our conjoined hands, and the smoke disappears instantly. I look up at Colton, who's looking down at the tapestry and then over to my father, who watches intently.

"It's done." Athalda reaches down, grabs the tapestry, and hands it back to my father.

"I'll see you both in the morning and escort you to the bridge." He makes eye contact with me for a brief moment, and I nod. He leaves the room, wrapping that tapestry back up.

I can only assume he's returning it to the vault for safekeeping. A heavy feeling of concern washes over me, and the air is suddenly filled with a tang of citrus and oakmoss. I quickly turn to Colton, realizing this is him. I'm not worried and have never smelled him like that before. It's like his scent has more depth to it. The smell dissipates quickly, and the feeling subsides as I watch him regain control over what he was feeling. I want to ask him what he's worried about, but we are still with Athalda, so I keep my thoughts to myself.

"Go, go, I have to clean all this up, and I'm sure it's going to be an interesting night for the two of you." Athalda swats at us to get out of her room. Colton helps me to my feet, and neither of us say anything as we walk back to our bed chamber. I stop on the way and pick up Chepi, who's still half asleep, so I carry him to our room. Once inside, I set him down on the end of the bed, and he curls up in a ball. Colton closes the door, and when our eyes meet an indescribable feeling washes over me.

CHAPTER
FOURTEEN

In the stillness of the room, my heart's beating feels so loud I'm convinced he can hear it. An indefinable energy hums between us, and warmth blossoms, starting at the nape of my neck and cascading downward. It's beyond the tactile; it's an emotional tug I feel deep in my chest. Every nuance of emotion he undergoes, I sense it, like a distant echo resonating within me. While I can't decipher his thoughts, the way I connect with him now feels unprecedented — deeper and rawer. A flash of surprise, a hint of amusement, a surge of...something else. Is it longing? It's a tangled web, and I can't quite pinpoint it, but I know it's coming from him.

The fresh blend of citrus and moss that defines his scent swirls around me, now deeply intertwined with the emotional whirlwind. This scent isn't merely olfactory anymore. It's an experience, a tangible reflection of the tether binding us.

"What are you thinking?" The moment the question slips out, his scent retreats as swiftly as it had intensified. It's as though he's returned to how he was before our bond.

He gazes into my eyes. "I sense a combination of awe and uncertainty from you, but, interestingly, no regret."

I can feel the heat rising to my cheeks. Regret was indeed absent from my emotions, and its absence surprises me. This newfound intimacy between us, as startling as it is, feels right, even if I'm not ready to admit that to myself.

"How did you cut off your emotions from me? One moment your scent was overwhelming, tangled with what you were feeling, and the next it vanished," I inquire.

"It's how you shield your feelings when you don't want to get hurt or when you're controlling your magic. But don't go too extreme. You don't need to construct an impenetrable fortress around your heart. It's more like closing a window," he says, a smirk playing on his lips. The thought of him trying to unravel the maze of my emotions is already making me cringe. I reflect on the barriers I've erected around my heart over the years, those protective walls that have seen me through tough times. Visualizing a window, like he suggested, I imagine it closing. Taking a deep breath, I focus, trying to find some semblance of calm.

"Is it working?" I ask quickly before I lose focus. Gods, this is going to be exhausting trying to guard how I'm feeling all the time.

"It's working." He nods.

"Did my scent intensify when you felt my emotions? Like the emotions were carried to you with my smell, and at first it was hard to decipher if it was what you were feeling or what I was feeling?"

"Yes. It was how you always smell, only more intense." He moves to the table and begins pouring two glasses of whiskey.

"What do I smell like?" I ask. I know I smell of honey-suckle, but I want to know how I smell to him, especially with it being more potent now.

"You smell of young roses, fresh dew, and honeysuckle..." His voice trails off, and he takes a prolonged sip from his glass. My cheeks flush with warmth. I want to approach him, to feel the touch of his skin against mine. Yet, the haunting memories of that night surge back to the forefront of my mind. Did he reject me because of my past? Because of the violations I've endured? Or did he truly believe I was yearning for Nyx?

He moves closer to me, offering the glass of whiskey. A sudden rush of emotion from him pierces my chest — sympathy. Damn. I'm clearly failing to shield my feelings.

"Don't pity me," I snap, snatching the glass and emptying its contents in one go.

He clears his throat, swiftly shutting down his emotions once more. "I apologize. I'll become more adept at guarding my feelings. It's... I hadn't fully understood." He hesitates, shaking his head as if dispelling a thought, then gently retrieves the empty glass from my grasp.

"Understood what?" I urge, narrowing the distance between us.

He tenderly brushes tangled strands of hair from my face, tucking them securely behind my ear. "Your pain. It isn't fleeting or superficial. Beneath everything, there's a profound sorrow, a persistent ache. I hadn't realized how deep-seated that hurt is."

I swallow hard, struggling to keep the sudden rush of emotions at bay. "You see, that's the thing," I whisper, my voice shaky, "so few people ever really see beneath the surface. I've become so good at wearing masks, at hiding the scars. But with you, with this tether, there's no hiding, is there?" I meet his gaze, searching for understanding. "Maybe that's what terrifies me the most— the thought of someone truly seeing me, all of me. Not just the broken parts but the strength that's kept me going."

His green eyes search mine, assertive and piercing. "Lyra," he says, voice firm and grounded, "from the moment I saw you, I recognized that fire in you. Even tethered now, I don't feel the shadows of your past. I feel that relentless strength, that fiery spirit that you've honed from every challenge thrown your way. I don't pity you. I admire your strength and resilience. I only wish I had been here for you sooner, to shield you from everything you've had to endure until now." He steps decisively closer, his body emanating a heat that beckons me.

His fingers tenderly brush my cheek, compelling me to look up at him. My eyes, heavy with anticipation, look up to find his. "Colton," I murmur, his name lingering on my lips, laden with desire. We are mere breaths apart, the touch of his hand on my face sending waves of electricity through me. A yearning consumes me, a hunger to feel the pressure of his mouth on mine, to savor the taste of him.

He releases my chin, taking a step back. "We should get some rest. It's late."

I search for anything from him, but he's much older and stronger than I am. From many years of controlling his Fae magic, he's obviously going to master blocking me out a lot quicker than I am. There's nothing to be found. Whatever he's feeling is trapped behind that window in his chest. He tears off his shirt and climbs into bed next to Chepi.

I go into the bathing chamber and clean up, my body hot with unfulfilled desire. Why doesn't he want me? He's just toying with me. He flirts and teases, but every time we get close he falls back out of reach. I don't understand. I blow out a breath, stripping off my clothes and donning a nightgown. I crawl into bed and turn away from him, pulling a pillow to my chest and closing my eyes.

I feel heat in my core, and my skin is flushed. I want to...

"Whatever you're thinking right now...stop. Or I won't be able to control myself and it'll be a long night."

Colton moves behind me, tugging my back against his chest. Gods, I need to keep my walls up and my window closed. I don't know what emotions I was projecting, but I have so much built-up sexual tension in my body right now. I want Colton more than I'd care to admit, his strong arms wrap around me, and I wish he was touching me lower.

"Stop reading my emotions if you can't control yourself," I snap.

"I'm not intentionally sensing them. It's how this works. You project, and I can't ignore it. You'll get better at controlling it. We both will." His fingers splay across my stomach, drawing me close until I'm nestled against his solid chest. Normally, we'd only gravitate to this closeness once one of us drifts into sleep, but tonight carries a different weight. It's clear why — we're navigating the unfamiliar waters of sensing each other's raw emotions. But this bond, though new, is something I'm determined to master. In due time, I'll perfect the art of shielding my feelings from him, revealing them only if I need to. After all, I got the impression this tether is more for him being able to locate me if I'm in trouble anyways.

Rest eludes me. My mind is relentless and won't shut off. Perhaps tonight is the opportunity to broach topics I've hesitated to discuss with Colton. He may be powerful, but he is still adjusting to this new bond, just like me. Maybe it's the ideal time to gauge his true feelings. Catching him off guard with my questions could give me a genuine glimpse into his emotions, should his shields momentarily falter.

Pushing his arm away, I flip over to face him. "Look, I'm not tired, and I'm certainly not ready to sleep." A huff escapes me, and an amused smirk dances across his face.

"You appear rather adorable when flustered. What has you so riled up?"

"Colton, it's maddening. One moment, you're close, and the next it feels like you're a million miles away. It's as if you're constantly torn between emotions. What are you truly feeling?"

"Can't you sense my emotions? You should know exactly how I feel, Princess," he retorts with a teasing grin.

"I don't find this amusing. You're clearly shielding your emotions from me. But that's not the main issue. I need to understand what you feel for me. Remember that night a few months ago? The night I bared myself to you and you rejected me? You've pulled me close every night since, and you flirt shamelessly during the day. I'm not in this for mind games. I'm already weighed down with the simulations and training. Do you feel anything for me at all?" My voice wavers a touch, revealing the vulnerability I'm desperately trying to hide.

He looks deep into my eyes, and the teasing glint is gone, replaced by genuine concern and intensity. "Lyra, I've never been good at these conversations." He pauses, and I feel something from him. It's powerful, possibly lust, but he's quick to keep his emotions locked up before he continues. "The moment I push myself away, it's because I'm terrified of the intensity of my feelings for you. It's not some light attraction. It's strong, possessive, almost overwhelming. The way I am drawn to you, it scares me. I fear becoming that overbearing, dominant lover who might end up smothering the very fire that draws me to you. But know this, every time I'm near you, it's a battle of restraint, not of disinterest."

He takes a deep breath, propping up on his elbow. "The night you speak of, it wasn't about you not being enough or about any past with Nyx. It was about me not trusting myself to stop once we crossed that line. I care about you more deeply than I've allowed myself to admit. But I've been trying to protect us both in my own flawed way."

Reaching out, he gently cups my face, the warmth of his touch melting away some of the tension. "You deserve honesty, and here it is. I want you, Lyra, not for a night but in a way that's all-consuming. But once we cross that line, there's no going back."

Swallowing hard, my eyes search his for any hint of deceit. "Colton, it's not about us or moving on from Nyx. It's about trust and understanding. I've been trying to figure out where we stand, deciphering these mixed signals. I mean, a few months ago I couldn't stand you, but somewhere along the way I think we became friends and now... I want something more. I want something real, and if that's not what you want, then tell me. But if you genuinely feel this way about me, why keep me at arm's length? Why this tug-of-war? I can't handle another heartbreak. I need to know I can trust you with my heart."

The last words come out as a whisper, betraying the depth of my vulnerability, although I'm probably projecting my feelings to him right now anyways.

His eyes darken briefly. "Lyra, my struggle has never been about trusting you. It's about trusting myself with you. Every time someone so much as looks at you, I want to mark you as mine to ensure no one else ever dares to touch what belongs to me. That level of possession, of dominance...scares me. Not because I think it's wrong but because I know I won't be able to control it once I fully give in. I've been holding back not to protect you—from the depth of my feelings and the force of my nature. But make no mistake, every fiber of my being screams to claim you, to make sure everyone knows you're mine. Can you handle that kind of intensity?"

The silence between us lingers as I digest his words. Gods, I was already attracted to him, but hearing him express his possessiveness like that? It's intoxicating. The urge to devour him is overwhelming, regardless of how reckless it might be.

"I've never shied away from intensity. In fact, I yearn for the very possessiveness you're talking about. I want to be the only woman in your eyes, the only one you touch in that way." Propping myself up on my elbow, I draw our faces tantalizingly close. In a sultry whisper, I challenge, "So if you're wondering whether I can handle you...why not show me how intense you really are?" I surprise even myself with how daring I am tonight. The words are barely out of my mouth, and he's pushing me back and climbing on top of me.

He captures both of my hands in one of his, pinning them above my head against the pillows. With his free hand, he hikes up my nightgown, revealing my breasts. He squeezes one, the weight of his touch both tender and demanding. He stares down at me, hunger evident in his eyes, as if he's starving and I'm the only feast that can satisfy him. Those eyes glow with an intensity I've never seen before. With his shields down, his emotions flood me— raw, unbridled need. And I reciprocate that need, wholly and fiercely. It's impossible to distinguish where his emotions end and mine begin; our desires are seamlessly intertwined.

He leans down, intending to close the distance between our lips. But before he can claim the kiss, I dart my tongue out, tasting his bottom lip then drawing it into my mouth with a gentle bite. The pressure isn't enough to harm, but it's sufficient to elicit a deep growl from him. His lips meet mine in earnest, his kiss nothing short of ravenous. His tongue sweeps in, strong and assertive, as if laying claim to every corner of my mouth. The sensation is dizzying, like experiencing a true kiss for the first time, drawing soft, involuntary moans from deep within me. I can sense his arousal, hard and insistent against me even through the layers of his clothes. Instinctively,

I arch my hips up, seeking friction against that enticing pressure.

He breaks the kiss, uttering, "Fuck," as he looks down, taking in our intimate contact. Encouraged, I grind against him again, feeling his grip on my wrists tighten in response.

"Don't forget what I said before. The first time I take you," he murmurs, his voice low and thick with desire, "it won't be in your father's palace, where you'd have to stifle your screams." His words make me writhe beneath him, the anticipation almost unbearable. I marvel at his restraint— every fiber of my being yearns for him, and I know he feels the same overpowering urgency.

"Colton, please," I plead, my voice laced with desperation and need.

"Shh," he whispers against my ear, his breath sending shivers down my spine. "You'll never have to beg, my little shadowmancer. I'll always give you exactly what you need." He kisses me tenderly, lips moving delicately against mine. His touch grows bolder as his hand trails down, fingers teasing over my sensitive skin, making my breath catch in my throat when his thumb presses against my clit.

A moan escapes me as he deepens his exploration, pressing a finger inside me and then another, each movement deliberate and intoxicating. "Look at me, Lyra," he demands, voice filled with authority. I meet his eyes, trapped in the glowing intensity of them. The connection is unbreakable, even as pleasure builds, threatening to overtake me. He thrusts his fingers in and out, curling inside me all while his thumb circles my clit, each touch designed to draw out sounds of pure ecstasy. As my climax approaches, his thumb finds the exact spot to send me spiraling. I bite down on my bottom lip, fighting to contain the scream threatening to escape.

He kisses me, a comforting kiss amidst the overwhelming

sensations, keeping me grounded until my body relaxes and the tremors subside. As he withdraws his touch, a feeling of emptiness emerges, my body already missing his presence. I rid myself of my slip, not wanting the barrier of fabric between us, craving the warmth of his skin. He rolls on his side and pulls me close to him, my head pressed to his chest, his heartbeat a soothing lullaby, pulling us both into sleep.

CHAPTER 15
COLTON

She's a vision when she sleeps, vulnerable and unguarded. I've been up for a while now, watching her, relishing in the tranquility that eludes her when she's awake. Last night was...intense, and the girl needs her rest. These relentless training sessions are grueling, not just for her but for me too. Every bruise, every mark on her feels like a punch to my gut. Euric and Athalda, those scheming bastards, treat her like some tool. Their intentions might be to strengthen her, but I don't trust them for a godsdamn second.

Zomea's in trouble, and what Drew has told me about Eguina, the lurking shadows in Cloudrum, it's clear danger is creeping closer to Nighthold. It's a damn good thing Lyra wants to see the Dream Forest. I don't like the idea of leaving her, but I don't like being away from home for this long. Bim and Dorian should have things under control there, unless Nyx pulls some of his usual stunts.

Speaking of Nyx, the mere thought of that prick sets my blood boiling. The idea of his hands on her... He had his chance and squandered it. She won't be his pawn again. I don't care what the prophecy says. His light won't be saving her. They cannot be destined to be together.

I think she is finally starting to heal from the pain he caused her. Lately, her sleep's been a bit calmer. I wonder if she even knows how fitful she is in sleep. Our tether lets me feel her inner turbulence now more than ever. There's a depth of pain she doesn't show the world, but I sense it. She's healing, bit by bit. For all the disdain I hold for Euric and Athalda, I have to admit that they've forced her to grow, to hone her strength.

It's hard to believe it's been only twelve weeks, but the change in her is undeniable...my shadow. I've noticed her reactions to my pet names for her—shadowmancer, dark enchantress, I think they're growing on her. But there's something simple and intimate about my shadow. I can't wait to witness the full force of her power once she learns to master those shadows she's destined to control.

I don't know what Nyx's plans for her were, but I'd bet he was scheming a way to harness her dark magic. That fucker is as power-hungry as the rest of them. He probably wants to wed her so he can be the king of all of Eguina, not just Nighthold. I don't necessarily think he's a bad king, but I don't trust him, especially not around her.

Lyra stretches and then nestles against my chest again. Gods, the sensation of her skin against mine... She's so incredibly smooth and beautiful. It's baffling how I got this lucky. I could've taken her that first night when she boldly climbed atop me, but the timing felt off. We had been drinking, and she was in pain. I didn't want any potential regrets on her end.

When Euric informed me about the tether a few days back, I wanted to share it with her, but it felt essential she came to her own conclusion, untainted by my influence. I hoped she'd be in favor, but I was mentally prepared for any choice she made. But last night, fuck... The overwhelming emotions she radiated as I caressed her, I'm surprised I held my composure and didn't embarrass myself like some inexperienced schoolboy.

I gently slide my hand over the back of her head, savoring the feel of her silky hair weaving between my fingers. Twirling a wavy strand, I then allow it to fall back into its place. It will be interesting to witness Nyx's reaction when he learns about our tether.

My shadow is awake. She is very bad at keeping that shield up, and the happy, content emotions she's radiating right now are making my dick hard. She sighs and stretches her body, pressing against mine like she craves the connection between us as much as I do. She tips her head back, and those eyes... Starring into her eyes is like plunging into the depths of a tempestuous sea, where the clear blue of the shallows meets the mysterious green of the abyss, beautiful and turbulent.

"Are you watching me sleep again like a creeper," she murmurs, peeking at me through lowered lashes.

I chuckle, "I think you like when I'm being a creep."

"Maybe." Her lips quirk up on one side, and she pushes off me, sitting up to look for Chepi. He's already jumping into her arms, pressing against her chest while she kisses his neck and murmurs sweet good mornings to him, lucky bastard.

"When do you want to leave for the tunnels?" she asks while rubbing Chepi's belly as he rolls around on the bed. Little Glyphie gets all the good attention.

"Whenever you're ready. I imagine you'll want to say your goodbyes to Euric and Anika before we go."

"Yes, and Athalda," she says. That cranky old woman doesn't deserve anything from her. Lyra goes into the bathing chamber, and I can't help but stare after her gloriously naked body. Man, practicing restraint every night in bed with her has been a true testament of my strength. I hear her get into the bath and decide she's going to be a while, so I pull on my pants, give Chepi a pet, and head to the kitchen for some coffee. Everything in the godsforsaken place tastes weird. The coffee and whiskey are the only tolerable things. I can't wait to be back home, can't wait to show Lyra the Dream Forest. For someone who's never been before, I know she's going to love it and all the creatures there. They'll love her too.

"You haven't even left yet and you're already slacking, letting her have a late start," Euric says, coming into the kitchen behind me.

"Give her a break. She's been killing herself for you for weeks." He's lucky Lyra loves him, because if she didn't I would really enjoy beating the shit out of him one of these days for what he put her through.

"It's for her own good. Now you're tethered to her like you wanted, so you better make sure she makes it back here in one piece. Don't waste any time. Once her dark magic awakens, you must come." He tries to stand in front of me, but I'm in no mood for him right now. I push past him and search for a mug.

"I'll make sure Lyra survives her dark magic for her, not for you, and we will return when she's ready," I say simply while pouring a cup of the dark liquid into my mug. I love pissing Euric off, him and Athalda both. It's too easy.

"If you don't, I'll tell her your little secret, and we both know where you'll end up then. We saw what happened when Nyx was caught in too many lies," Athalda says from behind me.

"This is different, and you know it. Nyx lied about everything, and I've only told Lyra the truth. I will tell her when the time comes," I say, not looking at the sneaky bitch.

"I'd love to see the look on Elspeth's face when that secret comes out. Your poor mother is going to be so disappointed in you," Euric says, and I grab a couple of weird pieces of fruit for Lyra and head for the door.

"She'll be down soon to say her goodbyes," I mutter on my way out. I can only imagine the scheming the two of them have been doing all these years in Zomea. Now with this fucking bridge unlocked— at least they both seem to think they need to stay here until we return with Lyra's dark magic activated. After that, I'm hoping Lyra will be strong enough to close the bridge somehow. I know it can be done, and the last thing I want is Euric coming back to rule over Cloudrum. I'll play nice for now, for Lyra's sake, but if there's one thing Nyx did right it was killing Euric. Lyra may trust him, but I think she's too damaged to face the truth. She doesn't want to see that her father might not be a good man. I believe he wants to save Zomea, and that's the only reason I'm playing along right now, but I know his reasons are purely selfish.

My shadow has been through enough, all these treacherous men. Thinking about Samael or Aidan gets my blood boiling. In my free time, I've been searching Zomea for either one of them, and still I come up dry. It's so much land to cover, and not being about to channel here is screwing me. Anika said she'll keep an ear out for me as well. If they are in Zomea, I want my time with them. The things I will do to them, slowly... I have no problem admitting I'm a sick fuck when it comes to torturing pricks who prey on the innocent. I will especially enjoy the pain I unleash on them.

I push the door open to our room, and Lyra's perched on the edge of the bed, running her hands through her wet, wavy hair. I want to tangle my hands in that hair and take her on the bed right now. Instead, I settle for tossing her a piece of fruit and heading to the bathing chamber. I need cold water this morning.

"Thank you," she says from behind me as I close the door. I

start to fill the tub with water and hear her leave the bedroom, probably going to spend time with her father before we leave. I relax in the cold water, and it instantly eases my muscles but does nothing to erase my erection.

Last night keeps playing over in my head. I stroke my cock and think about how it felt pressing my fingers inside her. Those perfect pouty lips and the way her teeth tugged on my bottom lip. Fuck, if there was ever a perfect woman, it's her. Her breasts and the way her nipples tightened beneath my touch, every little breathy moan I coaxed out of her with my touch. She was so wet for me and so tight—fuck. I stroke myself until I find my release. Maybe now I can get through the day without thinking about being inside her...not likely.

I get cleaned up and dressed, ready to leave this place finally. I look over the room one last time, not like I can forget anything since I didn't bring anything with me. I think I will miss this bed though. I've grown quite fond of the bed we've shared together first by force and now by choice.

I find Euric and Lyra in front of the fireplace talking, but as soon as they see me the conversation dies off. Lyra gets to her feet. "Ready to go?" I nod, moving closer to her.

"I'll channel you as close as I can get to the bridge without getting sucked into it," Euric says, placing a hand on my shoulder. Lyra wraps Chepi in her arms, I wrap my free arm around her waist as the icy chill of Euric's wind sweeps up, and darkness consumes us.

We land in the tunnels. I don't take my hand off of Lyra in the dark, not wanting to risk anything happening to her. Euric pulls her into a quick hug, and his eyes harden on me over her shoulder. I nod at him, and he vanishes. The dank smell in these tunnels is far worse than the smell in the Lamias' hive, and even that takes some getting used to.

"What do we have to do?" she asks, clutching Chepi and taking the hand I extend to her.

"I imagine we walk closer to where we first fell and something will happen." I don't feel any fear coming from her, maybe anxiety.

"What's wrong?" I ask as we start walking in the direction of the bridge.

"You can't hear it?" she says, and I'm immediately on guard.

"Hear what?" I ask, slowing my steps.

"Nothing," she shakes her head, brushing me off. I want to demand she tells me what she's hearing, but then the ground starts to tremble beneath our feet. She has a frightened look in her eye for a moment, but I pull her and Chepi close to me, wrapping my arms around them. Then the weightless feeling takes over, and I can feel the wind pushing past us. It's the opposite feeling of falling. It feels like we are pushing through a barrier, and then my back hits the grass and the sun blinds me.

"Always one to gain the upper hand, aren't you, enchantress?" I taunt, narrowing my eyes playfully. She smiles down at me then. I'm hurling her and Chepi aside moments before an explosion of fire roars where we were. I jump to my feet, pulling her with me as I take in the scene around us. The Lamia realm is under brutal assault. Demons, mortals, and Lamia engage in a frenzied battle of death and bloodshed.

"Stick to me," I urge her, my voice a low growl. But the glint in her eyes speaks of defiance and a readiness to unleash her fury. Splitting my essence, I summon two duplicates of myself, dispatching them to find Drew. With Lyra at my side, we weave toward the castle, desperation mounting as I struggle to make sense of the carnage that has befallen the land during our time in Zomea.

A guttural snarl makes me freeze. I see Adira fighting a

Spider Wraith to our left, her blade glinting in the firelight as she battles the ghost-like creature. I've never heard of a Spider Wraith in the Lamia Realm before. In fact, they are rarely able to cross the boundary around the Shifting Forest. The forest around us is aflame, grotesque Monstrauths rampant, slaughtering hapless humans who don't stand a chance against them— I hate those fucking rotting skeletons with horns.

A desperate shout wrenches my attention. "Soren!" Lyra's voice is filled with anguish, and I can feel her panic. Without a second thought, she dashes into the heart of the forest, and I curse as I chase after her. I watch as flames erupt from her, incinerating a pair of looming demons. Soren, his sword gleaming, tosses her a blade. She infuses it with her fire magic, turning it into a deadly weapon. As she cleaves through enemies, her fierceness is undeniably alluring. Fuck, she has become quite the vicious fighter, and it is hot. They seem to have things under control for the moment, so I close my eyes and look through the manifestations I sent out.

Neither of them have found Drew yet.

Forcing my focus back, I dive into the fray. Conjuring roots from the earth, they constrict and immobilize the fiends, allowing me to decapitate them with ruthless efficiency. Lyra follows suit, ensuring no remnant of the beasts remains, setting the corpses ablaze.

Catching a brief lull, I turn to Soren. "What in the gods' names is happening?"

He's panting, eyes wild. "It's the bridge. It's drawing them here. It's happened twice now while you've been away. Hordes emerging from the shadows, laying waste to everything they get their hands on."

Lyra's voice quivers with disbelief, "What are these creatures with wings?" She slams her blade down the throat of one of the Sarrols, its fanged face contorting before catching fire.

Damn, I can't remember the last time I saw a Sarrol in Eguina; the demons are unmistakable with their humanoid form and pointed, membranous wings. And I'd forgotten how ugly they are, too—with their elongated, goblin-like snouts and black, frothing mouths full of needle-sharp teeth.

Soren, his sword slick with ichor, responds, "Blood-sucking fiends, believed to have been purged from the realms. Now they emerge from the bridge. We have to have several people on guard at all times to kill them when they climb out of the ground." That's unusual. All the time spent in Zomea, we never saw such creatures. Where the fuck are the Sarrols coming from?

Above, Chepi swoops and dives, his agile form distracting the creatures long enough for either Lyra or me to deliver the killing blow. The haunting shrieks of dying demons and the cacophony of battle echo around us.

One of my duplicates found Drew. I focus my attention through him.

"About time you came back after that stunt you pulled," Drew says. She's near Blood Lake, blocking the entrance to the human village.

"I couldn't let her go alone. Besides, we both know we can't trust Euric," I tell her.

"Get her out of here. We have it under control, and I'll come to you when I can. We'll talk then."

"I'm taking her home with me. You know where to find us."

Drew nods, and I let my manifestations disappear. I'm back next to Soren and can feel Lyra's exhaustion as if it's my own. "Lyra, no," I yell, but I'm too late as I watch her thrust her palms forward, and from it a gust of wind picks up debris, hurling it at the enemies.

She's going to be too weak to help channel us out of here, and I'm useless alone until we make it closer to Nighthold. I run to her, and then with a swift motion she draws moisture from the air, freezing it into razor-sharp icicles that she launches with precision at the group of Monstrauths before us. It doesn't kill them, but it slows them down and drops several to the ground. I grab her by the arm right before she drops to her knees...fuck.

"You're not strong enough for this yet. You're using too much magic, and it's weakening you." I pick her up, tossing her over my shoulder and nodding to Soren before taking off toward the shoreline.

"Let me down. We can't leave them." She kicks in my arms to get free, but she's no match for me. We make it to the edge of the cliffs, and it's a steep descent to the dock, but I know I can channel us there.

I put her down and grab her by the shoulders, forcing her to look at me. "They have it handled. We need to get you out of here. You're too weak to channel us back to the Faery realm, and I can't channel that kind of distance without your help. So until we get all our strength back or make it closer to Nighthold, we have no choice but to get in a boat. Do you understand?"

The anger she radiates is palpable, but she lifts her chin and takes my hand.

Chepi flies into her chest, and I let my essence encircle us with the wind until we channel to the boats down below.

"Untie that side." I point to the other side of the boat where the rope is tied up, and Lyra gets to work on it while I unravel my side. Once detached from the dock, we push off, and I start to row us in the direction of Nighthold, but several Sarrols swoop toward the boat, their grotesque appearance instantly identifiable by their black, frothing mouths and spiky, deformed wings.

"Keep paddling! I've got this," Lyra shouts, determination

clear in her voice. But there's no chance I'm going to leave her to fend for herself.

One of the beasts lunges into the boat, making for Lyra. To my surprise, it doesn't seem intent on hurting her. Instead, it appears to be trying to capture her. What the fuck? Another Sarrol swoops from above, talons outstretched, aiming for her. Reacting instinctively, my wings unfurl, and I soar upward, colliding with the creature midair. I snap its neck before it can whisk Lyra away.

Meanwhile, Lyra battles the Sarrol in the boat, breaking its wing with a swift, powerful motion and sending it tumbling into the water. I dive down, plunging into the depths to ensure it doesn't come back up.

Emerging, I can't help but wonder how these Sarrols are crossing the bridge and for what purpose. I need to consult Drew about this anomaly. A part of me is tempted to return to Zomea and confront Euric about the true nature of these events. But, for now, the priority is to get Lyra out of this danger and bring her safely home.

The Feral Sea is angry, and the choppy white caps keep flooding the boat with water. We need to get far enough out to sea for things to calm down. The shores around the Lamia realm are always rocky with swift currents. I look across the boat to Lyra, and she's shivering, drenched in seawater, probably still in shock from what we were just thrown into.

"Are you alright?" I ask, feeling bad for scolding her earlier, but she wasn't listening, and we needed to get out of there. She nods, her lips pressed together. I release an oar and wave a hand at her, sending my magic to dry her clothes.

"I need to learn how to do that," she says, perking up a bit now that she's not wasting energy shivering to death. I row on in silence for the next hour until the Lamia realm disappears behind a fog bank and we are surrounded by the sea. The water is calm now, and I get a good rowing pace going.

"I didn't know you could channel outside the Faery realm," she says, drawing my attention back to her.

"Is that another lie Nyx told you?" I ask, immediately regretting bringing him up. I don't like the punch-in-the-gut feeling his name has on her. She's not shielding anything right now.

"We can only channel places we've been before or can picture in our mind, and if Nyx wasn't channeling it's because he didn't want anyone to be able to track him. Magic always leaves a trace," I tell her, wanting to be honest with her.

"I do recall Nyx saying we couldn't channel because he didn't want Samael to trace his magic, but with all the confusion along the way I guess I forgot he could channel in the other realms because I never saw him do it." She looks down at her hands in her lap, and I fight the urge to go to her, to wrap her in my arms.

"I can channel us far, but we are very far from Nighthold right now. I need you to help me. We can put our magic together and channel further," I tell her.

"How long until we can try? Sometimes when I exhaust my magic like this it takes hours before I feel strong again." She runs her hands through her hair, tucking it behind her ears.

"Don't get frustrated. It's fine. I don't need to paddle us anymore. We can just float with the current and relax until you're ready. There's no rush." I climb over the bench and grab several cushions to make a comfortable spot for us in the center of the boat. Once I settle down on the cushions with my back pressed against the side of the boat, I motion for her to come lie between my legs. She drapes her body across me and rests her head back against me. Chepi stays perked up next to the oars like he's keeping watch.

"Do you think they'll be okay?" she asks, and I know she's talking about everyone in the Lamia realm.

"Yes. They are more than capable of taking care of themselves and protecting their land." I try to ease her worry, but I do believe Drew will be fine.

"Do you think what Soren said is true, they are attracted to the bridge?" she asks.

"I don't know. They must be able to sense it somehow." I run my hands through her hair, massaging her scalp until she relaxes enough to fall asleep. We always recharge quicker in sleep, and a nap should do the trick so we can get off this fucking boat before one of us gets seasick.

"Sound the alarm if you see anything, boy," I say to Chepi, and he gives me a quiet yip. I trust the little creature, and he has an undeniable love for Lyra, so I try to rest my eyes.

CHAPTER 16
LYRA

My eyes flutter open, the once-blinding sun now hidden behind ominous clouds. Chepi barks urgently, nudging my shoulder with a paw. I rise, taking in the thick fog encircling us. "Colton..." I say, my voice a whisper of concern. Taking a seat on one of the benches, I grip the sides as the boat rocks, the increasing swells reminding me of the unpredictable nature of the open sea.

"Damn it," he mutters, rising to scan the horizon.

"Chepi woke me, and by the looks of it the weather's deteriorating fast," I inform him.

"Storms can creep up quickly in these waters. Can you swim?" he teases, trying to lighten the mood.

"That's not funny," I retort, swiping at him. My balance wavers as the boat tips with another large swell. He positions himself between the oars, beginning to row with purpose. However, our little boat, designed for calm harbor fishing, feels pitifully inadequate against the might of the encroaching storm.

"It's just one thing after another, isn't it?" I murmur more to myself than anyone else. Strength still courses through me; I

176

don't feel the exhaustion I expected. Maybe I can attempt to channel us out of here. I glance at Colton, hoping his plan isn't too intricate. Sharing magic is unfamiliar territory for me – I hadn't even realized it was feasible until now.

The air grows cold. I'm about to ask him to explain how we can channel combining our magic, then the first drop of rain catches my attention as it splatters against my cheek. Soon, it's no longer a drop or two but a deluge with water pouring from above, drenching us within moments. The waves grow taller, more ferocious, rocking our small boat back and forth as if it were a mere toy. The menacing roll of thunder overhead makes Chepi growl, the fur on his back standing straight up.

"We're not safe here," I shout over the sound of the storm, my voice barely audible even to myself. The sea has become a wild creature, angry and unrestrained. Each swell threatens to toss us overboard, and the wind howls, whipping my hair around my face, blinding me.

Colton's eyes meet mine, filled with determination yet also a hint of worry.

"Hold on, Lyra!" He suddenly stands, tearing off his tunic, unfurling a pair of massive, wyvern-like wings from his back. I've never seen his wings before today. They remind me of Nyx, and I push the thought aside. Black as the night, they glint with a subtle iridescence, making them shimmer even in the dim light. His drenched dirty-blond hair clings to his skin, and when he shakes his head, the locks break free from his face. I'm momentarily in a daze watching him, the storm forgotten.

As the boat teeters on the edge of a particularly massive wave, Colton acts. With a swift movement, he wraps an arm around me and snatches Chepi with the other. Then, with a powerful beat of his wings, we're airborne, leaving the tiny boat to the mercy of the tempestuous sea below.

The rain pelts us from every direction, but Colton's wings

shield us somewhat, and his grip is ironclad. We soar through the storm, lightning illuminating the skies around us, revealing the dark clouds rolling and crashing like the waves below. The sensation is both terrifying and exhilarating. I cling to him, Chepi tucked safely between us, his small body trembling.

"Do you think you can channel us if I funnel some of my magic into you?" he asks, and I tip my head up to study his face, but he's focused ahead.

"I've never channeled anyone else before, especially from the sky in a storm while using someone else's magic to help," I yell over the thunder echoing around us.

"You've got this. I'm holding you and Chepi, so imagine somewhere in Nighthold and try to channel there. My magic will give you a boost, and we'll automatically channel with you." I think he has way too much faith in my abilities, but I nod and close my eyes.

The feeling of his magic is warm and perfect. The moment it settles in my chest, I feel whole and powerful. I can't believe we have never shared magic before. This feeling is—

"Now, Lyra!" His voice is urgent, sending a surge of panic through me as the lightning flashes around us again. I try to think of somewhere in Nighthold, and all the places coming to mind are bad places... The star-gazing tub flashes in my memory, and I think of the snow in the Fate Fields. "Hurry." He grunts, and this must be taxing on him, fuck. I shake my head and feel the warm wind start to twirl around us. I open my eyes as darkness, my darkness, takes us.

THE SCENT of cedar infused with subtle mango undertones greets me before my feet even touch the ground. I exhale deeply as Colton releases his hold on me. Surveying our surroundings, a familiar tug of emotion hits me, prompting a quick mental check of my shields. It's crucial that I don't project any feelings right now.

"Of all places, you thought of this one?" Colton says, waving his hand to dry us instantly. He walks over, drawing back the translucent black curtains to look outside.

"In my panic, I defaulted to what I knew. I spent a lot of time here in Nighthold, so here we are." I can't gauge his emotions—he's become increasingly adept at keeping me out—but the tension in his jaw suggests he's not thrilled. My gaze falls on the bed, its black silk sheets still a jumbled mess. Someone's been sleeping here. Or perhaps Nyx simply hasn't bothered to tidy up. The room remains unchanged, and I suppress a swallow, pushing back the residual sadness it evokes.

"We should leave before we're discovered. Or would you prefer to stay?" His question catches me off guard. Part of me believes he might actually leave me here, that he would allow me to go back to Nyx if I wanted. But would Nyx even want me after everything with Colton? Such thoughts are pointless. I chose this place because it was familiar and safe, not out of longing for him.

"I want to leave. Please," I reply, stepping closer and enveloping myself in his embrace, Chepi nestled between us.

"Well then, my shadow, let me take you to the Dream Forest." Colton's comforting citrus aroma temporarily drowns out the cedar, until a gust of wind playfully tousles my hair and we prepare to channel.

The moment we appear, it feels as though we have entered another dimension altogether. I blink several times, letting my eyes adjust to the mesmerizing hues surrounding us. Trees stand tall and lush all around. Their bark shimmers in shades of purples and greens.

The air is thick with an intoxicating aroma, a blend of

sweet nectar, and an undercurrent of something else, possibly mint. A soft crackle of electricity travels on the wind rustling through the tree branches overhead, and they respond by sending out little sparks, like fireflies that dance about before settling back onto the branches.

"What is this?" I whisper in awe of my surroundings.

"The Dream Forest might not be as vast as some other parts of Nighthold, but its magic is unrivaled," Colton says, taking my hand in his. Chepi jumps out of my arms and starts flying off ahead of us.

"Be careful," I yell, but after all this is his home too. I wonder if he remembers it.

He leads me down a path paved with large stones that seem to illuminate our way.

"This is where I come to think," he says, gesturing toward a glen where the water flows upward, defying gravity, from a pool into the air where it splits into shimmering droplets that playfully return to the ground. I have an urge to run my hand through the shower of droplets, but I refrain.

I'm so taken aback by the beauty that I almost miss the villa itself. This is merely his backyard. His home looks as though it's almost grown organically from the forest floor. Enveloped in windows, nature seamlessly blends with the interior. He pulls me along through the ground floor of the villa, and I have no words.

The soft gurgling sound of water draws my attention as we step into a grand room filled with incredibly comfortable-looking furniture organized around a flagstone fireplace. I gasp as a pristine pond comes into view, winding through the villa's ground floor.

"Watch your step," Colton chuckles as I nearly trip, mesmerized by the radiant fish that swim beneath the glassy surface, a myriad of colors. He gestures to the staircases spiraling up toward the villa's heart, a colossal dome made entirely of glass.

"This is my favorite part," he admits, and I can see why. The dome brings the outside world in, showcasing towering cliffs and cascading waterfalls that seem within reach. I can't wait to lounge on the settee and stare up at the stars in here at night.

We continue down countless hallways, through the kitchen, guest quarters, and study. Vines covered with luminescent blossoms drape a few of the walls, turning them into vertical tapestries of life. Chepi suddenly comes running down the hall and then back toward the pond, already getting the lay of the land.

"I'll show you to your bed chamber where you can get cleaned up," he says, and I follow him up the stairs, glancing out the windows still in shock at how incredibly beautiful this place is. Once upstairs, we pass a couple of doors, then he leads me into the room I'll be staying in, and it doesn't disappoint.

Behind the bed rises a towering flagstone partition, punctuated by a grand arch carved directly into its surface. At its heart, sleek black marble weeps with a gentle cascade of water. Underfoot, planks of richly-hued timber span the expanse, and floor-to-ceiling windows stretch two stories high, offering an unobstructed view of nature. A slender, ebony staircase spirals upward, leading to an overlook balcony bathed in the room's upper half, granting incredible views of the Dream Forest.

Colton pushes one of the windows open, and I realize I'm in a daze again taking it all in. "Do you have anything I can change into?" I ask, looking down at my leather clothes from Zomea that have seen too much for one day already.

"I can have clothes brought here for you tomorrow. For tonight, will some of my clothes do?" he asks, and I nod, giving him a soft smile. "Okay I'll leave them on the bed for you. The bathing chamber is just through there."

He points to a door beyond the staircase, and I waste no time heading to it, wanting to get clean. Of course, the bathroom is as amazing as the rest of the home. I strip off my clothes and notice the green tiles underfoot are warm to the touch. I fill the bath, the gigantic bath that three people could easily fit in, and make use of the soap. I lather my hair and body and breathe in the relaxing scent of lavender that will always remind me of Tempest Moon.

I finish up in the bathroom and go back into the bedroom to find a white tunic and brown pants neatly folded on the light-gray sheets. I slip the tunic on over my head and pass on the pants altogether. No one else is here that I've seen, and the tunic falls basically to my knees. I venture back to the large staircase and see Colton relaxing on one of the large couches, his clothes fresh and hair damp from getting cleaned up as well.

"On second thought, maybe I won't have any clothes brought for you," he says, his eyes slowly trailing down my body. A fire is already roaring to life, and I glance over to see Chepi already passed out on his side in front of the fire. He is always a sucker for heat.

"Come, sit with me."

I plop onto the cushion, sinking into the soft fabric.

"I could get used to this." I muse, lying my head back to rest on the cushion behind me. This may be the most comfortable I've been ever. In this beautiful house, in a place I've always dreamed of seeing with someone who feels like home. My heart feels warm and happy, content for the first time in a long time. Colton smiles next to me, and I realize I must be projecting. I roll my eyes and let my head fall back again, smirking. Keeping a constant shield up is exhausting, and I've earned this time to relax. I don't miss Zomea at all right now, or anything else.

"I could get used to this too." He tugs on me until my head falls into his lap, and I stretch my legs out across the cushions, staring up through the glass dome at the twilight sky.

"The stars will be visible soon." I say mostly to myself, because I'm sure he's looked through these windows at the stars for centuries.

"Yes, Brysta better not disappoint for your first night." He strokes my head through my hair, and the massage could put me to sleep.

"Brysta?"

"The goddess of the cosmos. Did you not study the gods?" he says but continues to play with my hair.

"I did but don't recall all their names. As a Sorceress, we are mostly taught about Ryella, the goddess of shadows, and Helrix, the god of luminescence. We learn about the other gods too, but nothing in depth. I don't remember them all," I tell him, reaching out and taking his free hand. I place it on my stomach and trace my fingers up and down his hand and arm.

"Why do you never have your wings out?" I ask, evoking a laugh from him.

"That is an incredibly random question."

"Today was the first time I've ever seen your wings, and at the dinner party your parents had I remember seeing many Fae with their wings out the entire time." I tip my head back in his lap more so I can look up at him better.

"Well, first of all, those Fae at the party with their wings out all have what we call aetherials. Their wings are smaller and more translucent. I have Wyvern wings, and as you saw today they are much more cumbersome. I only materialize them when I need them, similar to what Chepi does." It makes sense, since his wings are rather large. I understand how they would get in the way.

"What makes someone have aetherial wings rather than

wyvern wings?" I ask.

"That's like asking why someone has red hair instead of blonde. It's what's passed down through our families."

"Does anyone stay here with you? Any servants or friends? Or do you live here all alone?" I continue playing with his fingers and trailing the muscles on his arm. It feels good to touch him like this, freely now that we have both professed feelings for one another.

"Yes, I have friends who visit and stay from time to time, as well as a cook and creatures that help me. No one is here now because I've been away for so long, but you'll meet everyone soon enough." That excites me. I look forward to meeting his friends and seeing what creatures help out around here. I want to meet all the creatures that live in the Dream Forest.

"Do you think I'll get to meet any Pixies?" I ask, rousing another chuckle out of him.

"It can be arranged." He laughs again, and then silence stretches on between us as we stare up at the stars together and listen to the hiss and crackle of the fire.

"Before all this chaos began, what did a normal day look like for you?" His question catches me off guard, and I have to think about it for a minute before I answer him.

"My lady's maid, Lili, would come in like clockwork before sunrise every morning to wake me. I'd then open my window and let Chepi out to stretch while I bathed. Once done, Lili would return to style my hair and help me dress. Typically, I'd grab a quick bite in my room before heading to my lessons with my tutor. After spending the majority of the day studying, I'd either relax on my balcony watching the birds in the forest or take a stroll in the garden. Dinner was usually served in my room, and then I'd retire for the night." I pause, taking a breath. "That might have been a tad more detailed than necessary, but that's a snapshot of my daily routine."

"Would you ever get bored?" he asks, and I crack a grin.

"Of course, I would get bored, but I wasn't allowed to go anywhere, and honestly so long as no one bothered me I considered it a good day." I think back about Samael, Silas, and my mother. It feels like so long ago we all lived together. It's hard to believe they're all gone now.

"Do you miss home?" He twirls a curly piece of hair around his finger.

"It hasn't felt like home in a very long time," I murmur, not wanting to think about it.

"What's a secret you've never told anyone?" he asks, probably sensing I wanted to change the subject. I look away, trying to think of something worth telling him something no one else knows. "When I was a child, I once found a wounded bird in the garden. Instead of telling anyone, I secretly nursed it back to health in a hidden nook of the castle. I was terrified Samael would find it and kill it, so I would use Chepi's invisibility to sneak out at night and care for it. When it was strong enough, I released it, and every evening after when I'd sit on my balcony, I'd swear I could hear its unique song amongst the others. It was our secret serenade."

I haven't thought about that bird in a very long time. It's one of the good memories from Tempest Moon.

Colton raises an eyebrow, looking down at me. "A secret bird healer within the castle walls? You never cease to surprise me." He pauses, his gaze growing cold and distant. "Samael should have been dealt with long ago. I had no idea how bad it was... I don't know how the council is ruling in your absence, but I do know it's surely better than having him on the throne."

"Can you somehow find out what's happening both in Tempest Moon and in the Lycan Realm? Especially with Larc now leading the Lycans?" I ask, the uncertainty evident in my voice. I believe Larc will be a good leader, but I worry for Rhett with all the recent attacks.

He nods thoughtfully. "I'll gather more information tomorrow. I'm having a few friends stop by who might know. I'll inform all the staff we are here as well so they can return." As he speaks, he brushes a strand of hair from his face, but I watch as it stubbornly falls back against his cheek.

"Hungry? The house might not be stocked up, but I'll scrounge up something for us."

As I sit up, my stomach growls, answering for me. "Yes, I could definitely eat."

Sometime later, we find ourselves in the kitchen where Colton starts making a quiche. To my surprise, he's quite skilled at cooking, and not just anything — he's preparing one of my favorites! Quiche holds a special place in my heart, rivaled only by a tomato and cheese tart. His version has cheese and spinach, and its rich aroma quickly fills the room. As the quiche bakes, we engage in light conversation, a welcome distraction from the pressures of Zomea and our intense training. It's a refreshing change, and the weight of our usual concerns feels momentarily lifted. I know we both should probably talk about the attack that was happening in the Lamia realm, but I think we've earned a night of peace.

"Would you like some wine?" Colton asks, serving the hot quiche onto the dining table.

"I would love some," I respond, recalling the sweet wine I once enjoyed in the Faery realm. He fetches a bottle and fills our glasses with its deep burgundy contents. The wine is bold, fruity, and carries a subtle hint of spice. "Thank you." I take a sip.

"This is one of my favorites," he says, but I can think of something better to talk about than the wine.

"Have you ever been in love?" My question momentarily

flummoxes him, evident as he nearly chokes on his wine.

Regaining his composure, he meets my gaze. "Once...a very long time ago," he admits.

His revelation tugs at something inside me, an unexpected flare of emotion I struggle to label. Jealousy? It seems ridiculous, especially considering his lengthy existence. I chastise myself for this irrational reaction. I'm being overly hypocritical right now.

"I suppose I don't need to ask you the same, considering I already know the answer," he murmurs, drawing me out of my inner turmoil.

I contemplate his statement, my emotions swirling. Did I love Nyx? I think I did, but I'm beginning to wonder if I even know what love feels like. With all the chaos and transformations of the past year, I feel like a stranger to myself. The naive girl confined within Tempest Moon's castle walls feels like a distant memory. Can that heart, which feels so shielded and hardened now, still hold love?

He interrupts my introspection, his voice soft. "What's on your mind?"

I quickly ensure my mental shields are up, hoping I'm not projecting too much, and they are. His question must be born out of curiosity. Taking a deep breath, I confide, "I'm not sure if I ever truly loved Nyx. And now I'm questioning if I'm even capable of love." My confession is followed by another sip of wine, hoping the liquid might drown my mounting uncertainties.

"Everyone is capable of love, Lyra. If you're unsure about your feelings for Nyx, perhaps you've yet to experience true love. When you do, it's unmistakable. Given all you've endured, it's only natural for your heart to be more protective now. The right man will understand that, and he'll be patient in earning his way in."

He offers this with a knowing look, and I'm tempted to ask about his own past love. Yet I hesitate, fearing the answer. Instead, I playfully challenge, "So, you believe you're that right man?"

His eyes glow a vibrant green. "Only time will tell, my shadow," he quips with a wink. I can't help but laugh at what's becoming his favorite pet name for me.

As Colton begins clearing our plates, a long yawn stretches from my lips. "Let's get to bed. Today has been exhausting," he suggests, his voice gentle. I nod, fatigue evident in my every movement, and together we leave the dining room.

"Should we wake Chepi?" he asks, nodding toward where he sleeps beside the fire.

"Let him be," I reply softly, my steps drawing me to the staircase. "He knows where to find me."

"Goodnight, Lyra," Colton mutters as he continues down the hallway.

I whisper, "Night," in return before slipping into my chamber. The bedding welcomes me, its luxurious softness contrasting with the unease growing inside. It's been months since I've slept alone, months since the last time the bed beside me was cold. Why doesn't Colton wish to join me tonight? Maybe he misses having his own space and I'm overthinking it?

I turn onto my side, staring out the expansive windows. The stars look so dreamy tonight decorating the inky night sky. I try to fall asleep, but my mind remains restless, thinking about last night with Colton. The progression of our relationship seemed clear. He said he didn't want to be just friends, he spoke of deeper feelings and hints of possessiveness, yet I'm alone in bed.

Was my admission — that I might be incapable of love — too much? Doubt grows. The bond I share with Colton is undeniable, an intensity beyond mere friendship. His presence fills the hollow spaces of my heart, spaces that have taken so long to mend.

I can't and won't replicate past mistakes. With Nyx, I lost myself. With Colton, I wish to stand my ground, to guard my heart while exploring the depths of what we might become. It's probably a good thing we have separate rooms now and take things slow.

But why do I feel as if a piece of me is absent without him here? Perhaps it's the new tether between us. I close my eyes, searching for our link. It's strange to feel such a tangible pull toward someone else. Since I can't sense any strong emotions from him right now, he's either still awake and shielding me or simply not feeling anything intense enough for me to detect.

Restlessness takes over. I throw back the covers and leave my bed. I need to understand why he chose not to sleep beside me, and instead of spending the entire night wondering I decide to find him and ask. He never showed me his room, but the floor above isn't extensive. Guided by the pull in my chest, I approach the door I'm certain he's behind. I pause, straining to hear any sounds, but there's only silence. I push the door open gently. The room is shrouded in darkness, and from what I can make out his bed hasn't been slept in. A muted glow illuminates the edges of another door, likely his bathing chamber, accompanied by the hushed sound of running water.

Peeking through a slight opening, I see he's in the shower. The steam fogs the glass, and the soft light from the candles flickers, disrupted by the humid air. I can't clearly see him, but I know he's in there. Showers are a luxury I've only experienced a few times in my life. Most people settle for bathtubs. However, after marrying my mother, Silas had one installed, and I sneaked in a few times when they were away on business.

The urge to join him is powerful. But even as I worry he might not want me there, I can't resist. I shed the tunic and inch open the misty glass door. A dense cloud of steam spills out, drawing Colton's immediate attention. His eyes lock onto me, a hungry intensity in them, and I involuntarily bite my lower lip as I appreciate the full view of him. Water cascades over his toned muscles, and my gaze travels downward, noting his undeniable arousal. His glowing eyes roam over me, exuding a desire that sends a warmth through my entire being.

I hesitate momentarily at the entrance to the expansive shower, which is almost like a room in itself. Yet, without uttering a word, Colton bridges the gap between us. He pulls me flush against him, one arm anchoring around my lower back while the other gathers my hair, tilting my head to face him. As he leans down, our eyes remain locked until the final moment, when his lips softly meet mine.

Yielding to the sensation, I push my tongue into his mouth, savoring his taste. My arms circle his neck, deepening our kiss. Water cascades around us, enveloping us in its warmth. Colton's grip on me intensifies, his hands firmly cradling my waist now, guiding me to a corner of the shower without ever letting our lips part. The backs of my legs make contact with a bench, and, breaking our kiss momentarily, he gently guides me to sit.

I can't help but watch intently as he kneels before me. He takes one of my breasts, letting his tongue tease over my nipple. His other hand journeys, tracing each curve and contour of my body, igniting a trail of goosebumps wherever he goes. Releasing my breast, he grabs my hips, pulling me to the edge. Leaning back, the warm tiles press against my spine, providing contrast to the streaming water. My legs part naturally, leaving me vulnerable, completely exposed to him. Any hint of self-consciousness dissipates.

The bond between us and the depth of his gaze make me feel safe.

He regards me through sultry, half-lidded eyes then slowly lowers his mouth. I can't suppress a sharp intake of breath when his tongue ventures into the most intimate part of me. I weave my fingers through his wet hair, involuntarily arching my hips off the bench as waves of pleasure surge within me. He stabilizes my movements, his hands strong and sure on my hips, anchoring me to the bench as he thoroughly explores every intimate crevice. Every stroke of his tongue, every subtle suck, draws moans and cries from deep within me. I can't hold back, nor do I want to.

He slides a finger inside me, and an involuntary sigh escapes my lips. My head tilts back, resting against the damp tiles, as I willingly yield to his touch. Another finger joins the first, stretching and filling me, their rhythmic thrusts synchronized perfectly with the teasing circling of his tongue on my most sensitive nub.

I can feel the crescendo of pleasure building, threatening to overwhelm me. His fingers delve deeper, while his tongue seems innately attuned to every quiver of my body. I'm on the precipice, teetering, and with one final concerted effort from him I'm falling over the edge. Sounds I didn't know I could make spill forth, my legs quaking from the sheer intensity of the release.

Even as the waves of my climax begin to recede, his fingers continue their thrusts inside me, prolonging the ecstasy. Once my shudders subside, he withdraws slowly. He raises his head to meet mine, and I catch the wicked glint in his eyes as he deliberately licks his lips, and a flare of heat courses through me.

He gracefully ascends to his full height, and impulsively I stand on the bench to level our eyes. We're nearly face to face, the heat from our bodies mingling with the warm mist from the shower. "Colton," I whisper, but he silences me, pressing a gentle finger against my trembling lips. For a charged moment, our gaze holds, the intensity palpable. But I can't resist the magnetic pull to let my eyes drift downward, taking in every sculpted plane and curve of his body. His impressive physique is matched only by his equally impressive cock.

Desire surges within me, I want to feel him, to be as close as possible.

Noting the hunger in my eyes, a smug grin forms on his lips. With a swift, confident movement, he wraps his arms around my waist, effortlessly lifting me from the tiles. Instinctively, my legs entwine around his torso, the solid length of him pressing tantalizingly against my stomach. The close proximity sends a thrilling rush through my veins, and I need more. I need him inside me.

My arms coil tightly around his neck as his lips blaze a trail of fervent kisses up the side of my neck. His hands, firm and deliberate, travel to cradle my ass, gradually lifting me. The very tip of him rests teasingly at my entrance, a promise of what's to come.

The warmth of his breath tickles my ear as he murmurs, "You're mine now, Lyra, and I intend to cherish what's mine." With that, he eases me onto him.

A sharp intake of breath escapes my lips, his size stretching me in a way that's both exquisite and overwhelming. My fingers dig into his shoulders, seeking some form of anchor against the intense sensation. Slowly, he fills me more, every inch of him I take inside causing me to tighten my grip. But once he's fully inside, a mixture of pleasure and adjustment courses through me. I exhale the breath I hadn't realized I'd been holding, my fingers relaxing their grasp.

His eyes search mine, a mix of concern and intensity.

"Are you well, my shadow?" he inquires softly, never looking away.

"Yes," I breathe out in response, barely audible.

He lifts me once more, leaving only the tip of him inside before lowering me onto him again. My breath hitches in my throat; he feels incredible. He repeats the motion, maintaining a slow pace to let my body adjust to his size. Drawing close to my ear, he murmurs, "Breathe." I heed his command, drawing in a shuddering breath.

I weave my fingers through his wet hair, guiding his mouth to mine. Our lips collide with an urgency, a fierceness that wasn't there before. Our tongues tangle, teeth occasionally clashing as our passion escalates. With each lift and descent, he quickens the pace. Then, shifting his stance, he presses me against the shower wall. The water spills over us, acting as a warm barrier on our intertwined bodies. Using the wall for leverage, he no longer lifts me but begins to thrust, driving deeper into me with each motion.

Overwhelmed by the sensation of him inside me, I can't hold back the moans and cries escaping my lips. The pleasure builds, threatening to crest once more, when he abruptly stops. With a quick motion, he shuts off the water, lifting me from the wall. Carrying me, without withdrawing from within, he places me gently on the bed, positioning himself above me.

His thumb grazes my face, wiping the water away, before his lips brush softly against my forehead. Then he captures my mouth in a heated kiss. Suddenly, passion takes over. Holding my legs aloft, he plunges into me with fervor, each insertion more powerful than the last. My cries grow louder, turning to screams, his name becoming a mantra on my lips, until waves of pleasure crash over me once more. Moments later, with a few deliberate thrusts, he finds his own climax, his movements slowing until he buries himself within me one final, deep time.

He rolls onto his back, pulling me with him so I lie draped across him, his cock still filling me. I rest my head on his chest, exhausted and utterly satisfied. I gently pull away from him, instantly missing the feeling of him inside me. Sitting up, I glance back at him, searching his eyes.

"Did you want to be alone tonight?" I inquire, a hint of vulnerability in my voice.

His brow knits together, casting a shadow over his striking features. "No," he replies, studying my face intently.

"You gave me my own room," I point out, recalling our earlier interaction. "And then you bid me goodnight and left."

"I thought you'd want your own space," he admits, his voice soft yet earnest. "But believe me, Lyra, I only want to share a bed with you every night. If you're okay with that, then this can be our room."

The sincere warmth in his eyes causes my heart to flutter. "I would love that," I confess. "Being apart from you tonight felt...out of place." A tender smile spreads across his face.

"Come here," he beckons, reaching out. Yielding to his pull, I settle next to him, resting my head on his chest. As he drapes the blankets over us, his arm encircles my waist, drawing me even closer.

The sensation of his fingers tracing delicate circles on the small of my back makes me shiver. "You feel incredible," he murmurs, his breath warm against my ear.

"I could say the same about you," I retort, eliciting a soft chuckle from him. "We're both drenched, and so is the bed," I observe.

With a graceful wave of his hand, he performs a minor miracle, drying us and the sheets instantly. I really need to learn that trick.

"Didn't I promise I'd have you screaming?" His tone is teasing, reminding me of our earlier intimacy. Thank the stars we're no longer in Zomea.

"Very funny," I grumble, playfully swatting his chest.

CHAPTER 17
LYRA

Something's coming! The whispers, once faint, now wind around me, vengeful, clawing at my sanity. Straining, my eyes fight the encompassing obscurity of this otherworld maze. The chilling embrace of the tunnels threatens to swallow me whole. Taking deep breaths, I steel myself, reminding my psyche this is a product of my midnight mind. I must remain master of it.

Ahead, a fork in the tunnel beckons, and I stride closer to it, though the whispers press in with increasing fervor, attempting to splinter my resolve. A frigid gust grazes the nape of my neck, its touch deathly cold. My heart leaps to my throat, and a scream tears from my lips. Without thought, my feet veer to the left, propelling me forward in a blind sprint.

As I weave through the maze, the scenery mutates. The once stone walls twist and morph into sinewy, dark roots and branches. They envelope everything, snaking from the ground and descending from above, secreting a viscous, warm substance. The unmistakable metallic tang of blood fills the air.

I want to race ahead, but the gnarled branches and roots are treacherous, lurking in the shadows to ensnare my feet.

My breath comes in ragged gasps, each exhale echoing in the claustrophobic tunnel. The ceaseless thud of my heartbeat becomes deafening, filling my ears—thud, thud, thud. But wait, there's a second cadence, a sinister symphony accompanying my heart's frenzied pace.

"What do you want from me?" I shout into the darkness. If this is a test, a reason my midnight mind summons me here, then let it be known. The dual heartbeat intensifies, now a frantic lub-dub, lub-dub, quickening my pulse further.

In the distance, a pinprick of light beckons. Like a moth drawn to a flame, I gravitate toward it.

"'It's okay. I have you.'" The sound of Colton's voice and the reassuring pressure of his arms bring me crashing back to reality. I gulp air greedily, each breath pushing the tendrils of panic further away.

"What happened?" Colton's voice is laced with concern.

I quickly recount the dream to him, keen to share every detail before they fade away. "Is the beating from the dream the same as the one you mentioned hearing in the tunnels? The one I couldn't hear?" He shifts slightly, pulling away to look at me, yet keeping his arms securely around me.

"Yes, the same. You know, one small comfort of being in Zomea was the absence of these nightmares. I didn't miss them," I confess.

His fingers glide gently down my side, a calming rhythm against my skin. "How often do they happen?"

"It's unpredictable. Sometimes there are days between them, sometimes months. The burning forest and bleeding trees I used to dream about... I now know those are the parts of Zomea that are withering away, and these new branches in the tunnel might signify something similar, but the heartbeat... It's a new, unsettling addition." The memory sends a shiver down my spine. The sound of that heartbeat remains hauntingly vivid.

"I felt you," Colton admits, releasing a weary sigh.

Confused, I scrutinize his face, searching for an explanation. "What do you mean?"

"You've always been restless in your sleep, but now with our tether I awoke immersed in your terror. I felt your fear as though it were my own. That's why I had to wake you," he says.

"Thanks for that." With a deep sigh, I run my hands over my face, noting the sheen of sweat on my forehead. Part of me thinks I should insist he doesn't wake me next time, that I should be diving into the depths of my midnight mind to decipher what I'm seeing. But with the creeped-out feeling still fresh in my mind, that's the last thing I want right now.

"What time is it?" I ask, scanning the windows, but they only offer back the dark, silent night.

"It's still early. The sun won't rise for a few more hours. Try to rest some more," he murmurs, gently urging me to lie back against him. But a dull ache flares in my side, prompting me to turn. Nestled between his arms, I press my back to his chest, drawing comfort from his warmth.

"After these nightmares, falling asleep again is a challenge," I admit, brushing against him. A mischievous grin forms on my lips as I press back a bit more deliberately. His answering growl is low and possessive, his grip tightening, making his intentions —and desires—crystal clear.

Last night was tender, and I needed that connection. But in this moment I crave the raw pleasure, the escape that only he can provide. I press against him again, hard.

His response is immediate, a familiar warmth spreading between my legs as his fingers travel south of my belly button and tease me. I arch back, allowing him better access, and he rewards me with a soft kiss on my forehead.

"Tell me what you want, my shadow," he murmurs, the intimacy of his voice contrasted with the urgency of his touch.

"Always with the nicknames." My words come out as a breath, and I bite my bottom lip, an attempt to conceal the smile that his pet names inevitably draw out.

"It's never mattered what I call you, Lyra, as long as I call you mine," he says, his voice deepening into a growl.

In an almost blinding motion, the blankets are discarded, and I'm flipped onto my stomach. He's on top, guiding himself into me. The initial sensation makes me gasp, but he waits, letting me adjust. When he moves again, he eases out of me slowly then slams into me, hard, rendering me breathless.

He leans in close, his breath a tantalizing caress against my ear, his voice hushed, "Is this what you desired?" The gentle graze of his teeth against my earlobe sends a shiver down my spine. His hands then secure themselves on the headboard, anchoring him as he surrenders to the rhythm of our connection—hammering into me.

"Yes," I manage to choke out, clinging to the sheets below.

His hands move to my hips, pulling me up, positioning me for a deeper connection. I feel him everywhere, inside and out, as he dictates the rhythm, each movement a testament to our shared desire. He tangles one hand in my hair, pulling my back up to meet his chest. I turn my head to see him, and his mouth descends on mine. I feel his fingers wrap around my throat, not hard but enough to keep me pressed to him. The sensation sends a thrill through me, and I moan into his mouth. He uses his other hand to tease my sensitive flesh again, and the feeling is almost too much.

"Colton," I whimper, desperate. He moves his fingers away, reigning me in and wanting to extend my pleasure longer.

I break the kiss, panting for air, and he releases my neck, running his thumb across my bottom lip then grasping my hair, pushing me back down on all fours. Grabbing my hips again, he holds me steady to meet his thrusts, while I bite into the pillow to muffle my screams.

"Colton," I cry out again between breathy moans.

"Are you ready to take more of me inside you?" he asks.

Gods, I want all of him, but I don't know if I can fit anymore. He presses into me again hard then stills. One hand leaves my hip and grips my ass then travels further, spreading me wider. His thumb presses against my backside, and an embarrassing noise escapes me as it presses into me. "Good girl," he whispers, and then he fucks me.

With every hard thrust of his cock, he works his thumb into my other hole, and every touch, every sensation is amplified. I surrender to the overwhelming tide of pleasure, and when it crashes, it's all consuming. I find my release twice before I feel him climax, grounding me back to the present.

He remains there for a moment, his soft breath warming my skin, a stark contrast to the wild passion from moments ago. He retreats gently, leaving a trail of soft kisses down my backside before heading to the bathroom.

After a few moments, he returns, climbing into bed and lying on his back. He motions for me to scoot closer, and I comply, relaxing on my back next to him while his arm wraps around behind me. "Are you alright?" he asks.

I tip my chin up to meet his stare. "Yes, why wouldn't I be alright?" I ask, my eyebrows furrowing.

"I just want to make sure. If you ever don't want to do anything, or if this is moving too fast for you, you can tell me. I'll never get upset."

I offer him a tender smile. "I know. I'm alright, really. I feel good, better than good." A smirk plays at the corner of his mouth.

For a while, we simply lie there, savoring the tranquility. Through the window, I watch the sky gradually brighten and the forest come to life. Birds begin to chirp, and animals stir amongst the trees.

"I'm going to send word that I'm back, and a couple of my friends are going to stop by today. I didn't want you to be caught off guard. I think you've already met one of them, Bim," he mentions.

Startled, I sit up straight. "What!?" The horror in my voice is more pronounced than I intended. Clearing my throat, I continue, "You're friends with Bim? Nyx's best friend? But you and Nyx can't stand each other. What am I missing?"

He laughs, adjusting himself to sit up against the headboard. "We all grew up together. Nyx and I might not get along, but that doesn't prevent Bim and me from being friends. Bim's always been smart enough not to take sides." He studies my face for a moment then adds, "If you're worried about him going back to Nyx and revealing our relationship, he wouldn't, especially if I ask him not to."

I exhale deeply. I'm not sure why I reacted so strongly. Bim had always been kind to me, and Nyx is bound to discover my relationship with Colton sooner or later. "No, it's okay. It took me by surprise, that's all," I explain, settling back against the headboard beside him.

"Clearly," he says with a chuckle. "I need to step out for a bit. Will you be okay here by yourself? Feel free to shower and make yourself at home. I'll be back before you know it."

"Of course, I'll be fine. Go on. I know you've been away from home for too long and have things to take care of." I gently prod him, urging him out of bed.

"Alright, alright," he relents. With a snap of his fingers, he's impeccably dressed in beige pants and a dark-green tunic. He leans down to plant a kiss on the top of my head. "I'll never get used to seeing you naked in my bed," he remarks, his smile widening.

"You'd better," I tease as he makes his way to the bedroom door. "Hey, will you leave the door open for Chepi? He'll probably be waking up soon."

"Of course," he replies, his voice fading as he disappears around the corner.

Now alone, I survey the room in the morning light. It's nearly a mirror image of my room down the hall, though this one boasts a full bar and a fireplace. The sheets, while equally plush, are a deep shade of gray, bordering on black. Last night was nothing short of perfect, and this morning? Absolutely decadent. The thought of spending the day cocooned in these sheets, enveloped in his scent, is tempting.

I rouse myself and shuffle to the bathroom. The water from the shower runs over me like a warm rain. I reach for Colton's soap, which carries the refreshing scent of the sea. After lathering up and rinsing my hair, I linger under the water, allowing the steam to sooth my muscles.

When I finally emerge, I scour the bathroom for a towel. Given that he probably uses magic to dry off, it's a minute before I locate one stashed in a cabinet. Dried off and wrapped in the towel, I return to the bedroom and spot a steaming mug of coffee accompanied by a piece of parchment on the bedside table. I take a tentative sip of the coffee, pleasantly surprised by its creamy sweetness—such a contrast to the harsh, black brew in Zomea.

Curious, I pick up the parchment and unfold it. It reads, "May this keep you warm until I return. P.S. My closet is on the other side of the bar. Feel free to choose anything you'd like."

A smile spreads across my face. I take another sip of the delightful coffee and move to explore his wardrobe.

I decide on one of his white tunics. Pulling it over my head, I fasten a leather belt around my waist, looping it twice and knotting it, fashioning the tunic into a makeshift dress. Coffee in hand, I make my way downstairs. The heartening warmth from the fireplace greets me, its flames still dancing with life. However, Chepi is nowhere in sight.

A clinking sound draws my attention, guiding me to the kitchen. "Oh my," I murmur, taken aback by the scene unfolding before me. The kitchen island and countertops are laden with an assortment of delectable dishes. Chepi is heartily devouring some freshly cooked bacon, while two Twig Wisps flit about, diligently stocking the pantry with a bountiful supply of fresh fruits and vegetables.

"Forgive us. We didn't mean to frighten you. Milord sent word he was back and instructed us to stock the house with food," one of the Twig Wisps says, looking so much like Twig with the same purple skin and silver wings, only his hair is black instead of gray.

"I am Rune, and this is my brother, Rix," the other says, his light-green skin and black wings setting him apart.

"It's a pleasure to meet you both. My name is Lyra, and I see you've already met Chepi."

"Indeed, he was hungry, so we cooked him breakfast. Can we make you something to eat?" Rix inquires.

"No, thank you. Though I'll take a piece of fruit and get out of your way," I respond, moving to grab an apple from the countertop.

"Don't worry. You're not interrupting anything. We're here to serve you. Whatever you need, we'll get it," Rune assures, his hands busy with bags of grain.

"Well, thank you. I appreciate it," I respond with a warm

smile then take a bite out of my apple. "So, what is it that you both do for Colton exactly?"

Rix, hovering nearby, answers, "Everything he asks. Primarily, we keep the house stocked with food and drink, cook for him, and ensure everything remains orderly."

"You've been with him for a while then?" I ask, glimpsing an unexpected path to learning more about Colton.

"Yes, for many, many years." Rix nods. "He saved our lives. Once, we were slaves to a cruel Fae family, but Colton freed us. Since then, he's taken care of our kin and ensured the Dream Forest remains protected from ravishers."

I recall our conversation in Zomea, where Colton told me about these so-called ravishers. The very idea of anyone wanting to harm or enslave such beings is beyond horrifying. It lights a fire within me, and I can't help but ask, "Being here with Colton... You don't feel trapped or like you're serving him against your will?"

Rix shakes his head emphatically. "No, not at all. We choose to work for Colton. He compensates us generously, and he's always fair. We serve him out of gratitude and genuine fondness, not obligation."

Rune, having positioned himself beside Rix, adds, "He may seem tough on the outside, but underneath, he's kind. Many in this forest, including us, owe him a great deal."

Rix, shifting the topic, asks, "Now, what can we prepare for you during your stay? You're staying, right?" His eyes shine with hope.

I laugh softly, "Yes, I'll be staying. But you really don't have to go out of your way for me."

"We insist," Rix counters with a grin.

Rune, not to be left out, prods, "Please, let us know your favorites. We enjoy cooking."

After a brief pause, I begin, "For drinks, it's mostly water for me. But lately I do have a soft spot for whiskey and sweet Faery wine. In the mornings, I prefer hot chocolate to coffee. But when it's coffee, I like it sweet and creamy."

Rix interjects, a gleam in his eye, "Ah, a fellow sugar aficionado!"

"And food-wise?" Rune presses, eager.

Remembering my favorites from back home, I say, "I have always had a love for tomato tart. Think of it as a pie crust filled with cheese and fresh tomato slices. Though I eat meat, I usually lean toward vegetarian dishes. Quiche, soups, and definitely soup paired with toast or bread rolls. Cheese melted on bread dipped in tomato bisque is a must. And fish... Any way you cook it, I'm in. Truthfully, I'll eat almost anything. I'm not too picky."

They both nod, taking in every word, clearly mentally cataloging my preferences.

"What about Chepi?" Rune asks.

"Oh, he'll eat anything," I say with a chuckle, glancing at Chepi, who's almost finished with his breakfast. "But he especially loves bacon and other meats."

"Righto," they say simultaneously.

"Hey, do you guys know Twig?" I shift the conversation.

"Yes, of course. He's with King Onyx, but we don't see him too often since the king rarely visits the Dream Forest," Rix shares.

I tilt my head, curious. "Why doesn't King Onyx visit the Dream Forest?"

"He isn't welcome here. He may be the king of Nighthold, but he knows the Dream Forest is loyal to Colton," Rune says.

"Why isn't he welcome here?" I ask, hoping to glean some insight into the tension between Nyx and Colton. They must have had some falling out if they once were friends and now have this palpable tension. And Bim being friends with both of them... I should probably ask Colton, but it feels like a raw topic right now.

"Things have never been the same since Z," Rix says, his voice tinged with sadness.

"What is Z?" I ask, rapt.

Rix hesitates for a moment. "Her name is Zaelinn," Rune interjects, a somber note evident in his voice.

"Who is Zaelinn? What happened?"

Rix sighs deeply. "The tale of Zaelinn is filled with pain and heartbreak. I'm not sure Milord would want us discussing it. Perhaps you should ask him directly."

"No, please," I interject, "I wouldn't want to upset him. Why make him relive such a sad memory when you could tell me now?"

They exchange glances, silently deliberating. Finally, Rune speaks up, "Have you ever heard of the Center Isles?"

"Only a bit. I know it's an island off the coast of the Noble Vale," I respond.

"It's a place few venture to because it's both dangerous and uninhabitable," Rune explains.

Rix chimes in, "But it's also breathtakingly beautiful. The underwater cave system there, the Brysta Trenches, draws those with adventurous spirits. I've never been, but it's said to be one of the most fantastical places in all of Nighthold."

"Brysta for the goddess of the cosmos?" I ask.

"Yes, the underwater amphitheaters are supposed to be comparable to the constellations themselves," Rix says.

"What's so dangerous about it?"

Rune explains, "The isles themselves are treacherous. If one wishes to explore the caves, they must swim extensive distances underwater to reach the various underwater amphitheaters. Cave diving alone has its risks, but the primary danger of this location is its ability to neutralize all magic."

I gasp. "A place that nullifies magic? Does it neutralize all magic only within the caves?"

"Yes," Rune clarifies, "so explorers have to embark on this dangerous journey without the safety net of magic, particularly challenging given the depths underwater."

I nod, processing the information, then ask, "So what exactly happened to Zaelinn there?"

Rune takes a deep breath, glancing to Rix. "Z... She was the love of Colton's life. They were deeply in love, inseparable. But then, for reasons none of us could understand, she got drawn to Nyx."

Rix cuts in. "Nyx, with his charm and title, enticed many. But he never truly loved any of them, not the way Colton loved Z." Rune's voice softens. "Colton was heartbroken. He wanted Z to be happy, and he might've forgiven King Onyx in time if it hadn't been for that night."

The two exchange a look before Rune continues, his voice dropping as if fearing someone might overhear. "Onyx and Zaelinn had been drinking and decided to visit the infamous Brysta Trenches. Maybe they were seeking romance or a quick thrill—no one knows. But Zaelinn drowned that night. Onyx couldn't use magic to save her in time."

"Oh gods... So Nyx is to blame?" I can feel a pang in my chest for them.

Rix hesitates. "It's not as simple as that. But in Colton's eyes, yes. He's never forgiven Nyx for leading Zaelinn into that place. And Nyx, despite his numerous casual affairs, was profoundly affected by her death. He might not have loved her the way Colton did, but he's lived with regret ever since."

Rune nods in agreement. "The rift between them has deepened over the years. Nyx might appear nonchalant, but there's undeniable guilt in his eyes whenever Zaelinn's name comes up."

I'm momentarily at a loss for words, stunned by the weight of their shared past. I had sensed that something had driven a wedge between them, but I hadn't imagined it involved a woman they both cared for, nor her tragic end. My heart aches for Colton, understanding his animosity toward Nyx. Yet I can't help but feel for Nyx too. The weight of his guilt, the loss of both a woman he cared for and a friendship, must be immense.

"How long ago did this happen?" I ask.

"Many years ago, maybe seventy," Rune replies.

Hmm, that's a very long time ago. I'm ashamed to admit that a feeling of jealousy begins to fester in my chest. Colton really did love another woman. I'm tempted to ask more about her, to know what she looked like, but perhaps it's better I remain ignorant. This woman came between the two of them, and now I've been with both of them as well. It feels as if history is repeating itself, but in reverse. Gods...

"I'm not sure when Colton will be back. Is it safe to go explore the grounds?" I ask, craving some fresh air.

"Of course, no one will harm you here. While it might be a tad more perilous if you venture deep into the forest, the manicured gardens around here are entirely safe," Rune assures.

"Would you like some company? Or is there anything else we can assist you with?" Rix inquires.

"I'm alright, but thank you." I walk out of the kitchen, apple in hand, with Chepi trailing behind, having already devoured all his bacon. The backyard beckons, and I take a seat on one of the benches by the pool's edge, entranced by the water's reflections.

"So, the rumors are true," a voice says from behind me, startling me. I turn and see a man with long, wavy brown hair and striking blue eyes that remind me of the Lycans, but he's clearly Fae.

"Which rumors are those?" I ask, clutching my apple a bit tighter while Chepi hops onto my lap, eyeing the newcomer cautiously.

"Colton mentioned he had a lady staying with him, but I had my doubts. I'm Dorian, by the way," he replies with a hint of amusement.

"You've spoken to Colton?" I press, curiosity piqued.

"Yes, I spoke with him a few minutes ago. That's why I'm here," he says while running his fingers over his beard.

"Are you two close friends?" I inquire.

"I'd like to think so," he responds, easing himself down next to me on the bench.

"Then why did you doubt I'd be here?" I ask.

"Colton doesn't bring women home, so you being here must indicate there's something quite exceptional about you," he remarks, his gaze intense yet not unkind.

"She is special," Colton interjects, seemingly materializing from thin air as he channels in front of us. In a couple of strides, he's right beside me, bending down to plant a kiss on my lips. This isn't a fleeting gesture, either; he lingers, relishing the moment before finally pulling away.

"Ahem." I shy away a tad awkwardly, my eyes darting between Colton and Dorian.

"I can certainly see that," Dorian comments cheerfully.

"You were only gone for a couple of hours. Did you manage to get everything done?" I ask, looking up at Colton.

"Enough for now," he replies, glancing toward the house as if sensing someone there. "Have you met Rix and Rune?"

"Yes, they're really kind. And quite adorable," I admit, smiling as I think of the two Twig Wisps.

"Adorable? They'll be thrilled to hear that," Dorian chuckles from beside me.

"So, what's on the agenda today? More training, or can we

switch things up and do something fun for once?" I ask, giving Chepi a gentle pat as I look up at Colton.

He raises an eyebrow, amusement flickering in his eyes. "Actually, Dorian has to take a little trip today, and I thought we would tag along."

"I'm intrigued. What kind of trip are we taking? Should I pack snacks?" I ask.

Dorian chuckles, giving me a playful nudge with his elbow. "Snacks? I'm starting to like this one already," he remarks.

Colton chimes in, "No need for that. We shouldn't be gone for too long, and I'm sure Rix and Rune are preparing a feast for this evening." I feign a pout, eliciting laughter from him.

"Does our journey involve the Dream Forest?" I continue.

"Indeed, it does," Dorian confirms.

With a burst of enthusiasm, I declare, "Then I'm in." Safely tucking Chepi under my arm and getting to my feet, Colton pulls me close, an arm wrapped snugly around my waist. I lean into his embrace, catching Dorian's cheeky smile before he vanishes.

"We're following him, I assume?" I say.

"Yes," Colton replies, leaning in for a quick kiss. "A heads up, Bim will stop by later. He might stay for dinner too. If you're uncomfortable with it, I can reschedule."

I shake my head. "It's okay. Let him stay." He nods before we channel away.

CHAPTER 18
LYRA

We land smoothly on a craggy ledge, Colton's arm securely around me until I find my balance. Chepi, restless in my embrace, wriggles free to explore our surroundings. We stand atop a high mountain range, and I'm drawn to the edge, mesmerized by the sight below. Endless mountain peaks pierce through a vast sea of rosy-hued clouds, their beauty breathtaking.

Muffled voices pull my attention back, and I realize we're not alone. Near what seems to be the entrance to a mine, Dorian converses with two miners, their clothes stained with deep shades of blue and black. After a brief exchange, the miners vanish from sight.

I turn to Colton, curiosity piqued. "What is this place?"

"It's one of Dorian's mines," he replies.

I glance back at Dorian, eyebrows raised in question. "And what exactly are you mining here, Dorian? What do you do?"

"I own a armory in Nitross," he replies, waving an arm for us to follow him.

"An armory? What does that entail?" I probe as we start to walk toward the entryway to the mine.

"In essence, I craft and forge weapons and other military gear. I also trade in unique weapons and magical artifacts. Beyond that, I manage my staff and handle any repairs that come our way," he elaborates. The profession sounds intriguing, and it strikes me that Dorian would be a valuable ally to have. His connection to Bim makes even more sense now. If Bim leads Nyx's military, they must collaborate frequently.

Colton chimes in, "Dorian could craft something especially for you – maybe a custom dagger or a light yet powerful sword. It's why I wanted you to come along today." I remember the physical training back in Zomea, where I had grown fond of wielding a sword. They could be cumbersome, but Colton often reminded me not to rely solely on magic, especially after hearing about Z. I wonder how many places nullify magic like that. The question irks me, but I hesitate, not wanting to sour the mood with memories of her.

"A dagger sounds wonderful. I prefer a sword, but they can be a hassle to lug around," I admit.

"How about I fashion you a sword paired with a magical sheath? When stored, it'd be no larger than a dagger, but once unsheathed it will reveal its full size," Dorian offers.

"That sounds incredible." I didn't even know that was possible, but nothing should surprise me anymore.

"What kind of magic do you have?" I ask, changing the subject.

"I have a bit of elemental magic in me. I can do very basic things with the elements. My primary gift is necromancy," Dorian says. As he says the word "necromancy," his blue eyes glow briefly in the dim light of the mine.

"I've never met a Faery with necromancy magic before. I

mean, I haven't known many Fae, but still... Is it a rare gift?" I inquire.

"Having necromancy magic isn't rare exactly. Many Fae possess traces of it, enabling them merely to sense the life force of another and gauge their strength. What's uncommon is the excessive amount of necromancy magic Dorian has," Colton answers.

I shift my gaze between the two of them. "So what kind of things can you do?" I ask.

Dorian drags his fingers along the wall as we start to descend further into the mountain. I try not to think about how being underground makes me feel. Gods, this is also a really tight cave, and that makes me even more uncomfortable. Colton wraps an arm around my shoulder, squeezing me gently, probably sensing my anxiety. I try to focus on Chepi flying up ahead while I listen to Dorian.

"Necromancy is often misunderstood and feared. I can't bring the dead back to life in their original form, contrary to what some believe. At times, I can act as a conduit, relaying messages between the living and the dead or obtaining information."

"Can you visit Zomea, like with midnight mind?" I ask. Then it strikes me, I wonder how much Dorian knows about me and what things Colton has told him about my magic and the power I'm destined to control.

He shakes his head. "No, it's different. I can meditate and beckon a spirit to communicate, but it's not always successful, and the interactions are fleeting. The most distinct ability I have is called Temporal Echoes."

That's a new one for me. "What does that entail?"

He pauses, searching for the right way to put it. "I can summon visions of past events that transpired in a specific location. Essentially, it's witnessing a spectral reenactment of history," he explains.

The idea of him being able to conjure up historical events is captivating. I hope I'll have the chance to witness that power in action one day. Such an ability is undoubtedly beneficial but could also be dangerous. I imagine many seek to take advantage of it.

Suddenly, the path before us reveals walls veined with glistening streaks. Scattered around are baskets filled with black and blue rocks, each emitting a faint, radiant glow. Colton gestures toward the baskets, explaining, "This, Lyra, is why we're here."

Intrigued, I approach one of the baskets, with Chepi cautiously sniffing them from a distance. "What are these?"

Dorian picks up a stone and, with a slight smirk, tosses it my way. Catching it, I'm entranced by its intricate pattern— bluish-gray with shimmering flecks. "Iron," Dorian clarifies, "specifically, the base of what I use to produce starforged steel."

"We call it starforged because this is the only mine located this close to the stars," Colton adds.

Drawing a connection, I pose, "So you're collecting this to craft specialized weapons?"

Dorian nods. "Right, but there's more. Colton approached me with a particular request."

Turning to Colton, I'm met with his reassuring gaze. "I thought it'd be fitting for Dorian to design something unique for you, a weapon that resonates only with your essence. While I can explain its significance, the intricacies of its creation are Dorian's expertise."

Dorian chuckles, stepping forward, "Indeed, let's leave the intricacies to me. For this weapon, I'll need you to select five of these stones and imbue them with your essence. Your choice will guide the weapon's character and capabilities."

"Five stones, infused with my magic?"

Colton chuckles softly. "Exactly. Pick them, channel a burst of your power into them, then drop them into this pouch," Dorian instructs, tossing me an ornate velvet bag. The task seems straightforward.

I peruse the baskets, selecting five intriguing stones. Holding each, I envision my magic flowing into it, feeling a responsive throb from the stone before letting it tumble into the bag. Once I've selected all five, I present the pouch to Dorian.

"That's all?" I ask in disbelief.

Dorian raises an eyebrow playfully. "It might seem simple to you, but crafting the weapon is where the real challenge lies." He winks, causing me to laugh.

"Didn't mean to belittle the process. I can't wait to see what you create," I respond, my anticipation evident.

"That's the spirit," Dorian replies, his eyes glowing. "It's not just about forging a weapon. It's about intertwining your essence with its very core. And that, dear Lyra, is an art." He carefully secures the bag, his fingers brushing over the pulsing stones inside. "Rest assured, it'll be something truly unique."

Colton smiles, pulling me closer. "Everything involving you tends to be extraordinary." I blush, nudging him playfully.

"Alright, I'll leave you two to it. I'll drop these off at my workshop then join you for dinner," Dorian remarks before vanishing, and I feel Colton's eyes on me once more.

"Well, we could explore the mines, but really there's nothing exciting to see. Instead, I have one more stop to make before heading back home. I need to visit my parents' house and grab a couple of things. Do you want to come with me?" Colton asks. I turn to face him, hesitating for a moment. It's not that I don't want to go; I'm just unsure about who we might run into. What if I see Nyx? Or what if I encounter Colton's parents and...

"My parents won't be home, if that's what's making you anxious," he says, smirking at me. I mentally check my shields. "Yes, take me with you. And I'm not afraid to meet your parents. I mean, I have met them before. It's just that now, after..." I'm not exactly sure what Colton and I are doing, what this is between us.

"I know," he says, pulling me close. Chepi flies into my arms, and then Colton's fresh citrus scent picks up with the wind as we channel. My feet touch down inside the elders' palace, and I recognize it instantly – we're inside the grand foyer.

"Make yourself at home, look around. Down that way," he says, pointing to a hallway, "you'll find a hall full of incredibly embarrassing family photos you can tease me about later. I need to grab something, but it'll only take a few minutes. I'll come find you afterward." He gives me a reassuring smile and a nod before taking off up the stairs.

Releasing Chepi, who flutters alongside me, I head toward the hallway of family photos Colton mentioned. Curiosity tugs at me about what he's doing upstairs and why he didn't want me along. I decide to wait and see what he retrieves and ask him about it later.

Crossing a grand sitting room, I turn a corner into a long hallway. True to his word, it's covered in pictures. Wooden frames span the entirety of both walls. The hallway is rather dark, so I conjure a small orb of light in my hand and toss it ahead to illuminate the photos.

Gods, I don't think I've ever seen pictures like these up close before. I've only ever seen paintings and sketches that attempt to depict people and places, but they don't always capture the exact likeness. It must be nice to grow up in a wealthy Fae family with the magical capabilities to capture such memories.

In the Sorcerer Realm, you would never find anything like this. It actually annoys me now, knowing my father was Fae and could have captured photos and taught me how to do it as well. I laugh, thinking about the family paintings we have in the halls of Tempest Moon Castle and how ridiculous I always looked in them. I thought the artists always painted me like a funny-looking doll, not the mischievous girl I actually was. The Fae are lucky to have the kind of magic that preserves memories in such a real way.

As I walk down the hallway, each photo of Colton alongside his parents strikes me as formal, almost harsh. The resemblance between him and his mother is undeniable. Granger, his father, has always unsettled me since our first meeting at the dinner party here. Thankfully, Colton bears little resemblance to him.

I pause in front of a photo showing a young Colton at a conference table surrounded by older men, including his father. Even as a teenager, he sits taller and broader than the others, his warrior-like build evident even then. "Pretty funny, huh?" I say to Chepi, tracing my finger over the photo.

Moving on, I find a picture of Colton's parents with another couple, unmistakably Nyx's parents, given the strong resemblance Nyx shares with his mother. But his father, Callum—if that's him—is imposingly large, towering over Granger and the others.

I toss the light orb from hand to hand as I cross to the other side of the hall, casting light on the wall. The photos get older as I walk further. Now, Colton appears as a child in a photo with a group of friends. Flora, with her curly red hair, stands out immediately. Next to her is Nyx, then Bim, and a young Dorian, identifiable by his blue eyes. At the other end is Colton, larger than the rest, and between him and Nyx is another girl—Z, with her light, strawberry-blonde hair in a tangled mess.

I chuckle, imagining what it must have been like growing up together as friends. A pang of longing hits me; I wish I had experienced something similar in my childhood.

I hear a sudden clang, like someone walking in heels in the distance. Quickly, I call my light back to me, plunging the hallway into darkness. Chepi drops to the ground and darts down the hall, his tail wagging. I whisper-yell after him, but he ignores me, prompting me to chase after him. I'm half-expecting to run into a servant, and I'm really hoping it's not Colton's mother, Elspeth. She was nice to me, but encountering her right now would be incredibly awkward.

"Chepi!" I hear her voice exclaim from around the corner. Instantly, I recognize it as Flora's. A mix of worry and excitement washes over me at the thought of being found here, but my steps don't falter. As I turn the corner, Flora's long red hair flips over her shoulder as she spins toward me. When our eyes meet, she quickly closes the distance and pulls me into a tight hug.

"Lyra, darling, how are you?" she asks, pulling back to hold my shoulders, her brown eyes scanning me as if looking for injuries.

"I'm good. I've missed you," I tell her as she releases me to pick up Chepi, showering him with pets. Chepi responds with a lick on her cheek, making her laugh. "What are you doing here?"

"Oh, you know me, always finding a reason to visit the library here. And what brings you here? If you're here, then the rumors about your recent company must be true," she says, her smile holding a coy edge.

"Oh gods, what rumors are those?" I ask, my internal cringe at the thought of Nyx hearing rumors about me.

"Just whispers of a certain Fae male being seen with you," she replies, setting Chepi down. He circles our feet, clearly delighted to see her again.

"Oh... Please, don't tell Nyx you ran into me here or that you ran into me at all," I quickly ask her. She's close friends and cousins with him, and he's her king. She's definitely going to tell him.

"Don't worry, Lyra. Your secret's safe with me, although I don't think it'll be much of a secret for long," she says, tucking a strand of hair behind her ear. I shift nervously on my feet, gathering courage for the question I dread to ask, but it tumbles out before Colton finds us. "How is he?"

Her eyes soften before she answers, "He misses you, but he's keeping busy." I nod, unsure how to feel about this revelation. He misses me... What has he said about me?

"Hey, I better get going. But don't be a stranger, okay? Come visit me anytime. You too," she says, bending to pat Chepi on his head.

"I will, and thank you for keeping quiet," I respond. She pulls me into another tight hug, a gentle smile gracing her lips as she prepares to channel. Just as she's about to disappear in her signature red wind, a look of concern crosses her face, and then she's gone.

I make my way back to the foyer just as Colton is descending the staircase. "Ready to go?" he asks, and I nod, my eyes drawn to the books in his hands.

"What did you get?" I inquire.

"I figured with everything going on it might be good to refresh myself on the history of the Luminary Council. I went to my dad's private chambers and grabbed what I could find. I'll read through them later and let you know if anything worthwhile comes up," he explains.

Picking up Chepi, I step closer to Colton, ready to leave.

"Do you think I should be worried...about the council?" I ask, concern in my voice.

"I'm not sure yet, but I'm going to find out," he replies, wrapping an arm around me. As he does, the foyer begins to fade away.

―――――

As we approach the dining room, the delightful aroma of food fills the air. Rix and Rune have laid out a spread of bite-sized snacks all over the dining table.

Rix spots me and beckons me over, pulling out a chair for me. As I sit, he places a plate in front of me. Colton, smirking at Rix's chivalry, takes the seat next to mine and starts describing each of the snacks spread before us. My stomach growls softly as I reach for toast topped with cheese and a slice of tomato.

As I'm about to take a bite, Dorian's voice interrupts, "Look who I found."

He enters the dining room with a bottle of whiskey in one hand and Bim following closely behind him. He looks the same as I remember, though maybe his facial hair is slightly longer.

I feel my heart race, an unwelcome wave of anxiety crashing over me. The sight of Bim, Nyx's closest friend, stirs something inside me. First Flora and now him. I sense Colton's touch beneath the table, a reassuring squeeze on my thigh. His green eyes find mine, narrowing slightly, as if sensing my turmoil. Taking a deep breath, I ensure my mental barrier between us is secure, and my window to him is closed, blocking any unintended projections.

Awkwardly, I start to rise from my chair to greet Bim, but when Colton remains seated, I quickly settle back down. Why am I so socially awkward in moments like this? I can navigate mazes and confront demons, but the appearance of Nyx's friend turns me into a bumbling mess.

Bim's handshake with Colton is firm, accompanied by a warm smile. Then, turning his attention to me, he nods slightly.

"Nice to see you again, Lyra," he says, his tone neutral and devoid of animosity. Maybe I've been misjudging this situation. Maybe Bim won't make things awkward after all.

"You too," I manage, painting a small smile on my face. To prevent any further verbal stumbles, I promptly take another bite of food.

The boys begin their exchange of small talk while Dorian pours a glass for each of us. Eagerly, I take mine and savor a sip. The whiskey is light, tinged with a pleasant sweetness that I appreciate.

I should've previously asked Colton how much Bim and Dorian were privy to. Our desire was to keep the bridge's unlocked status a secret, but I'm unsure if maintaining that secrecy is feasible now, especially after seeing the state of the Lamia Realm and all the evil the bridge is attracting. It won't be long before Nighthold sees the arrival of malevolent beings.

Colton has mentioned trusting both of them, so I suspect they're aware we've been in Zomea for the last few months. Nevertheless, I listen intently, trying to discern the nuances of their conversation.

Colton breaks my train of thought, directing a question at Bim. "So what have I missed?" he inquires.

Bim pauses, glancing at me then back to Colton, as if communicating something with his eyes.

"It's alright. Anything you have to say to me you can say in front of Lyra," Colton says, and I sit up a little straighter.

"A Sarrol was spotted in the Dream Forest a couple of weeks ago," Bim reveals, downing his glass.

"Impossible," Dorian spits from across the room, shocked.

Colton remains silent for a moment, and I can tell he's pondering the same thing I am. The Sarrols we battled in the Lamia Realm—we don't know where they originated since we are still waiting to speak with Drew. All we know is some of them came out of the bridge. I don't understand how it's possible when we didn't see or hear anything in Zomea or the tunnels.

"Are you sure?" Colton asks, directing his gaze at Bim.

"I am. At first, I was skeptical when one of the Pixies informed me. I tracked it for two days before confronting and eliminating it. Regrettably, several creatures fell prey to its hunger in the process," Bim recounts, shaking his head.

"Damn," Dorian mutters across the table, proceeding to refill everyone's glasses.

"As you both are aware, Lyra unlocked the bridge to Zomea, and we spent the past several months there. However, what I haven't shared with you is that upon our return through the bridge, the Lamia Realm was under siege," Colton begins, taking a moment to run a hand through his hair. "Monstrauths, Spider Wraiths, and even Sarrols were causing mayhem. We emerged right in the midst of the battlefield."

"Soren believed they were drawn to the bridge and that they've been manifesting in waves ever since," I say, my eyes shifting between Dorian and Bim.

"Fuck. I'm sure Drew was thrilled," Bim sighs, scratching his head.

"She's not pleased, that's for sure. But she understood that unlocking the bridge was necessary. We didn't get a chance to talk given everything that was happening. I expect she'll be paying me a visit soon," Colton comments, reaching out to grab a slice of cheese.

Rune pops in, asking, "Will you all be staying for dinner?"

Considering the abundance of food on the table, I'd assumed this was dinner.

"You're both welcome to stay as long as you'd like," Colton offers, surveying the table.

"Yeah," Bim responds to Rune, while Dorian nods in agreement before Rune swiftly exits the room. I glance around the table to see Chepi following at his feet and hold back a laugh. I bet he's following Rix and Rune around, eating scraps and treats while they cook.

"I think I'm going to go change before dinner," I whisper to Colton, rising from my seat.

I start to push my chair in and make my exit, but Colton catches me, pulling me back into his lap. He cradles me, places a soft yet assertive kiss on my lips, briefly exploring my mouth and running a hand down my bare thigh. Only when he's satisfied does he allow me to stand once more. This act, reeking of sheer dominance, sends a pulse of heat through me, especially when he momentarily drops his shield, letting me feel a wave of desire.

Without turning back, I make my way down the hall and ascend the staircase, headed for a change of clothes. A thought tugs at the back of my mind — how will Nyx react when he discovers the tether?

CHAPTER 19
NYX

"He's been gone for hours," I hiss through my teeth.

"Come on, dear, relax. I'm sure he'll be back soon, and it's not going to change anything," Flora says, peeking up from her book in the corner chair.

"You don't understand. I need to know if she's with him. I smelled her. I'm telling you she was here, in her old room," I say, continuing my restless pacing in front of the fire.

"I believe you," Flora replies, flipping a page in her book. "I'm just saying, what will it change if she is with him?"

"Everything," I mutter under my breath. She chooses to ignore my statement, recognizing it for the lie it is. The truth remains: it changes nothing. I love Lyra and want her back. I shouldn't have left her at Drew's. I should have made her listen, forced her to understand how deeply I feel for her. Maybe I should have locked her in that room until she grasped the depth of my love. No, that would have been wrong. But the image of her hands trembling while asking me to leave is still fresh in my mind. It took everything in me to leave when every part of my being wanted to stay close to her.

I'm overcome with frustration and need to get a grip. Running a hand through my hair and down my face, I move to the cart and pour myself a whiskey and water – minus the water.

I take my drink and move over to my desk, taking a seat. There should be enough work here to distract me until Bim returns. I start reading through complaints and incidents of attacks in Nighthold. But then I smell him even before he appears in front of my desk.

"Well?" I say, raising an eyebrow when he doesn't immediately divulge if she's with him.

"I stayed for dinner. That's why I was gone for so long," Bim explains, but my frustration is mounting.

I take a drink from my glass, trying to contain my temper. "Was Lyra with him?" I enunciate each word, inhaling deeply for patience.

"Yes, Lyra was there. Now, Nyx, damn it, don't put me in the middle of this. It's hard enough being friends with both of you. I've managed to maintain that friendship this long without betraying the other's trust," Bim argues. I glare at him over my glass, downing the rest and welcoming the burn it leaves in my chest.

"Tell me if she's okay," I finally say.

"She looks well, better than well. If you're going to stress about this every day, then go see her for yourself," he suggests, and I can't deny that the thought has crossed my mind.

"A lot of good it did me last time," I mutter.

This time, it's Flora who speaks up. "Last time was different. Everything was fresh, and she was hurt. She felt betrayed by you. But now she's had time to heal. As he said, she looks well. Maybe you'll feel better if you see that she's doing fine." Yeah, but doing fine with him, when she should be here with me. I don't say that part out loud though.

"He's only using her to get back at me for Z. I don't believe she's safe with him," I stress, and both Flora and Bim give me a look as if I'm taking it too far.

"Forget it. It's late, and if you're not going to tell me anything about the dinner..."

"I'll tell you what I can. But I won't overshare, because you wouldn't want me doing that if our roles were reversed," Bim responds, and I nod for him to continue, even though I'm irritated. After all, I'm not only his best friend but also his king. Regardless of his years of friendship with Colton, his allegiance should be to me.

"She did complete the final ceremony and unlock the bridge. The reason you haven't heard anything about her whereabouts all this time is that she's been in Zomea for the past few months," Bim reveals. The thought of her spending all that time with Euric makes my skin crawl. That bastard was probably trying to turn her against me the entire time, playing his mind games with her.

"If there's nothing else, I'm going to bed," I declare, rising to my feet.

"Do you want us to stay? We can have breakfast together tomorrow," Flora suggests, and I restrain myself from glaring at her. I've been insufferable these past months without Lyra, and I'm amazed they've tolerated me.

"No. Go home," I tell them, heading to my bedchamber without another word. I change out of my clothes and put on a pair of black shorts before settling into bed. Occasionally, subtle hints of her sweet honeysuckle scent linger in the room, evoking powerful emotions within me. I've never felt such a strong desire to have someone. While I might've said "I love you" in the past to appease women, with Lyra I genuinely feel it with every fiber of my being. I yearn for her presence.

A knock at the door interrupts my thoughts, and Twig flies

in, a tall mug in hand. "Your Highness, I thought you might appreciate this," he says, extending the mug toward me. Every night, he's been preparing a special tea for me— a concoction of herbs and magic meant to help me sleep and alleviate the tension I've been grappling with.

"Thanks, Twig. Have a good night," I reply as he departs, and I swiftly consume the soothing beverage.

The draught starts to work immediately, and I'm grateful for it. Otherwise, I'd be up all night with my mounting frustration.

———

I MUST'VE CONTEMPLATED VISITING her more than a dozen times. It's challenging to concentrate, knowing she's nearby. I could channel there within minutes and take her with me. However, such a move might be in vain. I want her to come to me willingly, especially before he has a chance to harm her. If he's genuinely entertaining a newfound infatuation with her to spite me—I won't hesitate to end him.

I need her to understand that my intentions were always to safeguard her. As my feelings for her deepened, I became hesitant to reveal the truth, fearing it might push her away. By the time I recognized the urgency of being transparent, it was already too late. Enough of this inner turmoil—I need to see her. I'll remain unnoticed and won't enter his home. I merely wish to catch a glimpse of her from afar, to reassure myself that she's truly well.

I get to my feet and channel to the Dream Forest. I stop on the outskirts of Colton's property. I've never understood why he's always preferred living so far away from everyone else. I channel to the other side of the grounds and look around. Seeing no signs of anyone, I channel closer to the house. Then I spot her. She's in the kitchen, wearing nothing but a long tunic...one of his tunics. Disgusted, I struggle to stifle my rage at seeing her in his clothes.

I take a moment to steady my breathing, focusing on the way her hair cascades down her back, how she moves gracefully from the counter to the stove. It's undeniable that Lyra has this ineffable allure about her. But right now, it's not her charm that's pulling me in. It's the worry, the anxiety, and the overwhelming need to ensure her well-being.

Watching her, I'm reminded of all our shared moments, the laughter, the secrets we whispered in the dark, the plans we made of a future together. The past few months without her have felt like an eternity, a chasm of emptiness threatening to consume me.

She reaches up to open a cabinet, and the tunic rides up slightly. I catch a glimpse of her legs and feel an even sharper pang of jealousy. The idea of Colton seeing her like this, or even more, is too much to bear. Yet I can't bring myself to look away.

Suddenly, she pauses, as if sensing something. Her eyes dart around the room, and for a moment I think she's sensed my presence. I push down the surge of hope. It's not possible, I remind myself. Yet, as she scans the room, her gaze seems to pause momentarily in my direction. The distance and the walls between us don't allow for our eyes to meet, but I swear there's a hint of recognition in her eyes. Or maybe it's my longing making me see things.

I retreat a few steps, keeping the house and Lyra in view but blending more into the shadows. She's the same Lyra, yet there's a difference in her demeanor, a new confidence. I miss her so much, and the weight of my decisions press on me heavily.

The moment is broken when someone else enters the

kitchen – it's Colton. My fists clench instinctively. He says something to her, his tone light, making her laugh. It's a sound I've missed desperately, but hearing it because of him is a knife to my heart.

As they continue their interaction, the reality of the situation sets in. I can't stand here and watch. The feeling of helplessness, mixed with anger and regret, becomes overwhelming.

I need a plan, something to bridge the gap between us. It's clear that merely waiting and hoping isn't enough. With one last look at Lyra, I channel away from the forest, the image of her laughing with Colton seared into my mind.

I settle back into my study. I was miserable without her these last months, but at least I knew she was in Zomea with her father. Now she's in my kingdom, so close. Knowing she's with him gnaws at my insides, especially not knowing the extent of their relationship. I've been so distracted. I need to focus on what I can control, and right now I can't control what Lyra's doing, at least not in a way that would be seen as good.

The door opens, and I look up from my desk to see Twig approaching with a stack of mail. "All of these came this morning, and Bim and Flora arrived wanting to see you again."

"Thanks, send them in," I say, taking the stack of parchment from him.

"Have there been more attacks?" Bim asks, glancing at the new stack of mail in front of me that I'm shuffling through.

"Yes." I pause, taking a deep breath. "It seems there have been, but I'll need to sort through all of these new ones and respond accordingly."

"Last night, Colton mentioned the unlocked bridge has been attracting waves of evil creatures, Sarrols included. Do you think that's what's behind the recent attacks here too?" Bim asks.

I think about that for a moment. "Granger told me there

have been whispers amongst the elders of getting the Luminary Council back together again. I don't think it's the bridge being unlocked. I think it's her—Lyra," I say, and it burns saying her name aloud. Gods, do I miss her.

"What do you need from me?" Bim asks, knowing better than to probe further into the topic.

"I need you to gather some of the men and look into these attacks." I hand him a piece of parchment with a list of recent incidents on it. "Whatever I find this morning when I finish going through this stack, I'll look into myself. Let's meet back up tonight for dinner."

"Consider it done." Bim takes the list and vanishes, channeling to the nearest army headquarters, I assume, to find a handful of men to assist him.

"What can I help you with?" Flora asks, dragging her finger across my bookshelf and examining the dust it leaves on her fingertip.

"You can go to the elders' palace library. I've already told Granger you'll be stopping by more frequently until we figure things out," I tell her.

"What do you want me to focus on? Dark magic still?" she asks, turning her attention to me.

"No, I need you to look for something more important." She narrows her eyes at me, sensing the seriousness in my tone. "Colton gave Lyra one of my father's journals that day she went with you to the library. She waited to tell me about it—"

"How did Colton get one of your father's journals?" she asks, cutting me off.

"That's not important. What's important is what it said. He spoke of a prophecy regarding Lyra. He always spoke of her darkness before his death, saying Euric's offspring would destroy everything. He never mentioned another way. But this journal said otherwise," I tell her.

"What did it say?" she asks.

I pull it from my desk. I retrieved it after everything that went down in Tempest Moon and must have read it dozens of times while Lyra's been away, looking for any clues but coming up short. I hand it to Flora.

"Turn to the last page and read it," I tell her.

She starts to read the passage aloud. "Born for darkness and destined to be with my son. Scarlett was right in questioning me. I banished Euric only to avoid the inevitable. Do I save my people or save my son? Why can't they be one and the same? Can his light save her, or will her darkness destroy him—destroy us all?" She looks up, her eyes locking with mine. "You think you can save her?"

I nod.

"I want you to find out anything and everything that has to do with this. Where did he get this information? What light does he speak of? Why did he believe her darkness would destroy everything?"

"I understand," Flora says, her magic at the ready to channel.

"I visited the Dream Forest this morning," I confess, drawing a sharp, surprised glance from her.

"And?" she prompts, anticipation evident in her eyes.

"I saw her. She seemed...vibrant, alive. Yet she was with him, in his clothes too," I admit with a hint of bitterness.

She counters gently, "Being with him doesn't dictate her heart's allegiance. And she wore his clothes? Maybe it's convenience, not intimacy."

"She donned his tunic, only his tunic, Flora. It felt like a betrayal," I retort, frustration mounting.

She steps closer, her voice soothing. "Lyra is young, wounded. Perhaps she's merely seeking solace or is momentarily adrift. And if your father's journal speaks the truth, fate ties her to you. Your paths will intertwine once more."

I want to believe her. That's why I need to know everything she can uncover about this prophecy my father spoke of. I need clarity. With a heavy sigh, I give a resigned nod, watching as Flora channels her powers and disappears on the wind.

I delve into my desk, retrieving the only other journal where my father has mentioned Lyra. I've perused every journal I could find, yet there are missing periods of time. And if Colton possesses one, surely more must be out there. I could directly approach Colton, inquiring about the journal's origin and if there might be more. Perhaps, if his feelings for Lyra are genuine, he'd assist me. Yet I hesitate. I don't want to alarm Lyra with this information. And knowing Colton, he'd likely give a sardonic retort instead of a straightforward answer.

I quickly navigate to the page I've earmarked, reading over my father's words once more.

The council grows overconfident. It has been an age since a dark Sorcerer held sway. Their underestimation of her potential threat is glaring. She won't simply control the dark power; she will become its epicenter, a focal point for every malevolent force. Her uniqueness, which Drew believes might be her salvation, only elevates my concern. Her unpredictability is precisely what makes her dangerous. The council must recognize this. I am resolute in ensuring she never reaches the age where her magic matures. If fate doesn't intercede, I'll ensure measures are in place to curb her rise.

I forcefully close the journal, pushing it back into my drawer with a hint of frustration. The ambiguity in my father's words is maddening. There's a ticking clock hanging over me. In a few short months, Lyra will come into her dark magic. I need to decipher what he meant when he said my light could save her. Perhaps all of this is merely the incoherent babbling of a madman, these prophecies nothing but fantasy. Maybe Lyra will be unaffected, requiring no salvation. Still, I have to brace myself for every conceivable scenario.

As much as I would like to center my attention solely on Lyra, my kingdom demands priority. The increasing frequency of attacks is alarming, signaling that I might have to resort to extreme measures sooner than anticipated, further compounding the situation. I sift through the pile of letters Twig handed over earlier.

Attacks in Nighthold were once a rarity, but a surge in malevolent beings suggests that the shadow hanging over Cloudrum might be spilling into the Faery realm. There have now been four Sarrol attacks. While Bim managed to eliminate the threat in the Dream Forest, two more incidents occurred in the Noble Vale and another in Nitross. A local farmer succeeded in taking down one, but the other two remain at large, necessitating my intervention today. The real question remains. How many more of these creatures are out there?

CHAPTER 20

LYRA

"I had Rix and Rune hunt for clothes for you today, though now I'm second-guessing that choice. Seeing you in just my tunic every day has its charm." He lifts the hem of my shirt just enough for his fingers to dance on the edge of my thigh, a tantalizing tease.

I lean into him, craning my neck to catch his lips. Swiftly, he pulls me close, lifting and settling me onto the kitchen counter. I part my legs to welcome him closer, my hands getting lost in his hair. The intensity of our kiss grows, heightened by the insistent pressure from his pants.

"Am I interrupting something?" Drew's voice shatters the moment. I jerk back, nearly coughing in surprise, while hastily pushing Colton away and hopping off the counter. My face feels as if it's on fire. When I chance a look at Drew, she's wearing a grin that stretches from ear to ear, her red eyes sparkling.

"Seems like there's a lot that's changed since our last meeting," she comments.

"I've been waiting for your inevitable appearance," Colton

retorts, looping an arm around my waist and drawing me into the protective curve of his body.

"Had some prior engagements to deal with." With a graceful turn, Drew heads toward the grand living room, her familiarity with the place evident. "Join me. We have much to discuss," she beckons, gracefully sinking into one of the plush couches.

Colton takes a seat on the couch across from Drew, and I perch on its edge next to him. Before I can settle, he tugs me close, wrapping an arm securely around me. Drew's eyes observe us keenly, though she doesn't seem the least bit surprised by our intimacy. I wonder if it's her mysterious echosphere granting her such insights, or perhaps she's secretly been harboring a seer.

"Is Soren okay? How's your realm holding up? Are you concerned about more attacks?" I barrage her with questions.

"Soren's fine. He'll be pleased to hear of your concern," she replies, a touch of warmth in her gaze. But it quickly shifts, her eyes hardening with a seriousness that makes my heart race. "My realm stands, for now. However, I believe we're in the calm before the storm."

"Is it true what Soren shared, that the creatures are drawn to the bridge?" Colton interjects.

"It seems so," Drew acknowledges. "But before I delve into the details of my visit, I need to know everything you both discovered in Zomea. You were away for quite a while."

Colton and I exchange glances, wondering where best to start. We then take turns narrating our experiences from the past few months: my intensive training in Zomea, the dire state of that land and our growing concerns that Eguina might soon follow suit, the significance of the Gholioth blood needing to be extracted from me after I awaken my dark magic to restore balance to Zomea and in turn Eguina. And of course we share

WHAT BEATS WITHIN THE TUNNELS

our tether with her too, but we stress its confidentiality, insisting Drew is the only other we've shared it with so far and trust her to keep it so.

Drew listens intently, nodding occasionally, taking in every detail but her face remaining stoic. "I knew Lyra's dark magic would play a pivotal role in all of this. However, I fear we might not have the luxury to wait until your nineteenth birthday," Drew says, her posture straightening with emphasis.

"What do you mean?" Colton inquires.

"I mean, there exists a method to awaken Lyra's dark magic before her nineteenth birthday," Drew begins, and my gaze flits between her and Colton.

"How? And what assures you it'll succeed?" I ask, eager for answers.

"I've witnessed it," she replies, her tone measured. I murmur, "The echosphere," drawing her focused gaze onto me.

"Yes, the future is fluid and ever-changing, but I am certain this is one potential future we should seriously consider," she advises.

"What precisely did you see? What does this entail?" Colton presses her.

Her lips curl in a hint of a smirk. "You might not be thrilled, especially given the scene I encountered when I arrived," she teases.

"Give us every detail," I urge, the anxiety building in my stomach.

"To achieve this, you'll need the Moon Grimoire, your family's treasured tome," she states.

"The last I heard, Samael was on its trail. I'm uncertain if he managed to locate it or even where it might be now," I admit.

"We could return to Tempest Moon, retrace Samael's steps. If necessary, I can employ Dorian's abilities to reveal past events, which could provide insights about the grimoire's whereabouts. But what's the part you believe we won't be fond of?" Colton asks, his voice laced with urgency.

"In the glimpses the echosphere granted me, I couldn't discern your exact location, but it's dimly lit, perhaps near some body of water. But there's one thing I'm sure of — you both were in the presence of King Onyx," Drew elaborates, causing my heart to plummet. Of all people, why him?

"There's no fucking way we're aligning ourselves with him," Colton declares vehemently. I lay my hand on his, attempting to calm him.

"I'm only conveying what I observed to aid your endeavors," Drew says, leaning back slightly. "My vessel is docked nearby. I can transport all of you to the Sorcerer Realm if you desire. However, you must decide by tomorrow night, for that's when I set sail," she says.

"And if we choose to exclude Nyx from the equation?" I question, anxiety evident in my tone.

"That's certainty an option, but I don't know what consequences it may cause," Drew admits. "The vision I received showed both Colton and Onyx present when your dark magic awakens. You're free to choose inaction, awaiting your birthday. However, that is still months away, and countless lives may be forfeit in the interim. Chaos is set to escalate before any semblance of order is restored."

My gaze drops to my lap, and almost immediately Chepi leaps up, sensing my anxiety and curling up for comfort.

"We'll take the night to deliberate and inform you of our decision by tomorrow evening," Colton states definitively.

Drew nods in understanding. "In that case, I'll grant you some privacy. Nighthold hasn't felt my presence in ages. I've some personal affairs to tend to." As she stands, a weighty sigh of vexation escapes from Colton. Drew gracefully makes her way to the exit, and I quickly bid her farewell, wishing I could ask her more questions. She casts me a playful wink, her lips curling into a mischievous smile before she vanishes from our sight.

I pivot to face Colton, curiosity bubbling. "Considering Drew's inability to channel, how does she move with such swiftness?"

"Lamias, by nature, possess exceptional speed, enabling them to glide over terrain seamlessly. Drew, with her age and immense power, can traverse distances at an astonishing pace. Her inability to channel hardly impedes her," he says.

"I want your opinion. What do you think we should do?" I say, though a decision has already crystallized in my mind. I need his thoughts to validate it, to know we're on the same page.

He brushes a strand of hair from my face, his touch gentle, eyes intense. "Whatever path you choose, I'm by your side. If you decide to barricade us here, to revel in each other's company, indulging in pleasures and waiting for your birthday, I'm all for it." A sly grin lights up his face as he continues, "In fact, I could easily be persuaded into that."

I laugh, wishing we could do exactly that forever. He always knows how to make me laugh, even with the prevailing darkness.

I absentmindedly pet Chepi, lost in thought. The widespread destruction in Zomea replays in my mind, alongside visions of the innocent girl, Anya. Her face under the blood moon still jolts me awake at night. The looming threat to Zomea and Eguina, the innocent lives in jeopardy— it all weighs heavily on my heart. My past haunts me, regret and guilt tugging at my soul.

I cannot bear any more loss when I could have acted to prevent it. I must see this through. I don't know if Drew's vision will come to pass, but I must do everything in my power to ensure it does. I believe I am strong enough to awaken my dark magic. I'm uncertain about Nyx's feelings after everything that has transpired, but I need to get him on board with this too, for the sake of the realms and what lies beyond.

Drawing a deep breath, I confess, "As tempting as that idea is, I can't...not with everything at stake." His arms wrap around me, pulling me close to his chest, holding me like I'm his anchor. "Say the word, my shadow, and I'll move mountains for you."

Gazing into his eyes, resolute, I reply, "I think we need to head back to Cloudrum, back to Tempest Moon, in pursuit of my family's grimoire."

Colton nods thoughtfully. "If come dawn you remain sure of this decision, I'll inform Drew that we're joining her. Using her ship will conserve our energy compared to channeling across vast distances. If we depart by tomorrow night, the Sorcerer Realm will welcome us by mid-morning. Drew's ships are very advanced."

"And what if I decide we need Nyx with us?" I ask, awaiting his reaction.

His emerald eyes darken momentarily then soften. "Then I'll personally see to it that our dear Nikki boy joins our endeavor." The commitment in his voice catches me off guard, but it's the reassurance I needed.

"No, I need to be the one to do it. I have to speak with him," I say, bracing myself for Colton's reaction.

"I understand. Would you like me to send word for him to come here tonight?" he asks. I can tell this isn't pleasing for him, yet he's handling it remarkably well.

"I'd rather go to him. The way we left things the last time I saw him wasn't exactly pleasant. I believe I should speak with him—alone," I respond, feeling Colton tense beside me for a brief moment.

"Whatever you'd like. Rix and Rune should have filled your closet by now. I heard them upstairs rummaging through things a little while ago. I assume you don't want to visit him in my tunic," he smirks. Gods, that would certainly not help convince him to join us.

"Okay, I think I'll go get cleaned up and dressed," I say. I lean in, giving him a soft kiss, then carefully shift Chepi onto the cushion next to me. As he stretches out, Colton begins to pet him.

I hurry upstairs, washing up and doing my best to brush my hair. Rix and Rune are nowhere in sight. Returning to my bedchamber, I find that the once-empty closet is now brimming with various outfits. I choose a cream-colored, long-sleeved gown with a laced-up, olive-colored bodice and matching sandals. It amazes me how they knew my size perfectly.

Sitting on the edge of the bed, I ponder what I should say to Nyx. The thought of seeing him again fills me with anxiety. I quickly ensure my barriers are in place, locking down my emotions.

Perhaps this could work out—for all of us to collaborate. I might even achieve peace between Colton and Nyx, reigniting the friendship they once had. Still, that might be too presumptuous of me. I won't truly understand the situation until I speak with Nyx. It's been months, and so much can change in that time. Perhaps he won't want to assist me. He might even be involved with another woman now. I'm uncertain about what I'll say, but I'm hopeful that the words will come once I assess the situation firsthand.

Letting out a long sigh, I rise. I should inform Colton that I'm ready to go. The sooner I get this over with, the sooner we can make a plan to move forward.

I find Colton and Chepi on the couch. Colton seems lost in thought, and I realize this can't be easy for him. "If you ask me not to go, if you tell me this will be too much for you, then I'll stay. We can manage without Nyx. Like Drew said, everything's an option. We can still search for the grimoire and awaken my magic. The echosphere isn't finite," I tell him, drawing his attention as I approach.

He stands up, wrapping an arm around me and placing a kiss atop my head. "I would never ask you to abandon something you believe in. I can handle whatever comes our way. If Nyx agrees, I'll work with him. Can't guarantee I'll be particularly friendly though," he says with a chuckle.

I squeeze him tighter, the comforting aroma of citrus emanating from him. "Thank you," I reply, tipping my head to meet his eyes.

He smiles softly. "You don't need to thank me. Remember, I know you want to handle this on your own, so I'm asking you to channel directly there and back. You heard Bim last night. There have been attacks in Nighthold. I need you to be cautious."

"I promise I will be. Look after Chepi for me. I'll return before you realize I'm gone."

I offer him a reassuring smile. He leans down, kissing me gently, then steps back to provide the space I need to channel. As the enveloping darkness stirs around me, lifting tendrils of my hair, I hold his gaze until I vanish.

CHAPTER 21
LYRA

My feet touch the cold floor, and I blink a few times. Unintentionally, I've landed in my old room within Nyx's castle. While I could have channeled outside and approached from the front door, this room was the easiest destination to visualize. Pushing down my rising anxiety, I step out into the corridor. Given the time of day, Nyx's study seems like the logical place to begin my search. As I navigate through the familiar yet foreign hallways, a touch of unease fills me—it feels odd wandering through his domain without an invitation.

Reaching his study, I take a moment to steady my nerves. As my hand grazes the doorknob, a voice breaks the silence. "He's not in there."

I startle at the sound of Twig's voice. "Oh..." I falter then recover. "Is he home?"

"No, but he should return soon. Come, I'll fetch you something to drink and eat," Twig offers, motioning for me to follow him. His ethereal silver wings catch the ambient light, shimmering as I fall into step behind him. In the kitchen, he delves into the pantry, seemingly on a mission.

"Twig, you don't need to go through the trouble. I can wait," I reassure him.

"How about a drink at the very least?" he counters, his hand resting on his pudgy purple belly.

I exhale. "Anything strong would be appreciated." I mutter the last part more to myself, but Twig seems to catch on. Handing me a chilled glass of Faery wine garnished with fruit.

"Thank you," I murmur, hesitating for only a moment before taking a sip. While I'm aware of Twig's uncanny ability to manipulate emotions through his essence, I take the risk. If anything, hopefully it will ease my nerves.

"Come, sit. I'll keep you company," he suggests, gesturing to a plush chair adjacent to the drinks cart.

"How has he been?" I venture, and Twig immediately knows to whom I'm referring.

"He misses you, Lyra. Physically, he's fine, but I see the weight he bears. His love for you...is unparalleled. I've never witnessed him care for someone the way he does for you," Twig shares.

It's painful to hear that. Despite the hurt he caused, guilt and longing intermingle within me. I take another deep sip of the wine, pushing those feelings aside.

I have feelings for Colton, and Nyx shattered any potential future between us. Now isn't the time to wade into this emotional mess, especially when lives hang in the balance. There are weightier concerns than my personal feelings.

"I thought you'd despise me," I admit to Twig, casting a tentative glance his way.

His smile broadens, revealing his slightly pointed teeth. "I could never hate you," he assures me.

Distracting myself, I ask, "And Flora? Have you seen her lately?" The question is both an attempt at casual conversation while we wait and a genuine inquiry. I wonder if she ever mentioned running into me.

"She's doing well. She was here this morning before she left for the elders' library," Twig informs me. I can't help but wonder about her latest research interests. It seems Flora spends an inordinate amount of time amid those ancient tomes.

Suddenly, Twig slips off his chair and reaches out, grazing my arm with his hand. "I'll give you some time to gather your thoughts. Once he arrives, I'll let him know you're here," he mentions, probably picking up on the storm of emotions within me. "Help yourself to the drink cart."

The soft patter of his bare feet fades away.

I down the remainder of my Faery wine and start to look through what the drink cart has to offer. It's not limited to whiskey; there's a range of enticing beverages. I opt for something with a sweet edge and pour myself a glass. As the liquid flows, my feet match its rhythm, tracing paths across the dining room floor as I pace. Each passing minute amplifies my anxiety.

Subconsciously, I perform mental checks, ensuring my emotional shields remain intact. Colton might attempt to sense my feelings, and I can't risk that vulnerability right now.

In the stillness of Nyx's home, memories flood me, each sharper than the last. The curve of his smile, the weight of his gaze, the touch of his hands—every recollection stirs emotions that I'm struggling to suppress.

Colton. His name emerges as an anchor, grounding me, reminding me why I'm here. Our newfound bond has been healing, a balm for the wounds Nyx left behind. And yet, standing here in his home, I can't help but question if I've truly moved on or if I merely sought refuge in the arms of Nyx's adversary.

Why does love have to be this complicated? Was it not enough to have my heart broken once, that now I'm teetering on the precipice of risking it again? No, I down my glass and shake my head. I'm not thinking clearly about this. Colton is a good man. He doesn't lie to me, and I care for him, not to mention the amazing sex. I don't want to love either of these men. I am not capable of love anymore. My heart cannot bare it.

I remember the pain in Nyx's eyes the day I told him to leave me be. It was real. Raw. But so was the betrayal, the web of lies he spun around us. Could I ever trust him again? Even if I wanted to? And with the very real risk of hurting Colton in the process? No, I could not.

But now, as I wait in the looming silence, I'm reminded that life isn't merely about black and white, love and hate. There's a spectrum of emotions, and right now I'm caught in its whirlwind.

What if seeing Nyx reopens old wounds? What if it doesn't? What if all it does is confuse me further, muddling the clarity I thought I'd gained over the past few months?

Deep breaths, Lyra.

But the weight of the unknown is paralyzing. What will Nyx say when he sees me? Will he be angry? Relieved? Indifferent? Worse, what if he's moved on? What if he's found someone else? Someone who didn't force him away? I don't care if he has, but I'm afraid of what seeing Nyx might make me feel, because I don't want to feel anything for him.

The decanter clinks softly against the drink cart as I set it down after pouring the whiskey. With swift, deliberate movements, I down its contents, the liquid fire blurring the sharp edges of my emotions. Another pour. Another swallow. But the numbness I'm chasing remains out of reach.

The room's fireplace offers a visual contrast, its warm glow opposing the icy weight settling in my chest. My steps carry me toward it, every footfall echoing the pounding in my head. And then the cold, unforgiving surface of the stone wall greets my back, urging me to slide down to the floor.

My knees press against my chest, my arms wrapping around them, as though trying to hold myself together. Nyx, with all the memories he represents, feels like an uninvited guest in my mind. The last time I was here, the shadows of the past with Aidan were still fresh, casting a dark haze over everything. An unwelcome tear makes its descent, the salty trail a testament to the overwhelming tide of emotions I'm struggling to navigate.

The heavy thrumming of my heart fills my ears. I can't distinguish if it's fear, anxiety, or some twisted amalgamation of both. My breaths come fast, the room feeling as if it's shrinking with each inhalation.

Then a chilling realization strikes. Twig's timely departure after serving me that drink can't be a mere coincidence. Could he have manipulated my emotions, intending to clear the fog of my feelings? I look down at my arm where his fingers grazed me. Did he believe that pushing me to confront my deepest fears and pains would pave a path to clarity?

But instead of enlightenment, there's chaos, an emotional storm I wasn't prepared to weather. If Twig's intention was to help, his methods have left me more disoriented, caught in the throes of an unexpected emotional break. All I can hope now is that the storm subsides before Nyx's return. I bury my face in my knees, close my eyes, and focus on my breathing.

I AWAKEN to the sensation of soft sheets caressing my skin. Instinctively, I stretch out, reaching for Colton, but the space beside me is empty. Panic grips me as my eyes snap open. I'm in Nyx's bed.

I sit up quickly, scanning the room. My gaze settles on Nyx, seated in a chair nearby, attentively watching me. I take a moment to study his appearance. He looks the same, yet there's a noticeable weariness about him. His black hair is disheveled, with strands sticking up haphazardly while others fall across his forehead. A coat of stubble covers his jaw, adding to his tired look, and his hand rests thoughtfully against it. His gray eyes glow upon meeting mine, and I suppress the urge to smile.

"This seems oddly familiar," he says.

"What happened?" I ask, rubbing my temple.

"You had a panic attack," he begins, his voice gentle. "It seems Twig unintentionally induced emotions you weren't prepared for. When I arrived, you were delirious, sprawled on the floor. I thought it best to let you rest here."

Noticing the darkness outside, I'm filled with dread. "Colton..." I begin, tossing the sheets aside, intending to stand. But Nyx's hand reaches out, restraining me.

"Where do you think you're going?"

"I need to return. It's late, and I didn't intend to fall asleep," I explain, my voice shaking.

"To him?" There's an unmistakable edge in Nyx's voice now.

"Yes," I say, trying to withdraw my hand from his. "He will be out of his mind with worry."

For a moment, Nyx simply stares at me, his jaw tight and his eyes filled with a mix of hurt and anger. But then, slowly, he releases my hand. "I see," he murmurs, looking away, but I can sense the walls building up around him once more.

"I didn't come here for this," I whisper, feeling a tug at my heartstrings. Seeing Nyx vulnerable, even for a fleeting moment, has an unexpected effect on me. "I came here because we need your help. Can we focus on that for a moment before I go?"

He nods, his face now composed, the raw emotion tucked neatly away behind a mask of indifference. "Of course, Lyra. I'm listening."

Taking a deep breath, I begin to explain everything – our quest, the threat, and why we need him. I tell him what Drew saw in the echosphere and how it may be our only chance at awakening my dark magic early. As I speak, Nyx's attentive gaze never leaves mine, and I'm reminded of how he always had this knack for making me feel like the only person in the world.

When I finish, there's silence except for the soft crackling of the fire.

"Why should I help him?" Nyx finally asks, his voice devoid of emotion. "After everything he's done to me, to us?"

"It's not about him or us," I respond, meeting his eyes. "It's about a greater threat that affects all of us, including you. I'm not asking you to help for Colton's sake or mine. I'm asking you to help for the sake of everyone in Nighthold, everyone in Eguina and Zomea."

Nyx seems to ponder that for a moment, his eyes distant. Finally, he looks at me and, for the first time since I arrived, there's a softness in his eyes.

"Alright," he says, "I'll help. But after this, I want you to promise me something."

I nod, heart pounding, waiting for him to continue.

"I ask that you consider the possibility that I am, in fact, your destiny." The sincerity in his voice stirs something within me, a deep-seated wonder at the intertwining of our fates.

I take a deep breath and give a small, thoughtful nod. "I promise."

"I'll meet you tomorrow night on the ship," he states, and I rise, preparing to depart.

"You will," I affirm, gifting him a gentle smile.

But his next words halt me cold. "You reek of him, you know." The warmth of my smile evaporates instantly.

"Excuse me?" I counter, incredulous.

"Colton. His scent clings to you. It didn't take you long to seek solace in another's arms, did it?" The accusation, the bite in his voice—it feels like a physical blow.

"Nyx," I begin, attempting to reason, but he cuts me off.

"You should probably address me as King Onyx now."

Taking a moment to collect myself, I refuse to let him see how deeply that affected me. "I believe we've inflicted enough pain on each other, King Onyx. I genuinely hope to see you on the ship tomorrow night. But if not...I wish you all the best." Without giving him the chance to have the last word, I channel.

CHAPTER 22
LYRA

I materialize beside Colton's home, adjacent to the pool. Rain cascades from above, its rhythmic patter a soothing backdrop to my turbulent thoughts. I pause, allowing myself a moment to recalibrate. Looking up, only a handful of the brightest stars manage to pierce through the angry clouds tonight.

Outstretching my arms, I let the rain embrace me, hoping its touch will cleanse the weight of the night from my soul. I lower my shields, opening that intimate mental window, and project my raw yearning for Colton. The atmosphere around me responds, and the familiar tang of his citrus scent wafts to me. Within moments, he materializes mere steps away, his torso bare and those loose-fitting pants that seem to be his favorite.

Our eyes lock, and the magnetic pull is undeniable. No words are needed. With a sudden surge of desire, I bridge the gap between us, wrapping my arms around his neck and surrendering to the urgent kiss that follows.

I press my tongue to his lips, and he yields, allowing me to explore him further. My fingers weave through his damp hair, pulling him even closer. A low growl vibrates from his throat, and I'm compelled to be even nearer. Without breaking our kiss, his hands deftly work to unlace my bodice. I pause and leave a trail of lingering kisses down his rain-dampened chest. Reaching his pants, I tug them downward.

He steps out of them, revealing himself fully to me. I tentatively reach out, feeling the warmth of his considerable arousal before taking him into my mouth. I revel in the taste, drawing him deeper until he reaches the back of my throat. My hunger for him is insatiable, and I find myself wanting even more.

His head tilts back, my name escaping his lips as his fingers weave through my hair, guiding my movements. A deep yearning surges within me, prompting me to seize his hands and tug him down to the forest floor. As he sinks to his knees, our eyes lock in a mutual understanding. Pushing my hands against his chest, I guide him to lie back.

With a swift movement, I gather the fabric of my dress, positioning myself atop him. Guiding his cock to my entrance, I'm overwhelmed by the depth of my longing, a soft moan slipping past my lips as I lower myself onto him. The cool, damp earth presses against my knees, while he fills me, eliciting a raw exclamation from him.

"Fuck," he murmurs, his hands feverishly tracing the contours of my body, desperate for a closer connection. In a sudden move, he seizes the front of my gown, tearing it open. My dress falls away, and without hesitation his hands latch onto me.

He grips my hip firmly with one hand, accentuating my rhythm with a push and pull of his arm as I move above him. His other hand gently traces my collarbone before cradling my breast, his fingers teasing and pinching my already taut nipple. Our bodies glisten, slick from the rain, and the soft, wet sounds as I ride him only intensify my pace. Strands of my hair cascade over my shoulders, brushing against his chest as I lean in, captivated by his glowing emerald eyes. The fervent hunger I see in his stare mirrors the fiery passion burning within me.

Locked in his gaze, I rise and descend, savoring the overwhelming yet delightful fullness of our connection. Colton, with newfound urgency, grasps my hips, urging me to meet him with even more fervor. I tilt my head back, allowing the rain to trace cool paths down my face and over my sensitive nipples. But, as if the forest sensed our passion, the nature of the rain shifts.

The once heavy droplets soften, and upon opening my eyes, I'm greeted by a surreal sight— a shower of flower petals descending from the sky.

Each petal glows, illuminating the surroundings in hues of light blue and purple. I'm awestruck by the sight around us. This is something I've never witnessed before. It feels fantastical, as if I've stepped into a dream. Extending my hand, I watch in awe as the petals settle upon it, creating a delicate mosaic against the rain-soaked earth.

Suddenly, Colton captures my hand, drawing me close before gently flipping me onto my back. My gaze leisurely travels over him, admiring the sculpted muscles of his chest, stomach, and then lower, anticipation mounting once more as I study his thick cock.

"Look at me, my shadow," he commands with a hint of urgency. Our eyes lock in an intense connection, made even more profound as he pushes inside me. The world slows, each movement is deliberate, and each thrust is deep and teasing. As I hold his gaze, Colton drops the barriers around his emotions, and an overwhelming surge of feelings envelops me. The intensity of our shared desires becomes palpable, our emotions intertwining so closely that the line between us blurs. Drawn irresistibly to each other, our lips meet, further deepening the bond that has forged between us.

I tease his mouth with mine, drawing his bottom lip between my teeth and eliciting a low growl that vibrates deep within him as I bite down on it again. His rhythm quickens in response. Suddenly, our kiss breaks. One of his hands anchors into the sodden ground, supporting his weight, while the other ventures downward, finding the sensitive apex of my desire. He watches our union intently, his touch bringing me to the brink of exquisite pleasure.

Gazing upward, the sky seems almost otherworldly, with dark clouds serving as a backdrop for the mesmerizing dance of rain and luminescent petals. As my orgasm nears, my focus returns to Colton. Our hands reach for each other, and as he leans down I embrace him, his damp hair creating a curtain around us.

"I'm close," I breathe, and he meets my eyes, holding the connection as an overwhelming rush of pleasure overtakes me. My cries are captured by his lips, and he follows me over the edge, finding his own release.

He remains inside me, his fingertips grazing my dampened skin. Gently, he sweeps the wet tendrils of hair from my face, his palm tenderly cradling my cheek, his thumb skimming my bottom lip.

"With the stars as my witness, I promise you, Lyra, no one will ever hurt you again," he murmurs, eyes intent on mine. Drawing my bottom lip between my teeth, I realize he must have sensed my emotions before.

"I know," I whisper back, finding comfort in the sincerity of his vow.

He pulls out of me gently and collapses beside me, pulling me close. I nestle into his side, resting my head on his shoulder, both of us catching our breaths.

"Colton," I say, exhausted, "why are petals falling from the sky?"

He strokes my back tenderly, drawing me even closer. With his free hand, he retrieves a glowing petal from my tangled hair, inspecting it closely. "It's the Celestial Blossom," he says with a hint of wonder. "It's an extremely rare phenomenon. It occurs when the emotions shared between two souls in this forest reach such an intensity, such depth, that the very spirit of the Dream Forest responds. The petals? They're its tribute to that bond."

I take the petal from him, studying it for a moment before letting it drift onto his chest.

"So the forest is...echoing our emotions?" I venture.

He nods, his eyes shimmering with intensity. "Exactly. The Dream Forest is bearing witness to our connection, celebrating it alongside us. Our tether must amplify its effects. I've only heard tales of this, never experienced it."

"It's breathtaking," I murmur, staring up at the vast night sky. As I listen to the rhythmic beating of Colton's heart and feel the comforting rise and fall of his chest, a sense of serenity washes over me. I drift into sleep, feeling an undeniable sense of belonging — as if even the forest itself confirms that this is where I'm meant to be in this moment.

I WAKE up nestled in the comfort of Colton's bed, his arms securely wrapped around me, Chepi snuggled at my feet. I don't recall how we ended up here, but it's clear Colton channeled us back after I'd drifted off in the forest. I shift to face him, finding his eyes already on mine.

"You're awake," I comment, a hint of surprise in my voice.

"It hasn't been long," he replies. The dim light accentuates the details of his face, and I realize the events of last night are somewhat of a blur.

"Ready to talk about it?" His question is laden with meaning, and I immediately understand the reference.

Taking a deep breath, I start, "I..." Words elude me.

Colton gently interjects, "All I need to know is whether I should expect to see Nyx on the ship tonight."

"Nothing happened," I rush to assure him, needing him to believe it. His gaze remains fixed on me, fingers idly playing with strands of my hair. "I'm not sure if he's coming. Things were left...unresolved. But I have a feeling he might."

"I see," he says, distant.

"I don't want any secrets between us," I say, my voice faltering but determined. "If the roles were reversed, I'd want you to be honest with me about everything that transpired." Taking a deep breath to steady myself, I continue, "When I arrived, Nyx wasn't there. Twig made me a drink, and as we talked, something about his essence—his magic—triggered a panic attack. The anxiety, the uncertainty about seeing Nyx again... It all weighed heavily on me. I must have drifted off while waiting because I woke up in Nyx's bed."

At this, I notice Colton's jaw tighten, a flash of distress in his eyes. "And?" His voice strains, revealing the unease beneath.

Pushing past the lump in my throat, I say, "And I immediately left his bed, requested his help, and hurried back here. I half-expected you to come after me, given how long I was gone."

He takes a moment before replying, "I wanted to, every minute you were away. But you said you needed to see him alone, and I wanted to respect that." The earnestness in his eyes brings a smile to my face.

"When I awoke in his bed, the only thing racing through

my mind was how out of place it felt. I yearned to be back here with you. I tried my best to persuade him to join our cause. I believe I might've succeeded, but there's no denying he harbors bitterness and pain from everything that has transpired. Before I departed, he made it clear I should address him as King Onyx from now on," I share, looking for any sign of reaction from Colton.

To my surprise, he bursts into laughter. My eyebrows knit in confusion, and I playfully slap his chest. "Why's that so funny?"

Through his chuckles, Colton manages, "Oh, Nyx... King Onyx? It just seems so characteristic of him. Always the dramatic one. I guess it's his only way to assert some control over you after everything that's happened."

I cast my gaze downward, memories of the previous night flooding back—how Nyx gripped me, clearly not wanting me to go. Perhaps I've now wounded him as deeply as he once did me. Maybe, in some twisted way, we're now on equal footing. I hate thinking of it as a tally.

"What preparations do we need to make before meeting Drew later?" I ask.

"I need to consult with Dorian. You can accompany me if you wish or stay here, maybe pack some clothes or relax," he suggests.

A pang of sadness hits me. Our time in the Dream Forest has been far too brief. I've always dreamed of this place, and now, just as swiftly as we arrived, we're departing again. "I'd prefer to remain here, if that's alright. I want to explore a bit more. Who knows when we might return?"

He plants a kiss on my head. "Do as you please. But if you venture far, take Rix and Rune with you."

"I will."

255

CHAPTER 23
COLTON

I lean down, capturing her soft lips with mine. After a quick shower and slipping into my clothes, there are things that demand my attention before we depart. Pulling back, I let my eyes roam over her one more time. Damn, that flawless skin, her tousled hair spread across my sheets – a sight I wouldn't mind waking up to every day.

But I can't indulge in those thoughts, especially not after she vanished on me yesterday... Nyx. That bastard. He and I are overdue for a discussion.

"Enjoy your day, my dark enchantress," I remark with a sly wink. The hint of a pout that forms on her lips whenever I tease her with a pet name never gets old. It's evident she secretly relishes it. The urge to claim those pouty lips once more is tempting, but if I give in, I know I won't be leaving this bed – or her – anytime soon.

With a final lingering glance, I channel away.

Without wasting time on formalities, I channel directly into his study. It's where I'd typically find him at this hour. I hear his irate voice before I even lay eyes on him, and the mere

256

knowledge that my presence irks him ignites a smirk on my face.

"Well, if it isn't a great morning, Nikki," I quip, turning to confront him. His expression is more tormented than usual. The loss of Lyra seems to have shattered him, and for a fleeting moment I almost feel a twinge of pity – then I recall our history, and that sentiment vanishes. "You look like you've missed some sleep. I've been up quite a bit myself as of late, though for entirely different reasons." I let an unabashed, smug smile stretch across my face, thinking of Lyra in my bed. At that, Nyx rises from his chair, tension evident in every line of his body.

"Is there something you need, Colton?" His voice drips with disdain when he says my name, and it's crystal clear I've touched a nerve.

"Got any plans to accompany Lyra and me on our little jaunt?" I ask, deliberately casual.

He narrows his eyes. "I can't exactly trust you to watch over her by yourself, can I?"

Leaning in closer, I reply with a smirk, "She seemed more than satisfied with my care thus far." His eyes darken, visibly affected.

"You might have had her in your bed, but I'm certain I'm the one she was thinking of. She loves me. To her, you're a temporary balm, a fleeting distraction from the anguish I've caused. And soon, she'll see that and come running back," he retorts with a bitter edge.

I refuse to let him rile me up. "Believe me," I say, voice low, "I had her so consumed with pleasure that the only name she could scream was mine."

The room's temperature drops noticeably, a clear indication that Nyx's control over his magic is wavering. The realization strikes me: this bastard might genuinely harbor feelings for her. I wouldn't have believed him capable. Despite the smoothness of his response, I don't miss the tight, white-knuckled grip he has on his desk.

"So, when's the ship setting sail?" he finally asks, trying to regain some semblance of composure.

"Before dusk," I state firmly, "whether you're there or not."

He meets my gaze with a defiant one of his own. "I'll be there," he snaps.

I decide it's time to cut the encounter short. There's no need to drag out this pissing match any longer. I prepare to channel, leaving him in the cold, but I hear him before I go.

"Just remember, Colton, every touch, every kiss, she learned from me. You're merely retracing my steps."

The door to Dorian's shop creaks open under my forceful push, announcing my arrival with purpose. What Nyx said still scratches at the back of my mind, fueling my irritation. But right now there are more pressing matters to attend to.

Front and center, Trilok and Goaty manage the shop's daily dealings. Goaty, with her uncanny ability to read anyone, immediately catches onto my mood. "Well, someone's feathers are clearly ruffled," she observes, her voice dripping with sarcasm and a smirk playing on her lips. The old woman has always had a sharp tongue and keen eye.

Trilok is ever the mediator. "Dorian's in his usual spot," he offers, casting me a sympathetic look. I knew I always liked the talented young Fae.

I spot Dorian immediately, hunched over a long table scattered with schematics, rare metals, and the glint of various tools. The air is thick with the smell of molten metal and aged wood, mixing with the distinct scent of magic-tinged leather. The rhythmic clang of a hammer against steel resounds from the opposite end, where a few apprentices are hard at work forging.

Dorian, always absorbed in his craft, doesn't notice me

immediately. He's engrossed in a design laid out on a work-bench, his hands deftly moving over various tools and metals. As I approach, he looks up, his sharp eyes instantly assessing my state.

"Rough morning?" he inquires with a raised brow.

"Nyx," I mutter by way of explanation, my voice low and laced with barely restrained annoyance.

Dorian nods, understanding the implication. "I see. If you're here for the supplies, they're ready. But if you're looking for a sparring partner to take out that frustration..." He smirks, indicating a set of weapons hanging on the wall.

I can't help but grin at that. "Maybe later. For now, let's focus on the task at hand."

He chuckles, motioning for me to follow, and we delve deeper into his workshop.

Dorian pauses in front of a hefty cabinet, its doors resembling cage bars. With a key pulled from his pocket, he unlocks it, extracting a compact sheath. He places it into my hand, and the weight is deceivingly light given its size, which is no longer than my own palm. The sheath, crafted from the deepest black leather, has a meticulously etched L—a signature for Lyra.

"I've custom-made this for her," Dorian declares, his voice betraying a touch of pride. "Your briefing on her abilities was quite enlightening."

Compelled by curiosity, I pull the handle. A blade emerges, cascading outward, black as a moonless night sky. Even in the workshop's subdued lighting, it gleams ominously. Its edge looks wickedly sharp, promising lethality in every strike.

Dorian watches my fascination before speaking again. "This blade," he says with care, "is crafted from Starforged Steel and is laced with essence crystals sourced directly from the Dream Forest's innermost sanctum. Its core is designed to resonate with its user's deepest emotions. When Lyra wields this, she isn't just holding a sword; she's channeling a conduit for her own potent magical energies."

Experimentally, I flick the blade, watching as it shrinks back seamlessly into its sheath. Dorian nods in approval. "The sword senses its master's intentions. It remains discreetly hidden on demand and readies for combat when the situation calls."

Slipping the sheath onto my belt, I meet Dorian's gaze. "This is perfect. She'll love it," I assure him.

AFTER A PROLONGED DISCUSSION WITH DORIAN, and ensuring Bim would oversee the Dream Forest in my absence, I barely managed to scrape together enough time to pack some essentials.

Throughout the day, Lyra's fortitude in maintaining her barriers impressed me. I only sensed her once, a whisper of melancholy brushing against my mind.

Upon my return, I questioned her about her day, needing to know she was alright. Her response, detailing a simple walk with Chepi and some relaxation, didn't quite sit right with me. I couldn't shake off the feeling that she had been lost in deep thought, perhaps wrestling with her own demons. This tether, as powerful as it is, frustrates me in its limitations. I crave a deeper connection, a way into all of her thoughts.

I yearn to know the secrets she holds close to her heart, the thoughts that weigh her down. Even when her face is illuminated by a smile, I can't miss the lingering sorrow in her eyes. It's a constant reminder of the pain she's endured. I wish I had the power to extract all her pain and anguish, and I'd like to torture everyone who has ever dared to hurt her.

I drop my pack onto the bed and sit, pulling Lyra close to stand between my legs.

"What's on your mind, my shadow?" I ask, wrapping her in my embrace and taking a deep breath, letting her sweet scent of young roses and honeysuckle fill my lungs.

"It's... I'll miss this place," she admits.

"But aren't you eager to see your home again?" I prompt.

"Tempest Moon hasn't felt like home in a long time. But Lili... If she's still there, I'm excited to see her," she says, sounding vulnerable. I sense her trepidation, probably old memories associated with Samael resurfacing. I might not know the depths of it, but the glimpses I've gotten are enough to tell me it was bad.

Gently, I cradle her face, pushing away those tousled waves. "Listen to me," I say, locking onto those entrancing eyes, "I swear, I won't let anything harm you."

She bridges the distance, her lips meeting mine with a tender kiss. Every part of me wants to lay her down and lose myself in her, but I resist. This isn't the time for that.

When she pulls away, a void instantly forms, reminding me how addictive her presence has become – her scent, her essence. "Is it time to go?" she asks, her fingers unconsciously tracing the outline of her necklace. It's a subtle tell; she twiddles with it whenever anxiety looms.

Perhaps she's wondering whether Nyx will make an appearance. While I'm certain he will, I don't disclose that. Not from a desire to hide anything but to shield her from potential disappointment. I'm well aware she sees Nyx as an ally, essential to our mission's success. I only hope that's the sole reason she wishes for his presence. Their past hangs heavy on my mind.

"Yes," I reply, my voice firm, "it's time."

She moves out of my hold to fetch Chepi. As I heft our

pack onto my shoulder, I pull her close, her arm wrapped around Chepi. In a breath, we channel.

We touch down on the dock, and Lyra immediately heads for the ship, a hint of excitement evident in her stride. I follow her up the ramp to the deck where Drew and Adira await, accompanied by several mortal crewmen. I see Lyra's gaze sweep over the deck, searching. It doesn't take a genius to know who she's looking for, and I'm aware he hasn't arrived.

Catching Drew's eye, she raises an eyebrow questioningly. I nod slightly, confirming my unspoken promise.

Drew clears her throat. "Shall I show you both to your rooms? Or would one suffice?"

Before I can voice my preference, Lyra speaks up, "Separate rooms, please." I reel from her sudden declaration, my mind bursting with questions. But now isn't the time nor the place, so I put on a façade of indifference.

"I'm glad you're both aboard," Drew says, genuine warmth in her voice. "This is the right choice."

A familiar, unsettling aura reaches me before the voice does. "Indeed, the correct choice," Nyx drawls from behind.

Lyra's reaction to him is almost imperceptible: a quick turn of her head, her breath hitching momentarily. But to me, it's a blazing flare of jealousy.

"Good of you to grace us with your presence, King Onyx," Lyra says, her voice steady.

Biting back a retort, I silently fume.

Drew intervenes, "I'll lead you all to your quarters. We'll be underway shortly."

She glides inside and descends a set of steps, with Nyx quick on her heels. I gesture for Lyra to go ahead, and she complies, her lips set in a tight line. Staying close behind her, I'm hyper-aware of every subtle shift and sound around us. The briny scent of the sea is pervasive, blending seamlessly with the aroma of freshly polished wood. The ship's gentle movement causes Lyra's hair to dance in the breeze that wafts through the small windows. The realization that we won't be sharing a room tonight stings, but I respect her wishes, even if they remain unspoken. The atmosphere feels thick, charged with unspoken words and lingering emotions.

Drew addresses Nyx first. "We have the captain's quarters for you," she states, indicating a grand door adorned with golden details. She then turns to Lyra and me, pointing to two rooms side by side. "For the two of you, the finest guest rooms on board."

I can feel the weight of Nyx's gaze as Drew speaks. It's clear he's surveying the arrangements, perhaps weighing the implications of our separate rooms or assessing the quality of his own quarters. But my focus remains on Lyra.

She hesitates momentarily before her room, taking a moment to absorb its facade. I can only imagine the thoughts swirling inside her head, especially with all that has transpired.

"I hope none of you get seasick. Have a good night," Drew says, smiling. Her red eyes linger on mine for a moment, and I narrow my eyes at her. I'm sure she's picking up on the complexities of the situation. I wait for Lyra to enter her room, closing the door. I glance over at Nyx and push into my own quarters.

The room is adequate. I've never been one for fussing over sleeping quarters. Throwing my bag onto the desk, I let myself collapse onto the bed. The weight of my emotions threatens to sink me into its depths. Falling for Lyra? It seems I might be falling deeper than anticipated. The boundary I swore not to cross, I've overstepped, and now I'm neck-deep in the aftermath.

She isn't truly mine. We've never defined what we are. It evolved from a genuine friendship into something more intimate. But now, damn it all, I fear I'm falling in love with her. Her request for separate rooms blindsided me, fucking gutted me. Sure, I have called her mine, but I don't know if that's truly what she wants, and if she were to change her mind and find her way back to Nyx, I couldn't hate her for it.

Above all, I want her to find happiness. If that means she's going to be with me, then I'll cherish her and guard her with my life. But if Nyx really is her person, this light that can save her, then I'll find the strength to bear it, as long as she finds her happiness.

CHAPTER 24
LYRA

I lean against the wall, staring out of the porthole window in my room, mesmerized by the waning hues of orange and pink as they merge with the deepening blue of the sea. My room, though dripping in luxury, feels almost too grand for my current mood. Polished wooden panels line the walls, and there's a spacious bed in the center, its deep-blue sheets reminding me of the vast ocean outside. Soft, silken pillows invite me to rest, but I feel restless. I change into a nightgown to try and get more comfortable.

Lying down on my back, I let Chepi settle next to me, his tiny warmth a source of comfort. My eyes fixate on the wooden panels above, thoughts swirling in my head. I long to be in Colton's arms tonight. But I thought I was making the considerate choice, given Nyx's presence. I didn't want to flaunt our newfound intimacy, not when the air is already thick with tension. But the brief flash of pain and surprise I felt from Colton when I made the request haunts me. Hurting him was the last thing I wanted. Maybe it's for the best that I sleep alone tonight, allowing me some space to gather my thoughts.

Closing my eyes, I let the gentle sway of the ship lull me into a light sleep. When I awaken, I'm still on top of the covers, the cold having seeped into the room. I'm sure it's this sudden drop in temperature that roused me. I snugly tuck Chepi under the covers, ensuring he's warm. Grabbing a throw blanket from the foot of the bed, I wrap it around myself, slip into my boots, and venture outside, craving the fresh night air.

Silently, I open my door and tiptoe past the rooms of Colton and Nyx. The stillness suggests they're deep in sleep. Climbing the steps to the deck, I'm struck once again by the grandeur of the ship. The deck gleams, every wooden plank polished to perfection. The ship's mast stands tall and proud, crowned with crimson sails that billow gently in the night breeze. Intricate rigging crisscrosses above, lanterns hanging and casting a warm, golden glow all around. Their gentle swaying in rhythm with the ship's movements adds a serene feeling.

Spotting a few crewmen on one side, I head to the opposite side, hoping for a moment of solitude. With no one in sight, I settle down on the deck, pulling the blanket tighter around me and leaning against the ship's side. The sea, an abyss of inky blackness, is barely visible, but the sky more than compensates. A tapestry of stars sparkles above, and the moon, in all its luminescent glory, casts a silver sheen over the water. It's a sight to behold, and for a moment I lose myself in its beauty.

It's hard to believe sometimes that the gods created all of this.

"Can I join you?" A voice startles me, and I look up to see Nyx approaching, dressed in his usual all-black attire. He reeks of whiskey and looks as if he hasn't slept in days, and I remind myself not to feel bad for him.

"Sure. You're King Onyx and can do whatever you wish," I

say, a tinge of sarcasm in my voice. He sits down next to me, closer than I anticipated, and leans back against the wall.

"You don't have to call me King Onyx. I was being an asshole," he admits, letting out a sigh.

"You think?" I turn my head to study his face, the bags under his eyes. He meets my gaze, his gray eyes shining even more brightly in the darkness of the night.

"Lyra... I'm sorry for everything. Truly. I know it's too late to fix anything, but I want you to know I regret lying to you. I regret hurting you. Trust me, I'm living with the consequences of my actions."

That takes me by surprise. I pull my lower lip into my mouth and look back out at the sea, unsure of what to say. After a long pause, I finally respond, "I forgive you."

Holding a grudge against Nyx only hurts me. I don't want to be angry, and I don't want to feel hurt by him anymore. It's time to let go. Nyx clearly isn't sleeping, and maybe my forgiveness will offer him some solace, if not a good night's rest.

"Lyra, you have no idea how much that means to me." I shift my gaze to the stars, taking a deep breath, the salty sea air filling my lungs. "Sometimes, we hurt the ones we love the most. Maybe it's because they're close enough to feel the pain. Or perhaps we take them for granted, expecting them to always be there no matter what. And sometimes they are. Some endure this pain out of fear or shame, but forgiveness is a choice. It's a gift we offer, not just to those who've wronged us but also to ourselves." He reaches out to touch my face, but I pull away, turning my gaze elsewhere. We sit in silence, each of us lost in our own thoughts.

I often wish I could find the strength to forgive everyone who has hurt me. I'm not there yet, but I cling to the hope that someday I will be. The pain and resentment I harbor toward Aidan, Samael, and even my own mother for her indifference to my suffering under her watch remains fresh when I'm not working to keep it buried. Yet, in the midst of this turmoil, I find space to forgive Nyx. As much as I try to deny it, he was my first love. While I wish I could forgive solely for the sake of love, it's more for my own peace. I realize that to truly heal from the wounds he inflicted, I must let go. So, for my own sake, I choose to forgive him.

Nyx shifts suddenly, pulling me from my thoughts. He turns to face me fully, his eyes intense. "Lyra, princess, I love you," he says, gripping my chin to force our eyes to meet. "Do you remember when you said you were mine?"

I wrench away, catching the unmistakable whiff of whiskey on his breath.

"You're clearly drunk," I snap.

"I'm not," he shoots back, voice tinged with desperation. "Look at me, damn it!" He tries to grab my face again, but I dodge his hand, leading him to seize my wrist instead. "I've never loved anyone but you, Lyra. Only you. You need to understand that I need you. You *will* be mine."

Releasing my wrist, I quickly stand, heart racing. "I'm going back to bed," I declare, trying to keep my voice steady. "You should too, before you do something you'll regret come morning."

He gets up as well, taking a step toward me. "Lyra, please understand I never meant to hurt you. You need to know how I feel." I back away, unsettled. I've seen signs of his possessiveness, but this intensity is new and unnerving. He clearly hasn't slept and has been drinking too much tonight.

Nyx's voice grows desperate, almost haunted. "You've read my father's journal, Lyra. The prophecy...must weigh on you, as it does me. You think you can be with him? Well, he's not the one destined to be with you, destined to save you. You're mine." The finality of his last words sends shivers down my spine.

This isn't the Nyx I know. Deciding there's no point in prolonging this confrontation, especially given his state, I turn to leave. Maybe he won't even remember this tomorrow. But he grabs the edge of my blanket, pulling it away.

As I pivot to reclaim it, he seizes my wrist, his eyes roaming over me. "Gods, Lyra, I've missed you," he mutters, yanking me into his embrace. Torn between the urge to flee and a twisted nostalgia, I momentarily allow his warmth to envelop me. Somewhere deep down, there's still a weakness for him, a trace of what once was.

Taking a deep breath, I plead softly, "Nyx, let me go."

He releases me abruptly, shoving my blanket at me. "I can't believe you let him touch you," he spits out, retreating to the ship's opposite side.

Wrapping myself in the blanket, I hurry back to my room. As I settle into bed, my pulse races, and my hands tremble visibly in the dim light. What the fuck happened?

The image of Nyx's possessive eyes lingers in my mind. One thing he said sticks with me. Whatever was written in Callum's journal does indeed haunt my mind. Destined for darkness, destined to be with his son—Nyx. How can I push it aside? Frustration surges within me, and I slam my fists down on the bed. Where did Callum even get this prophecy, and how can it be true? If I'm truly destined to be with Nyx, then why am I so drawn to Colton? I can't deny my past feelings for Nyx, the depth of our connection, but that's not how I feel now. With Colton, there's an undeniable pull, an unexpected spark, a fire that I can't ignore.

I really can't sleep now, and I need a distraction. I focus on practicing my magic. Instead of stressing about the two men on this ship. I need to concentrate on honing my skills. I must be ready when my dark magic wakens—whatever that will bring. I focus on the candles flickering about in my room, drawing the flames to me, I gather them into my palm, creating a tiny orb of fire. I play with it, tossing it upward and guiding it back to its wick repeatedly until fatigue finally takes over and I fall asleep.

SOMETHING'S COMING! A chill creeps down my neck when a voice whispers in my ear. "Don't come back," it seems to say, but the gusty winds steal the clarity. The voice is joined by others, echoing from the dark recesses of the tunnels. I'm determined to uncover the reason behind these recurring visits. This time, I refuse to let fear dominate. I hasten my steps, my fingers grazing the cold, stone wall, guiding me to the familiar spot.

It doesn't take long before the rhythmic thudding starts. At first, I mistake it for my own heartbeat echoing in my ears. But it's not. Lub-dub, lub-dub. Drawn to it, I follow the sound. It magnifies, resonating with the accelerating beats of my own heart. The environment shifts — I'm getting closer. The pungent iron tang of blood becomes palpable. Underfoot, a sticky fluid makes each step a challenge, and the tunnel as before takes on the semblance of dark, writhing roots and branches.

Deep breaths, I tell myself, as dread crawls up my spine. The chilling feeling of impending doom envelopes the tunnel, compelling every ounce of my courage to keep moving forward. Overhead, bleeding branches drip crimson, staining my clothes and skin. I sidestep the treacherous tangle of roots below.

Suddenly, the heartbeat's tempo diminishes, drawing my attention to a faint glimmer ahead — a beckoning glint of light. Its pull is undeniable. But the whispers mount in volume, evolving into familiar, terrifying screams.

My mother's voice pierces the cacophony, "Don't touch it, Lyra!"

Then Luke's desperate whisper, "Don't come back."

Another voice, unfamiliar, bellows, "Run!" I'm overwhelmed.

"Don't touch what? Run where?" I shout back, defiant.

Without warning, a powerful gust propels me toward the light. But then an eerie silence reigns. The whispers, the wind, all cease. Straining, I discern a distant thud, thud, thud. Out of the blue, an unseen force collides with me, sending me sprawling. The wet ground greets my back harshly, and a scream rips from my throat as I scramble to regain my footing.

My eyes fly open at the nudge of a wet nose to my cheek. I blink a few times as Chepi nudges my face again and licks me.

"Aw, come here, squish." I draw him close, turning onto my side. "Thanks for waking me. Things were getting a bit intense in Zomea."

He responds with a lick then stretches out, settling down for more sleep. Dawn isn't far off; a soft glow filters through the porthole, lighting up my room. Leaving Chepi to rest, I decide to rise and prepare. I'm uncertain when we'll arrive in Cloudrum today, but I want to be ready.

I slip into black leather pants with my black boots then don an off-white tunic and cinch a black bodice around my waist. This attire would be far more practical for combat than a gown, especially if anything unpredictable arises during or en route to Tempest Moon.

Chepi, with his tail wagging enthusiastically at the foot of the bed, catches my attention. "Alright, go have fun but stay close. After speaking with Colton, I'll meet you on deck. If you run into Drew, she might have some breakfast for you," I tell him.

I cautiously open the door a crack to survey the hallway. With the rest of the doors shut tight, I release Chepi, watching as he silently soars up the staircase.

Hesitating, I find my eyes drawn to Nyx's door, pondering how his night might have unfolded. Instead of knocking on Colton's door, I simply turn the handle and step in, hoping to avoid any chance of disturbing a possibly still-sleeping Nyx.

As soon as I enter, my eyes lock onto Colton. Awake and shirtless, the sight of his chiseled physique still leaves me breathless. Perched at the edge of his bed, he's donning his pants, busy lacing up his boots. He stops momentarily as he catches my entrance, eyes meeting mine. Drawn to him, I bridge the gap between us, climbing onto his lap. As he encircles me with his arm, I lean in, capturing his lips with mine. Breathing in his scent, I'm reminded that last night was the first we've spent apart in months. I missed him more than I anticipated.

"I missed you too, my shadow," he murmurs, his lips tracing a path down my neck. An involuntary shiver runs through me as he nibbles my earlobe.

"I want you, every inch of you," I admit with a soft moan.

"That can certainly be arranged," he responds with a hint of mischief, gently flipping me onto my back. As he hovers over me, our gazes lock. I lose myself in the unique freckles within his eyes – little specks of gold and brown swirling within the vivid emerald irises. How did someone as breathtakingly beautiful as him become mine? Is he mine?

His hand drifts up my thigh, fingers reaching for the laces at my waist. As he moves to untie them, I catch his wrist, stopping him.

"What's wrong?" he asks, concern evident in his eyes.

Drawing a breath, I reply, "It's not that I don't want this – believe me, I do – but not here, not with Nyx so close by." He props himself up beside me, and I push up on my elbows to face him. "That's why I slept in my own quarters last night. I wanted to be with you, but we can't let anything jeopardize the mission. We need Nyx's cooperation, and flaunting our relationship feels...cruel. He's struggling with this. Last night, he..."

I search for the right ones to convey my thoughts.

"He what?" Colton asks, brows furrowing with a mix of curiosity and concern. "What happened last night?"

"Nothing really happened. I was on the deck, taking in some fresh air because I couldn't sleep, when he joined me. He'd had too much to drink and seemed...out of sorts. It's not like him," I explain, but I can see Colton's face hardening with every word.

"How did he act? What did he do?" he questions, trying to keep his voice calm.

I sit up straighter, hesitating for a moment. I don't want to hide anything from Colton, but I'm also wary of causing tension. "Promise me you won't confront him about it, okay? We need to get along. He was drunk, and it seemed like he hadn't slept for days. He was kind one moment then shifted suddenly. He grabbed me, but it's okay. He wasn't himself. He's in pain, Colton," I plead.

His eyes flare with a protective rage. "I'll keep quiet, but only because you've asked me to. If he ever lays a hand on you again, he'll regret it," he says, his voice firm.

Hoping to diffuse the tension, I gently touch his cheek. He leans into my hand, planting a tender kiss on my forehead. "Thank you," I whisper.

Colton's demeanor might sometimes seem possessive, but I truly believe it's his way of showing he cares. He has far more self-control than he admits. "Anything for you," he murmurs, taking my hand and delicately kissing each fingertip, drawing a smile from me.

"You know, I'm really proud of you. As tempting as it is to get under Nikki's skin, you made the right choice not to share a room with me last night. If we're going to make this work with him, we all need to be understanding and shouldn't flaunt what we have in front of him," Colton concedes.

My smile widens, and I pull him closer, kissing him deeply, lingering on the moment and knowing it might be the only intimate moment we share today.

Eventually, I pull away and stand, saying, "I'll see you upstairs," and offering him a playful smile. He dramatically clutches his heart and falls backward onto the bed, feigning devastation. I can't help but giggle at his theatrics as I head for the door.

In the hallway, Nyx's door remains shut. As I approach, it swings open, and he steps out, nearly colliding with me.

He extends an arm, motioning for me to proceed. "After you," he says. I pause to meet his eyes briefly before moving ahead. He looks as if he managed to catch some sleep after our encounter last night, which is a relief. I ascend the steps to the deck, which bustles with activity. Crew members move with purpose, and I spot Drew at the ship's helm, Chepi with her. When she turns, I see she's feeding him some kind of biscuit. Typical. She grins at my approach and sets down Chepi, who eagerly finishes his treat.

"Restful night, I presume?" she jests, glancing between Nyx and me.

"Something like that," Nyx replies. I glance his way, but he avoids my eyes. I gravitate to the railing, taking in the familiar sights of Cloudrum's coast with its rocky shores and the subtle scent of pine on the breeze.

"You all should be able to channel from here to your castle. I plan to dock my ship and accompany you for the time being," Drew proposes. The idea excites me. Not only will I get to know Drew better, but she might also serve as a useful intermediary between Nyx and Colton.

"Sounds perfect. When do we depart?" I inquire.

Colton appears behind me, his fingers brushing my back ever so briefly before moving ahead. "Imminently, if we're all prepared," he says.

Drew nods in agreement. Nyx's lips tighten, but he offers a curt nod. "Very well. King Onyx, would you channel me to the castle?" Drew emphasizes Nyx's title with a hint of flattery.

Without a word, Nyx grasps Drew's hand. A swirling dark wind envelopes them. As they start to fade, Drew's crimson gaze finds mine, ending with a conspiratorial wink. I can't help but chuckle to myself.

Colton draws me close, wrapping an arm around me. He tenderly cradles my face with both hands. "Remember, nothing will ever harm you when you're with me. You're always safe," he says, sensing the anxiety gnawing at my heart about returning home. I give him a soft smile in response.

"I know," I murmur. Chepi flies into my arms. Nestling against Colton's chest, I close my eyes, allowing the sensation to envelop us as we channel to Tempest Moon.

CHAPTER 25
NYX

Drew and I land in the pathway in front of the castle moments before Colton and Lyra. My eyes fixate on Colton's hand as it moves from her lower back to her arm, holding her for a moment longer than necessary. A surge of jealousy bubbles up, and I fight the urge to order him to remove his hand.

Taking a deep breath to quell my emotions, I ask, "Shall we head inside?"

I remind myself of her destined place beside me. There was a moment last night, a flicker of what used to be. When I pulled her close and felt her hesitate against my chest, I knew her feelings for me still lingered. Though she might resist, I am resolute. By the end of this journey, she'll be by my side, as I vowed to Colton.

"Yes, let's," Lyra says, advancing toward the front doors. She stops momentarily, and I fight back the instinct to approach her, to offer the comfort of my embrace. The weight of the painful memories she must associate with this place, particularly given our last visit, presses on my heart. A fleeting smile

276

touches my lips as I notice Colton's hesitation, most likely clue-less to the depth of her past sufferings here. When she falters within, needing someone to rely on, I'll ensure I'm right there for her.

Without knocking, she pushes open the doors — after all, this is her domain. Drew steps in swiftly behind her, and I follow, deliberately entering before Colton.

"Princess Lyra," a servant's voice echoes, laced with surprise. "I'll inform Kaine of your arrival." The servant hastens up the stairs.

Naturally, Kaine is present, serving as the head of the Regency Council. No doubt he's reveling in the interim power, acting as a placeholder ruler until Lyra reaches her rightful age. The man's always had a penchant for power plays. And with this title, it's inevitable he'll secure a spot on the Luminary Council. Just my luck. But to my surprise, Lyra appears unfazed by this revelation. Perhaps she had anticipated this move.

She doesn't hesitate. Taking the initiative, she begins her ascent up the stairs, showing everyone that this is still her domain. We fall in step behind her, tracing her confident steps to the throne room. It's somewhat unexpected, given the cruel memories that room holds for both of us, particu-larly with Samael's torment. Yet there's a shift in her demeanor – a strength that wasn't as apparent before. It seems the once timid and reserved Lyra might truly be a thing of the past.

She boldly strides into the throne room, and there stands Kaine in conversation with the young servant we met earlier. "Kaine," I murmur disdainfully under my breath.

He raises an eyebrow, smirking. "It's Lord Regent Kaine now actually, King Onyx." He approaches with an air of arro-gance, not that I'm surprised. "Lyra," he addresses her with feigned concern, "we've been fraught with worry. It's a relief to see you've returned safely."

She counters coolly, "It's Princess Lyra actually."

I can barely suppress my grin at her assertiveness. Kaine seems momentarily taken aback, but he quickly regains his composure. "Of course, Princess Lyra," he corrects himself, his voice dripping with condescension. "To what do we owe this unexpected visit?"

Lyra stands her ground, unflinching. "This is my home, isn't it?"

He tilts his head, attempting a show of magnanimity. "Naturally, so will you be gracing us with your presence indefinitely?"

She nods, undeterred. "Myself and my friends will remain for a brief period. We have matters to attend to. I'll be reclaiming my old quarters. Please ensure suitable accommodations are arranged for everyone else."

I glance at Colton, catching a flash of approval in his eyes. This new side of Lyra, strong and unyielding, is undeniably attractive.

Despite her tough facade, I can detect the subtle signs of Lyra's inner struggle. The almost imperceptible tremor in her hand, the way she fiddles with her necklace, all reveal the undercurrent of emotions she's battling within. Yet, to the unsuspecting eye, she remains steadfast and strong.

Suddenly, Drew steps forward, drawing attention. "Lord Regent, it's come to my understanding that my daughter, Citlali, has been here. Might I inquire about her whereabouts?"

Lyra's gaze sharply turns to Drew, surprise evident in her eyes, clearly unaware Drew was going to ask this.

Kaine, idly toys with the gems on his sleeve. "Ah, that troublemaker. Yes, she did stir up quite the commotion in the village. At present, she's confined to the dungeons. Should you wish, I could make arrangements for a meeting."

"We would all like to speak with her," Lyra interjects, her voice carrying an assertiveness I hadn't expected. Every time I witness this newfound dominance in her, I can't help but be intrigued about how the imminent awakening of her dark magic will further change her. If she chose, she could rule Eguina beside me as queen – with Cloudrum pledging loyalty to her and Nighthold to me. Coupled with her emerging dark magic, our reign could be unparalleled. Still, I recognize it's her choice. For now, my aim is to gently weave my way back into her life.

Kaine, sensing his position, nods in agreement. "Very well. When you're prepared, I'll ensure a guard escorts you to her cell." His voice barely hides his reluctance, but he knows he can't deny her this.

Unable to contain my own curiosity, I press, "And Samael's body? What became of it?" I'd relish the thought of spiting on that fucker's grave.

I notice Lyra's hand quiver even more at the mention of Samael. The urge to soothe her is overwhelming, but I hold back, focusing on Kaine.

He appears genuinely puzzled. "I'm not certain what you're referring to."

Frustration bubbles up. "His corpse. It was here in the throne room when we last departed – right there." I point to a conspicuously refurbished section of the wall.

Kaine's surprise seems genuine, unsettling me further. "I apologize, King Onyx, Princess Lyra. While I'm aware of the ordeal you encountered during your previous visit, we haven't found any trace of King Samael's remains."

The thought is confounding, and I scramble through my memories of the last moments in this room. During the chaos

279

after Lyra channeled, my primary concern was chasing her, especially once Chepi resurrected and I could take him to her. Handling Samael's remains seemed secondary. I had assumed the palace staff, many of whom loathed him, would see to it – be it burial or cremation. Citlali, seemingly harmless with Samael gone, wasn't even on my radar. Now, it seems she must've claimed his body, yet another vile scheme in her relentless pursuit to torment Lyra.

But he was dead. I'd witnessed the life ebb from his eyes, watched him crumple lifelessly. Panic seizes me momentarily at a horrid thought. What if we had been wrong? What if he was not truly gone? But the thought is too inconsistent. If Samael still lived, he would've already seized the throne and plunged everything into chaos.

It's clear Citlali has taken his remains, likely a part of some twisted game. When we confront her, I intend to find out.

Lyra, deflecting the conversation from Samael, shifts the topic. "Is Lili still here?" she inquires.

Kaine, recognizing the name of the woman who's devoted her entire life to the service of the castle, replies, "Yes, of course, I believe she's gathering supplies in the village with a few other staff members."

"I'd like to see her in my chambers. Can you send word for her to meet me there when she returns?" Lyra's voice is almost steady, but I detect a subtle tremble that seems to go unnoticed by Kaine. He merely nods.

Colton interrupts the lingering tension, "Can we see Citlali now? There's no point in delaying."

While I expect Kaine to find some excuse to avoid the request, he simply responds, "Yes, of course." Gesturing at two guards stationed by the entrance, he adds, "They will take you to her." He then casts a lingering glance in Lyra's direction, an expression that reads more calculating than concerned.

"Should you require any further assistance, don't hesitate to ask."

Lyra acknowledges him with a nod, and we fall into step behind her as she leads the way, following the guards. The corridor is silent, the air thick with unspoken thoughts and tension.

Suddenly, I halt, compelled to address something. "Stop," I command, surprised when everyone obeys. Standing directly behind Lyra, I meet her gaze as she turns to face me. "We need to talk. Privately."

Her eyes scan the faces of our group before answering. "Alright."

I spot an adjacent door leading to what looks like vacant guest chambers. Without hesitation, I push it open, ensuring its emptiness. "We'll continue in a moment," I tell the group, casting a pointed look at Colton before ushering Lyra inside. Though Colton's expression remains inscrutable, I can sense the simmering displeasure beneath, and I flash him a smile.

Inside the chamber, I swiftly guide Lyra to the room's far end, ensuring we're well out of earshot from any potential eavesdroppers beyond the door. Her eyes, searching mine with evident concern, prompt her to ask, "What's wrong?"

Pausing for a brief moment, I reply, "I wanted to give you a breather. Seeing Kaine, discussing Samael... It's a lot."

Her eyes, now glistening with tears, meet mine. "It's...overwhelming," she whispers. Unable to resist, I enfold her in my embrace, the feel of her is amazing, and I bend my head down and breathe in her sweet scent.

"Everything's going to be okay," I assure her. She leans into the solace of our closeness.

But Lyra steps back and out of my arms. "I know it is. I appreciate the moment, Onyx. You're right I needed it, but I need to stay focused. It doesn't matter how I feel. There are more important things that need our attention," she says, her voice firm yet soft.

I nod, brushing away her tears with my thumb, grateful when she doesn't recoil. "Right," I agree, allowing a hint of determination to seep into my tone. "Let's go talk to the bitch about where she hid the body."

A faint smile graces her lips at my words. As she heads to the door, I lightly place my hand on the small of her back. She doesn't shrink from the touch, solidifying my hope that it's possible we can mend what was once broken.

Continuing down the torch-lit corridor, the oppressive atmosphere of the dungeon is a familiar reminder of the time I spent down here, helpless to help her. I try not to remember her screams, the feeling of not being able to protect her, I clinch my fists at my side. The cell that once imprisoned Lyra now holds Citlali, who stands with an air of forced nonchalance.

As she catches sight of us, a facade of cheerfulness lights up her face, "Mother! What brings you to my humble abode?" Her tone drips with saccharine sweetness, masking the venom beneath.

Drew, not one to be swayed by Citlali's charade, retorts sarcastically, "It's nice to see that associating with a deranged man, obsessed with his own sister, has brought you to such great heights." The biting edge in her voice is unmistakable, and I can't help but stifle a chuckle at the sharpness of her words.

Citlali sneers, "You understand nothing, Mother."

With a stern expression, Lyra steps uncomfortably close to the cell bars and demands, "Where is Samael's body?" Citlali's gaze flickers over me before settling on Colton, a mocking smile tugging at her lips.

"Ah, look who it is—his little bird. Found a new man to stand beside you, have you?" She sizes Colton up, her voice dripping with disdain. "What's so special about her? Why do men like you keep gravitating to this bratty princess?" I resist the urge to enter her cell and extract the information from her by force. Instead, I lean casually against the wall, feigning indifference.

Suddenly, with a forceful push of her palm, Lyra sends Citlali crashing against the stone wall. The impact is so fierce it leaves a visible crack. "I'll ask once more. Where is Samael's body?" Lyra's voice is steady, authoritative. Her mastery and control over her magic astonishes me; she's clearly improved. Slowly, Citlali picks herself up, dusting her garments with a haughty air.

"And why," she mutters with a sly grin, "should I reveal anything to you?"

"Your life," I answer before anyone else can. "Keep playing games, and it might be the last thing you do."

Citlali smirks, deliberately running her tongue over her sharp canines. "Thinking of joining me in here for a little fun?"

"You're revolting," I retort.

Drew takes a step forward, her posture radiating both authority and a mother's concern. "Citlali, beneath all your anger and bitterness, you're still my daughter. I hope that some vestige of decency remains within you. Assist us, and we might find a way to help you in return."

A mocking laugh escapes Citlali. "And what do you propose, Mother?"

Drew squares her shoulders, determination evident in her eyes. "I'll repeal your banishment. If you cooperate, once this is over, I'll welcome you back to the Lamia realm."

Citlali raises an eyebrow, intrigued. "How noble of you," she replies, sarcasm evident in her voice. "But how can I trust you after all that's transpired between us? Perhaps your promise is as fleeting as the love you once claimed to have for me."

Drew's expression tightens, the pain visible in her eyes. "I never wanted things to turn out this way. I always hoped for reconciliation, for a chance to mend what's broken between us. I don't like this path you've chosen to go down."

Lyra steps closer, reinforcing Drew's plea. "You know, Citlali, the choices you've made have led you here, to this cold cell. But this offer... It's a chance to change, to be part of your family again."

Citlali leans against the back wall of her cell, clearly pondering her options. Her eyes, filled with a mix of defiance and contemplation, flicker from Drew to Lyra, and then to me. "And what if I refuse?"

"Then I have no problem killing you," I mutter.

Citlali casts a sly glance in my direction. "Being at your mercy, King Onyx, would be a blend of pleasure and pain, I imagine. A tantalizing proposition indeed."

That makes my blood boil. If this were Nighthold, she'd already be dead, information be damned. No wonder she served Samael. They are both equally deranged.

Colton steps forward, his patience visibly waning. "Enough games. Either you share what you know, or we leave you here to rot."

Her laughter, eerie and mirthless, reverberates through the stone walls. "Ah, the quiet one finds his voice," she mocks.

Suddenly, the bars she clings to begin to glow a fierce red, emanating intense heat. She yelps in pain, dropping her grip and stumbling back. The unmistakable scent of singed flesh fills the air.

"My apologies," Lyra says coolly, her eyes flashing with controlled rage. "I seem to have inherited the short temper of a bratty princess." The heated bars serve as a stark reminder of the untapped power she wields... Fuck, I want her.

"You know, I will tell you what you wish to know, but only because I can't wait to see the expression on your faces when you learn the truth," Citlali declares, a malevolent grin creeping across her features. I instinctively move closer to Lyra, bracing for the possibility of her magic flaring up in response to Citlali's provocations.

"Your betrothed still draws breath," she reveals with a gleeful cackle.

"Betrothed?" Colton interjects, his voice laden with confusion.

"Samael. He lives, likely still searching for ways to possess you," Citlali continues, seemingly enjoying every second of our dismay.

"How can you be so certain?" Drew challenges.

Amused, Citlali glances between Lyra and me. "In your lover's spat, you were so consumed by concern for each other that you both departed without ensuring Samael's end," she taunts.

I remember that night vividly. The blood, the chaos, the swirling emotions. It all played out like a nightmare. But there was no way... We watched him fall.

"He was at death's door," I growl, my voice low and dangerous. "I saw it with my own eyes."

Citlali tilts her head to the side, studying me with those dark, red eyes. "Eyes can be deceived, especially in the midst of chaos. But what do I know?" she muses, that same wicked grin pulling at her lips. "After you two dashed out like scorned lovers, I approached him. I expected to find a corpse, but instead I found a very weak, very much alive Samael. And with a little...assistance, he was revived enough to flee this castle."

"But why save him?" Lyra demands, her voice barely above a whisper, her face pale.

Citlali shrugs, a nonchalant glint in her eyes. "It's in my best interests to keep him around. Besides, the chaos he brings is always entertaining."

The dungeon grows silent. Samael alive. The thought is irritating, but the thought of him wanting to "own" Lyra, as Citlali put it, fills me with a fury unlike anything I've ever known.

Chepi catches my eye as he nuzzles Lyra's leg. He seems to intuitively understand her emotions. Without another word, Lyra picks him up and swiftly exits the dungeon. She doesn't meet my eyes as she hurries past me. Colton follows closely behind her. As much as I yearn to comfort her, there are more pressing matters at hand. The last person to possess Lyra's family grimoire was Samael. I'm determined to uncover his whereabouts, regardless of the methods required.

Drew and I exchange glances, and I know she's here with the same intent. I'll cooperate for the time being, but if her tactics prove ineffective I won't think twice about entering that cell and giving Citlali a taste of the torment she subjected Lyra to.

CHAPTER 26
LYRA

Without exchanging a word with Colton, I keep my composure and rush to my bed chamber. If I believed Colton could find his way to my room without me, I'd use Chepi to make myself invisible. I should grab them both and channel there now.

Instead, I keep my chin up. I don't want to look distraught, and I avoid eye contact with the servants as I pass. Thankfully, no one stops me. Once inside my room, I unravel.

I release Chepi and attempt to regulate my breathing, but the panic is already consuming me, making my skin scalding hot as if I'm about to combust. Seeing my distress, Colton steps in front of me, gently cupping my face and tilting it upward to meet his gaze. "Breathe," he commands. I focus on the sprinkling of freckles in his eyes, trying desperately to steady my frantic heart, before I lose control of my magic and burn this entire castle to the ground.

Suddenly, a soothing warmth envelops me, and the distinctive scent of Colton becomes more pronounced. He projects his emotions on to me with such intensity that they begin to intertwine with my own. My heart rate steadies, and I draw a deep, calming breath, all the while holding his gaze.

"How did you do that?" I ask, letting the calming feel of him wash over me.

"I wasn't sure it would work, but I dropped my shields and tried projecting my feelings, hoping they might calm you if you could sense my emotions strong enough," he explains. His arms encircle me, and I nestle my face into his chest, finding comfort in being this close to him.

"I couldn't bear to be down there any longer. There are so many questions still unanswered, and Samael, if he has the grimoire... It's just too much," I confess, my voice wavering.

"But you don't have to shoulder everything yourself," Colton soothes. "Drew and Nyx stayed behind. They'll do whatever it takes to get the information we need from Citlali."

Lifting my head to meet his eyes and drawing in a deep, steadying breath, I try to center myself. Colton, sensing my internal struggle, gently prompts, "Talk to me. Whatever's on your mind, let it out. I'm here for you."

"I can't wrap my head around it. How can he not be dead? And if he isn't, why isn't he here, trying to seize power? Why would he run?" I say, my voice trembling with confusion.

"Perhaps he realized he'd crossed a line and assumed the council wouldn't back him," Colton muses.

Shaking my head, I reply, "You don't get it. He's mad and fixated on me. He doesn't just want a marriage; he craves the power of my dark magic. He's always several steps ahead, plotting who knows what."

Colton's voice grows firm. "He won't get to you or your magic. We'll find him, get your grimoire back, and I swear I'll put an end to him." I hope it turns out to be true.

Do you think the others will come up here once they're

done with Citlali?" I ask, the thought of going back to the dungeons unsettling me.

"If you want to stay here and maybe take a bath, get comfortable, I can head down and see how things are progressing. I'll return as soon as I know something," he offers, sensing my hesitance.

"Alright," I reply, and he slowly pulls away from me. He gently kisses my lips and eyes me one more time, as if he thinks I'm not in my right mind. I give him a small reassuring smile, and satisfied by that he turns to leave. He nods at Chepi as he heads out.

"Keep her safe while I'm away." Then he's gone.

Alone in my room, I take in the surroundings. It's been ages since I've been here. Everything is as I left it, yet it feels different, as if it's wrapped in a layer of the past. Chepi silently follows me into the bathing chamber, and his presence always comforts me.

Deciding to heed Colton's advice and trying to relax, I begin to fill the tub. The hot water is inviting, and I sink into it, letting it soothe away some of the day's tension. Chepi settles by the door, always keeping an eye out.

I think I started having a minor panic attack earlier. That's the second time this has happened now. Thankfully, Colton was able to calm me somehow through our tether. I don't like feeling out of control of my emotions like that. I lie back and close my eyes. How is it possible that Samael's alive? I'm kicking myself for not making sure he was dead, but my father... I can't remember exactly what he said, but he insinuated that he believed Samael to be dead too. Did he lie, or does he have no connection to him anymore?

Why does all this chaos keep unfolding? I wanted to stay in the Dream Forest, wanted to spend my days lounging among the magical creatures there and my nights having amazing sex with Colton. I wanted to meet a fucking Pixie. Damn it all.

Frustrated, I stretch out, hardly noticing as water spills over the tub's edge.

Anger bubbles up, thinking of Samael still out there, and the impending awakening of my dark magic. And whispers suggesting I won't be able to handle it don't help. Then there's Nyx, suddenly pulling me aside earlier. The tormenting memories in the throne room were something he likely shared, and though his gesture provided momentary comfort, I don't want him to get the wrong idea. I hope for friendship with him and harmony between him and Colton.

I don't care what the prophecy says. I can't imagine choosing Nyx over Colton. I'm not Z and don't want them reliving the past through me either. Something serious would have to happen for that destiny to come true.

Once my dark magic is fully awakened, if I don't choose to be with Nyx will I really destroy us all? Maybe his light can save me without us being together. Maybe a friendship is enough. Fuck prophecies—I don't even have my dark magic, yet I can understand why the dark sorcerer before me was so misunderstood.

Taking a deep breath, my thoughts focus on the root of it all: Samael. The sleepless nights, the relentless fear, the burden of shame — it started with him. And if that's where it began, it's where it should end. Once I embrace my power, my first act will be to put an end to him, once and for all. That dark magic he craves so badly, I'm going to give it to him in the worst way imaginable.

The water in the bathtub begins to boil, and I suddenly realize that my own unchecked emotions and magic might scald me. I leap out, my skin burning to the touch. Grabbing a towel, I dry off quickly and pull a robe from the closet. As I begin to pace my bedroom, a flood of thoughts threatens to pull me into a deeper spiral. When did my thoughts turn so dark?

Fortunately, a soft voice interrupts my inner turmoil.

"Lyra?" Lili gently asks, peeking into the room.

I rush to her, wrapping my arms around her neck. The comforting scents of lavender and vanilla surround me, that smell that will forever remind me of home. "It's so good to see you. You look well," Lili remarks, inspecting me as I step back.

"I've missed you," I confess, moving to sit on the edge of my bed. She joins me, and we spend the next couple of hours effortlessly falling into conversation, updating each other on everything that transpired during my absence. Lili has always felt like a second mother to me, and confiding in her brings a deep sense of comfort. I'm grateful she steers clear of discussing the unsettling events from our last encounter.

Lili looks thoughtful for a moment. "You know, with Samael out of the picture, the library should be open to you. Many of your father's old journals are still there, waiting. I know you spent time with him in Zomea, but if you're still grappling with doubts about his intentions, perhaps diving into those journals could give you clarity or peace of mind."

I had almost forgot with everything that's happened that Lili was reading through all of my fathers old journals, looking for answers.

"Did you ever uncover anything else noteworthy in them?" I inquire.

"No, nothing that stood out too much. But he seemed very captivated by Zomea, often going on about the source of all magic and something about unlocking gates. It was all a bit confusing," she says, causing my eyebrows to raise in intrigue. Maybe she's confusing gates with unlocking the bridge.

"The source of all magic? And which gates?" I press, eager for details.

Lili shrugs slightly, her expression contemplative. "I can't be certain. He doesn't mention discovering anything specific, but he keeps referring to his search for the source of all magic, implying he was on a quest to find it in order to unlock these so-called gates. He repeats it several times. It's...strange, to say the least. Perhaps you could bring it up the next time you see him? After everything transpired during your last visit, I took a hiatus from the castle. Things took a turn for the worse here," she adds, a shadow crossing her features.

"Are things better now with the council stepping in and Kaine staying here as regent?" I ask.

"Yes, Kaine has certainly brought some stability back to the Sorcerer Realm," Lili says thoughtfully, her fingers gently pushing back strands of my hair. The touch is so reminiscent of simpler times, back when she would style my hair and offer motherly comforts.

"He's doing his best, but he's aware he's not the permanent solution. Once you come of age, everyone expects you'll take the throne. Will you?" she inquires, looking into my eyes with a mix of hope and concern.

I don't have the heart to tell her we are going to awaken my dark magic early and I might never come back. "I'm not sure what I'm going to do yet. A lot has happened, and I still have time to decide," I say instead, and it's mostly the truth.

Lili studies my face for a moment, probably sensing there's more beneath than what I'm letting on. With her nurturing nature, she has always had a way of reading between the lines when it came to me. "Promise me you'll do what's best for you, Lyra. You've faced so much, and all I wish for you is happiness and peace," she says softly, her eyes filled with genuine concern and love.

"I will," I say, letting a smile spread across my face and it's not forced.

"I overheard some of the servants mentioning guest room preparations. Who's the other man you came with, and what's the situation between you and Nyx?" Lili's voice is laced with keen interest.

I let out a soft chuckle, searching for the right words. "Well, it's complicated. I'm not really committed to either of them. Nyx hurt me, though I've since forgiven him. But Colton... Lili, he radiates a genuine warmth and honesty that's rare. And, not to mention, he's undeniably attractive and makes me laugh. The idea of love feels so complicated right now. Sometimes I wonder if I'm not cut out for it. For now, I'm trying to enjoy the good moments and face each day as it comes."

Lili's eyes soften. "Lyra, your heart is vast. You've always spread love and understanding, whether to people or animals. No matter what you've been through, your heart has always remained kind. Such a heart is meant for love, and you deserve someone who can love you just as deeply."

I'm not so sure anymore. The girl Lili once nurtured seems to be fading away. My heart has grown harder over time, but I can't bring myself to tell her that now. Instead, I offer her a small smile.

Colton strides in without knocking. Lili, caught off guard, quickly rises from her seat. I suppress a chuckle as I introduce them. Lili, seizing the opportunity, insists on taking Chepi with her, citing a night of bonding and treats. I know she probably misses him a lot. As she makes her exit, Chepi trotting by her side, she promises to see me later. Before closing the door, she sneakily gives me a thumbs-up and winks, ensuring Colton doesn't see.

"Did you manage to take that bath I suggested? How are you feeling now?" Colton inquires, settling down next to me on the bed.

"I did, and I'm feeling much better. You were away for

quite a while. Learn anything useful?" I ask, eager to know more.

"We did. And unfortunately we didn't have to resort to any form of torture," he reveals, a hint of regret in his tone. I find myself conflicted. While part of me wants her to pay for her actions, another part recognizes that she's a small player in the grand scheme of things. Letting go might be the wiser choice...at least for now.

"Drew has a way of being an intimidating interrogator. Coupled with the looming threat of Nyx's violent tendencies, Citlali was quick to spill what she knew," he says, a smirk pulling at the corner of his mouth.

"And? Do we know Samael's location? Does he even possess my grimoire?" I press on, anxious for answers.

"I believe we've discerned his destination. First thing tomorrow, we'll devise a plan and pursue him," he declares.

"Why wait until tomorrow? We can prepare and strategize now," I counter quickly.

"Because the upcoming days will be difficult. We need to track down your grimoire, handle Samael, and then determine how to awaken your dark magic," he explains, a grin taking over his face.

"And..." I prompt, hungry for more information.

He leans in slightly. "We all felt that, tonight, you deserve some levity. Tomorrow's challenges will be daunting enough. It's time to do something fun. Drew's joining, and I even extended an invitation to dear old Nikki." His laughter fills the room.

"Where are we headed?" I ask, curious.

"Alchem Hollow," he answers, his eyes shimmering with mischief. The village lies on the edge of the Black Forest. My memories of it are faint, limited to glimpses from a carriage when I was a child. The thought excites me.

"It's almost ironic. One day, I could ascend as the queen of Cloudrum, yet I'm unfamiliar with the village closest to my home. While tales of Princess Lyra circulate, few could match the name to my face. How can I be expected to lead when most don't truly know me or my values? And now with whispers of my dark magic..." I muse more to myself than to him.

Colton reaches out, gently cradling my face. "They'll adore you, Lyra. But only if and when you decide the crown is what you truly want."

"When do we head out?" I ask, swiftly rising from my seat, still draped in my bathrobe.

"As soon as you're prepared. A servant guided us to our chambers, and we're all adjacent to one another in the east wing. I'll freshen up and change, then we can reconvene here once everyone is set. Does that work?"

"Sounds perfect," I affirm with a smile. He gives me with a swift peck before making his exit.

The emptiness of my room feels strange without Chepi, but I move along to get ready. I brush through my hair, letting it fall naturally in loose waves. Skimming through my closet, my eyes settle on an emerald-green gown, reminiscent of Colton's eyes. Sleeveless with a fitted bodice and a daring slit up one thigh, it's a perfect choice. Slipping it on, I make minor adjustments in front of the mirror, pleased with the reflection staring back.

I head to the balcony and watch as the sun sets over the gardens and listen to the soft chirps of the birds. I find myself wishing I could invite Rhett along. Technically, I could channel to the Lycan Realm and attempt to reach him, but that feels like an overwhelming task. Besides, he likely has his own life and pack politics to navigate. I hope he's well and that Aidan's absence has improved things for them. Once I get a moment, I'm determined to pay him a visit.

If tonight is truly the last chance for fun before embarking on our quest to awaken my dark magic, then I'm determined to be carefree. For tonight, I'm granting myself permission to set aside everyone else's concerns. I'll prioritize my own desires and simply do as I wish.

A knock at the door disrupts my thoughts, sending a jolt of anticipation through me. When I swing the door open, I'm met with Nyx, immaculately dressed in black.

"Hi," I greet, a hint of nervousness seeping into my voice, but I'm not sure why.

"May I come in?" he inquires, and I realize I'm inadvertently obstructing his way.

"Yes, of course." I move aside quickly to grant him entry.

"You look beautiful," he says, advancing further into my room and giving me an appreciative once-over.

"Thank you," I reply, straightening up.

"Are you ready to visit the Center Isles tomorrow?" he inquires as he steps out onto the open balcony.

I follow him and ask, "Do you believe Samael is there? Why would he choose that location above all others? Colton didn't mention that," I respond, looking out toward the horizon. "He just said we'd discuss details tomorrow and that tonight should be about having fun."

Nyx leans against the balcony railing, the cool night air tousling his hair. "The location has always been a touchy subject for Colton."

I turn to him, my curiosity piqued. "Because of Z?"

A hint of surprise flashes across Nyx's features. "He spoke of her?"

"Not in depth. But I'm aware of her, and I know she died in the Brysta Trenches...with you," I add gently, noticing the pain that briefly crosses his face.

Nyx meets my gaze squarely. "It was a tragic accident," he says, his voice heavy with emotion.

"I believe you," I say softly, reaching out to touch his arm. "You don't have to explain anything to me."

He clears his throat, shifting slightly. "It's the Brysta Trenches that make the Center Isles an ideal hideout for Samael," he says, steering the conversation back to the present issue.

Curiosity bubbles up within me again. "Why would he choose the trenches, knowing full well that magic doesn't work there?"

"Given his injuries, Samael likely sought refuge in the trenches to recuperate. It offers him a sanctuary where others can't exploit magic to track or attack him," Nyx explains thoughtfully.

"That makes sense," I reply slowly. "But it's also risky for him, isn't it? Going to a place where he himself can't use magic?"

Nyx nods. "It's a double-edged sword. While he's vulnerable without magic, so is anyone coming after him. In the trenches, it's all about sheer strength, wit, and cunning. Without magic to aid you, even simple tasks become perilous. Samael probably believes it's fair ground since everyone would be at the same disadvantage."

I consider this for a moment. "I don't need magic to end him."

"I can see that you've grown stronger, both in skill and character," Nyx observes, breaking the brief silence between us. His tone is measured, but a hint of curiosity tints his words. "You trained intensely in Zomea, didn't you?"

Searching his features, I'm taken aback by the realization that he might not know much about my time there. "Every single day," I confirm.

He steps closer, and I can feel the intensity of his presence. "And you and Colton, how did that transpire?"

I hesitate, gauging how much to reveal. But the weight of our history urges me to be honest. "When Drew brought him to aid in my training before the blood moon ceremony, I couldn't stand him. But when I unlocked the bridge and was ready to face Zomea on my own, he stepped in without hesitation. I thought he had ulterior motives, but time proved otherwise."

Taking a deep breath, I continue, "I didn't just jump into bed with him, like you said, Nyx. After everything that happened between us, my heart was shattered. I'm still mending it. And Colton...is a good man. Whatever animosity you may have toward him, you can't deny his sincerity." I watch his face, bracing myself for any potential outburst.

Nyx's eyes search mine, a vulnerability piercing through the usual mask. "I can't undo the pain I caused, Lyra," he admits, pausing to find the right words. "But if you gave me a chance, I'd spend every moment trying to make it right."

I swallow hard, Nyx's gaze remains fixed on me, the familiar intensity of his glowing gray eyes piercing through the defenses I've built. "Every day, I regret letting you go," he continues, voice soft yet heavy with emotion. "I never intended to hurt you, Lyra. I was blind, lost in my own bullshit. I wish I could turn back time. I wish I had fought harder for you, for us."

My breath catches in my throat, emotions swirling within. "Nyx," I start, taking a slow inhale. "So much has changed..." I trail off, and he places a finger to my lips silencing me.

"Shh, don't say anything right now. Be open to the idea that you are destined to be with me. Whatever this is with Colton, I can forgive it, for us," he says.

I take a step back, removing his hand from my face.

"You can forgive it?" I echo, my voice dripping with disbelief.

"Yes, Lyra. I will forgive you for everything if you just allow me to hold you, let me show you I can be the one to mend your heart." He reaches for me again, but I shake my head, resisting.

"Nyx, I'm the one who forgave you. I didn't do anything wrong. You don't need to forgive me for Colton. What the fuck does that even mean? There's no more 'us.'"

There's a quick knock at the door, and then Drew glides into the room. She looks stunning in a long black gown with little rubies on the bodice. They sparkle red, like her eyes.

"Sorry, am I interrupting something? Should I come back later?" Drew asks, her crimson eyes shifting between Nyx and me. I move inside from the balcony.

"No, we were admiring the sunset. Colton should be joining us soon, and then we can head out," I reply, though Drew gives me a quick, skeptical glance, as if sensing there's more to the story. Regardless, she takes a seat at the small table by the window, and I join her in the opposite chair. I'm thankful she interrupted us when she did.

Nyx remains on the balcony, his silence speaking volumes. Truly, if the fates have decreed that Nyx and I are destined to be together, they have a strange way of showing it. Every time I believe we're making progress, like we could have a friendship, we seem to end up at odds again.

Colton makes his entrance, and my heart skips as I notice the glimmer in his eyes when they land on me. It's clear he wants to approach, likely to embrace or kiss me, but a quick glimpse of Nyx lingering on the balcony makes him hesitate.

"Everyone ready to go?" he inquires.

Rising to our feet, Drew and I exchange glances. "Yes, but I'll need one of you to channel me there. It's been a very long time since I passed through the village, and I can't quite recall the way," I admit.

Nyx steps in, inching closer to me. "I'll guide you. Colton, you can assist Drew. Let's rendezvous outside Lore's Bindings."

Colton's eyes meet mine, seeking assurance. Although part of me wants to refuse Nyx's offer, I nod in agreement, offering Colton a reassuring half-smile. He gently takes Drew's hand, and for a brief moment the familiar, intoxicating citrus scent of Colton fills the room. Then they vanish.

Nyx pivots to face me, his eyes earnest. "Lyra—"

I raise a hand, stopping him before he can continue. "No, Nyx. This evening is meant for everyone to have a good time. I don't want any apologies, explanations, or arguments. I want peace, everyone to be happy, to coexist without tension. Is that too much to ask?" I exhale, the weight of my emotions evident in my voice.

Nyx smirks, raising an eyebrow. "Expecting harmony in one night, Princess? Life's not a Faery tale, but I'm game to play along...for now."

I don't even know what he means by that, but before I can say anything back he grabs my waist, pulling me tighter to him than necessary. His darkness envelopes us with his sweet earthy scent, and we channel with the wind.

CHAPTER 27
LYRA

We touch down in Alchem Hollow, outside of Lore's Bindings. I soon realize it's a bookstore – the name is clever indeed. The village buzzes with life, exactly what one would expect of a Sorcerer Realm settlement. Crooked cobblestone streets are bordered by aged, leaning buildings that host an array of magical shops. Above, floating lanterns glide languidly, their gentle light reflecting off the shimmering surface of a river that winds through the village center. The mingled aroma of campfires and herbs fills the air, making me smile. Being among fellow Sorcerers is heartening.

"I knew you'd love this place," Colton observes, noting my joy and beckoning me to walk alongside him. Gratefully, I distance myself from Nyx. Drew, to my relief, engages Nyx in conversation, and they trail a bit behind us.

"I'd always dreamt of visiting these shops when I was younger," I share with Colton, watching the lanterns dance overhead. "But I was always restricted. I could only glimpse them from our carriage, left to conjure up tales of the wondrous items they might contain."

He looks at me, a hint of sadness in his eyes, understanding the confines of my upbringing. "Well, tonight, you're free. Let's explore to your heart's content," he says, his voice full of warmth.

The energy in the village is alive. Groups of people are huddled together, trading spells or exchanging vials of unknown potions. Children dart through the streets with tiny, sparkling creatures trailing behind them, their laughter echoing in the crisp night air.

A sign ahead reads, "Mystic Crystals & Rare Stones," and next to it is another displaying "Brews & Elixirs of Alchem Hollow." I'm pulled toward a stall where an elderly woman is selling woven dreamcatchers, each one infused with its own enchantment.

Every so often, a patron exits a shop with a scroll, carefully sealed and radiating magical energy, while others haggle over the price of an antique grimoire or a rare magical artifact.

"I think there's a potion shop around this bend," Colton says, gently guiding me through the crowd. "And further down, a renowned seer. I've heard she has the gift of unveiling the deepest desires and truths of one's heart."

I look over at him, excitement evident on my face.

"Let's check it out!" I say, eager to dive into the magical wonders this village has to offer.

We round the bend, and an old wooden sign comes into view for The Potion Parlor.

"Let's go in there," I practically squeal. I've seen potions and tonics brewed before, but only on rare occasions. I find it incredibly fascinating.

Glancing back, I spot Nyx and Drew engaged in conversation with a vendor under a tent, a curious scroll in his hand. Pivoting to Colton, I arch an eyebrow in curiosity.

"Let them be," he suggests. "They'll find us later. Let's explore the shop."

Upon entering, the sight overwhelms me. Glass bottles of varying shapes, sizes, and colors line dusty wooden shelves, and the rich aroma of spices fills the air. As Colton and I go our separate ways down the aisles, I occasionally pick up intriguing potions, reading their descriptions.

Nightshine Nectar: Infuses the drinker with a soft luminescence, lighting up their vicinity in the dark. Mirthful Muddle: A playful potion causing temporary, harmless fits of laughter in its consumer. I can't help but chuckle, imagining slipping this to my mother or Silas right before one of their insufferably long dinners. I would have loved to have access to this as a child. Elixir of Euphoria: Uplifts the consumer into a state of gleeful abandon for several hours. Serendipity Syrup: Bestows fleeting bouts of luck upon the drinker, leading them into fortunate situations.

My laughter at the Serendipity Syrup's description catches the attention of the shop's proprietor, an older gentleman with spectacles resting atop a pronounced nose and a gray mustache. "What tickles your fancy, Miss?" he asks.

"These...really work?" I reply, slightly skeptical.

He offers a knowing smile. "Potions are a revered craft. If they weren't effective, customers wouldn't return."

Locating Colton amid the shelves, I find him engrossed in some bottles, occasionally letting out a chuckle. "Ever sample these?" I ask.

"Indeed." He grins. "Much like in Nighthold with our Stardust beverage and other magical brews. The main distinction? We infuse our elixirs with our innate magic. Here, potions are meticulously brewed and enchanted. But, remember, too much of anything is never good."

I smirk. "In that case, I'll take a hundred vials of the

Serendipity Syrup and another hundred of this Elixir of Euphoria!" I laugh.

I snatch the bottle from his grasp, curious.

"What's this?" I scan the label. Whimsical Whiff: This potion, upon uncapping, exudes a fragrance evoking the inhaler's most cherished memory.

I arch an eyebrow, challenging him with a playful smirk. "And what would your nose catch, I wonder?"

Colton leans in, his voice a sultry whisper. "You."

My heart skips, but I prod further, feigning innocence. "A young rose garden? Perhaps honeysuckle in bloom?"

His eyes glow slightly as he shakes his head. "I'd be reminded of your come, intimately intertwined with me."

A hot flush creeps up my neck, and I steal a glance at the shopkeeper, hoping he's oblivious to our conversation. Suppressing a laugh, I give Colton a playful shove.

"Insufferable," I tease.

"Here, this could bring a new twist to the bedroom," Colton suggests, lobbing a bottle my way, his eyes lighting up. Catching it, I read. Chameleon Concoction: Temporarily alters the drinker's hair or eye color.

"Very funny," I retort, playfully throwing it back to him. He chuckles and returns it to its spot on the shelf. "See anything you want?"

I shake my head. "Nothing's caught my eye."

Just then, I pause, my attention captured by a familiar bottle. Serenity Soak: One Twilight Use; Empty into Evening Waters. This is what Lili used to pour in my baths when I couldn't sleep. It always relaxed me, and I used to love how it changed the water's color.

Gently, I pull out the cork top and breathe in the lavender and vanilla scent. I love that smell. I push the cork back in and place the bottle back on the shelf. Colton watches me. "Do you want that? We can use it later," he winks.

"No, that's okay," I tell him, giggling. Although the idea of getting in a bath with him is definitely appealing.

"Then shall we?" He gestures toward the exit.

Nodding, I head to the door. "I'll be right out," he says, pausing at the counter.

Once outside, I'm curious about his purchase, but I resist the urge to peek. Nyx and Drew are nowhere in sight. They've likely lost themselves in the magical allure of another shop.

Drawn by an inexplicable feeling, I cruise toward a series of tents by the creek. One in particular nestled closest to the water beckons me. I hesitate, feeling I should wait for Colton. Then I remember our tether. He'll know where to find me when he's ready.

The entrance to the tent is decorated with little silver bells that chime melodiously even in the absence of a breeze. Inside, amidst the dim, smoky ambiance, sits an old woman with iridescent eyes. Her face is half-hidden beneath a hood.

"Are you here for a reading?" she inquires. I glance around, momentarily taken aback, ensuring she's addressing me. "Oh, no, I..."

This doesn't seem like a typical shop, and there aren't any items for purchase.

"You should be," she states with quiet conviction.

"Why is that?" I ask, unsure if she's a seer or possesses some other ability.

"I recognize the darkness lurking within you. Even now, the shadows sense their kin," she replies, causing my heart rate to quicken with unease.

"What does a reading entail?" I ask, pushing past the instinctual part of me that urges me to flee the tent.

"Whatever the gods show me, you too will witness. It varies

for each person. Sometimes, I see nothing. However, with you, I believe we might glimpse something profound," she intones. I take a few tentative steps closer. "Please, have a seat," she beckons, motioning to the chair across the table from her. Despite my apprehension, a compulsion to comply takes over, and I find myself seated. "Your life is entwined with another's," she observes. Uncertainty grips me. Is she sensing the tether I share with Colton or alluding to my fated bond with Nyx?

Before I can voice my question, the table vibrates ominously. My eyes dart to hers as they widen in anticipation. "Place your palms flat on the table," she commands. I hesitate, but then I do as instructed. Her hands cover mine, and abruptly the table morphs into a milky abyss.

We're pulled forward, plunging into its depths. Overwhelmed by a rising panic, my surroundings blur and darken.

We're cast into an all-encompassing void. My heart beats wildly, each thud echoing in the engulfing silence. What feels like forever, yet could have been mere seconds, elapses before my eyes acclimate. I'm isolated in the tunnels, as if ensnared by one of my midnight mind visions. Tracing the intricate branches on the walls, I brace for the whispers, but they remain eerily absent.

Instead, the soft rhythm of a heartbeat resonates, heralding the appearance of a shadowy female figure. Though her face remains concealed, her words are clear. "You must choose, Lyra." It evokes memories of my past encounter in the burning forest.

"Choose what? I don't understand!" I exclaim, irritation seeping through.

"You stand apart from your predecessors. Your willpower is unmatched. Choose wisely, and you'll harness the darkness in unprecedented ways. Yet, a wrong choice will lead the darkness to consume you—and doom all."

Grasping for understanding, I press on, "Is this about Nyx? Should I be with him? Can his light save me?" As I seek answers, the figure recedes. Desperation propels me forward as I chase after her.

"Only one holds the light that can save you. Yet, remember...darkness is drawn to darkness and will seek to change you," she says before dissolving into the void.

Suddenly, I'm back in the tent, seated across from the seer. Her previously iridescent eyes now appear clouded, seemingly exhausted by our shared experience. Breathless, we sever our linked hands.

"What the fuck was that? Why must everything be so cryptic?" I shout, my voice warbling.

"Visions are never clear, and they are not always certain," she says, wiping her brow. "Lyra, you are at the heart of a great shift. Tread carefully. Ryella does not appear to just anyone."

Regaining my composure, I face her defiantly. "How do you know? Ryella—do you mean the Goddess of Shadows?"

Her response is serene, "I possess vast knowledge, young one. Indeed, Ryella, the Goddess of Shadows and Darkness, whose shadows you unknowingly bear. I see them now beneath your skin, waiting to be released." I glance down at myself, half expecting a revelation, but nothing appears amiss. When I raise my eyes to the seer, she has vanished.

I quickly exit the tent. It feels like I spent an eternity inside, but it might have only been a few minutes. The remnants of the encounter leave my head spinning. As I approach the cobblestone street where I left Colton at the potions shop, I spot him, Nyx, and Drew deep in conversation. The moment they notice my approach, their chatter fades, giving me the sense they were discussing something they'd rather I not hear.

"We were about to come looking for you," Drew remarks,

her eyes narrowing on me as if trying to decipher my recent experience.

"Let's head to a nearby tavern. I believe we could all use a drink," Nyx suggests, leading the way.

Colton hangs back to walk beside me, a few steps behind the others. "Are you okay? For a moment, I felt our connection, then it vanished. I couldn't feel the tether at all. I didn't want to alarm Nyx, since you've been insistent on keeping it a secret, but then the connection returned." He scans my face with concern, wrapping an arm around my waist for comfort.

"It's nothing. I'm fine. I'll fill you in later when we're alone," I reply, not ready to discuss it in such a public space. He nods in understanding, and we follow the others to the tavern.

We reach the tavern, and a large sign outside reads, "The Crystal Chalice," then just below that it reads, "Known for our magical performances and drinks that play tricks on the senses." Interesting. Once inside, I glance around the dimly lit room. There are tables everywhere and a stage on either side of the long room. A few women dance on one stage, minimally clothed in garments made of purple smoke.

On the other stage, there's a man playing a musical instrument. I'm not sure what it is, but the sound is upbeat and pleasant enough. A few people dance in front of the stage, swaying with the music and holding cocktails in their hands. Nyx walks straight to the long bar and pulls out a stool, motioning for me to sit at it instead of trying to get a table. I take a seat, and he takes the one to my left. Colton takes the seat to my right, and Drew sits on the other side of him.

The bartender, a tall male with silver-blue hair cascading down in waves, moves gracefully from one end of the bar to the other, conjuring drinks as much as pouring them. Wisps of smoke swirl around some glasses, while others glow softly in the dim light, illuminating the faces of their drinkers.

"I've heard of this place," Drew says, leaning over to speak to Colton. Her eyes follow the movements of one of the smoke-clad dancers, fascinated. "They say the concoctions here can let you taste the stars or relive a fond memory."

Nyx beckons the bartender over, sharing a few words in hushed tones. The bartender nods, disappearing momentarily, only to return with a tray bearing four drinks. They all glow red, and I'm half afraid to drink it.

"Don't worry. It's supposed to make you feel good for a couple of hours. We could all use a break. Isn't that why we're here?" Nyx says, pushing a glass to each of us. I take mine, trusting Nyx wouldn't give me anything that would harm me, and Colton and Drew take theirs too. I'm kind of surprised at how trusting they are being, but then again they probably don't care and want to have a good time.

"To new adventures," Nyx toasts, lifting his glass.

"And to defying prophecies," Colton adds whispering in my ear.

The four of us clink our glasses, and the atmosphere momentarily lightens, the weight of our journey temporarily forgotten in this little tavern.

Drew speaks up, "I think I'll find some entertainment for the rest of the evening. I'll see you all at breakfast." She heads over to one of the female dancers she'd been exchanging glances with.

Colton orders another round of drinks for us, as we'd drained our first ones rather quickly. "This time, it's a sweet ale," he assures me. "It doesn't have any altering effects."

I sip my drink, the rhythm of the music captivating me. I suspect the first drink Nyx got us might have already started to take effect — I feel elated and can't seem to keep still. Though I'm not typically one to dance in public, I'm compelled to move to the beat. Seeing many already dancing in front of the stage, I decide to join. Grasping my drink, I weave through the crowd, ignoring the surprised expressions of Nyx and Colton as I rise from my seat. Finishing the ale, I place the empty glass on a nearby table, preferring my hands to be free.

Surrendering to the music, I let my hips sway and my hands trail through my hair and down my body, reveling in how good I feel in this moment. When I glance back at our spot, I notice Colton still at the bar, but Nyx is nowhere in sight.

"Looking for me?" Nyx whispers into my ear from behind. His hand wraps around my waist, and he spins me to face him.

"Yes," I reply, caught in his gaze.

"Dance with me," he urges, drawing me close. I let him lead, our bodies moving in harmony to the music.

"So how's Colton in bed?" Nyx inquires.

"Amazing," I respond immediately then slap a hand over my mouth, mortified by my frankness.

"You've been intimate with him then?" His eyes narrow as he assesses me.

"Many times," I confess and internally cringe. Something isn't right. I'd know better than to say that when we're trying to keep everyone happy. "Nyx, what did you do to me?"

I halt our dance, awaiting his explanation.

"I might have asked the bartender to add a touch of truth to your cocktail. There are things I need to know for this...arrangement to work," he admits. As I attempt to distance myself from him, he tightens his grip on my waist, steering me deeper into the crowd, probably out of Colton's line of sight. "There is no 'arrangement' between us," I say, and realize that in my current state I can only speak the truth.

"Did you ever love me?" he presses.

"Yes," slips from my lips before I can even process the question. The realization stuns me. I have to get away. "Was this truth serum only in my drink?" I demand.

"Yes," he confirms, subtly encouraging me to keep dancing with him. Although I'm fuming, the cocktail's effects keep me relaxed. If not for the drink, I might have found an instrument to stab him with or taken a shot at a low blow before bolting.

"Are you still in love with me?" As I twirl, trying to dodge his question, he grabs my hand, drawing me back.

"I don't know," I admit, cursing myself internally. But deep down, I do know, and the answer is no.

"That's more hopeful than a flat no. Are you in love with Colton?" he continues, his question making my eyes widen.

My treacherous mouth replies, "I think so."

His expression remains unreadable, but he seems neither angry nor pleased, "That could be problematic."

I bite my lip, torn between the urge to escape and a morbid curiosity about what he'd ask next. "Do you believe we're fated to be together?" he asks.

I respond candidly, compelled by the potion's effects, "I'm still trying to figure that out." He hums in thought.

"Did you ever lie to me when we were together?" The weight of the question makes my stomach twist, but the truth refuses to be caged.

"Yes," I confess.

A brash dancer tries to cut in, hoping to dance with me, but Nyx growls, positioning himself between us. The dancer, reading the room, turns away.

"Did you deceive me more than once?" Nyx persists. I intend to shake my head, but the words slip out against my will.

"Yes."

"So you resent me for the pain I caused, for my lies, but you're no better, a hypocrite," he remarks, more an accusation than a question.

Yet the answer forces its way out. "Yes."

"Perhaps I've met my equal. Maybe we truly are destined,"

he muses. His grip tightens around my waist again, drawing me nearer, his breathing irregular. One hand ventures to the slit in my dress, caressing my thigh. "Do you enjoy that sensation?" he inquires.

"Yes," I whisper back.

"Last question," he murmurs, his lips almost brushing my ear, intensifying the intimacy of the moment. "What do you desire right now?" His fingers dance lazily over my skin, sending shivers up my spine.

Struggling to maintain composure, I admit, "I wish it was Colton's touch, not yours."

He abruptly releases me, and I catch a chilling glimpse of his eyes—hues of gray with enlarged pupils that make his eyes look almost black. Without waiting for his response or reaction, I weave through the crowd, darting out into the cool embrace of the night. Gulping down air, I take a few steps and lean against the side of the building.

I realize I'm not even angry with Nyx for his actions. In a strange way, I'm grateful. That potion forced out confessions I'd never have had the bravery to utter on my own. Now, he knows how I truly feel about Colton. I don't plan to flaunt those feelings, but neither will I suppress them. He deserved the truth, and my fears had held it captive. I'm relieved he didn't question me about our tether. That revelation might've pushed him too far.

"Hey, what's wrong?" Colton asks, appearing beside me outside.

"Nyx had the bartender mix a truth serum into my drink. He cornered me on the dance floor, interrogating me," I admit, surprised at my own candor. The potion's effects linger.

"Do you want me to handle him?" Colton asks, dead serious.

I laugh. "No, he's already tortured enough. Let him be."

Colton chuckles, "He seemed anything but tortured when I left."

I raise an eyebrow. "What do you mean?"

"See for yourself," he says, guiding me to glance through the door's window. Nyx is dancing, surrounded by three women, looking far from despondent.

"And Drew?" I ask.

"She left earlier with one of those smoke dancers," he replies with a knowing smirk.

"Can we go? Anywhere but here?" I request.

"It would be my pleasure, little enchantress," he responds, pulling me close. He grips my hair gently, tilting my head back. Our lips meet, and as his tongue ventures deeper, a gust of citrus wind swirls around us, and we channel.

CHAPTER 28
COLTON

I relish the sensation of her lips against mine as I channel us to the perfect spot. Knowing my shadow as I do, I'm confident she'll be enchanted here. The instant our feet make contact with the ground, I gently release her hair, giving her the space to immerse herself in our surroundings. We stand amidst the Nocturne Willow grove, a hidden treasure of the Black Forest.

Her face lights up with genuine wonder, and I can't help but watch her intently. Towering above us, the trees mirror the traditional weeping willows, yet they're distinguished by their unique attributes. Their elongated branches sway with the night wind. What makes these trees special are their shimmering black leaves. Each leaf glistens, reminiscent of stardust, and under the moon's silvery touch they appear as cascading waterfalls of twinkling stars against the night.

Her delight is undeniable as she turns slowly, her head tilted upward, absorbing the magical display above. "I've never seen anything so mesmerizing," she confesses, her voice imbued with awe. I hold back for a moment, allowing her the pleasure of this first encounter, appreciating how the night air seems to invigorate her spirit. The more she's bathed in the moonlight and shadows, the more her essence seems to resonate, as if the darkness within her finds its kinship in the night.

Thoughts of Nyx's deception earlier in the evening fleetingly cross my mind. I should have known the bastard would try something sneaky, but to tamper with her drink... When he approached her on the dance floor, I chalked it up to mere longing. I can't fault him for that. I long to be close to her too. But now I don't care what he's doing, because right now it's just her, this grove, and me.

A yearning surges within me, an urge to pull her close, to brand her as my own. I want the world, especially Nyx, to recognize the bond that has formed between us. Yet I sense the turbulence within her, the mix of emotions and questions vying for space in her heart and mind. I must be patient, allowing her the time and freedom to come to terms with her feelings and to approach me when she's ready. The weight of the prophecy looms, and I have to resist the urge to share the entire truth with her. The ramifications of that revelation keep me silent.

The lie casts a shadow between us, a wedge that I fear might split us apart. I cannot— I will not hurt her the same way Nyx did. I will not keep the truth from her for much longer. I have to make it known before we get too much further down this rabbit hole.

Her delicate hand wraps around mine, guiding me deeper into the heart of the grove. "Aren't you concerned? This forest has a reputation for danger," she teases, her voice a playful lilt. I can't help but chuckle, glancing at her.

"I have a feeling you're more than capable of facing anything this forest has to offer." My belief in her is unwavering. Her lips curl into a playful smile, and for a brief moment her eyes sparkle — a blend of cerulean and emerald, against the forest's inky backdrop.

"Besides," she says with a hint of teasing, "I have you by my side to protect me." My gaze fixates on those pouty lips, an irresistible pull drawing me closer, yearning to claim them with my own.

"Do you believe that truth cocktail is still in effect?" I inquire, moving a step closer.

She smirks, mischief lighting up her eyes. "Yes, I think so... Why not test it out? Ask me something."

"Aren't you afraid of the questions I might pose?" I murmur, sliding a hand through her silky tresses, allowing my fingers to linger on her cheek.

She takes a breath, the playful facade fading slightly. "When I'm with you, I don't feel afraid of anything." By the way her eyes widen, I sense that wasn't what she'd intended to say. The truth cocktail's influence, no doubt.

The temptation to dive deep, to ask all of the questions simmering in my mind, is overwhelming. Yet I want the answers to come from genuine emotions, not the lingering effects of a drink, so I refrain from asking anything too deep.

"What do you desire at this very moment?" I ask, bending down to press a chaste kiss on her forehead, savoring the unique scent of her hair.

Her heartbeat accelerates, and I can feel my dick harden at the way her body responds to me.

"I want your touch," she says, her voice barely above a whisper.

Cupping her face gently, I tilt her head, ensuring her eyes lock with mine. "Tell me, my shadow, where exactly do you crave my touch?" My voice drops, laden with intensity and promise.

"Everywhere," she gasps. Without hesitation, I hoist her up, her legs instinctively wrapping around my waist. Our lips collide, and I stake my claim on her mouth.

"Colton," she murmurs, pulling away, the light catch in her breath making my name sound almost like a plea.

Gently, my fingers find the ties at the back of her dress, and I work them loose. The fabric slips, pooling at her waist, revealing the soft contours of her chest.

I lower my head, capturing one of her breasts with my mouth and teasing her nipple with my tongue until it hardens in response. The sensation draws a soft moan from her, which fuels my desire even more. Carefully, I set her down, ensuring she's grounded before I push the gown off the rest of the way, leaving her completely nude. I take my time looking at her. She's incredibly perfect.

"Your turn," she murmurs.

In mere seconds, my boots are off, my tunic pulled over my head, and pants discarded. "Do you trust me?" The question falls from my lips with a touch of uncertainty.

Her eyes meet mine, filled with desire and a hint of vulnerability. "Yes," she whispers.

Promising safety, I lean in, brushing a gentle kiss against her neck, backing her until her skin touches the cool bark of one of the Nocturne willows. "Stay still," I instruct.

As my lips travel down her neck, I let my magic call upon the roots. They emerge, wrapping gently but securely around her ankles. The sensation causes her to gasp, but she remains still. At my command, the roots part her legs just slightly, and I kneel to explore her more intimately with a tender touch. I press a finger into her pussy, and it's wet, her body already responding to me. Fuck, I want to be inside her, but I settle for tasting her. I want to have her squirming and begging for my cock. I part her flesh with my tongue, and she tastes as sweet as she smells. I work her clit until her legs are quivering and her hands are in my hair.

She arches into my touch. The moans that escapes her lips are evidence of her pleasure. Before she can react, slender branches descend from above, twining around her wrists and pulling them upward. Her pulse quickens.

"I told you not to move," I whisper against her skin, resuming my slow exploration, drinking in every sound, every tremor, every breath.

I lick and suck on her clit, pressing and curling my fingers inside her. When I sense she's on the brink of an orgasm, I pull away, rising to my feet and stepping back. Her intense gaze and evident desire intensify my own cravings.

"Colton, please," she pleads, breathless and wanting — exactly the way I want to see her.

"Tell me what you want," I command in a low voice, yearning to hear her admission.

"I want you, all of you, inside me," she begs. With a wave of my hand, I command the roots. They respond, and her eyes widen momentarily as they lift her legs, spreading them wide for me. With the assistance of the roots, my hands are free to explore her body, and I position myself between her legs. The wet warmth of her entrance beckons, and I press my cock to her threshold. I watch as she draws her bottom lip into her mouth, the anticipation almost too much for her.

I hold my position, teasingly pressing against her while bending to tantalize her breasts with my lips. My hands explore her, occasionally nibbling on a nipple with just enough pressure to elicit a response. "Colton," she murmurs, a plea lacing her voice.

Yielding to her desires, I thrust deeply, giving her no time to adjust to my size. I pull back only to drive into her once more, her pleasure evident in her screams. Her head tilts back against the tree trunk, her breaths coming fast. No more teasing. I take her fervently, one hand grasping her ass and the other stimulating her clit. Even as I feel her pussy tighten around me, signaling her climax, I continue my rhythmic movements, carrying her through the waves of pleasure.

She pants and writhes against her restraints, but I crave more. I yearn for every part of her. Gripping her thighs, I capture her mouth, resolute in my intention to drive her to her limits. My goal is to bring her to another climax, and I'm confident in my ability to achieve it.

Releasing her mouth long enough for her to draw breath, I seize her hair, pulling her head to the side. I trace a path up her neck with a mix of gentle sucks and firm bites, teasing her earlobe between my teeth. My thrusts become deliberate and slow, yet they remain deep, ensuring she feels every inch of me. I want the memory of our intimacy to linger, a reminder every time she moves tomorrow.

"Oh gods," she rasps, and as she tightens around me once more, it sends me over the edge with her. I remain there within her for a moment, letting both of us catch our breaths. Holding her face, I gently kiss her damp forehead.

As I pull out, she winces, making me second-guess my intensity. "Are you alright?" I inquire, and she looks at me through half-lidded eyes.

"Yes," she whispers, her voice soft and sleepy.

With a snap of my fingers, the roots and branches vanish. Gently, I cradle her in my arms—one beneath her knees, the other supporting her back. Her head rests on my chest, and I bend to kiss the crown of her head. She makes no move to escape my embrace, and I revel in her willingness to stay within it. My resilient little shadow, I could hold her for an eternity.

"Ready to retire for the night?" I ask. I can faintly sense her emotions when she momentarily drops her barriers, and all I perceive now is fatigue.

"I think so," she replies. As I slowly set her down, ensuring she's steady. I gesture, and our clothes materialize upon us. She grins, as she often does when I wield my magic, as if she doesn't realize the powerful magic she holds within herself.

"Take me to your room. I don't wish to sleep in my old room tonight," she murmurs, a subtle reminder of the scars and memories that room must hold for her. The injustices she's suffered enrage me, and for her I would lay waste to all of Eguina—my shadow. She scrutinizes my face, that ever-present hint of sorrow in her eyes a painful reminder of all she's endured. I yearn to eradicate that pain. With an arm wrapped securely around her, I channel us back to the castle.

We return to my room, and neither of us bothers to change. We simply undress and climb into bed, exhausted. I'm not certain if Drew or Nyx ever made it back to their rooms, but I don't particularly care as long as they show up at breakfast. I want to get this over with. I suspect the Luminary Council will want a meeting concerning the awakening of Lyra's dark magic. Drew hinted as much. I hope they don't pose another threat to her. Drew is generally level-headed, and Nyx seems infatuated with her in his own way. However, the opinions of the others remain uncertain, especially my parents. It'll be telling to see where their heads are at.

I haven't spoken to my father in months, and although I wish to speak with him before any meeting, it seems improbable now. I'm confident in Lyra's strength and her ability to control her magic, but I'm unsure how it might alter her. I draw her close, tracing slow circles on her stomach, relishing the feel of her soft skin beneath my fingers. This might be the last night I embrace her like this before her magic awakens. It's hard to believe such powerful dark magic lies dormant within her even now. I think we all struggle with the unsettling possibility that awakening her magic could irreversibly change her.

"Nyx knows about us," she whispers, shattering the silence.

"What do you mean?" I question, although I am well aware that Nyx isn't naive. I implied as much back in Nighthold when I intended to provoke him. I never explicitly stated I was intimate with her, but I reckon he understood. Regardless of our efforts to remain discreet in his presence, it may only provide him with deceptive hope. Frankly, I can't determine if his hopes are misplaced or not. Lyra might be fated to be with him, and the thought disturbs me; it feels like history repeating itself in a twisted manner. The idea of another man touching her, being inside her. I can't let myself think about it.

"I might have mentioned to him earlier how skilled you are in bed and that we've been intimate numerous times," she confesses, followed by a soft giggle. The sound brightens my mood.

"I would've relished seeing his reaction to that. He had it coming, trying to force the truth from you."

"He did have it coming, and honestly I don't regret telling him," she says. She turns in my arms to face me, and every time she gives me that look I have to suppress the urge to assertively claim her as mine. I desire a commitment from her, but I can't suffocate her with my wishes. I need to be patient and see how things unfold over time.

A deep breath escapes me when her delicate hand lifts to trace the contours of my face. "I'm so fortunate to have you," she whispers, causing that familiar stirring in my chest.

"I'm the fortunate one, my sexy little enchantress," I tease. Her giggle resonates in the quiet room again, the sound so pure and joyful. She doesn't laugh nearly enough. How could anyone ever harm her? The very notion churns my stomach. "I'll never let anyone harm you again."

Her eyes soften, and she offers a gentle smile, tucking her hair behind her ear and caressing her necklace. I yearn to delve deep into her past, to understand her history with Samael, Aidan, and her parents. But it seems inappropriate to bombard her with questions right now, especially given the pain these memories might evoke. She revealed a fragment of her past to me in Zomea, and I unintentionally witnessed snippets of her traumatic experiences during her time in the simulation maze. I wish to understand her completely, the good and the bad alike.

"Are you afraid of the aftermath once my dark magic awakens? I've read the book about the last dark Sorcerer. Many have been consumed by the darkness, and then there's the prophecy," she says.

I take a moment to consider carefully. "I fear for your safety but never fear you."

"Watch out, I can be pretty scary," she teases, her voice accompanied by another soft giggle. However, her face soon adopts a more solemn expression. She lowers her lashes, avoiding my gaze, and begins to fiddle with her necklace. I sense her unease but choose not to press her on the matter. "Colton, can I ask you something?"

"You can ask me anything," I assure her, curious about what's prompting her newfound seriousness.

"Can you tell me about Zaelinn?" she inquires, catching me completely off guard.

"How do you know about her?" I ask, sidestepping her question momentarily. I wouldn't have expected Nyx to divulge that information. It doesn't paint him in the best light.

"Rix and Rune might have mentioned her a bit. But please don't be upset with them," she adds hastily. Those Twig Wisps always seem to be at the center of gossip.

"I'm not upset," I reassure her. "You have every right to ask about her. I suppose it's only natural you'd want to know more." I pause, considering my next words carefully.

"We all grew up as friends. Nyx, Dorian, Bim, Flora, Zaelinn, and me. As time passed, Zaelinn and I, being slightly older than the others and always closer, naturally gravitated toward each other. Eventually, our bond evolved into something more intimate," I pause, searching her face for any reaction. She simply gazes back, urging me to continue with her eyes. "We got engaged. But Zaelinn, with her free spirit, seemed to have second thoughts. Not long after our engagement party, she ended things. Soon after, I learned she was with Nyx."

"Were they having an affair?" she inquires.

"I never got a straight answer, and honestly I never pushed for one. Knowing wouldn't have changed how I felt. Nyx, once a good friend, felt like a traitor, and so did she. I had loved Zaelinn deeply, and though she shattered me I wanted her happiness. I wanted them both to be happy, and I could have forgiven them." I take a deep breath, steeling myself for the next part.

"But..." she prompts.

Swallowing hard, I try to put my pain into words. "One day, tired of the rift that had formed in our circle, I visited Nyx's house. I wanted reconciliation – for all of us to move past the hurt and be friends again. But Twig informed me they'd ventured to the Brysta Trenches." I sigh, frustration evident in my voice. "It was always off-limits to us as kids. Too many have perished there. But their daring natures always overrode caution. By the time I arrived, it was too late."

The chilling memory plays out before my eyes. "Navigating from the first to the second amphitheater is the most dangerous part. The darkness can be disorienting. One mistake and you run out of air. You're so far below, no one can help you, magic is useless, and you can't channel." The scene is still so vivid to me even after all these years. "Zaelinn...she didn't make it. Despite Nyx's desperate attempts at reviving her, she was gone. The guilt and anguish on his face said it all – he blamed himself. As did I."

"I couldn't look past his role in her death. Especially when he moved on so fast – numerous flings, drinking, living recklessly. Our group fractured after that."

"I'm so sorry," she murmurs, her touch a comforting presence on my shoulder.

"It was a long time ago," I reply.

Since she's asking difficult questions, I decide to redirect our conversation and ask one I've been avoiding, "Do you still have feelings for Nyx?"

She hesitates for a moment, looking away. "I don't know," she whispers, avoiding my stare. "There's always going to be this part of me that cares for him, despite his recent actions. Yet I'm drawn to you. My biggest challenge is the uncertainty about the prophecy and the awakening of my dark magic. Often, I'm on the verge of immersing myself fully in 'us,' but something deep inside gives me pause. I'm afraid of the potential pain – both inflicting it and experiencing it. Sometimes, I wonder if I'm not meant to be loved."

"Lyra, love awaits you, in its purest, fiercest form. I hope destiny allows me to be the one to show you its depth."

I'm consumed by the desire to tell her I love her, to urge her to choose me, to truly commit. I wish I could unveil the entirety of the prophecy to her, but, damn, I can't. She's so close, so seemingly within my grasp. She's right here in my bed, nestled in my arms, yet she's still out of reach. She's with me yet not wholly mine.

"Me too." She draws closer to nestle against my chest. I hold her and stroke her back until she falls asleep in my arms.

CHAPTER 29
LYRA

Before the first light of dawn breaks, I find myself rousing from the warmth of Colton's embrace. I carefully slip out from his grip, ensuring I don't wake him. Standing there for a moment, I admire the chiseled contours of his face, accentuated even in sleep. The urge to dive back under the covers with him is strong, but I remind myself of the day's significance.

Last night may have been fun, but today everything changes. I don't bother changing into my dress. Instead, I channel into my bedroom for a refreshing bath. Given the impending events of the day, I decide to dress more practically. I opt for fitted black tights, matching boots, and a dark tunic cinched at the waist with a black leather bodice. If I'm about to embrace my dark magic, I might as well look the part.

After tying my hair into a long, side-swept braid, I sit at my vanity, returning to the ritual of makeup application—a practice I've neglected recently. I emphasize my eyes with deep shadows, adding a flush of color to my cheeks and a dark hue to my lips.

I'm not entirely familiar with how Kaine has been

managing this place, but since the four of us agreed to meet for breakfast, I venture toward the dining room, assuming that's where the gathering would be. Upon entering, Drew sits at the table, fingers drumming impatiently. She looks impeccable, as always. I'm curious about her evening, particularly about the dancer she seemed interested in, but I bite back the question.

"Morning," I greet. "Remember, no one specified a time for this breakfast."

She waves a dismissive hand. "The kitchen's prepared some dishes. Eat up before we head out."

Nodding, I pick up a muffin as Nyx strides in wearing the same attire from last night. Drew's eyebrow arches. "Interesting night?"

Nyx smirks, a twinkle in his eye. "You could say that."

I can't quite pinpoint the emotion bubbling within me. It's not jealousy—more like a sense of relief. Soon after, Colton materializes beside me, having channeled directly into the room. With a swift motion, he shuts all entryways and then takes a seat, motioning for me to join him. As I sit, our hands find each other beneath the table—a silent reassurance.

Nyx, with his usual audacity, helps himself to a generous portion of bacon, not missing a beat. Between bites, he inquires, "Alright, who's going to kickstart this briefing?"

Clearing her throat, Drew sits up straighter, ready to dive into the plan.

Drew outlines the plan, her voice steady, "You three are headed to the Brysta Trenches today. My ship will get you there swiftly. About an hour's sail should bring you close enough to the Center Isles to channel. Once you retrieve the grimoire, the crew will transport you back to the Lamia Realm. I've arranged a safe location where the magic awakening can occur without endangering others." She glances in my direction, eyes filled with an unspoken message.

"You're not accompanying us?" I ask, surprised.

She shakes her head, "I have urgent matters to address. However, I'll be there with you by nightfall."

Nyx leans forward, his eyes narrowing. "You're assembling the Luminary Council, aren't you?" His tone is pointed.

There's a palpable silence before Drew responds.

Nyx's impatience surges. "I'm a fucking member of that council, Drew. It's only fair Lyra and I are informed. This matter concerns her after all."

Reluctantly, Drew nods. "I've initiated conversations with a few, including your parents, Colton."

Colton's brow furrows. "Invoking the council seems risky. What if things don't go as planned?"

My gaze flits between them, apprehension growing. "The council's convening is precautionary, in case I lose control and you're forced to...what? Kill me?" My voice cracks.

Drew hesitates. "It's more for your safeguarding." I'm not convinced.

Fed up, I push away from the table. "Then let's get this over with," I declare, standing. "I have to find Lili and bid Chepi farewell. I doubt the trenches are an environment suitable for him."

Drew nods in agreement. "It's a wise decision."

Colton's fingers wrap around mine, "Once you're done, find me," he says.

I nod, eager to get this over with. This day has loomed over me for too long.

As I weave through the corridors toward the kitchen, I'm almost certain that's where I'll find Lili, likely spoiling Chepi with bacon strips and other delicious morsels. The aroma of sizzling food grows stronger with each step, and as I turn the bend the familiar scene of the duo at the kitchen island confirms my suspicions.

The sight prompts a sense of déjà vu, and I approach with a mix of urgency and hesitancy. "Lili, I'm sorry for asking again, but can you look after Chepi for me? It might be a day or two, maybe longer," I request, my voice quivering slightly.

Lili's face softens, her eyes filling with concern. "Of course, I'll care for him. But you need to be careful. The last time you left him in my care..." The memory is unspoken but hauntingly clear in the air between us.

I gently place a hand on her arm, stopping her from saying more. The nightmares from that time already plague my sleep. I don't need to hear the details now. "I'll do my best to be safe," I promise, even though a nagging voice inside me wonders if it's a vow I can genuinely uphold.

Holding Chepi close, I feel the soft rhythm of his breathing and the comforting warmth of his small body. "Behave for Lili, squish. I'll come back as soon as I can. I love you." I plant soft kisses atop his furry head. Setting him down next to Lili, I offer him a strip of bacon as a parting treat.

Lili pulls me into an embrace, and as we pull away her hands frame my face. Her eyes, earnest and filled with concern, lock onto mine. "Always remember, Lyra, your heart is pure and kind. No matter the challenges or darkness you face, nothing can alter your true essence. I love you."

That touches a place deep within, providing a much-needed reassurance. "Thank you," I manage to say, choked with emotion. After giving Chepi one last affectionate pat, I force myself to turn away. As I near the hallway's end, I cast one last lingering look at them.

A foreboding sensation tightens around my heart, whispering that everything is about to change, and I can't predict when I'll be reunited with them. The weight of the impending unknown threatens to break me, but I steel myself, pushing the pain and uncertainty aside, I blink back my tears before they can fall.

Ready to find Colton, I focus on the tether that binds us. It guides me like a beacon, and I can sense he's in his quarters. Bypassing the castle's winding corridors, I channel directly into his room. Being in a place so familiar that I can channel anywhere I want without much thought really comes in handy.

The instant I materialize in the room, Colton swiftly crosses the gap, concern etched on his face. "Are you okay?" His fingers glide tenderly over my hair, settling gently on my cheek, the touch both soothing and grounding.

I force a nod. "Yes." I keep back unspoken fears and rising apprehension. My anxiety is already festering in my chest, and we haven't even left yet.

Seeming to sense my unease, he tries to divert my attention. "I have something for you," he says, producing a finely crafted sheath. The details on it are beautiful, an L intricately carved into the leather and a stunningly designed handle peeking out. Its lightweight nature puzzles me.

Colton explains, "This blade is unique, crafted just for you by Dorian. He is the very best. It will extend and retract based on your will. It's magically bonded to you, amplifying your power and resonating with your emotions." Drawing the blade from its sheath, the black gleam catches my eye. Light as a feather and impeccably balanced, I admire its craftsmanship before sliding it back into its sheath.

"Thank you," I say, touched. "It's perfect." With his help, I secure it around my thigh, the leather melding seamlessly with my attire, becoming a part of me.

"Drew's gone, and Nyx is probably getting restless downstairs. Say the word and we can vanish. Start anew somewhere beyond the boundaries of Zomea and Eguina," he proposes, hopeful and seriousness. For a fleeting moment, the idea is incredibly appealing, and a serene image of that life flashes before my eyes.

Reality pulls me back, and I whisper, "I'm ready."

He extends his hand, which I grasp firmly, letting him guide me back to the dining hall. As anticipated, Nyx is there, pacing with growing impatience. "Took you long enough," he grumbles.

With a flash of defiance, I smirk, "See you on the ship." Drawing on my inner power, I channel, the familiar sensation sweeping me away. As soon as I arrive, both Colton and Nyx materialize next to me. The ship's crew, efficient and prepared, springs into action the moment they see us.

CHAPTER 30
NYX

We ought to be hashing out a strategy right now, but predictably we're not. That would be too logical. Instead, we're dispersed across this ship, each mired in deep thought. Silence has gripped us for what feels like an hour.

Lyra has staked out a spot at the deck's edge, her gaze lost to the water below, probably grappling with the weight of our fates. It's a bit out of character for Colton to let her be, especially given their recent...closeness, as our conversation last night revealed. The mere thought of him touching her unsettles me.

While they might be burdened with dread, I'm impatient to move forward. I'm eager for Lyra to fully embrace her dark magic. I believe once she does, she'll realize the prophecy doesn't lie. I'm her protector, the one she's destined for. As for Colton? Memories of Z, and now fears regarding Lyra, must torment him. Though Lyra's not destined for death, I sense a change coming. She's bound to leave him behind. It's inevitable.

I can sense we're nearing the point where we can channel

to the Center Isles. There's an inherent connection I feel when close to my realm. Without hesitating, I stride over to Lyra, beckoning Colton as I move.

"It's time." I don't engage in prolonged conversation, merely wrapping an arm around Lyra, pulling her to me, and initiating the channeling. I'm certain Colton will be right on our heels. To my surprise, Lyra doesn't resist my touch, showing no preference to channel with Colton over me. Perhaps she's starting to see reason.

Our feet find the sandy shores a moment later, but today nature isn't in our favor. What's typically a serene beach is now tumultuous with raging waves. I sense immediately that this endeavor may not go smoothly. Colton arrives moments after us, looking equally aware of our grim circumstances.

"Alright, since you seem to be taking charge, why don't you outline the plan for us?" I challenge Colton, trying to mask the edge in my voice.

"I've never ventured beyond the first amphitheater, Nikki," he responds, the nickname grating on my nerves. He's well aware of how much I detest it. "It's you who should be leading. You've been there."

Hesitating slightly, I almost admit, I haven't been past the first amphitheater either. But there's no point in sharing that with Lyra right now. We can tackle it when we get there.

I brace myself, pushing forward with the plan. "Alright, you want the plan? Well, there is no fucking plan. Here's how we proceed. I'll lead, Lyra follows directly behind me, and Colton, you bring up the rear, ensuring Lyra is safe." A fleeting thought crosses my mind about the usefulness of a rope to tether us together, but given our rushed departure, it's an oversight we'll have to live without.

Turning my attention to Lyra, I ask, "Can you swim proficiently? How long can you hold your breath? I'm beginning to wonder if it might be wiser for you to stay here, while Colton and I undertake this." I notice the faint trembling of her fingers, unsure whether it's the cold or her nerves.

"No," she declares defiantly. "This is my journey, my mission. I'm going with you. I can swim and hold my breath. I might not be an expert, but I'll manage."

"Listen," I assert, "if you feel you're running out of breath down there, signal either me or Colton. Do you understand?" It's time they realized I'm not merely their peer – I am their king, and they should heed my command.

"I need to explain what it'll be like down there," I announce, barely suppressing my irritation as I watch Colton take Lyra's trembling hand. "First, brace yourselves for the cold water. We'll venture beyond the waves to a sharp underwater drop-off. As we descend, the cold will intensify, and the pressure will mount. Remember, we can rely on our magic only up to the cave entrance—beyond that point, it ceases to function."

I study their faces, weighing how much to reveal about potential challenges.

"The breath-holding—is that our primary concern?" Lyra asks, her feet shifting in the sand.

"No, there's more. We must be wary of powerful currents, drastic temperature shifts, and something called portal pools. But if we maintain our formation and stay close, we'll overcome them," I reassure her.

She tilts her head, curiosity evident. "Portal pools?"

Before I can respond, Colton interjects, "They're like short-cuts within the caves, pools that transport you to different sections. But a wrong move and you could become disoriented, even risk drowning."

"Remain close to me and they won't be a problem," I insist, hearing a rare fragility in her voice. The impulse to console her surges, but I push it down.

"Lighten your load. Shed anything that might hinder you," Colton suggests, stripping off his boots and tunic. Always seeking an opportunity to undress.

"Lyra, retain your shoes. Though I'd enjoy the sight of you in fewer layers, the cold will bite, so best to keep them on," I counsel, a protective edge to my voice. "Also, don't part with your weapon. Without magic, it might be our best defense."

As he stows a dagger, Colton chimes in, "I can fend off the cold, but you'll feel it. And indeed, keep your weapon accessible."

"Shall we proceed?" I propose, motioning toward the water.

"Get on my back. Hold tight until we're farther out," Colton tells Lyra, helping her find a grip. A rush of envy washes over me as I watch Lyra wrap her arms around his neck and her legs around his waist.

The instant the initial wave grazes me, the water's cold bite pierces my skin, despite it reaching only to my waist. The last time I dared this journey, intoxication numbed the cold and suppressed my apprehensions. Memories of Z threaten to surface, but I squash them. Now isn't the time. My focus needs to remain unyielding, especially with Lyra's safety on the line.

"We'll need to begin our swim soon!" I call out, raising my voice to cut through the wind's howl and the waves' clamor. Choosing my moment, I dive deep, evading an impending colossal wave. Breaking the surface on its other side, I'm relieved to find Colton and Lyra mirroring my maneuver. Several repeats later, battling both waves and a treacherous current, the seabed eludes my feet, pushing us further into deeper waters.

"Tread water momentarily. I need to ensure we're aligned correctly." Without waiting for acknowledgement, I submerge to scan our surroundings. Despite my keen vision, the murky water limits clarity, but as the seabed plunges I confirm our position. Resurfacing, I beckon them forward. "Only a bit further!"

Diving once more for reassurance, I find our entry point. With determination, I summon my magic, hauling three massive rocks from the adjacent cliff. They hover weightlessly before us. Addressing Lyra directly, since Colton is versed in this tactic, I explain, "Take one of these stones, clutch it against you, and dive. Its weight ensures rapid descent. Use your feet to maneuver, hands clutching the stone. When we approach the entrance, I'll guide you. At that point, you release the stone."

Her response is swift, eyes determined. "Understood."

Securing a boulder, I inhale deeply, meeting Lyra's gaze one last time. With a wink, aiming to diffuse the tension even by a sliver, I plunge into the abyss below.

Lyra is at the forefront of my mind, but I resist the urge to glance back. I have to trust her capabilities, and knowing that Colton shadows her offers some semblance of reassurance.

The technique works remarkably well as the chilling grasp of the water intensifies. In the muted light this deep, the faint luminance ahead signals the cave entrance. The closer I get to the cave's mouth, glowing ever-so-dimly, the more its details become visible. I let go of my boulder, propelling myself to the entrance, and grab onto its rocky perimeter.

In the dim glow, I see Lyra tailing closely. Her resilience fills me with pride. As she nears, she drops her rock, and I extend my arm, drawing her into the embrace of the cave and myself. What comes next is something I hadn't disclosed, an opportunity I've been yearning for.

I place my hand firmly yet gently on the back of her head, pulling her face closer. The surprise in her eyes is evident as they widen, but under these circumstances resistance isn't an option. I signal her to exhale, mimicking the action myself.

Calling upon the remnants of my magic, I take a deep breath then press my lips against hers. As she opens to me, every instinct screams to explore, to savor this intimate moment, but I suppress the urge.

Instead, I concentrate on the purpose, transferring the magically imbued air into her lungs. This will be the last time we can call upon our magic until we make it back out of here.

As we part, I glimpse at Colton, his stoic expression betraying nothing, though I'm certain I've pissed him off. Meeting Lyra's eyes, I offer a reassuring nod and guide us deeper into the cave.

Schools of Neostripes encircle us, their bodies emanating a radiant neon green. These peculiar fish seem invariably drawn to these intricate caves. It's a mystery why, but their bioluminescence is crucial, making the treacherous journey somewhat bearable.

The cave's constriction isn't for the faint of heart, a tight squeeze that forbids the luxury of standing or any extensive movement. A full rotation of one's body within this narrow recess would be a commendable achievement. I latch onto submerged rocks, propelling myself through the water, striving to conserve the limited air we have by maintaining a brisk pace.

Every now and then I pause to steel glances into the depths below, windows into eerie aquascapes teeming with unseen life. This unique landscape is one of the wonders of Nighthold, its elusive beauty concealed by the difficulties of reaching it. These aquatic apertures are like portals into cosmic canvases, the creatures below illuminating the water in a symphony of lights and flashes, resembling the constellations, a living homage to Brysta.

As I swim over one of these windows in the cave floor, I point downward, hoping Lyra glimpses the spectacular view beneath us. Despite our mission, the surreal allure of this concealed world is worth a moment of marvel.

I count the windows as we pass over them. After the third one, we approach a small fork, and I guide us to the right. I learned the hard way the left leads you back out, and going straight results in a dead-end. The cave narrows uncomfortably, and I sense we're nearing the first amphitheater when a current begins to tug at me. I yield to its pull, and soon we emerge into a vast pool — the first amphitheater. Swiftly, I reach back for Lyra's hand, drawing her up to the surface with me.

We clamber onto the rocky shore, taking in the striking darkness. This place could be the epitome of romance if not for the haunting memories of my past experience. My eyes involuntarily drift to the black sand beach, the very spot where I tried to resuscitate her. Pushing away the recollection, I turn to Lyra as Colton joins us.

"Are you alright?" I inquire.

"Yes, this place is mesmerizing. It feels like an entirely different world. Hard to believe we're submerged beneath so much water, yet here we are, breathing and on solid ground," she says, her eyes taking in the glowing plants and creatures.

The only light source stems from the fish and crustaceans. The amphitheater's dome ceiling stretches up about fifty feet, and though it's said to be the smallest of its kind here it teems with luminous crabs and snails, each radiating its own unique glow, reminiscent of stars.

"It truly is unparalleled," Colton acknowledges, echoing Lyra's sentiments. I can tell his mind is likely also burdened by past events.

Shaking the water from my hair, I ask Lyra, "Did you ever feel short of breath or uncomfortable?"

"No, I felt perfectly fine. I could've swum even further," she responds, settling on the dark sand.

"That's good to hear. Our journey to the next amphitheater will be longer," I inform her.

"How many openings like this are there? And you both believe Samael is just hiding in one of them? How does he even survive down here?" she inquires, posing valid questions.

Colton says, "No one knows the exact count. We're certain of at least three, but considering the portals and some caves being too deep for a breath-hold, there could be many more."

Jumping in, I add, "Indeed, and the third room we're aiming for is believed to be the most expansive. If the rumors hold any weight, he could comfortably sustain himself there, feeding on fish and relying on the plant life for oxygen."

Lyra, appearing somewhat skeptical, asks, "So neither of you have been to this third room? You're basing this on the assumption that it's the largest amphitheater?"

I chuckle. "When you frame it that way, it does sound a bit sketchy. But, no, neither of us have. However, I am confident in its existence. I've reviewed maps and spoken to those who have ventured there."

Impatiently, she retorts, "Then what are we waiting for?"

I glance at Colton, sensing our shared hesitation. Memories of Z resurface. She had been intoxicated and panicked underwater. Unlike then, we are sober now, and Lyra is prepared. The belief that we'll all pull through steadies my resolve.

"The next stretch is longer and considerably narrower than the previous one. It's imperative to remain calm, stay alert, and keep pace. We'll need to move swiftly," I caution.

Lyra's expression hardens, her determination evident. "I understand," she declares. And with that it seems we're committed to continuing on.

I'm itching to leave this suffocating chamber. I nod to Colton, who returns the gesture with a firm glance. I then lock eyes with Lyra, instructing, "Deep breath."

Without hesitation, we plunge into the water.

The entrance in the cave wall isn't far, and I find it effortlessly, darting through with a fleeting glimpse to ensure they trail close behind me. I use the walls and floor to my advantage, pushing and propelling myself forward against a resistant current that fights to push us back.

Only moments in, an uneasy sensation creeps over me. Schools of Neostripe fish, which once illuminated our path, now dart past, spooked. A shadow seems to loom ahead, turning our illuminated path into complete darkness. The stark absence of their luminescence reveals my worst fear. The path is blocked. I momentarily panic but brush it off. The icy water feels like a million tiny needles on my skin, and the weight of it presses against my chest.

With the one-minute mark approaching and the familiar dull ache reminding me of my lungs' limit, I scour the blockade in front of us, trying to find a way through. My fingertips, numbed by the cold, trace over the rocks, feeling for weak points.

Behind me, a sudden frantic tug—Lyra. Fuck, her breath is running out. Quickly, I find her face in the darkness, pulling her body up mine in the tight space and pressing my lips to hers, giving her the last remnants of my air.

Desperation seeps in, and I guide her hands to the rocks. Together, we claw, pull, and tear at the blockade, each second stretching into what feels like eternity. The cold water weighs heavily, causing my ears to ring and my heart to thud loudly in the confined silence.

As hope seems to be dwindling, the wall gives way. An overpowering rush of water propels us forward into the awaiting chamber. The faint, eerie glow from the marine life lights are way again.

My vision blurs, and spots cloud my sight. A fierce grip on

my hand pulls me upward. It's Lyra. Together, we breach the surface, gasping and choking for air. Colton surfaces right after us, coughing up water.

We all take a moment, relishing the sweet taste of oxygen. Lyra's eyes reflect an intensity I haven't seen since we were tied up in the throne room together, and I know she's shaken. Reaching out, I reassure her, "You're okay." She nods, still catching her breath, and Colton grabs her face, embracing her in a tight hug, pressing her head into his chest. The display of affection makes me want to vomit, and I have to look away.

Lyra's voice cuts through the moist air like a shard of glass. "We all could've died if we didn't get that wall down. I can't lose either of you." She clings to Colton, her damp face emerging from his embrace to lock onto mine. The weight of her stare — my fiery princess, whose strength still manages to surprise me every day.

With a grunt, I pull myself up, the gritty feel of the shore beneath my boots grounding me. "Let's move," I declare, my voice echoing in the cave. While shadows dominate, the cave's light-emitting foliage casts a soft glow, lighting our way.

"We might find another route – one above water," I suggest, noting the uncertain terrain.

Colton, always the strategist, nods in agreement.

"Hidden paths aren't uncommon in places like this." We venture deeper into the cave.

Suddenly, Lyra's voice rings out. "Here! There's something!" She gestures toward a possible passage. I signal for Colton to lead the way. And though our journey is met with dead ends, we push on, searching cave after cave.

"Good thing we haven't gotten trapped so far," I comment, trying to lighten the mood. Lyra shoots me a look, both playful and warning.

"Don't jinx us." I smirk, raising my hands in a jesting surrender.

But the mood quickly turns somber when the path narrows, forcing us into a crawl. And when I think we've faced enough challenges, Colton's voice stops me in my tracks. "Nyx, we've got a situation."

Straining my neck, I try to glimpse past Lyra. "What now?"

"It's a portal pool," Colton answers tersely, confirming my dread.

"Carefully move around it," I order.

He replies with a mixture of frustration and urgency. "There's no way around. It's a dead end."

The sight of that ominous, swirling black void leaves us with few options. But it's Lyra's unexpected proposition that catches me off guard. "Do we risk it?"

I flash back to our last disastrous portal encounter. But before I can voice my concerns, Colton, ever the daredevil, dives in. Fuck.

"Lyra, wait. Do you remember what happened the last time I let you go into a portal before me?" I say, thinking about Samael in the dungeons. The things he did to her haunt me.

Lyra's outstretched hand beckons me, her eyes reflecting our shared memories and unspoken promises. "Together?"

I don't like this. Colton, as much as I can't stand the bastard, already went through, and we can't not follow him. I firmly grasp her hand. "Always." Together, we plunge into the unknown.

The sensation of the portal is chilling, akin to diving into deep water, yet we can breathe unhindered. The bizarre sensation occupies my mind for only an instant before gravity takes over, and we're plummeting. Instinctively, I coil my body around Lyra, cushioning her from the brunt of the impact as we crash onto rocky terrain then tumble into the water below.

Almost immediately, Colton surfaces, wrenching Lyra from my grasp and dragging her to safety.

Rising to my feet, I take in our surroundings. The cavern we find ourselves in is immense. It's a vast, aquatic expanse nestled deep within the bowels of the earth. Stalactites descend from above like nature's own chandeliers, periodically shedding droplets that cause ripples upon the serene lake beneath. Mineral veins streak across the cave walls, emitting a soft glow. Their muted illumination casts cerulean tints around the chamber, making particular areas of the rock face gleam mysteriously.

Scattered stone platforms emerge from the water, differing in height and reach. Farther away, strands of kelp dangle from the ceiling. Impossibly, they flourish even outside the water, transforming this part of the cavern into a verdant forest.

"Stay close," Colton murmurs to Lyra. With caution, we venture away from the water's edge, heading closer to the kelp-laden expanse.

As we delve deeper into the kelp forest, a faint, irregular rasping catches my ear. It's someone, or something, trying to stay hidden yet struggling to breathe. Instinctively, I step in front of Lyra, Colton mirroring my movements. We're her shield.

The sound leads us to a secluded alcove surrounded by dense curtains of kelp. Inside, scattered remnants of makeshift meals – fish bones, shells, and some edible underwater plants – litter the ground. This place isn't just an alcove; it's a hideout.

And there, in the center, a shadowed figure sits— Samael. But he's...different. The intimidating force he once was is now gaunt, his powerful presence dimmed. But his eyes— those are unchanged. As they latch onto Lyra, they gleam with the same hunger, the same dark obsession.

I step closer, anger fueling my voice. "What are you doing here?"

A weak sneer plays on Samael's lips, and even now it manages to irritate me. "Even at my lowest, I knew you'd come," he rasps, his focus locked on Lyra. "Euric may have taken much, but she is the key to what I desire."

Colton's voice, deep and threatening, interrupts, "You're in no position to demand anything."

Lyra, not one to be intimidated, moves forward, her voice firm. "Where is my family's grimoire, Samael?"

He chuckles, the sound more like a cough. "The grimoire? Ah, so you're still chasing shadows. Why am I not surprised? I knew you would come for it eventually."

My fists clench. "Answer the question."

"We're not leaving her here with you, if that's what you're after," Colton says, placing a hand on Lyra's back

His seedy leer grows more menacing. "Who said you had a choice?"

That's when I notice them. Emerging from the shadows are several figures – Samael's followers. They might be as magic-deprived as he is, but together they pose a threat we can't ignore.

With a swift motion, I yank a dagger from my boot. Simultaneously, Colton draws one from within his trousers. But it's Lyra who truly catches me off guard. From the sheath secured on her thigh, she draws a full-length sword. Dressed in sleek black leather, with her wet hair and now wielding a blade... Fuck, she's distracting. I shake off the trance.

The three of us form a defensive triangle, our backs touching, ensuring no angle is left unguarded as the Sorcerers begin their menacing circle around us. Quickly, I tally the numbers in my head: seven against three. The odds could be worse.

"You all cower here, devoid of your magic. Outside this

refuge, you wouldn't stand a chance against us," Colton taunts. "You've become nothing more than lost, delusional Sorcerers, trailing behind a madman who's lost his power."

My chuckle reverberates eerily off the cave walls.

One of the Sorcerers steps forward, a malicious look in his eyes. "Don't think we'll end you swiftly. We intend to make a show of it, especially with your precious princess."

"Yes, I think we should make them watch while we take turns playing with her," another says. Dark rage forms within me. Oh, he's definitely the first one I'm taking down.

The smug Sorcerer's words linger in the air, echoing faintly off the cave walls. A surge of anger courses through me, further fueled by Colton's low growl.

Without hesitation, I charge at the taunting Sorcerer, our blades clashing with a resounding clang. He's agile, but I've sparred with better. On the slick cave floor, our violent dance commences – each move, each step calculated to wound or incapacitate.

In my peripheral vision, Lyra engages with two adversaries. One attempts a swift lunge, but she counters with her impressive sword, its blade gleaming in the dim light. Her movements are solid. She's certainly learned a few things in my absence.

Colton, however, faces overwhelming odds. Three Sorcerers close in on him. He navigates the space with a unique brutality, leveraging the rock formations. Suddenly, one Sorcerer makes a bold move. He dives into the water, attempting to use it as a cover to strike from beneath. But Colton anticipates this, throwing a dagger that pierces the water, producing a muffled cry.

Yet, as I deflect and parry, a realization hits me. These Sorcerers, even without their magic, aren't entirely defenseless. They're using the cave's acoustics, the misleading echoes, to disorient us.

An unexpected pain sears through my leg. My opponent has managed a shallow cut. This fleeting victory on his part only fuels my resolve. With a feigned leftward lunge, I shift forward, sinking my dagger deep into his thigh. His agonized scream fills the chamber, but I've no time to savor the triumph, as another one approaches.

Lyra's fierce battle cry resonates as she dispatches one of her attackers. But her moment of dominance is fleeting. The remaining Sorcerer sees an opening, exploiting it to slice her arm. Blood stains her leather attire, the wound superficial but enough to stagger her momentarily. Sensing her vulnerability, he moves in for the kill, but Colton intervenes just in time, his blade meeting the Sorcerer's in a powerful clash.

Away from the immediate fray, my eyes are drawn to Samael. He stands aloof on a raised platform, gawking with relish despite his evident weakness. He's holding the grimoire, probably ready to flee with it like a coward.

Amid the cacophony of clashing blades and cries, I engage another Sorcerer. We circle one another slowly, our intentions clear. A sudden shout captures my attention.

"The grimoire!" It's Colton, having managed to get close to Samael. Despite his weakened state, Samael isn't helpless. He produces a dagger, charging at Colton, their clash intense, desperate, and utterly chaotic.

Gradually, the tide turns in our favor. One by one, the Sorcerers are defeated, until only Samael remains, cornered and outnumbered.

Breathing heavily, weapons slick with the remnants of battle, we close in on him, intent on concluding this conflict and securing the grimoire for Lyra.

She speaks first. "Samael, hand over my grimoire. It's done." She's gasping for breath, her face pale but resolute.

Samael's lips curl into a wicked smirk. "As you wish, little bird," he sneers, flinging the book toward her with a flourish. As she catches it, a sudden, unsettling transformation begins. Her fingers tremble violently, and from the book, a searing light erupts, threatening to consume everything around it. The very walls of the cavern respond, shuddering as if alive, a symphony of vibration and dread.

"You damned fools!" Samael's laughter, twisted and unhinged, rips through the cavern, but my entire focus is on Lyra. Every instinct in me screams to help her, but when Colton lunges to wrench the book from her, I stop him.

"Don't you dare touch her!" My voice comes out sharper than I intend.

"She's in pain, Nyx! Can't you see?" Colton's desperation echoes my own, but there's a gnawing thought in the back of my mind.

"Just...wait," I force the words out, my heart pounding. "Maybe... Maybe this is meant to be."

Before I can process the implications, a tremendous quake threatens to tear the cavern apart. Lyra, the epicenter of it all, collapses, the grimoire slipping from her limp grasp. The world seems to slow, every minute detail etched into my memory. Her fall echoes the haunting image of Z's lifeless form— a memory I've fought to bury. It's paralyzing.

Colton, frantic, reaches her first, shaking her gently, desperately searching for signs of life. I'm beside her a split second later, my world teetering on the edge of oblivion. And then, the gentle rise and fall of her chest—she's breathing...she's alive.

CHAPTER 31
LYRA

The moment the book brushes against my fingers, a sharp jolt of pain surges through my hands, radiating upward. This isn't right, isn't how one should feel upon touching the grimoire. The searing sensation snakes its way up my arms, causing them to tremble uncontrollably. When it reaches my heart, I gasp, overwhelmed by a feeling of constriction. Without warning, a blinding light erupts from the book. The earth seems to tremble beneath me, though I can't discern if it's my own quaking limbs or the ground itself.

My gaze locks with Colton's, his expression clouded with alarm. Then I seek out Nyx, and in that split second the world tilts, sending me plummeting toward the ground. I don't recall the impact of hitting the ground. Instead, it feels like an endless descent with a gentle darkness wrapping around me. It's unexpectedly comforting, reminiscent of being nestled within the plush embrace of the softest blanket. My senses are sharp, every nuance of sound and sensation amplified to an incredible degree. But the solitude is short-lived. In a heartbeat, I realize I'm not alone and have fallen into somewhere serene.

The beauty of this garden contrasts sharply with the danger of the purple nightshades, creating an eerie ambience. As I stand amidst the towering plants, the peculiar sky casts a dusky haze over the entire scene. It's hauntingly beautiful.

From the shadowed corners of the garden, a figure begins to emerge. Her movement is graceful, yet there's a distinct power in her step. "Lyra," her voice resonates, soft yet commanding. The very air seems to hum at the sound of her voice.

I squint, trying to make out her features. "Ryella?" My voice wavers with uncertainty and hope. She responds by letting the shadows enveloping her dissipate, drawing nearer with every step.

I'm taken aback by her mesmerizing appearance. Cascading down her back, her hair is a fiery cascade of strawberry waves. A dusting of freckles decorates her face. But it's her eyes that capture my attention the most – they're a void, an endless abyss of black. No whites, no irises, an infinite swirling darkness.

"As I see, you've made contact with the sole dark grimoire. You seek the awakening of your magic before your nineteenth year, don't you?" Ryella's words are gentle but probing. I manage a nod, my voice eluding me.

"Do you truly think you're prepared to harness such might?" Her obsidian eyes penetrate mine, probing for truth.

"I have to be ready," I reply, determined not to avert my gaze.

"Follow me," she instructs. We walk together, surrounded by plants, each more captivating than the last, all possessing a potent mix of beauty and danger.

Eventually, we approach a gazebo, distinguished by its unique pillars—carved figures of a serpent, an eagle, and another creature I can't quite identify but am sure I wouldn't want to encounter. The heart of the gazebo doesn't feature a typical fountain but one that seems to flow with pure, shifting shadows.

Ryella takes a seat, gesturing for me to join her. The situation feels surreal, but I move to sit beside her.

"Dark magic wasn't born from wickedness. It was humans who tainted its reputation," she muses, watching the dark tendrils weave around her fingers.

"I think they're scared of what they can't grasp," I observe, intrigued by the shadows that move as if they have a life of their own.

"I have limited time. Staying separated from your body for too long could have consequences," she warns. I simply nod, bracing myself for what's to come. "Since my time on Earth, numerous dark Sorcerers have arisen. All of them, unfortunately, were overwhelmed by the very power they sought to control, leading to their undoing," she reflects, a weight of countless ages behind her words. The unsettling sensation in my chest deepens. "This magic won't inherently be evil, nor wholly good. Instead, it will mirror the essence of its wielder – your innermost nature."

Her words strike a chord in me, reminding me of something I'd read in Drew's book about the last dark Sorcerer and the Luminary Council. "While dark magic isn't malevolent by nature, it's compelling and yearns for dominance. Yet such desires aren't detrimental if harnessed correctly," she continues.

Desperate for guidance, I ask, "But how will I discern the right way to harness it?"

"You are special, Lyra. The light will be your salvation," she says.

"The prophecy?" I ask, voice tinged with anticipation.

"Do you ever wonder where prophecies come from?" she begins, her eyes deep pools I can't look away from, "They're either the dreams of the gods or mere superstitions crafted by mortals. In your case, I've dreamt of you for a very long time, Lyra Lewis.

"I must caution you. Your journey will not be an easy one. The dark magic will incessantly attempt to lure you in, seducing you with tantalizing promises of power and domination. There will be others too, who will try to ensnare you, coveting your unique abilities for their own ends. But take heart, for you won't be contending with the shadows by yourself. Should you choose wisely and truly unite with the light bearer, a soul untouched by the relentless shadows, his illuminating presence will be your salvation. His unwavering light will empower you to resist the allure of the darkness, ensuring that your heart stays resolute and your motives remain untainted. For he is your destiny," she declares.

I gulp, the weight of her words pressing down on me. "And if I fail, if I choose wrongly?" I venture, dreading her response but knowing I must face the truth.

"Should that happen, not only will you doom the one you've chosen, but you will also be your own downfall. The darkness will swallow you whole, and Eguina will be irrevocably altered, becoming unrecognizable. There's so much more I'd like to share with you, but our time is running out. Are you prepared?" she asks.

I have a torrent of inquiries in my mind, but I muster the courage and utter, "Yes."

She rises suddenly and moves to the fountain's edge, motioning for me to follow. "Once you immerse your hands in this fountain of shadows, your dormant magic will manifest. You will inherit the wisdom and skills of past dark Sorcerers. With each passing day, your strength will flourish," she intones, her voice rich.

As I hesitantly approach, she suddenly reaches for the pendant around my neck, pulling it free. My heart races, and I instinctively try to reclaim it. "It's alright," she soothes, holding the stone aloft. "You will become far more enduring than this mere trinket. Consider this my gift." With a fluid motion, she casts the necklace into the swirling shadows below. "It's only fitting that your pet partakes in your newfound strength. From now on, his fate will be intrinsically linked to yours."

My fingers graze my bare neck, feeling its absence sharply. Chepi will now have a life tethered to mine, and perhaps even some unique powers of his own. As I begin to articulate my flood of questions, Ryella insists, "It's time."

I cast her a final, lingering glance, sensing an inexplicable bond with this enigmatic goddess. The urge to embrace her, to convey my gratitude, is strong, but the beckoning shadows of the fountain urge me on. Taking a deep breath, I plunge my hands into the engulfing darkness.

As soon as my hands plunge into the shadows, Ryella vanishes. Everything around me becomes intangible, leaving only the fountain and me in a void. The inky tendrils rush forth, enveloping my hands, climbing my arms, and then wrapping my entire being, leaving a chilling caress in their wake. As the fountain overflows, my body becomes a canvas of moving darkness.

Then a torrent of experiences engulfs me. It's not merely witnessing the lives of past dark Sorcerers but inheriting their essence. I don't watch from the sidelines; I live their moments after the awakening of their dark magic. I feel their triumphs, their tragedies, and their ultimate demises. With each memory, I am imbued with the understanding of harnessing this arcane power. It's an education unlike any other, a lifetime of knowledge gifted in mere moments.

It's a sensation that defies description, a profound merging of emotions, knowledge, and sheer power. It's as if the universe has whispered its ancient secrets directly into my soul, leaving me both overwhelmed and enlightened. The weight of centuries and the wisdom of ages flood through me, making it impossible to articulate the depth and magnitude of what I've just experienced.

I take a sharp inhale, my eyes flying open to find myself cradled in Colton's arms. "You're awake. You're okay," he murmurs, his gaze locked onto mine. As I take in our surroundings, the vast chamber enveloping us, it feels as if everything has shifted. It's as though I'm perceiving the world anew. The rich green of Colton's eyes seems even more intense, every nuance of the cave stands out in stark detail, and the distant rumbling is punctuated by the delicate sound of dripping water from overhead stalactites. Everything feels heightened, more vivid.

Nyx suddenly pushes Colton aside, his glowing gray eyes scanning me intently. As I reach out, he draws me into a tight embrace. "Everything's okay, Princess," he murmurs soothingly. Even though I know this closeness might pain Colton, I take comfort in Nyx's words. He's my light, the one I am destined to be with.

Pulling back slightly, urgency tinges my voice. "Where's Samael?"

"He took off when all of this began. We've been trying to ensure you're okay," Colton replies, studying me as if I'm a book he wishes to read.

The tremors in the chamber persist, hinting that the structure could crumble at any moment. The danger of our situation snaps me back to the present. I try to gather my bearings, pressing my fingers to my temples, as if that would somehow help me process everything that has transpired. It's dizzying. Everything feels more real, more vivid, more immediate.

"He ran," Nyx clarifies, his gaze sharp. "When he saw what was happening to you. When the magic began to pour out."

I glance at the grimoire, which now I know I no longer need. It still needs to be kept out of the wrong hands.

"You shouldn't have touched it," Colton mutters, his voice tinged with concern.

I shake my head, struggling to reconcile the rush of emotions coursing through me. "It had to be done," I whisper, more to myself than anyone else. "It was meant to be."

Nyx tightens his grip on my arm, pulling me closer. "We need to leave. Now. This place isn't safe."

As Nyx finishes speaking, a massive stalactite above us detaches, crashing into the waters below. "Wait," I command. Both halt and turn toward me. I grab the grimoire, tucking it securely under my arm. "Take my hands." Their skepticism is written all over their faces, but they comply.

Closing my eyes, tendrils of darkness emanate from me, enveloping Nyx and Colton. Frozen in astonishment, they don't resist as we're whisked to the surface. We materialize on the beach, the impact forcing us to our knees in the cool sand. Relief washes over me as I breathe in the familiar salty air.

Colton, still reeling, asks, "How did you manage that? You shouldn't be able to use magic down there."

Nyx interrupts, "That wasn't mere channeling. It was something entirely different."

I give a casual shrug. "I suppose the old rules don't bind me any longer."

"Let's head back to the ship," Colton suggests, his gaze lingering on me, his expression inscrutable. Without hesitation, I take both of their hands, and in an instant we're aboard the ship. "Honestly, I believe I could've transported us straight to the Lamia Realm," I muse, feeling a newfound energy pulsating within me.

"Regardless, we had to come back here to instruct the crew

for the return journey," Nyx says, his gaze steady and devoid of the apprehension I see in Colton's eyes.

A sudden urge for solitude overwhelms me. Without another word, I head to the far end of the ship, to my favorite spot. I settle down, leaning against the ship's wall. I study my hands, my arms. On the surface, I appear unchanged. But deep down, I feel different.

Although my mind should be consumed with the pressing matters of Zomea, the Gholioth blood coursing through me, and the spreading devastation I need to stop, my thoughts are consumed by Colton and Nyx. Onyx being my destiny, the necessity of our union, weighs heavily on my mind. How soon must I make a choice? As much as I care for Colton, knowing Nyx is my destined partner has shifted something within me.

With a sigh, I rub my face, feeling the grime and remnants of saltwater. I need to cleanse myself of the day's ordeals. Rising, I grab the grimoire next to me, and without a second thought I throw it overboard into the sea below. I watch it sink, knowing I won't need it anymore, but I don't want it falling into the wrong hands. I somehow feel a sense of relief.

I find Nyx and Colton in an unusual conversation given their typical aversion to one another. "Can we go to Drew's? I need a shower and a change of clothes," I request, only to be met with bewildered stares. "What's wrong?"

"You can freshen up before any discussions," Colton replies, his voice distant and guarded. His cool demeanor troubles me.

"Why meet with the council if my powers have already manifested?" I challenge.

"How can you be certain? We've only witnessed your ability to channel from the caves," Colton retorts.

His skepticism frustrates me. "I just know, alright? I can feel it." I almost divulge my encounter with Ryella but decide it's information best kept to myself for now. "What were the two of you discussing without me?"

My gaze lingers on them with suspicion.

"I believe it'd be best if you came home with me instead of going to Drew's. You should take some time to understand your newfound abilities, away from the prying eyes of the council. A council we don't even know if we can trust yet. We can always visit Zomea later when you're prepared," Colton suggests, and the idea tempts me.

Nyx quickly counters, "I am a member of that council, and I assure you, they won't be dissecting you. We need to show them that there's nothing amiss and that there's no need for further scrutiny. Besides, you being the subject of their discussions isn't ideal."

The notion of being in the spotlight is far from appealing, but after weighing the options Nyx's logic wins out. "We should head to Drew's. They need to see I'm alright, that I can manage this. And either way, I need to ensure Chepi is returned safely, before or after our trip to Zomea," I decide.

Nyx's lips curl into a satisfied smile. In contrast, Colton sighs, ruffling his hair in mild exasperation.

"Can I use my old room?" I inquire, turning to face Colton. He nods. "Drew probably expected your return. I doubt anything's been moved."

"Perfect. I'll seek you out once I'm settled," I say, my gaze shifting from Colton to Nyx.

"Are you sure I shouldn't be worried about the council meeting? Did you ever find anything in those books?" I ask, suddenly recalling the books Colton retrieved from his father's chambers at the elders' palace. I can't believe I forgot to ask him about them until now, with everything else that's been occupying my mind.

"What books?" Nyx inquires.

Colton responds, "I never found anything in them that's worth worrying you over. The council will have many new members now, especially after Aidan's death and with your parents' departure. I don't trust the council, but I trust Drew. With her and Nyx both on the council, hopefully they can sway the others to see reason."

"We won't let anything happen to you, Lyra. Let the Luminary Council think they're in control," he continues.

I nod in agreement. "Colton's right. Frankly, I'm not entirely sure what to expect. It could go either way. When you get a group of power-hungry people in a room, and they have too much control, they might see you as a threat, regardless of what we say. But we have to face it and at least know what we're dealing with," Nyx adds, and I find myself agreeing with him. If the council, or at least some of its members, are going to be my enemies, then I'd rather know about it now and face it head-on, rather than have it surprise me later from behind.

"Alright, I'll see you soon." Not wanting to bump into anyone or be cornered by the council prematurely, I channel directly into the familiarity of my previous quarters.

I immerse myself in a prolonged bath, relishing the embrace of the warm water. After cleansing my hair, I step out and approach the mirror for a closer inspection. I draw near, fixating on my eyes. They appear normal until I beckon the shadows lurking within. Almost instantly, black veins animate, converging to form swirling inky voids reminiscent of Ryella's haunting gaze. Intrigued, I summon even more of my shadows, watching as tendrils of smoky blackness cascade over my skin, ensnaring every inch of me. With a sharp intake of breath, the darkness dissipates. The face staring back is once again my own.

Tempted to experiment with my newfound abilities, I decide this isn't the right place, especially with the Luminary

Council congregating. I comb through my hair and move into the adjoining bedroom, hoping to find some dresses. To my surprise, Nyx is lounging on the edge of the bed.

"Feeling refreshed?" he inquires with a hint of amusement.

Taken aback, I let out an involuntary yelp, not having anticipated anyone's presence.

Retreating into the bathing chamber, I hastily snatch up a towel, draping it around myself.

Nyx chuckles. "Come now, it's nothing I haven't seen before." He advances closer with an impish grin.

Pushing aside his teasing remark, I ask, "Have you spoken to Drew or any members of the council?" I ensure the towel stays securely in place.

Nyx leans against a wooden dresser, his posture relaxed. "I spoke with them. There's a council meeting in an hour, but you won't be attending," he says with an air of casual dismissal.

I stare at him in disbelief. "What? Why? If they're discussing me, shouldn't I be present?"

He meets my eyes, his own filled with understanding but also a hint of frustration. "Many on the council still see you as merely a young girl. Besides, it's been ages since they've convened. The initial reunion might be filled with pleasantries. They intend to summon you afterward."

I cross my arms, resolute. "I'm more than just 'a young girl.' They need to recognize that. I'm attending that meeting."

Nyx smirks, the mischievous glint back in his eyes. "It's three floors down, second door to your left," he supplies, almost as a dare.

Raising an eyebrow, I challenge, "You just told me to wait. Why give me the location now?"

He steps closer, the space between us charged with intensity. "I said you *should* wait. But..." He tucks a wet lock of hair behind my ear. "...you are, undoubtedly, a force to be reckoned with. I won't dictate your choices."

I let out a soft sigh, "Nyx." I lower my gaze, the weight of him this close to me pressing heavily on me.

Gently, he tilts my chin upward, compelling my eyes to meet his. The depth of emotion in them is undeniable. "Lyra, where do you stand with Colton? Does sharing an intimate moment with him bind you to him?"

Taking a breath, I say, "No, we aren't committed to anything. But that doesn't mean I'm ready for something with you either. I care for him, and I care what happens to both of you."

He steps closer, the gap between us lessening. "I love you, Lyra," he confesses, his voice raw with emotion. "It's a love that feels destined, as if written in the stars. I'll wait, give you the space and time you need. Even if you wish to further explore things with Colton or anyone else. But know this. I won't let the encroaching darkness consume you. I will remain close by, until you're ready to embrace me as your light."

I swallow hard. He places a hand gently on my cheek, his thumb caressing my skin. "We get so caught up in the 'what-ifs' of tomorrow, we forget to live today. Let's be in this moment, right now, together."

He leans in slowly, maintaining our eye contact. I sense he's gauging my reaction, giving me every opportunity to step away. But curiosity, coupled with a surge of unexpected desire, keeps me rooted in place. When his lips gently touch mine, there's a softness in the gesture that takes me by surprise. The kiss deepens, our breaths mingling, the intimacy undeniable.

His hands slip into my hair, fingers, tangling in the damp strands, drawing me closer. He lifts me off my feet, and my legs wrap around his waist as he backs me into the wall. As the intensity grows, I feel the towel slip slightly, his fingertips brushing the curve of my shoulder. His kiss is tender yet insistent, capturing my complete attention, and for a few heartbeats the world fades away. All that matters is the connection between us.

His fingers trace a gentle path to my breast, and a soft moan escapes my lips as he gently toys with my nipple. "Lyra," he murmurs, his voice thick with desire, "I need you. Now." As he speaks, his other hand begins to fumble with his pants.

"Stop," I whisper, catching his hand. He pauses immediately, our eyes locking. The intensity in his gaze is unmistakable.

"What's wrong?" he asks, concern filling his glowing eyes.

Taking a deep breath, I say, "It's not that I don't want this, Nyx. It's... Everything feels so rushed. We need to slow down. I don't know what I'm doing. I don't know what I want."

He exhales, stepping back and allowing me to readjust my towel. "I apologize, Lyra," he says with genuine regret. "I got caught up in the moment. I promise I'll respect your boundaries."

"I'm not playing games, Nyx. It's all so overwhelming right now," I confess.

He raises his hand to caress my cheek. "I know," he replies softly. "Take all the time you need. I'm here, always. I should prepare for the council session," he says, briefly touching my shoulder in a fleeting yet intimate gesture. With a soft wind, he disappears—probably transporting himself to his chambers. I sink into the bed, hands covering my face, my mind a whirl of confusion. How did I get here? What the fuck is happening to me?

Every part of me is torn in different directions—my newfound powers, the burdensome prophecy, my tangled emotions with both Nyx and Colton, and the looming council meeting. Each thought weighs heavily, like chains trying to pull me under. Not to mention Samael is still out there somewhere, and I need to get to Zomea soon. I slam my fists onto the bed, and the bed frame trembles slightly. I didn't mean to do that.

This isn't the time to unravel. I have responsibilities, promises to keep, and dangers to confront. Pushing off the bed, I stride to the wardrobe, determined to find an outfit that screams confidence. Whatever awaits, I'm facing it head-on.

CHAPTER 32
COLTON

A surge of emotions hits me through the tether, an intense mix of passion and anxiety. My fists clench involuntarily. Nyx must be close, most likely in her room. The dominant urge to barrel through that door and drag him away is overwhelming. But as much as every piece of my being screams at me to intervene, I can't dictate Lyra's choices.

Still, there's a distinct difference between Nyx and me. He's been weaving his way back into her heart, especially after the incident in the caves. He's drawn to her newfound power, seeing an opportunity to seize control of Eguina.

But my desires are primal, stripped of ambition. I couldn't care less about ruling lands or wielding unmatched power. I crave her, just her. The thought of her being with someone else, especially Nyx, sets my blood on fire. It's a testament to my restraint that I don't march over there.

Though I don't sit on the Luminary Council, my heritage and power have their weight. Instead of chasing after Lyra, I need to strategize. I need to go find my parents and have a word with my mother.

Drew has already informed me of where they'll be staying. I channel to the designated room's entrance and give a firm knock. The door swings open to reveal my mother's radiant face, her golden eyes twinkling with delight at the sight of me. She pulls me into a fierce embrace, her warmth engulfing me for a moment. "Granger!" she exclaims with playful reproof, "Your son has graced us with his presence."

Drawing back with a chuckle, she tugs me inside. "Had to journey halfway across Eguina to get a visit from you, did we?" my father remarks, his voice a mix of jest and genuine pleasure. He firmly claps my shoulder in greeting before returning to the mountain of paperwork spread out on the desk. True to his nature, always engrossed in some study or research. He's undoubtedly prepping for the upcoming council gathering.

"How long do you suppose you'll both be staying?" I inquire, glancing between them.

My father sets down a stack of papers, eyeing me gravely. "Not long. The Faery Realm has had far too many attacks. It's unsafe for us to be away."

I turn to face him, eyebrows drawn in concern. "Attacks? What kind?" Memories of the event Bim had mentioned in the Dream Forest flash in my mind, but this sounds much worse.

He hastily organizes his papers, a troubled look in his eyes. "You haven't spoken with Nyx? Check with him later, must've slipped his mind. I've got to prepare, but we'll catch up soon, alright?" Without waiting for a response, he strides toward the door, pausing briefly. "Elspeth, don't be late," he advises, shooting her a knowing glance before exiting.

My mother chuckles lightly, gracefully seating herself on the plush settee. "He worries too much. I've still got time." She grins, pulling me close. "I've missed this face of yours." She motions for me to join her. "Come, sit. Share what's been happening."

I settle beside her, recounting tales of Zomea, the bridge, and the whirlwind of events since our last meeting. She listens intently, her eyes sparkling with interest.

She interrupts gently, curiosity evident in her gaze. "But what's this new bond I sense, this connection to another?"

Caught off guard, I stammer, "What do you... How?"

She arches an eyebrow, unimpressed. "Over a millennia old and a mind-walker, did you really think such an emotional tether would elude me?"

I sigh, realizing the futility of hiding anything from her. "It's complex but manageable. We've become quite adept at keeping our feelings in check," I admit, feeling her comforting understanding envelop me.

"Tread carefully," my mother warns, her gaze piercing. "I've ventured into her mind. I went searching for the Fae magic Euric concealed but glimpsed much more. She might have a pure heart, but darkness pursues her relentlessly. She's weathered storms you can't even fathom. Before she wholly surrenders her heart, she has inner battles to face."

I feel the need to stand up for Lyra, but deep down a part of me acknowledges my mother's words. "I understand," I concede, "but I'm patient. I'll do what it takes."

Her eyes, always so discerning, seem to see right through me. "You're in love with her," she states more than asks.

I nod, feeling almost vulnerable in my admission. "Yes, and that's why I'm here talking to you. She deserves to know the truth. I can't risk losing her."

She looks down, seemingly lost in her thoughts for a moment. "Oh, Colton," she murmurs, lifting my face to meet hers. "I love you dearly. But revealing our truth might shatter our family. If you truly love her, you'll find a way without ever telling her the truth. Do you understand?"

I rise abruptly. "I can't promise anything," I respond, my

voice harsher then I mean for it to be. "If I lose her to Nyx, I might never know the truth myself."

Her expression softens, and there's a visible sadness in her eyes. "You've always been a fighter. First loves are intoxicating and unforgettable, you know that. Remember your journey after Z. Just because Nyx claimed her heart initially doesn't ensure he holds onto it forever." She offers a reassuring smile, trying to lift my spirits.

"Now, escort me to this meeting and cheer up." She wraps an arm around my elbow. We ascend the several flights of stairs needed to reach the meeting hall.

As my mother and I approach the chamber, the heavy doors open to reveal the familiar grandeur of a vast round table. Memories flood back of those tedious elders' meetings I'd often try to escape from when I was younger.

Sybil, the Sorceress and Kaine's wife, quickly strides toward us. It's evident her place here is more due to her marital ties than her own merit. Kaine himself, having a seat at this council, doesn't sit well with me. But with Lyra's parents gone and Samael off the throne, the council seats seem to be filled with second choices.

I count the chairs and look around the room, taking note of who is here. There's my parents, Nyx, Drew, Roland, and Auelina. The last two, a pair of Elders from Nighthold, I haven't seen in years. And I imagine normally Aidan would be here to represent the Lycan Realm, but I presume Larc will be present tonight if the rumors are true of him taking over as leader of the packs. I don't know if he has a wife or not, will be interesting to see if he shows.

Observing the room, I realize just how Fae-dominated this council has become. Given our longevity, it's not surprising, but the imbalance is noticeable.

Pushing aside my growing unease, I settle into the chair

next to Drew. The wood beneath me feels hard and cold, reflecting the atmosphere of the room.

Kaine's voice slices through the tension. "Since when did you become a member of this council?" His condescending tone grates on my nerves.

Drew, always the pillar of calm, retorts, "He may not be an official member, but he knows Lyra better than most. He's earned his place here, even if just to listen and offer insights." I cast her a grateful glance. Our bond is time-tested. We've always stood up for one another.

Kaine's eyes narrow, but he doesn't push it, instead letting out an irked grunt. The rest of the council finds their seats.

I can't help but feel Lyra's absence. This entire assembly is for her, about her. Yet she's not here, not given a voice. It's a continuation of the life she's always led, where decisions are made for her. The injustice of it pisses me off, but for now I bite my tongue, waiting to see how the events unfold.

It's my father who speaks first. Always accustomed to running things, he finds it odd that this council doesn't really have a leader. Everyone is supposed to have an equal say. However, only a small handful of people here were even alive to witness the last dark Sorcerer's rule. "Thank you, Drew, for filling us all in and calling this meeting. I understand it was originally convened to ensure Lyra's safety during the awakening of magic. But with her magic already intact, that is no longer necessary. However, there are still many matters that need discussing today. The first, what do we plan to do with her?"

"Actually, I believe what needs to be discussed first is the situation in Eguina—the deaths, the attacks, and the unmistakable sense of darkness looming. I know I'm not the only one who has seen it, felt it," Drew asserts.

Before anyone can respond, Nyx interjects, "Indeed.

Nighthold has experienced an increase in attacks over the past few months. Creatures not typically found in Nighthold are appearing there. We've had several unfortunate fatalities, with new reports of disturbances coming in daily."

"And you don't believe this dark shroud spreading across the lands is due to the girl?" Kaine poses, skepticism evident in his voice. My gut churns with discomfort. I don't like where this conversation is heading.

"No, what's happening now feels identical to what I felt prior to the War of the Realms. Roland, Granger, surely you both remember?" Drew inquires, seeking confirmation from the seasoned elders present.

Roland dismissively responds, "The past should remain in the past. What we need to discuss urgently is the prospect of neutralizing the girl. Most here might not recall the havoc of the last dark Sorcerer, but I do. As each day passes, her power grows. If we delay, there might come a time when we're powerless against her. If King Onyx had done his job, this wouldn't be an issue right now."

My blood boils at his implication. Before Nyx can react, I interject, "Lyra has Gholioth blood in her, placed there by Euric. He's convinced that once she's back in Zomea, he can extract it. Doing so could restore Zomea's stability, consequently bringing stability to Eguina. Perhaps history is repeating itself. Who's to say Euric didn't steal something during the War of the Realms?"

"Why then, did he not act during your visit, son?" my father questions, his tone cool and indifferent. His lack of immediate support grates on my nerves, but he's always been this way.

"Because Euric believed Lyra wouldn't have survived the process; she wasn't strong enough without her dark magic," I

WHAT BEATS WITHIN THE TUNNELS

reveal. Nyx's gaze snaps to mine, his eyes piercing, as if he believes I'd have let Euric endanger her in any way.

"How can you be so sure she'll withstand it now?" Nyx challenges, making me wish we could've had this conversation privately.

"It's irrelevant whether she survives or not," my father interjects coldly. "If there's any merit to the procedure and it can halt the devastation to our realms, it must be attempted. If her life is the price for restoring balance, so be it."

Drew subtly taps my hand beneath the table, a silent plea for restraint. Yet, my patience is wearing thin.

"If she perishes in the process, it might solve two of our concerns," Roland smugly adds. I'm on the brink of eruption, especially seeing Nyx, who professes profound love for Lyra, maintaining an infuriating calm.

Nyx is accustomed to handling difficult individuals in meetings. I'm not. As I rise, poised to give Roland a piece of my mind, the Lycans enter the room. Drew instantly stands beside me, saying, "Larc and Libby, I'm glad you could join us. Please have a seat." As she settles down, she pulls me to sit beside her. Drew always appears composed, even if she's internally churning.

Larc nods in acknowledgement. "It was a challenge to slip away, but your ship proved invaluable. Thank you." I study Larc for a moment. Lyra has spoken of him in a positive light, indicating they share some history. However, the depth of their connection remains uncertain to me.

My father quickly brings Larc and Libby up to speed on the discussion thus far. "From what we've gathered, the Lycan Realm has borne the brunt of the recent disturbances. While Nighthold grapples with escalating attacks and the Sorcerer Realm witnesses dying vegetation, we'd like to understand the full extent of the situation in your territory," Drew prompts, her gaze fixed intently on Larc.

"It's been an arduous few months, especially following Aidan's death—our previous pack master—and the challenges his passing brought. Our pride in safeguarding the realms by containing the monsters within the Shifting Forest is being tested as we speak. The very essence of magic in our territory is undergoing a transformation. This looming darkness you allude to? I've witnessed it firsthand. As our forests wither away, malevolent creatures expand their territory, encroaching beyond our borders. Some of our younger Lycans struggle to control their shifting abilities, resulting in unfortunate casualties," Larc recounts.

Drew's mention of the events preceding the War of the Realms resonates in my mind. The circumstances then were different—Lyra wasn't in the picture, and the Gholioth blood wasn't a factor I was conscious of. Euric had previously sealed Zomea and mended Eguina, yet no one truly investigated the methods he employed.

What is he concealing? Despite Lyra's inclination to trust him, my instincts warn me of his potential duplicity. I'm also skeptical of my father's intentions. His longstanding alliance with Euric, during and post-war, coupled with his reluctance to delve into those times, leaves me wary. History should be our guide, ensuring we don't replicate past mistakes. But how can we benefit when our leaders seem to veil the truth? I exhale deeply, forcing myself to stay present, attentive, and above all composed.

Out of the corner of my eye, I catch a shadow moving, but with no windows and only the dim glow of candles, my eyes could easily deceive me. Roland breaks the thick tension, "It pains me to hear of the troubles in your lands, but this is a foreshadowing of what awaits all our territories. Forget Zomea, forget Euric. The girl must be eliminated. Everything traces back to her and that nefarious magic she wields."

Nyx's calm voice counters, "Lyra is not your typical dark Sorcerer. She's different, and if you'd give her a chance you'd see it for yourself." I feel my fists clenching beneath the table, trying to restrain the rising anger.

Drew chimes in, "Killing her won't end this. Another dark Sorcerer will emerge in her stead. She's not the problem." I can't help but nod in agreement, frustrated by the narrow-mindedness of the conversation.

Larc speaks thoughtfully, "I may not know the princess well personally, but she has faced betrayal from the Lycans and still chose kindness over vengeance. That says a lot about her character. Is it not possible that she can harness this dark magic you all fear?" A sense of relief washes over me hearing Larc's rational perspective. Roland might have met his match.

"No, it's impossible," Roland spits out. "No one has ever tamed such a force, and now it's in the hands of a woman. She'll be consumed by the darkness, and you all will regret the day you didn't act when she was vulnerable."

What he says about Lyra ignites something feral within me. Before I even process my own actions, my magic responds to my fury.

His chair is violently pushed backward, crashing into the wall. From the corners of my eyes, I swear the shadows part for him. I channel my power and summon roots from deep within the earth. They rupture the solid concrete walls of the hive, seizing him in their grasp. They wrap around his limbs, snaking their way up to his throat.

Auelina's horrified scream pierces the room. It's the first time I've heard her voice since the meeting started. I can't help but feel a pang of pity for her—spending a millennium married to this insufferable man must be a fate worse than death.

"Colton," my mother's voice is stern, her eyes reflecting her disapproval, "that's enough."

But my rage is focused solely on Roland. The roots constrict tighter around his throat, his gasps echoing my fury. Auelina's desperate attempts to free him are in vain. Her power always seemed weak compared to the other elders.

"Colton, release him!" my father's commanding voice booms.

With a surge of effort, I relinquish my hold, letting my magic dissipate. The roots retract, sinking back into the earth from whence they came.

"You've always been nothing more than a petulant child, easily set off by the slightest provocation. It's a wonder how you're not the biggest disappointment to your family, and it's exactly why you're not a member of this council," Roland taunts, the malice evident in his voice.

"Enough, Roland," my mother interjects, her voice carrying a mixture of anger and exhaustion.

I catch the slight slump in my father's posture, a fleeting sign of his embarrassment. I can sense his unspoken wishes — he's always desired a son more like Nyx, the picture of poise and restraint in such matters.

But I've had enough. Without a word, I tap into my magic, channeling out of that suffocating room. The weight on my chest lightens slightly with distance, and I take a deep breath. I know Drew will keep me informed of the council's conclusions later. There's only so much one can endure.

The echoing footsteps along the corridor remind me of how vast this hive is. I'm heading to Lyra's door, drawn to see her, to hear her voice. But as I approach, doubt creeps in. I'm unsure about her state of mind, and the unresolved matters with Nyx hold me back. I can't face her yet. I need to cool off.

Passing both of our rooms, I head toward the library. It's the sanctuary I need right now, a place where I can find some peace and maybe answers. I think about Drew's echosphere. Maybe it can offer me insights, help me see clearly.

My mother wants me to hide the truth, keep the secret buried. But everything in me screams against that. Love has always been about honesty. And even if I haven't told Lyra how I feel yet, there's no denying it to myself. I love her.

CHAPTER 33
LYRA

Perched on the edge of my bed, impatience gnaws at me. I long for Chepi's presence, I miss him so much already, and the temptation to channel to him is tempting. However, a gut instinct tells me it's best to wait until things stabilize in Zomea. Lili keeps him safe, I reassure myself. Ryella's words echo in my mind, veiled and mysterious. Although Chepi's life is intertwined with mine, she hinted he might inherit some of my new abilities. Could he possibly manifest his own dark magic?

A heavy sigh escapes me. The council meeting drags on, and the thought of them discussing my fate a few floors below is maddening. Through our tether, I sense Colton's departure from the gathering. He's close, somewhere down the hall, and he's upset. Panic sets in. If he left without seeking me out, the meeting's outcome must be bad. Or perhaps he's learned of my indiscretion with Nyx.

I need to speak with Colton, to apologize, to confess that I'm confused and am unsure of my actions. Yet, right now, the urge to eavesdrop on the council meeting intensifies. I channel myself to the precise location Nyx mentioned, positioning myself outside the meeting doors. Earlier, I experimented with manipulating the shadows. Theoretically, they should aid me in seeing, hearing, and even concealing myself. Regardless of what the shadow fountain taught me about dark magic, I'm no expert—yet.

My previous attempts showed me mere fragments of conversations until the moment Colton thrust Roland against the wall. Being closer now, it should, in theory, be more effective. I glance at the shadow cast by a wall candle and tentatively touch it, feeling its cool embrace. Pushing my senses deeper into the shadow, I sense a faint vibration, reminiscent of a guitar string's hum. This sensation reverberates through the hidden matrix of shadows throughout the castle, creating a complex tapestry. Refocusing on the council room's door, I allow my consciousness to glide along one of these threads, and soon I find myself tucked in a corner of the council chamber. My proximity has amplified my perception. Everything seems clearer.

As I tune into the discussion, the voice of the woman next to Roland breaks through, "If the rumors about the Gholioth blood prove true, we should seal the bridge and end the girl's life. There's no need for extraction. If she dies, she'll return to Zomea, taking the blood with her." I haven't caught her name yet, but her casual dismissal of my life stirs something inside me.

Auelina, as Roland identifies her, continues, "Granger, do you have a method to close the bridge? We can simply cast her back down, and she can sort it out with Euric. As long as we can seal it forever afterward, that solves everything. We rid ourselves of dark magic and restore the Gholioth blood to

Zomea. With the blood back, Zomea will revive, and consequently Eguina will heal."

Every time they refer to me as "the girl," it feels like a slap
in the face. Don't I deserve the basic respect of being addressed
by my name?

Granger's voice fills the room, "Flora's been persistent in
seeking a solution, and she's on the brink of a breakthrough."
My heart plunges. Flora, trying to shut the bridge? Despite my
complicated past with Nyx, I thought she was my friend. Why
would she wish such harm on me?

Nyx's eyes sharpen as he turns his head to Colton's father.
"Flora hasn't mentioned any of this to me. She's working on the
prophecy to protect Lyra, not to thrust her into harm's way.
This entire conversation is ludicrous. Granger, you've met her,
and you're aware of my feelings for her."

"I apologize, Onyx," Granger replies, a touch of regret in
his tone, "Flora's concern for you is genuine. But she also
acknowledges the greater good. The bridge has become a
threat, what with Sarrols and potentially even Euric emerging
from it. It's a risk we can't afford."

I feel betrayed. Granger was supportive when we sought to
unlock the bridge. Was his kindness a ruse, a way to earn Nyx's
trust? But Nyx already trusted him wholeheartedly... And why
would Elspeth help me with my Fae magic if in the end all they
wanted to do was find a way to get rid of me?

Nyx's voice cuts through the room, firm and pleading.
"But you know of the prophecy. My father believed in it.
There's a chance I can save her. She's destined to be by my
side. If she ever loses control, I'll be there to guide her back. I
can control her if you give me time." His words wrap around
my heart, squeezing tight, and for a moment I want to believe
him.

But I don't like where this is going. Control me? I've had

enough of being controlled, manipulated. The sting of past memories lingers. But is he simply posturing to sway them?

Granger's sneer is audible. "Onyx, the prophecy isn't certain, and for it to work she'd have to make the ultimate vow to be with you and only you. And as of now, the girl isn't even with you. Last I heard, she's been warming my son's bed, not yours."

My cheeks burn, a mix of anger and embarrassment. I struggle to keep my breathing even, my grip on the shadow threads taut.

Suddenly, a distant voice beckons, echoing like a whisper carried by the wind. "What are you doing?"

I'm yanked back, the threads of shadow slipping away as I find myself outside the council room. Colton towers over me, his gaze sharp with suspicion, studying every inch of my face. It's then I realize that I've been caught.

"I felt your anger, saw the swirling shadows in your eyes," he says, his voice laced with concern. "Were you...listening in?"

Drawing a shaky breath, I nod, pushing a stray lock of hair behind my ear. "I was using the shadows to eavesdrop."

A wicked grin spreads across his face, transforming his features from concern to amusement. "Of course you were, my shadow." He leans in, capturing my lips with his. When he pulls away, a wave of guilt crashes over me, and I'm about to confess when he raises a finger to my lips, silencing me.

"You don't need to tell me about Nyx," he says. "I've seen his attempts, and I know you're torn about the prophecy." I'm relieved, yet the weight of uncertainty remains.

His eyes search mine, full of questions. "What did I miss?"

Taking a moment to collect my thoughts, I reply, "Not much. Discussions of throwing me into the bridge or ending my life. But why should I care about their opinions?" I attempt a playful tone, but the strain is evident.

Colton's jaw tightens momentarily then softens. "You care more than you let on. This council... It's all bullshit. Let's put an end to this talk of harming you."

Before I can protest, he's thrusting the doors open and grabbing my hand, pulling me into the room.

The tension in the room thickens as the members of the council shift their gazes between Colton and me. The heavy drapes and ornate decorations of the chamber seem oppressive, with the central table acting as the barrier between the council and us.

Roland's piercing stare never wavers. I can see the skepticism in his eyes, mingled with something darker—contempt, perhaps. He's a tall man with a severe face and silver streaks in his hair. Power emanates from him, and I can sense that he's used to getting his way. His hate isn't hidden, rather on full display, challenging me with its intensity.

When Drew extends the invitation to sit, his tone carries a hint of mock politeness, his eyes twinkling with barely suppressed amusement. "Lyra, Colton, come take a seat. Join us."

But I'm not in the mood for their games. "I think I'll stand, thank you." I reply, firm and unwavering. My posture is tall and confident, feet planted firmly on the polished marble floors. The last thing I want is to appear submissive or meek in front of them.

Colton's hand brushes against mine, a silent offer of support. I appreciate his presence, but right now I need to stand my ground, alone.

The swirling tempest of emotions inside me is hard to suppress. On one hand, there's the instinctive urge to shield myself, to appear unthreatening and gain their favor. On the other, a sense of defiance grows, urging me to show my strength, to let them see the storm they're recklessly provoking.

A sharp voice cuts through my inner chaos. "You weren't invited to this meeting for a reason. What are you doing here?" The woman next to Roland, draped in flowing robes of deep emerald, freely shares her disdain. Auelina, I presume.

Taking a deep breath, I ready myself to reply, to face the council and assert my place. No longer the girl they think they can toy with but someone with power, resilience, and a will that won't be easily broken.

"Apparently, the most important conversations about me happen when I'm not in the room. It's time I change that," I say with a smile, cool and distant. Auelina's face contorts, barely masking her contempt.

As the meeting progresses, I glance over at Kaine and his wife, Sybil. They are Sorcerers from my realm, and I am destined to be their queen, yet they remain silent, offering no defense on my behalf. In fact, they haven't uttered a word throughout the entire meeting. When my gaze finally meets Kaine's, he clears his throat, and for a brief moment I anticipate him speaking up for me.

"Lyra, if I may," he begins, and I brace myself. "We all witnessed the toll that practicing dark magic took on Samael. Do you truly believe that you embody what's best for Cloudrum? Perhaps we should explore ways to rid you of this dark magic." His words strike me like a blow, and anger courses through me. It's clear now—he only seeks to maintain his control, and of course he would attempt to suppress my power...but to compare me to Samael.

Nyx attempts diplomacy, "Lyra, perhaps you should return to your quarters. I'll fetch you when this is over." His voice is soothing, but I can't ignore the undertone. He's parading me, showing them he has some semblance of control. Yet, he doesn't grasp my exhaustion from constantly being told what to do.

"I'd rather stay, especially if you're plotting my demise. At least have the audacity to discuss it in my presence." My gaze flits between Granger, Roland, and Auelina, finally settling on her. "Or are you afraid of what my shadows might do?"

Granger shakes his head in disbelief then addresses Nyx directly. "Nyx, if you think you can reign her in, you're deeply mistaken." As Nyx casts me a desperate glance, seeking understanding, I spot Larc, and genuine warmth fills me.

I yearn to discuss the Lycan Realm and ask about Rhett, but Roland, bristling with agitation, interrupts. "Drew, the time to secure her in the magical tomb is now. That's what it's designed for. We'll debate her destiny while she's confined." That startles me.

"What tomb?" I demand, sidestepping his aggression and focusing on Drew. She's unfazed, her signature nonchalant expression intact.

"The magical tomb deep within the hive. Constructed ages ago in anticipation of a formidable dark Sorcerer. Its power surpasses the bars that held Onyx. Once inside, all magic is rendered useless."

"Try it, and you'll have to contend with me," Colton declares, advancing defiantly.

Drew, ever the peacemaker, interjects, "Let's not resort to rash decisions. Lyra isn't a threat if treated with respect." But as Drew attempts to stabilize the rising tension, I sense the fire within me blazing hotter and the shadows cocooned beneath my flesh writhing, eager to burst forth.

Roland and Auelina, in unison, rise to their feet, confronting us. "Facing you is no concern of mine, young man. To me, you're as volatile as she is," Roland spits out.

The restraint I once had wavers, allowing a surge of my arcane energy to ripple through the chamber. An icy chill settles, and shadows cascade, swallowing some of the chamber's light. This partial unleashing of my dark capabilities feels invigorating, and I revel in the immediate relief it brings to my being.

In a heartbeat, Roland and Auelina unleash their powers, catching me off guard. Roland hits Colton with a magic surge so potent that I sense Colton's shock and pain through our bond, and I involuntarily let out a scream. Almost simultaneously, Auelina's magic crashes into me, feeling like a shard of ice piercing my heart. Though Colton quickly regains his footing, Granger intervenes. I catch fragments of their exchange, but my ears are muffled by my rising fury and the onslaught of my dark magic.

Drawing all ambient light toward me, I absorb its essence, casting the room into complete darkness. I think I hear a gasp—perhaps from Colton's mother—but it barely registers. Channeling the gathered energy, I shove my arms forward, releasing a dense, pitch-black orb of viscous energy straight at Auelina. I simultaneously release the light back to the room, wanting to witness her reaction. The sheer terror in her eyes, right before my magic engulfs her, is a sight to behold. She clutches her chest, stumbling back into the table before collapsing to the ground.

I tilt my head back, a grin spreading on my face. The electrifying sensation of sheer dominance ripples through me, feeling almost euphoric. This intoxicating power of darkness is something I've never experienced before, and in that moment I succumb to the seduction. I grasp its allure. Embracing it, even briefly, is profoundly exhilarating—orgasmic even.

"Her eyes... What's happened to them?" the woman beside Larc murmurs. My fingertips graze my face, and I'm confused about what she means, but it's the reactions of Colton and Nyx that really ground me. Colton, no longer restrained by Granger, and Nyx, poised, looking like he's ready to intervene, with Drew at his side.

I glimpse Roland beside Auelina, motionless, and a surge of realization and intoxicating power courses through me, beckoning me, caressing every fiber of my being. The stares of everyone are intrusive, making my skin crawl, but the darkness within feels like a lover's embrace, promising ecstasy and might.

Larc's voice slices through the thick tension, "Everyone, take a breath. Let's talk this through." But I can barely hear him against the symphony of power playing within me, urging me to dance to its seductive tune.

Roland's voice, dripping with venom, pierces my thoughts. "She's gone because of you!" His charge toward me is halted by an instinctive lash of my shadow tendril. As it tightens its grip, Roland's voice, desperate and filled with dread, shouts, "She must be stopped now!"

I'm captivated by the sight before me—Roland, choking on my power. The thrill is electrifying, addictive, a siren's call beckoning me into deeper waters of dark magic.

A distant murmur, "Lyra, my shadow," reaches me. It's Colton, his presence a gentle anchor, but the lure of my power pulls me away.

Nyx, trying to be the mediator, steps closer, hands raised, voice soothing. "Lyra, let's resolve this. Release him. No one will harm you, I promise." The seductive promise of the darkness makes me revel in Roland's plight. Each gasp he takes is an affirmation of the power I've embraced. I morph my shadow into something with more substance, a dense suffocating force. As I consider deepening my grasp, Larc is upon me. My shadows retreat as he clamps his arms down around me from behind. Roland coughs out remnants of my essence, gasping for air, and Larc's grip tightens around me.

In Larc's grip, I thrash, momentarily disconnected from my magic. Cast to the floor, I try to remind myself of his alliance, that he doesn't seek to harm, only to halt my descent. Yet, as he struggles to pin me down, his form warps grotesquely.

His face twists, and those piercing blue eyes staring into mine become hauntingly familiar. A torrent of memories featuring Aidan floods my mind, and a debilitating panic grips me, suffocating every breath, until I surrender once more to the intoxicating pull of my dark magic.

CHAPTER 34
NYX

In the tense stillness of the room, Roland's violent coughs, filled with a black, tar-like substance, echo eerily. Every gaze fixes on Larc and Lyra, their struggle evident. Despite Larc's intentions, every fiber of me screams to intervene. Her screams of anguish pierce the silence, echoing with a terror that's hard to describe. I watch Larc's face begin to warp, hinting at an imminent shift.

Glancing to my right, I see Colton's parents shielding him protectively or restraining him from intervening. I can't tell which. Drew, Granger, and Elspeth exchange hushed words—maybe pleading for Colton's release? Kaine and Sybil flee the room, fucking cowards.

Feeling a surge of urgency, I get ready to step in. But before I can, Lyra sends Larc soaring through the air. His pained howl fills the room, and a consuming darkness engulfs her. It's not just any shadow—it's alive, swirling around her as if she's its very core. Dark tendrils emanate from her, entrapping Larc. His growls, though menacing, don't seem to shake her.

She rises, and the sight captivates me. Her eyes, no longer

recognizable, appear as infinite wells of swirling obsidian. Dark veins mark her face, and the shadows wrap around her, as if they're part of her very being. Her once white-blonde hair flows like a torrent of night itself. She's both hauntingly beautiful and terrifying.

Pushing past my shock, I try to reach out to her. "Lyra, Princess, let's release Larc and talk. I know your emotions are running high, and this new power is overwhelming. But I believe you're stronger than this. Control it." I take a step, hoping for a glimmer of recognition. Yet she seems utterly lost, distant, oblivious to my pleas.

The room's tension spikes as Roland's voice cuts through, "Forget caging her. She needs to be put down!" With a furious yell, he launches himself at Lyra, his hands alive with power. A rush of his magic surges past me, aimed directly at her. But instead of the expected impact, she remains unyielding, barely moving an inch.

"All of us, Granger! We need everyone!" Roland's voice is tinged with frustration.

My heart races, fearing for Lyra. They might actually harm her if they deem her uncontrollable. Determined, I extend my hand, reaching through the thick shadows to grasp hers. I pull her gently, urging her to face me. Her gaze falls upon me, but it's distant, curious—as if she's never met me. Even so, I'm not afraid. My love for her is unwavering.

"Lyra, come back to me," I whisper, and for a moment there's a hint of recognition. The blackness in her eyes begins to recede.

But the moment is shattered as Libby, in her shifted form, lunges. Colton, breaking away from his constraints, intercepts her, pinning the she-wolf to the ground. She rises quickly, but Lyra's focus has shifted back to the Lycans, her connection with me lost.

The room devolves into chaos. Elspeth and Drew wrestle to subdue Granger, while Roland, with a war cry, makes another charge at Lyra. But Drew's voice rises above the din, "Stop attacking her! If you keep this up, we're turning her into the very monster you fear!" It's rare to hear her voice so forceful, but she's right.

Drew's call fades into the background as I make my move, getting between Lyra and Roland. His power collides with me, a frigid onslaught that knocks the wind out of me. I'm bent on subduing him, but without resorting to my own magic. The last thing we need is more chaos.

High above the table, Lyra's dark tendrils still ensnare Larc, suspending him helplessly. On the ground, the scuffling and growling signify the ferocious tussle between Colton and Libby. Everything's spiraling, and it's tangible in the sudden drop in temperature. The once flickering candles now stand extinguished, and puffs of cold mist accompany every breath I take.

As I attempt to regain my footing, another burst of Roland's power strikes my midsection, forcing a painful grunt out of me. But that discomfort is just the precursor. A subtle hum gives way to a room-shaking tremor that reverberates through the very foundations. This is not a good omen.

A yelp of pain breaks through the rumbling. Libby's teeth have found their mark on Colton, as the acrid scent of blood begins to permeate. The vibration amplifies, a testament to Lyra's mounting distress. We have to act—before her unbridled power threatens to tear the very hive apart.

The council chamber's doors burst open, revealing a seething Adira, likely drawn by the pandemonium. She unsheathes her blade with practiced swiftness, aiming the back of it squarely for Lyra's head. A part of me rationalizes that perhaps knocking her unconscious might be the solution. Such a blow would be non-lethal, merely incapacitating.

Roland, seizing the distraction, regains his balance and lands a brutal blow of pure magic. The force collides with Lyra, causing her to stagger backward, making her even more vulnerable to Adira's incoming strike. As I lunge toward Roland, aiming to thwart any further assault, Lyra's cry of raw anguish echoes through the chamber. The countless shadowy tendrils that once bound Larc suspended break away, tearing him into pieces as they descend. Blood mists into the air, and his flesh rains down in ribbons all over the table—fuck.

The gut-wrenching aftermath leaves me in disbelief. Roland, too close for comfort, receives the brunt of her wrath next, disintegrating instantly into ash that coats the bloodstained surfaces. The fallout continues as Libby, still in her wolf form, combusts into searing flames. The chamber is consumed by mayhem, and Colton can only recoil in horror, his face twisted and distraught.

Lyra's shadows lash out behind her, casting Adira beyond the threshold before dissipating. The dim chamber flares back to life, illuminated by the rekindled candles. As I meet her gaze, the darkness remains, yet a hint of her essence lingers. Sensing her intention to flee, I recognize the familiar aromatic blend of her presence giving way to her signature honeysuckle scent. Driven by instinct, I launch myself at her, grabbing hold as she initiates her escape—taking us both into the unknown as she channels.

We crash onto the forest floor, the distant sounds of waves signaling our proximity to the shore. Lyra quickly positions herself atop me, pushing me deeper into the soft earth beneath. Our eyes meet, hers mostly familiar but with faint tendrils of darkness still dancing in the whites. Before I can utter her name, she silences me, her lips crashing into mine.

Her tongue explores, asserting her dominance, while her hips move rhythmically against mine. Her fingers entangle themselves in my hair, pulling me even closer. Every coherent thought is chased away by the sheer intensity of her desire and the overwhelming sensation of her body pressed against mine.

She's intoxicated by the rush of dark magic coursing through her veins, and every part of me wants to embrace this pleasure with her. Damn, she wants to claim me, and I want to let her. I've never felt her so dominant like this, and it's fucking hot. I have to fight the urge to lose control alongside her.

I'm aware that she's not entirely herself right now. When she momentarily breaks our kiss to breathe, I seize the opportunity. Grasping her face gently between my hands, I compel her to meet my eyes. "Lyra," I say, seeking the depth of her soul.

For a moment, I find her there, fully present, as she whispers, "Nyx."

We lock eyes, both of us momentarily lost in a shared silence. Her gaze penetrates mine, searching for something I hope she finds. Slowly, she begins to pull away. Sitting up, I instinctively reach out, enveloping her in my arms, pulling her close. I sense the tears before they even form, her eyes glistening. "Oh gods."

Stroking her hair, again blonde, I whisper, "It's okay. I've got you."

But she's already rising to her feet, distance creeping into her eyes. I stand too, trying to anticipate her next move. "Nyx, I... They're gone. I took their lives." The weight of realization hangs heavy between us.

Larc, Libby, Roland, Auelina – I might not have mourned the latter two, but the truth is, death, especially one caused by someone you care about, is never easy to swallow.

"Lyra—" I try to bridge the growing distance between us.

But her eyes, so filled with anguish and turmoil, tell me

she's spiraling. "No, Nyx... I can't," she stammers. And before I can reach out, she channels away, leaving me alone in the forest of the Lamia Realm. Damn it.

I return to the hive, materializing instantly in the council chamber. To my astonishment, most evidence of the recent horrific scene has been cleared away. I would say this meeting was an epic failure. My father would be disgusted by everyone's behavior today. They let their own prejudices and greed for power obstruct their ability to see reason. I really thought I could sway the others into at least giving Lyra a chance. I've never before witnessed such a display of fear, hatred, and irrationality from them.

Colton paces, his eyes narrowing instantly as they land on me. He advances. "What happened?"

Drew's attention also shifts to me, her expression expectant.

"She's okay, herself again," I begin. "Grappling with the aftermath of her actions today is going to be hard for her. By the time she comprehended the full scale of what she'd done, she was in tears and channeled away before I could reach her. Now, I have no idea where she's gone."

Drew suggests, "Colton can find her."

Surprised, I retort, "How? If I can't trace her, how can he?" Colton and Drew exchange a brief, knowing look before Colton offers a response.

I nod for him to explain, though resenting it. "Euric and Athalda tethered us in Zomea to safeguard Lyra," Colton says. The notion that he's connected to her in this intimate way sends a surge of jealousy through me. He can feel her emotions, sense her presence.

"Well, find her now," I order.

He closes his eyes, raising a hand in a gesture for silence. Though my patience is thin, I exhale a deep breath.

Moments later, he says, "She's crossed the bridge. She's in Zomea."

I know instantly that I have to go after her.

Elspeth's voice, calm yet filled with concern, echoes across the room. "What will you do next?" She looks to me, her gaze seeking answers.

Granger, sitting beside her, chimes in, "We might need to get Flora involved, consider closing the bridge while she's still in Zomea."

Drew speaks up, "That's not going to solve anything. If Lyra can't master her dark magic, especially after what we've seen today, then the prophecy is our only hope."

Granger, ever the strategist, brings up another concern. "And the Lycan Realm? How will this affect them?"

"I say we deal with their reactions later," I shoot back. The immediate crisis at hand is Lyra, not Lycan politics.

Colton steps forward, determination evident in his voice. "I need to be the one to go after her."

I whirl to face him, ready for another clash. But it's Granger who settles it. "Onyx is the one she needs right now. His light is the counter to her darkness. Colton, you played a part in today's events, getting between them when you know they are destined to be together. Perhaps it's best you step aside."

I can't help but smirk in Colton's direction, anticipating his retort.

"I'm sorry, Mother." Colton's voice is heavy with emotion as he addresses Elspeth. Instinctively, I tense, half-expecting an outburst or an attack from him. He seems dangerously on edge, like he might snap. Elspeth's face, however, is etched with pain, and her eyes are shimmering with unshed tears. I struggle to make sense of the situation.

"We can't be certain the prophecy is about Nyx," Colton continues, desperation clear in his voice.

I scoff, irritation flaring up. "Really, Colton? You sound pathetic. Lyra never loved you. You were just a temporary distraction while she tried to get over me. It clearly didn't work."

Colton grimaces, scratching his chest as he struggles with something he doesn't want to say.

"Nyx," he pleads, taking a deep breath, "you've got it all wrong. The prophecy might refer to either of us. Because...Callum is my biological father too."

I swear my heart stops for a split second. I'm ready to dismiss it as another of his ludicrous tales, but then Drew, usually so composed, steps forward, confirming his claim.

Elspeth's tear-filled eyes move to meet Granger's, who looks equally stunned. "Elspeth, this is madness! What's going on here?" Granger demands.

She hesitates, tears spilling over as she confesses, "After Callum passed, his magic transferred to Colton. We... Callum and I... It was only once, after a late-night event. Granger, I'm so sorry. I love you."

I'm in shock, trying to digest the implications. "But my father's magic... It came to me," I say, suddenly unsure.

Colton's face is earnest as he approaches me. "Nyx, I was just as taken aback. When the magic manifested in me, I confronted my mother. Initially, I couldn't accept the truth either. I wanted to tell you sooner, but our relationship was already so strained. I couldn't risk tearing our family apart with this secret."

Even with his explanation, I find it hard to believe. My world feels upended, and all I can do is try to process this revelation.

My eyes dart between Colton and Elspeth, grappling with

the revelations. "So you're saying I inherited all of my mother's magic, not my father's?" The implications dawn on me, and I'm staggered. "And the only reason I didn't get my father's magic was because Colton is older?"

Elspeth nods, her face pale but resolute. "Had Colton been younger than you, you might have inherited Callum's magic. I might never have had to reveal the truth about Colton's biological father."

The room feels like it's closing in. I always believed I had all of my father's magic. I remember those times I'd tried and failed to conjure illusions like he could. I assumed it was a unique gift, a talent that might've skipped me. But then there was Colton—had I ever witnessed him wielding such powers?

"Prove it," I challenge, trying to assert some control over the situation.

Colton's eyes lock onto mine, the intensity visible. "Have you never questioned why our wings bear such resemblance? Why we can both discern auras, a trait unique to our line?"

I'm doubtful but refuse to show it. "Demonstrate it then. Show me something that only my father could do."

He hesitates, exhaling a deep sigh. But then, to my shock, three identical versions of Colton materialize before me. They speak in perfect harmony, their voices echoing in the chamber. "Is this enough proof for you?"

The illusions fade, leaving the real Colton. And as the truth sinks in, realization washes over me. My adversary, my rival, my brother. And we are both in love with the same girl— Lyra.

Suddenly the door slams shut behind Granger. Elspeth's apologetic gaze lingers on Colton for a moment before she rushes after her husband, leaving an awkward silence in her wake.

"Does Lyra know about this?" My voice sounds louder than intended in the quiet of the room.

"No." Colton's reply is simple, and I'm taken aback. Why wouldn't he have used this information as leverage to play on her emotions?

Drew, her voice low and thoughtful, adds, "I think he might've hinted at it once, but it was ages ago. Lyra probably never connected the dots."

I snap my gaze to Drew, eyebrows furrowing. "And how the hell are you in on this secret?"

Colton speaks up, his voice defensive but weary. "She's an old friend. I needed someone to talk to after I found out. Nighthold wasn't exactly brimming with confidants."

Shaking my head, disbelief threatening to drown me, I declare, "This revelation doesn't make us family, Colton. Don't expect any brotherly bond."

His eyes harden. "I never expected it to change things between us. But for Lyra it changes everything."

Despite the animosity between us, I can't deny what he's saying. Drew steps in, her voice eerily calm. "It's more than a torn heart, Nyx. Lyra's destiny involves choosing between the two of you. The fate of all of us hangs in the balance."

Colton and I exchange a long, searching look.

"Looks like it's time we go to Zomea to get our girl," Colton says with a maddening smirk. The audacity to refer to Lyra as "our girl!" I suppress the urge to snap at him, reminding myself that there are bigger things at play here.

Even if he is my father's son, even if we might share some twisted brotherly bond, Lyra is not up for debate. She's mine. Everything between us, every moment, every touch... It can't all have been for nothing.

The memory of our recent intimate moment rushes back, igniting a fire within me. It's a clear sign, isn't it? A sign that despite everything, despite Colton's sudden revelations and the prophecies, she still feels something for me.

Without another word, I reach for the door handle, ready to put this room and its stifling atmosphere behind me. Throwing it open, I step aside, offering a sarcastic bow to Colton. "After you, brother." The word tastes like ash in my mouth, but I force it out, challenging him with my stare.

CHAPTER 35
LYRA

My heart thrashes wildly, its every frantic beat echoing the horror of what I've done. Panic pushes me to the cliff's edge, where the bridge is located. Without a moment's pause, without allowing my mind to replay the awful scenes, I jump. I surrender to the void, letting the darkness pull me in, enveloping me until the world shifts and I find myself in Zomea.

My feet touch the cold stone of the tunnel floor, and I'm running, running away from the monster I fear I've become. Tears streak down my face, each salty drop an emblem of my remorse and pain. If only I could distance myself from the memories, from the dark power that surged through me, from the lives it claimed.

The tunnels whisper, their eerie voices chasing me, almost as if they're sharing my anguish. In this strange way, they offer solace. Their haunting presence is a distraction from the crushing weight of guilt threatening to tear me apart. I don't know how to get to the surface. I need to find a portal, or my father needs to find me as he did before. *Keep running.*

I scream his name, my voice a desperate plea echoing through the winding pathways. But there's no immediate answer, just the pounding of my heart — or is it? A distinct, calmer heartbeat resonates through the tunnels, so different from my own racing pulse. Its steady rhythm beckons me, drawing me deeper into the labyrinth than I've ever been.

Getting lost in these depths seems insignificant compared to the chaos I'm fleeing. I welcome the fear, wanting to feel anything other than what I'm feeling in this moment. I let the rhythmic heartbeat guide me, latching onto its steadiness, yearning for it to calm my own frenetic heart, hoping it might somehow drown out the memories of the council room's horrors.

In a flash, I stumble, my foot snagging on something unseen. Momentum throws me forward, arms flailing to brace my fall. My palms smack against the wet, cold ground. Trying to catch my breath and reorient myself, my eyes adjust enough to identify the thick, dark substance coating my hands—blood. Oh gods, the council room flashes in my mind, the blood staining nearly every surface.

I push the memory aside and rise on shaky feet, acutely aware of the intricate mesh of roots that have started to dominate the ground. As I tread further, the entire tunnel transforms. Roots and branches envelop the walls, ceiling, and floor, creating a natural cave that seems to pulse with life—or maybe with dread. I recall the hauntingly vivid dream that has often consumed my nights and have a realization.

This place, this eerily familiar setting, it's the very scene from those dreams. Why has my midnight mind brought me here? What does it want me to see?

Droplets fall from overhead, the same viscous blood splattering against my skin, confirming my worst fears. The distant heartbeat, that rhythmic *lub dub*, grows more pronounced, pulling me deeper into this nightmarish landscape. Every ounce of my being tells me to run, to flee from the escalating horror, but I can't. I need answers. Steeling myself, I let the heartbeat guide me, desperate to confront whatever lies at its source. I need to know what beats within these tunnels and why I'm the only one who can hear it.

I round the corner, and the thick web of roots and branches in this part of the tunnel immediately demand my caution. With every step, I'm forced to navigate over, under, and around the maze of organic obstacles. The squelching sound beneath my boots is the only other sound accompanying the now deafening *lub dub* that reverberates through the tunnel.

Up ahead, I can see something, the faintest shimmer at the end of the tunnel. It's like my dream, and I have the strangest feeling as I work to approach it. It's as if an invisible wind has picked up and is tugging me forward, tugging me closer to the shimmering glow in the distance.

I reach the end of the tunnel and push through a tangled web of roots crisscrossing the entryway. I have reached it and stare for a moment, unable to move, while I try to comprehend what's in front of me. I've stumbled upon an object unlike anything I have ever seen before.

It's large, roughly the size of a boulder, yet its texture is unlike stone. The surface appears slick, glistening with a wet sheen that shimmers with light coming from within the object itself. It's a deep red, almost black in some places, interspersed with patches of white and gray tendrils and vessels. These vessels creep over its surface like winding rivers and then break free at the top, where the branches extend out all the way to the ceiling and then branch off and spread across every surface of this place.

Its most astonishing feature is its rhythmic movement. Every second or so, the entire structure contracts and then releases, pulsating with a life of its own. This movement is accompanied by a deep, resonating thud, which sends subtle vibrations through the ground. This is the heart. This is the heartbeat I've been hearing, the heartbeat I've been searching for. The whole entity seems fragile and strong at the same time, as if it's brimming with raw power.

It's suspended in the very center of the room, and where branches break free at the top a lattice of roots stems from its base, snaking and intertwining, fusing with the tunnels from where I came. Parts of it are semi-transparent, revealing a maze of inner chambers, and with each pulsation I can see a surge of shimmering translucent fluid being pushed through them.

In a strange, mesmerizing way, this bizarre structure seems both otherworldly and deeply familiar. There's an undeniable organic quality to it, reminding me of the inner workings of a living being. Energy radiates from it and the bleeding black, tarry substance pools at the ground beneath it and drips off the roots and branches.

"I knew you would be drawn here when the time was right," a voice says, startling me. I spin around to find my father stepping into the dome-like chamber. Without a second thought, I rush into his arms, seeking comfort in his embrace.

"Oh, Father, I've done something terrible," I confess, tears threatening to spill.

"There, there, Pixie," he murmurs, holding me close. "Tell me what happened."

The weight of my actions press down on me, and I struggle to find the words. "The Luminary Council was meeting. I thought... I believed I could control the dark magic, but they were hostile and threatening, and... I killed them, Father. I killed half of the council." The reality of my confession knots my stomach as remorse threatens to undo me, and I can't bring myself to meet his gaze.

"I hadn't wanted to kill them, but they were discussing killing me, confining me in a no-magic chamber, simply because of their concern over not being able to control me," I say in defense.

He places a hand gently but firmly under my chin, forcing me to look at him. "My darling, you were destined for this," he says, a sinister smile slowly spreading across his features.

I blink in disbelief. "What did you just say?" I ask under my breath. I instinctively take a step back, wishing I had misheard him.

He tilts his head, studying me. "You were born for darkness. There are shadows that stir within you, a hunger for power. Embrace it, let it consume you, and you will achieve greatness beyond your wildest dreams," he says with an eerie calmness.

I search his face, trying to find the father I once knew, but there's a gleam in his eyes that I've seen before, one I've tried to ignore. Memories of the intoxicating power of the dark magic rush back to me. The shadows, the overwhelming ecstasy as they coursed through my veins. But the destruction, the loss, it was all too real. I shake my head, torn between the allure of power and the consequences of surrendering to it.

I swallow hard, the weight of my thoughts heavy on my chest. "I can't let myself hurt anyone else," I murmur, mostly to myself, feeling the pain of my actions. "If I go down that path again, I might never find my way back."

Father's voice cuts through the tension, dripping with disdain. "Look at you, so weak. This isn't the Lyra I raised. You were meant to embrace your dark magic, not cower from it. Resisting its pull will only delay the inevitable. Your magic even led you here."

I take another step away from him, unsettled yet desperate to understand what's truly happening and how to save Eguina.

The urge to purge this blood from me grows stronger. If being with Nyx is the key to mastering my magic, then maybe I can accept that. But first I have to address the situation at hand.

"What is this place? What is this thing?" I question, though I'm unsure whether I can trust any answer my father provides.

"This, my dear, is the heart of Eguina. It's the source of all of Eguina's magic, the very force that powers the lands and breathes life into the continent," he explains. The heart's overwhelming presence in the room is strong.

"Why was I drawn here? Why has my midnight mind been leading me to this place?" I press on.

He takes a deep breath, "Because it's in your blood, Lyra. You're bound to this heart, much like I am. The heart of Eguina calls out to those who possess the power to either save or destroy it. Your midnight mind dreams were not random; they were the heart's way of summoning you." He glances at the pulsating organ, its rhythm echoing through the cavernous space. "Your connection to it is deeper than you realize. It's beckoning you because of the power you carry within." I stare at him, my mind racing, trying to piece together what he's saying.

"Now," he intones, drawing me back to the present, "you're prepared to uncover the reason behind all this."

I find myself wanting to know more.

"As you can discern, the heart of Eguina is in dire straits," he states, his voice heavy. "I never needed your Gholioth blood, but the truth would've been too much for you then. Athalda's tale seemed a fitting lie, so I played along."

My internal alarms go off. "What made the heart sick? What did you do?" I ask sharply.

As he begins to circle the heart, I keep a safe distance between us. "I had envisioned our meeting unfolding quite differently," he says with a sigh, "but now that we're here, it's only fitting I begin at the very start." He pauses, and for the briefest moment, an unmistakable shade of sorrow crosses his features."Do you recall how, during your time here, you didn't experience any midnight mind visions?"

"Yes," I respond tersely, growing impatient. "I remember."

He nods, slowly. "That's because while you are in Zomea your midnight mind remains dormant, saving its revelations for when you're back in Eguina. It always delves deeper... After my demise, after my arduous journey into Zomea, I resigned myself to this being my final resting place. But then my midnight mind showed me something more. It took me deeper."

His eyes lock on the heart.

"Deeper?" I echo.

He glances at me, his eyes searching mine. "There are gates in Zomea, ancient and mysterious. Their final destination is known to none. I used to believe they led to the realm of souls lost to the final death – those too weak to seize a second chance in Zomea. The Gholioths, however, hold a different belief. They believe the gods live beyond the gates."

"The gods?" I interject, the mention catching me off guard.

He nods, taking a moment before continuing, "Indeed. The Gholioths were once Fae, powerful beings who harbored a relentless ambition for even greater power. They sought to unlock these very gates, aspiring to dwell alongside the gods. But their attempts were in vain, and their failures transformed them. They were cursed, morphing into grotesque creatures, forever tasked with guarding the depths of Zomea. Eternity stretches before them, void of solace or respite."

"But why? I don't understand."

His face tightens. "That's beside the point at the moment. They failed because they were too weak. No one has ever successfully opened the gates," he retorts with evident irritation.

"You think you can? How does this tie into me or the heart of Eguina?"

"The heart of Eguina is deteriorating, dying. That's the reason behind the chaos in Eguina. The situation will continue to worsen unless the heart regains its magic," he insists.

"But how did the heart fall into this state in the first place?" My gaze narrows, suspecting his involvement.

"To breach the gates, I need unparalleled power. So I've siphoned nearly all the magic from this heart, and it isn't the only one. There are three hearts in total, each powering a distinct continent. Eguina's heart is but one. My dear, there are lands even grander than Eguina. Two other continents, two other hearts," he reveals.

I try to wrap my mind around the existence of other places like Eguina.

"How can that be?" I stammer.

"It's a vast world, one that Eguina's inhabitants, including you, are oblivious to. I too was ignorant for a significant part of my life," he admits.

"Why disclose all this to me now? What's the endgame?" I demand, my patience wearing thin.

"Having drained all three hearts, I stand on the threshold of unlocking the gates," he declares. A chill sweeps through me, dread sinking into my bones.

"So you'd doom everyone for a shot at living amongst the gods?" My disbelief evident.

His smile is cold. "No, not merely to live with them. I'd condemn them all for a chance to ascend as a god."

"I don't understand," I whisper, maybe not wanting to. It sounds ghastly.

His eyes gleam with fervor. "I believe my midnight mind has taken me deeper, to another realm entirely, one that lies beyond the gates. I've had visions of the gods, even conversed with some. I'm convinced that with the hearts' power, I can open those gates and ascend. I'd become an entity of unimaginable might, dwelling in a place beyond your imagination."

My temper surges, a protective instinct for the innocent blazing within. "You'd condemn everyone, obliterate entire continents, all for your ambition to ascend as a god. You never truly cared about me, did you? Why drag me into this? Why unlock the bridge? Why reveal this to me?" I demand, struggling to keep the quiver of fear from my voice.

"Pixie," he murmurs, taking a step closer, "you are my daughter, and I love you. That's why I've done all of this. I'm offering you a choice." I narrow my eyes.

"If you truly loved me, you wouldn't have embarked on this path. What 'choice?'" I spit out.

"With your dark magic, you've become formidable," he continues, and I fight the unsettling sensation building in my stomach.

"Formidable enough for what?"

"You can choose to join me. Together, we can unlock the gates and ascend," he says. I shake my head vehemently, certain he's deluded to think I'd ever agree, especially knowing the destruction it would entail. "I anticipated this reaction, which is why I awaited the awakening of your dark magic for you to be capable of a choice. If you decline my offer, then you can rejuvenate the heart of Eguina and return as its savior."

"And how, exactly, do I rejuvenate this heart?" I inquire, desperation evident.

"Simply touch it with both hands. It will draw the necessary magic from you. Your dark magic is more potent than you realize. By sharing a portion of it with the heart, you'll restore Eguina. And it won't be fatal. It'll merely drain you temporarily, while your magic recovers," he adds.

"Why should I trust a word of what you say? It feels like

my entire life has been a web of deceit. How can I possibly trust you now?" I challenge.

"Give me your hand, and I'll demonstrate." He offers his arm, and despite every instinct telling me to flee I'm compelled to confront this. I grasp his hand, and we channel. Suddenly, we stand before a dark, pulsating stone barrier. As it reshapes and the stones start to bleed until they morph into a portal, recognition hits me.

"This is the barrier Colton and I encountered when we first came here. You claimed it was one of many portals to the surface," I say.

"Indeed. But had I not intercepted you then, you'd have discovered it's not merely an exit from these tunnels. It's a conduit to Drikora," he declares. Startled, I whip my head to face him.

"Drikora," I echo.

"Precisely. One of the other realms I mentioned. Let me show you I speak the truth." Hesitantly, I grip his hand once more, following him through the chilling liquid veil ahead.

CHAPTER 36
LYRA

The instant wave of scorching heat assaults me, even before I can plant my boots firmly onto the unfamiliar terrain. Blinking against the burning sensation in my eyes, I force them open.

As far as I can see, crimson sand sprawls out, its surface shifting and contorting to form whirlwinds of fiery dust that dance menacingly on the horizon. The sky above is no refuge, either; it's a chaotic blend of charred black and ashen gray with occasional sparks and ashes falling like sinister confetti, remnants of a firestorm I cannot see but can undoubtedly feel.

This... this is not the world I know. This place is so broken, so desolate. Every part of my being aches with a sorrow I wasn't prepared for, mourning for the life that once thrived here, now erased from existence.

Drawing a shaky breath, the taste of ash and despair fills my mouth. "What have you done?" The whisper escapes my lips, a lament more than a question. A lone tear breaks free, tracing a hot path down my face.

"This is what will become of Eguina if the heart is not restored."

Shadows stir through my veins, and I can barely contain the rage festering from deep within. "I should kill you for this," I seethe, every word dripping with venom. "You don't deserve ascension. You deserve your final death, an eternity of torment for the destruction you've unleashed." I can feel the inky tendrils of my darkness starting to twist and writhe beneath my skin, urging me to surrender to my emotions.

A twisted grin spreads across his face. "Ah, get angry, Pixie. Let those shadows emerge. I bet that darker part of you is eager to ascend alongside me."

I tremble, torn between revulsion and an eerie understanding. There's a seductive pull from within, tempting me to release all restraint, to avoid feeling this pain, to embrace the void and its apathy. The allure of darkness is overwhelming, threatening to drown my very essence.

Shaking my head and mustering every ounce of my willpower, I manage a defiant whisper, "No." In a blink, I step back, retreating through the veil and into the tunnels again.

"How can I trust that this wasn't merely a desolate corner of Zomea? How do I know you're not trying to deceive me?"

He materializes beside me, effortlessly crossing the veil as I did.

A smirk plays on his lips. "Deep down, you know that wasn't Zomea. But if your instincts aren't convincing enough, allow me to dispel your doubts." Before I can protest, he firmly clasps my shoulder, transporting us again.

The chamber we emerge into eerily mirrors the one where I found the beating heart, yet its essence couldn't be more different. A stifling silence engulfs us, devoid of the comforting rhythm of a heartbeat. My breath catches in my throat as I take in the horror before me. I'm confronted with the heart, but it's a grotesque shadow of the one I'm familiar with. No longer floating with vitality, it languishes on its side, drowning in a pool of inky, viscous liquid. My hand flies to my mouth in shock.

"Oh gods," I barely manage to whisper.

His voice, dripping with feigned affection, pierces the silence. "You see, my dear, I do possess a semblance of love for you. The heart of Eguina still pulses, albeit weakly. I left it with just enough life, giving you the choice to rejuvenate it and reclaim the life you once knew if that is what you wish."

Whirling around, I confront him, my eyes blazing with fury and revulsion. "Your wickedness knows no bounds. The very blood that runs in my veins feels tainted, knowing I share it with you. How can you have no remorse for the destruction you've caused."

His grip tightens on me once more, as the wind surges with alarming force, ensnaring us both, channeling us back to where the heart of Eguina lies.

The sight of the black ichor dripping from the heart, trickling down the tendrils of roots, is chilling. Fuck. Even if I can't trust him, the main reason I hastened the awakening of my dark magic and returned to Zomea was to prevent further devastation in Eguina. Whether he's telling the truth or not is irrelevant. I'm committed to doing whatever is necessary to protect the realms, and he's well aware of that.

"Sentimentality, remorse – they're mere impediments, Lyra. Flaws I've long since discarded." His voice is steeped in arrogance. "The question remains, will you accompany me to the gates, embrace the chance to ascend, or will you linger here and nurse your beloved Eguina?"

My father's voice, once overpowering, now sounds distant, inconsequential, drowned out by the overpowering rhythm that courses through my mind and soul.

There's a harmonious connection, a synergy that builds as I draw nearer. It's as though the heart senses my resolution, feels the determination coursing through me, and amplifies its own energy in response. All else fades. The only reality is the mesmerizing pulsation of life before me, the gentle glow of fluid coursing through its chambers.

Guided by an instinct deeper than thought, my hands rise of their own accord. Time seems to stretch and warp. With a heart full of purpose and a resolve that's unbreakable, my fingers make contact with the very essence of Eguina as I touch the heart.

A barrage of unfathomable images surges through my mind. Suddenly, it feels as though I'm plunging deep within the heart, becoming a part of its liquid essence, navigating its many chambers. I am caught in a maelstrom, akin to being dragged through chilling rapids. Each pulse threatens to drown me, making it nearly impossible to draw breath.

Then I find myself back on solid ground, gazing up at the heart. It seems more expansive than before, as though it's engorged with vitality and magic. A radiant glow emanates from it, its rhythm steady and commanding, stronger than before. My chest fills with relief, especially when a lone flower sprouts in the tunnel out of the corner of my eye. *My gods, I think it worked.*

I think Eguina is going to be okay, and I'm still alive. I try to move, but my body feels treacherously heavy, every limb pinned down by fatigue.

My eyes dart around, seeking out my father. There, in the shadows, he emerges, hands clasped around the heart with a disturbing grin plastered on his face. I panic, but my muscles refuse to cooperate, leaving me helpless. My attempts at screaming come out as feeble whispers. It's heartbreaking to see the heart, so freshly rejuvenated, start to wilt again under his grasp. Each drop he siphons feels as if he's tearing away a piece of my very soul, and the heart begins to ooze again.

But then, abruptly, he releases it. He throws is head back, and his cold laughter echoes across the room, and when he drops his chin to meet my eyes his stir black for a moment. A chill creeps up my spine, and a gnawing dread takes root, leaving me wondering and fearing what he might do next.

A smug satisfaction radiates from him, filling the space between us with an almost palpable tension. "Oh, my naive Pixie," he coos, taking deliberate steps closer to me. "Always the righteous one. Predictable, as I'd hoped. Your entire life, dancing on the strings I've set."

My heart thuds heavily, each word a dagger embedding deeper into my soul. "Your belief in saving Eguina, in touching the heart, was all I needed. To unlock the gates, I required a taste of your essence, your darkness. And now, thanks to you, I have it."

Rage, pure and white-hot, courses through me. I yearn to leap up, to confront him, to make him pay for every transgression. But my strength betrays me. All I manage is to roll onto my stomach, the weight of my weakness anchoring me down, rendering me helpless before his gloating stare.

"Fear not, my dear Pixie. Your strength will return in time, and you might even have a shot at saving Eguina," he sneers, circling me like a predator. "But by then, I'll be far beyond your reach, transformed and all-powerful. And when your darkness eventually consumes you, as it inevitably will, I'll revel in the wicked irony of watching you obliterate the very world you once bled to protect. You see, your fate is sealed, regardless of how noble your intentions might be— destined for darkness, and destined to destroy it all."

I grip my hands into fists, my nails digging into my palms. "The prophecy... I have to trust in it," I barely whisper, clinging to the sliver of hope I have left. "There has to be a way out of this darkness, a chance to find balance. I know there is."

Father's cold cackle chills me to the bone. "Your naivety is astonishing. The power coursing through your veins doesn't desire balance. It craves supremacy. The sooner you come to terms with that, the stronger you'll be."

I shake my head.

"You're mistaken. There's undeniable strength in kindness and doing what's right," I say, holding my ground.

"And where has all your righteousness led you?" he retorts, venom in his voice. "Looked down upon by your own mother, tormented by your stepbrother, manipulated by the two men who profess to love you, and defiled through unspeakable acts that Lycan subjected you to. All the kindness in the world hasn't spared you from these fates. Even now as you lie here, you still want to do the right thing. Pixie, give in to your dark side and you'll feel so much better."

I pull myself together, finally able to sit up and press my back against the wall, wiping away my tears defiantly. "Those are tragedies, indescribable pains that no one should bear. But, Father, those trials didn't weaken me. They molded me, made me stronger. Today, I stand before you as a woman not willing to be controlled by the shadows," I declare.

He chuckles, a mocking tone in his laughter. "After all you've endured, you believe you're formidable? Such innocence." And without warning, I lash out at him, throwing my fire in his face.

"Using my own essence against me? Naive. Only the darkness that dwells within you can challenge me," he taunts.

A forceful wave of his magic collides with me, feeling as if every cell inside is aflame. The burning sensation radiates, settling deep within, causing me to convulse in pain.

Gasping for breath, I claw at the wall, using the protruding branches to pull myself upright. "You're going to regret that." My voice takes on a tone I wasn't expecting as I speak. Without warning, another surge of his magic slams into me. I can't dodge in time, and the impact sends me crashing back to the ground, blood filling my mouth. Every part of me feels ablaze from the inside.

"Unleash your shadows and fight me, if it will make you feel better," he taunts, looming above. As he forcefully presses his boot into my back, every breath becomes a painful effort. Desperation fuels my attempts to wriggle free, but he's always been the most powerful force in my life, and now is no different.

"Stop...please," I rasp, tasting blood and bile. The dark, thick liquid already staining the floor mixes with the fresh blood spewing from my mouth.

"Begging? Not the response I expected. Fight me, Pixie," he growls, driving his heel deeper. An agonizing jolt runs through me, amplifying the sensation of my skin tearing open under the force of his magic.

As he raises his foot, preparing to crush me once more, desperation pushes me to the brink. I surrender to the shadows lurking beneath my skin, the ones I've been fighting to suppress. The darkness surges forth with a force unlike any other, catapulting him violently against the wall. A wave of exhilaration washes over me, the power of the night coursing through my very being.

The sensation is intoxicating, a blend of terror and exhilaration, and I never want to be rid of it. As I glance downward, shadowy tendrils wrap around me, acting as an armor against the world.

"There she is," he comments, advancing toward me. But I don't retreat. The fear that once controlled me is now replaced by a newfound strength.

"Fuck you," I retort, standing tall, our eyes locked in defiance.

"Such spirit suits you far more than kindness." He smirks, but it doesn't bother me.

With the dark magic enveloping me, I feel transformed. It's as if I'm still me but free from the shackles of regret and remorse. Empowerment courses through me, and visions of retribution for those who wronged me dance tantalizingly in my mind. This newfound drive delights me. With the shadows at the helm, who could possibly challenge me? There's a shift in my gaze, one of pure abandon, as I truly surrender.

His voice is laced with a sinister glee. "Off to Eguina with you now, to let your shadows wreak havoc. I must leave, but rest assured, our paths will cross again, dear daughter." As he begins to summon the power of the wind, without a second thought, I lunge at him. The moment before he channels, I clutch onto him, ensuring he doesn't escape without me in tow.

The impact jars me as we crash onto the solid terrain, but instinct drives me upright in an instant. And while we both spring to our feet, my agility gives me the edge. Shadows erupt from my core, slithering out like dark serpents to ensnare him. They wind around his limbs, tugging them wide and leaving him vulnerable. I slide my sword from its sheath, and a twisted satisfaction surges within me at the fleeting flash of alarm in his eyes, taking in the sword's impressive span and ominous sheen.

"You've wrought devastation," I hiss, the timbre of my voice a chilling fusion of my own and something more sinister. "A swift end by my magic won't suffice. You should feel every ounce of pain you've inflicted." I prepare to strike, savoring the moment, but he somehow wrenches free, countering with a blade of his own.

His smirk returns. "You seem to forget. Your darkness courses through me as well. You won't defeat me easily." With a mocking flourish, he adds, "But please entertain me with your attempt at swordsmanship."

He thrusts at me, the air singing with the speed of his swing. But I'm quicker, swerving away as the blade slices mere inches from my face.

The ground beneath us is hard-packed dirt, and above the skeletal remains of trees loom, their gnarled branches creating a canopy against the stormy sky. Thunder growls, each rumble resonating deep within me, echoing the chaos of our confrontation. In the gloom, my eyes catch the silhouette of the gates he mentioned. Even bathed in darkness, they're unmistakably intertwined with familiar, branch-like tendrils, reminiscent of the tunnel. What significance could this hold? My thoughts scatter as a swift move from him sends me crashing to the ground, jolting me back to the immediacy of our fight.

He sweeps his arm forward, and a force akin to a gravitational pull seizes me, suspending me midair. He's lucky my magic is still recuperating, otherwise I'd obliterate him on the spot. I can sense my magic's strength returning incrementally, and it's a ticking clock before my darkness takes over.

Reaching out with my shadows, I latch onto the trees, dragging myself back to solid ground. Euric makes a hasty retreat downhill, evidently aiming for the gates. I can't let him reach them.

Before I can intercept him, Nyx and Colton emerge from the tree line, positioning themselves as barriers between Euric and the gates. The bond between Colton and me must've guided them to our location.

"I've killed you once, and it seems I'll have to do so again," Nyx declares, lunging at my father.

Euric evades Nyx's magic with ease. "Your victory was only possible because I permitted it," he says. An aura of dark energy swirls around him, becoming more pronounced and potent. "Your two misfits won't be enough to stop me."

Colton steps forward, his eyes glowing with determination. "It doesn't matter how powerful you've become. We'll stand together, always." He raises his hand, conjuring a barrier of ethereal energy that shields them from Euric's next onslaught.

I can feel my strength surging back, the darkness within me clawing at the surface. I focus on Euric, ensuring that if he makes another move I'll be ready to strike him down. The thought of unleashing my full power is exhilarating, and with every passing second it's becoming more irresistible.

Nyx and Colton coordinate their attacks, keeping Euric on the defensive. But I can see the gates glimmering ominously in the background, and I have an urge of my own to move closer to them.

I race down the hill, and by the gods, Nyx and Colton look hot in the throes of combat. "Lyra, are you present? Are you in control?" Colton inquires, concern etching his features.

I chuckle. "It's me, Colton. I'm here. I'm in control."

"Your eyes have that shadowy tint, and your hair's transformed," Nyx points out, eyes still on the enemy, my father.

I glance down, noting the writhing shadows embracing me. There's an undeniable temptation to surrender, let them dictate my actions. It's as though every worry dissipates, replaced by the comforting cocoon of darkness. A distant call, barely perceptible, lures me a step closer to the gates.

Suddenly, Nyx's cry of pain slices through the tension. I spin, stomach churning at the sight of my father's blade grazing Nyx's abdomen. It's a superficial wound. Nyx will recover quickly. But my tolerance has reached its limit.

With a piercing stare, I fixate on Euric, channeling my power. In moments, he crumples to his knees, blood oozing from his ears and eyes.

"How... how are you doing that?" Colton breathes, awe and fear mingling in his voice.

I don't answer. My entire focus narrows to the defeated form of my father. Despite any power he might've absorbed, in this moment I'm certain he stands no chance against me.

"You wanted my darkness? Here it is, Daddy," I taunt, his fate teetering in my grasp as my magic bears down on his mind.

"Ah, Pixie, you're finally embracing your true self," he manages through gritted teeth, and despite the pressure I'm exerting, a twisted smile forms on his face. "Don't hold back now. Finish it. Give in."

"Lyra, don't," Colton pleads. "No matter how monstrous he's been, he's still your father."

I barely register his words, my focus solely on Euric.

"Lyra, Colton's right. We'll handle him. You don't need this," Nyx intervenes.

Their voices are distant, but I answer without breaking my gaze from Euric. "You have no idea of the horrors he's committed. A swift death is too merciful for him, regardless of our ties." Out of the corner of my ear, I catch Nyx muttering a curse.

"Lyra, you don't need this burden," Colton says. "Savoring this power might feel invigorating now, but when the darkness recedes, you'll be left to grapple with the aftermath."

Their concerns begin to penetrate my resolve, but I shake off the doubt, frustrated by their insistence on intervening in this intimate reckoning.

I raise my hand, and blood begins to trickle from Euric's nose, staining his chest. Yet, through the pain, he manages to laugh — a sound that reverberates hauntingly with the roll of distant thunder, igniting the rage within me even further. He's responsible for the deaths of countless beings, for the obliteration of entire realms, and for every twisted turn in my life.

Every semblance of goodness he's shown has been a facade, a shield to hide the power-hungry demon that dwells beneath.

"What's it like, Father, dying in Zomea? I wager you won't have the luxury of a second return. But you're about to find out, aren't you?"

His grin remains, even as he spits out blood, eyes bleeding. "If I were to truly die, what better way than at your hands, watching you become everything you hate about me."

"I'm nothing like you," I retort. "You're sick, taking lives for mere amusement and the pursuit of power. I am not that monster."

"Alright, release him. We'll handle this now," Nyx urges, taking a step toward me. But when I growl, he halts, rooted in place.

"Keep telling yourself that, Pixie," he whispers.

I surge forward, thrusting my hand into Euric's chest. The grisly crunch of bone and the squelch of torn flesh echo hauntingly. I clasp his heart firmly.

"I'm not the monster here," I whisper, my breath a cold promise against his face. In one swift motion, I wrench the heart from its cavity.

"Fuck," Nyx murmurs, shock evident in his voice. I sense Colton retreat, muttering a curse under his breath. Slowly, Euric's body tilts, collapsing face-first into the earth.

I glance at the heart — its grotesque resemblance to Eguina's. With a mixture of revulsion and resolution, I drop it then nudge it with my foot toward Euric's lifeless form. My gaze drifts, settling on the looming gates ahead.

"Okay, my shadow, it's time to rein in the darkness again. You don't need any more dark magic to protect you," Colton urges. But his voice becomes a distant echo as my feet, seemingly of their own volition, want to close the distance between me and the gates. I can't resist the pull emanating from them.

"Lyra, what are you doing?" Nyx's voice fades against the allure of the gates.

"I...I need to know what's behind them," I reply, the words coming out involuntarily.

"No, Lyra, you don't. We have no idea why these massive, creepy-looking gates exist in Zomea, but you really don't need to know what's behind them," Colton insists, gripping my arm. I react instinctively, my shadows leaping to my defense, pushing both Colton and Nyx away. They're not harmed, but they're kept at a distance.

"Lyra," Nyx implores, "whatever is behind those gates can't be good. Think about it. If Euric wanted to open them, then there's danger lurking behind."

Deep inside, I understand their warnings, but the dark magic surging within craves power. Ascending to godhood, gaining unparalleled strength... Such thoughts tantalize my shadowy side. However, buried within me, a sense of caution and something—someone—else beckons, I think Euric was wrong about what's beyond the gates.

Desperately, I cling to thoughts of Nyx and his light, recalling the prophecy we've been trying to unravel. As these images flood my mind, I sense the dark magic ebbing, and a semblance of control returns. I stand in front of the gates, captivated by the intricate roots and branches woven around them.

Colton's voice breaks through again. "You look like yourself now. Are you okay?" My eyes drop to my feet, noting the absence of swirling shadows. A sigh of relief escapes my lips.

Nyx's soft voice reaches my ears, "I was worried there for a moment. Thought we'd lost you to the darkness."

Grinning, I turn to him, "See? I told you I could control it."

But my moment of triumph is cut short by Nyx's alarmed shout. "Lyra, no! Stop!"

Confused, I follow his gaze to my arm. Once again,

shadows spiral around it, reaching, yearning for the gate. I panic.

"I can't stop it," I whisper, terrified, as my fingers brush against the cool metal bars.

Suddenly, Colton is there, grabbing me and yanking me away, turning to face him. Our eyes lock, his filled with concern.

"Are you alright?" he breathes out, studying me.

Gazing down, I see my hands are free of shadows once more.

"Yes, I... I'm sorry. I don't know what came over me. Thank the gods you were there. I can't imagine what might have been unleashed if those gates had opened—"

All of us freeze.

The unmistakable, slow screeching sound of the gates opening pierces the night.

Ashley R. O'Donovan is an author of fantasy romance currently working on her next novel. Drawing inspiration from her love of travel, Ashley enjoys exploring new cultures and experiences, particularly in Kenya and Uganda, where she finds endless inspiration for her stories.

Born and raised in Monterey, California, Ashley loves spending time with her friends and family, and when she's not writing, you can almost always find her cuddled up with one of her dogs reading a book, or catching the latest horror movie with her husband.

If you enjoyed this book, please consider leaving a review on Amazon and keeping in touch with Ashley on social media. She loves hearing from readers and is excited to share more of her stories with the world.

For more books and updates:
www.AuthorARO.com

Made in the USA
Middletown, DE
11 September 2024

60217951R00255